D0193184

The Hideaway

Sheila O'Flanagan

The Hideaway

REVIEW

First published in Great Britain in 2018 by
HEADLINE REVIEW
An imprint of HEADLINE PUBLISHING GROUP

1

Cataloguing in Publication Data is available from the British Library

ISBN 978 1 4722 3538 1 (Hardback)
ISBN 978 1 4722 3537 4 (Trade Paperback)

Typeset in ITC Galliard Std by Palimpsest Book Production Limited,
Falkirk, Stirlingshire

Printed and bound in Great Britain by Clays Ltd, St Ives plc

Headline's policy is to use papers that are natural, renewable and recyclable
products and made from wood grown in well-managed forests and other
controlled sources. The logging and manufacturing processes are expected
to conform to the environmental regulations of the country of origin.

HEADLINE PUBLISHING GROUP
An Hachette UK Company
Carmelite House
50 Victoria Embankment
London EC4Y 0DZ

www.headline.co.uk
www.hachette.co.uk

The Hideaway

Chapter 1

There was a long queue at the car rental desk and I was at the back of it.

I'd congratulated myself on being first off the plane and thought I'd be first in line at the rental desk too, but I'd forgotten there would be other flights into Alicante airport and that those passengers might also be hiring cars. Now it seemed that everyone who'd landed that evening was in the queue ahead of me. And it was moving at a snail's pace.

I was standing immediately behind a family of four whose flight had arrived nearly three hours late and who were feeling very cranky about it. The little girl, aged about two, was holding on to her mother's leg, whimpering pettishly, while her slightly older brother was aiming his bright-green plastic laser gun at the waiting adults and whooping 'gotcha' every couple of seconds. The parents were venting their annoyance in equal measure at the airline and the car rental agency, asking each other why it was taking so bloody long to hand over a set of keys. The last comment was pitched loudly enough for everyone in the line to hear, and there were plenty of approving nods as well as a few mutters of 'bloody disgrace' from the waiting hordes.

The two people currently at the desk had been there for at least twenty minutes. If everyone ahead of me took that long, I'd be waiting for nearly two hours. Which would mean that it would be after midnight before I got my car, and at least another hour before I reached the Villa Naranja. So my time on the ground would be practically as long as the flight itself – longer if, as I feared, I got lost.

'You won't get lost, Juno,' Pilar had assured me as she'd highlighted the route on Google Maps. 'Once you're on the road to the house, you'll be fine. The hardest part is the turn just before the town because it is quite sharp and easy to miss in the dark. But you'll know you've passed it if you end up in Beniflor.'

'Is there a hotel nearby if I do lose my way?'

'Not in Beniflor itself,' she replied. 'But there's a lovely one about fifteen minutes past it. La Higuera. Small, but very chic. Even though it's expensive it's always booked up. Honestly, Juno, you'll find the Villa Naranja, no problem. Don't worry.'

I wasn't exactly worried, but despite my limited budget I wished I'd opted for the chic and expensive option, at least for tonight. I supposed that if things took too long, I could always drive into Alicante city, check in to the first hotel I saw, and leave looking for the Villa Naranja until the morning when it would be bright and everything would seem better and easier. Even as I considered it, I told myself not to be stupid. The drive was straightforward enough and I was perfectly capable of finding a country house, even in the dark. I was a strong, competent woman, wasn't I? It might be true that both my strength and competence had been called into question of late but I shouldn't be such a . . . a

. . . the disparaging word I was about to call myself was lost as, out of nowhere, the pain and the grief enveloped me like a tidal wave, literally knocking me sideways. I gasped an apology as I bumped into the mother in front of me.

'That's OK,' she said. 'It takes it out of you, doesn't it? Travelling. And all this hanging around is ridiculous. Sometimes I wonder if going away on holiday is worth the hassle.'

She kept talking without waiting for me to answer, which was just as well because I wasn't listening to a word she was saying, and I couldn't speak anyhow. My throat had constricted and there was only room in my head for my anguish. The problem, of course, was that I had no right to be anguished and no right to be in pain. Yet it caught hold of me when I least expected it, and wouldn't let me go.

Without wanting to, I was replaying the moment I'd heard the news. The moment I'd seen the photograph flash up on the screen and my life had been turned upside down. I was utterly unable to stop the memories or the images filling my head. It was all I could do not to cry.

The queue moved forward again.

'We're staying at my sister's.' The woman's voice broke into my thoughts. 'She has a place in Altea Heights. It's beautiful. Views of the sea. Lovely terrace. And a private pool.'

'It sounds great.' My voice came out as a croak but she didn't seem to notice.

'Oh, it is,' she told me. 'Sadly, we won't be able to come this time next year. Cooper will be in school then, and they fine you for taking them out in term-time now. It's ludicrous. Everyone knows the airline companies scam you on flights during school holidays.'

'It's the nanny state at work,' said her husband.

I nodded in agreement. As a single woman just past her thirtieth birthday, school holidays were irrelevant to me, but I understood her frustration.

'Are you on your own, then?' She looked at me, inviting conversation.

To my enormous relief a second window at the rental desk opened at that moment. The queue split and hustled forward and I didn't need to answer. To avoid any possibility of talking, however, I took out my phone and looked at it. But I already knew the most recent message would still be the one from Pilar, sent just before I boarded the plane in Dublin.

Slight problem. Mum didn't get to the house today so electricity is still off. No fresh food either but there is coffee and tea. Best pick up something at airport for snack and brekkie. Hope you have great time. Px

I'd bought two extra Danish pastries on the flight. They'd looked soggy and unappetising even before I put them in my bag but I didn't care. I wasn't hungry. I wouldn't be hungry in the morning either. I'd lost my interest in food along with almost six kilos in weight over the past couple of months. I knew that I couldn't really afford to lose any more. I've always been on the slender side, and dropping almost a stone didn't really suit me. But the last thing I cared about was how I looked.

I scrolled through my other messages, even though I told myself not to. I stopped at the last one in the conversation with Brad.

Tonight's dinner location. Joining them shortly. Love you. Miss you. Bxx

The wave of grief hit me again. I clenched my teeth and

4

tightened my grip on the handle of my luggage. At that moment, it was the only thing keeping me upright.

A final move forward and then it was my turn at the desk. I gave my details and was handed the keys to a Ford Fiesta, which the rental agent said was on the third floor of the car park. I thanked him, and walked towards the exit. The family of four was still at the desk. The little boy was bashing their suitcases with his plastic laser gun and the father was arguing with the agent about the insurance excess charge.

The car park was busy. I checked the bay number for the Fiesta and strode along one of the rows. The dark blue car was where it was meant to be. I gave a sigh of relief, popped the boot open and hefted my case inside. I opened the door and slid into the seat before I realised I was on the passenger's side. I got out and walked around to the driver's door.

I'd driven on the Continent before, so left-hand drive didn't bother me. The first time – in France with my closest friends, Cleo and Saoirse – had been a little scary, but after the initial anxious minutes I'd been fine. I'd been the one to do most of the driving through Europe with Sean, my fiancé, a few years later. Sean became my ex-fiancé after that trip, although it hadn't been on account of my driving. It had been on account of him deciding he wasn't ready to marry anyone. Or at least that he wasn't ready to marry me. Of course I'd had broken relationships in my life before Sean, but I'd never felt as devastated as I'd felt then. All the dreams and plans of the life I'd expected to lead had come crashing down around me. I'd felt battered and bruised and despairing. Humiliated, too – though I tried to tell myself that it wasn't a reflection on me that Sean had changed his mind. And better at that point than after we were married. Still, it was a difficult few months. But I'd got over it. I'd rebuilt my life, advanced my career and moved on. Now my heart was broken all over again, and this time it was much, much worse. This time I didn't know how to get over it, I didn't know if I'd ever recover.

I took a deep breath, then put the Fiesta into reverse and eased out of the parking bay. It was good to have something to concentrate on, something to pull my mind away from the dark places it still wanted to go. Besides, I like driving. I'm a better driver than Sean ever was. I'm alert and confident and I don't let myself be bullied on the road. That was why Cleo and Saoirse always made me drive on holidays. And I honestly didn't mind, because I like being the one in control. I'm much better at giving orders than taking them.

I hadn't been on holidays with the girls since I'd started going out with Sean. But after Brad, Cleo had asked me if I'd like to go away for a weekend with her. To a spa, she suggested. Somewhere top-notch. Somewhere I could be pampered.

'I don't deserve to be pampered,' I'd told her in a voice that was tight with the effort of not crying.

'It wasn't your fault,' Cleo protested.

'I know. But it feels like a judgement somehow.'

'You've got to give yourself a break, Juno,' she said.

'They didn't get a break, did they?' I asked.

And Cleo hadn't said any more about pampering.

'At the roundabout, take the second exit.' The female satnav was a welcome distraction from my thoughts.

I concentrated on my road positioning and followed her instructions. Most of the route to Beniflor was by motorway, which made things fairly simple. I like motorway driving. I like putting my foot down and giving the car its head.

But I didn't put my foot down too heavily in the Fiesta. I was afraid to drive too quickly. There was a chance I might burst into tears, and I didn't want to be travelling at 120kph when that happened. Nevertheless there was a tiny, tiny part of me that thought driving off the road and into oblivion had its merits.

I fixed my eyes on the road ahead. I wasn't going to think like that. I'd had those thoughts in the darker days but I'd told everyone that I was much better now. The thing is, I wasn't, not really. The reason I was here was because I wasn't at all better, and because I couldn't do my job properly. Because I'd felt obliged to hand in my resignation before I did something really stupid. And before they fired me.

I was really good at my job before. I know women aren't supposed to blow their own trumpet and say they're brilliant at anything – like driving, or our jobs. We're meant to be self-deprecating and modest and put it all down to luck rather than being super-capable. But I was one of the best radiographers at the private hospital where I worked, and I knew it. I knew it because the patients said so. The staff said so too. And I loved my job so much, I was always trying to improve my skills and to make the experience better.

The patients are the most important part of my work. They're either nervous or in pain, or both, when they come to radiology. A big part of what I do is to make them feel relaxed. But how could I make anyone else relax when I was as tight as a coiled spring myself? And how could I be cheerful and positive with them when I was unable to come up from the depths of my own misery?

7

I tried, I really did. But it was asking too much. One day, after I'd finished an ultrasound of a young woman with abdominal pain, I burst into tears right there in the room beside her. The patient, not surprisingly, thought I'd seen something terminal in her ultrasound, and she burst into tears too. She was utterly inconsolable and wouldn't believe that she wasn't about to die.

Afterwards, I was called in to see the head of the department. Drina O'Driscoll is in her fifties; she's cool, professional and a role model for everyone in radiology. She looked at me without saying anything. I handed her the letter and she placed the envelope on the desk in front of her.

'I know you've had some personal issues, Juno.' Her voice was steady. 'I realise they have affected your work.'

I was gripping the edge of the seat with my hands in an effort to keep my composure. I wondered what she knew about my personal issues, and how she knew it.

'I'm very sorry,' I said. 'I shouldn't have allowed a private matter to affect me professionally.'

Drina looked at me from grey eyes that were soft with kindness.

'We don't live in a bubble where everyone can come into work and shut out everything else,' she said. 'It would be nice if we could. But we can't.'

'I totally traumatised the patient,' I said. 'She could sue us.'

'Hopefully she'll be so relieved her ultrasound was clear that she won't.' Drina smiled slightly. 'Having a health scare can change your perspective quite a bit.'

'Even so,' I said. 'I was totally unprofessional.'

'And now?' asked Drina. 'How are you now?'

8

I indicated the envelope with my resignation letter inside.

'I'm not a safe person to be around,' I told her. 'You can't afford for me to be on the team.'

'I see that you need some time away.' Drina shuffled some papers on her desk. 'But I hate to lose someone as skilled as you.'

'That's the thing.' I tightened my grip on the seat. 'I'm not skilled any more. I've lost it. I may never get it back.'

'You haven't lost it, and there's no question of not getting it back,' Drina said. 'I suggest that you take three months' unpaid leave. We can use agency cover for you until then. If, after that, you still feel you can't cope, we'll replace you.'

It took a few minutes for her words to sink in, and then I felt the tears well up again. I choked them back.

'I thought you'd be pleased to get rid of me,' I said.

'Get well, Juno.' She handed me the unopened envelope. 'Come back better.'

'Thank you.'

I stumbled out of her office and went to the hospital café. Cleo and Pilar, two of the other radiographers, were waiting for me. We're a tight-knit bunch in the radiology department, and they'd been there to pick up the pieces when I'd made a show of myself.

'That's a great outcome.' Cleo's words were encouraging. 'I'm sure you'll feel completely different by the end of the summer. What will you do?'

I shrugged. 'I don't have any plans. Just stay home, I suppose. Think about it.'

'For God's sake, Juno, you know I'm totally supportive and everything, but you can't spend three whole months with nothing to do but think about it.' Cleo looked at me in horror. 'You'll go mad. You're not the wallowing sort, and you don't spend time thinking about stuff you can't change.'

'I won't be wallowing,' I objected. 'I'll be . . .'

But Cleo was right. Thinking too much had got me into my current situation. I needed to figure out how to stop thinking and start living, not continually analysing my choices and wondering how things could have been different.

'You should do something new,' Pilar said. 'Something creative perhaps. Like writing a novel or learning to paint.'

For the first time since I'd left Drina's office, I smiled.

'The only writing I'm any good at is technical reports,' I said. 'As for painting – well, unless it's a wall, I'm hopeless.'

'It doesn't have to be painting or writing,' Pilar pointed out. 'You could just as easily do rock climbing or white-water rafting.'

'Or I could sit at home and read,' I said. 'To be honest, that's all I want to do. Be on my own. Do nothing.'

'This is an opportunity,' said Cleo. 'If nothing else, Juno, you should go to counselling.'

'Oh, please.' I snorted. 'I don't do counselling.'

'There's no need to turn your nose up at—'

'I have an idea!' Pilar sounded excited. 'You could stay in my grandmother's house. And you could read as much as you like and go for walks and explore my country.'

'Huh?' I looked at her.

'My grandmother's house,' repeated Pilar. 'I have told you about it before. It's in a small inland pueblo on the Costa Blanca. Not completely remote but on its own. Nobody has lived there since she passed away last year, and I know my parents would be happy to rent it. You could sit in silence and let the sun and the sea and the orange groves heal you.'

10

'D'you really think so?' I asked, as I imagined the bliss of a warm evening on the coast with the scent of orange blossom in the air. Where I wouldn't have to meet people I knew and could grieve by myself without pretending that my sorrow was over something else entirely.

'Of course,' said Pilar. 'My mother would love to have someone stay there. She feels bad that it's empty.'

'Where is it exactly?' Cleo licked her fingers as she finished her croissant.

'It's in the hills but not too far from Benidorm,' said Pilar. 'Beniflor is a rural community but there are also quite a lot of foreign homeowners in the neighbourhood. My grand-mother left her house to my parents when she died, but it's difficult to sell. Most of the foreign buyers want something on the coast or with views of the sea. And they want modern homes too. Grandmother's house is old-fashioned. It has views of orange groves and the mountains. It's not what they're looking for. And for local people, well, there are some who would take the orange groves – one of the local farmers harvests the oranges – but they don't need the house. So it is still on the market but unlived in. My mother spends occasional weekends there but it has become a little . . . a little . . .'

'Neglected?' suggested Cleo.

'Yes.' Pilar nodded. 'And I know this distresses my mother because she would like to keep it nice for my grandmother's sake but she lives now in Valencia, which is about an hour and a half away, and she cannot simply visit whenever she likes.'

'All the same, she might not like a complete stranger staying there,' I said.

11

'You're not a stranger, you're a friend,' said Pilar. 'She would be happy, I promise you.'

It was appealing but it seemed like an easy way out. Why should I get to spend three months in some country idyll – even a neglected country idyll – while everyone else was working? I didn't deserve it. It would be totally wrong.

That was what I said to Saoirse when she came home that evening. We shared an apartment which was close both to the hospital and to the accounting firm where she worked.

'Three months in the sun!' cried Saoirse. 'You'd be crazy to say no.'

'All the same, I don't know if I should. It's like being rewarded for—'

'For crying out loud, Juno, don't be ridiculous!'

'But—'

'No buts. You need to get away. You really do.'

I looked at her uncertainly.

'You can't say no,' she said.

So I said yes.

And that was why I was driving along the AP-7 at midnight to a place I didn't know.

Alone.

It was exactly an hour later when Jane, as I'd christened the very prim-and-proper-sounding satnav, jolted me out of my thoughts by telling me to take the next motorway exit. I dragged my mind back to the present and followed instructions that left me on a wide deserted road. I shivered slightly, very conscious of my solitary state and suddenly spooked by the fact that, apart from the car's headlights, the only other illumination was from the crescent moon, half hidden by

12

scrappy clouds in the sky above. The road ahead looked completely different to the Street View version on Google Maps but I reassured myself that it was only because it was dark. I was on the right track, all I had to do was listen to the satnav. And then Jane directed me on to a narrower, twisting country road, lined with orange trees. At least, I thought they were orange trees. The sliver of moon had disappeared behind a thicker cloud, so it was difficult to tell.

I slowed down. Jane remained silent but, according to the screen, I was supposed to stay on this road for another five kilometres. There were occasional dots of brightness in the distance, which I supposed were house lights. Perhaps they were the foreign homeowners Pilar had talked about. Or perhaps they were the local residents who wanted her grand-mother's oranges but not her house. Or ghosts moving around the countryside.

I tried not to think about ghosts. It should have been easy because I'm a rational, logical person who decided a long time ago that there is no such thing as an afterlife or restless spirits or any of that nonsense. People who claim to get in touch with the departed are charlatans. My view has always been that when it's done, it's done. But things had changed for me over the past few weeks, and I wasn't in complete control of what I believed any more. At that moment, alone in the middle of the unfamiliar countryside, the idea of ghosts roaming around the place wasn't half as fanciful as it was when I was safe at home in my apartment. And besides . . .

Get a grip, woman! I interrupted my own thoughts as I changed gear. Just because it's dark and lonely, you don't have to lose the plot completely.

I slowed to a near crawl when Jane told me to take the

next left, because I was afraid of missing it. I hoped this was the difficult turn Pilar had spoken of, and when the Fiesta's headlights picked out a sign pointing to Beniflor, I sighed with relief. I drove forward cautiously.

'You have reached your destination.'

Jane sounded particularly self-satisfied as I brought the car to a halt in the middle of nowhere. There was nothing in sight. Not a barn, not an outhouse, and certainly not a two-storey house matching the photo that Pilar had given me.

'Great,' I muttered. 'I hate satnavs. I really do.'

Given its isolated location, it had been impossible to enter the exact address of the Villa Naranja, so I guessed Jane had just dumped me on the road that led to it. Or at least had dumped me on the road that led to the road that led to it, because I knew the house was down another narrow track. Pilar hadn't been able to show me the track on Google Maps because it wasn't mapped.

A sudden glare in the rear-view mirror almost blinded me as another vehicle drew up behind me. My heart began to thump as the plot of every scary movie I'd ever seen raced through my head. I was resigning myself to being dragged off into the dark night by a marauder or a ghoul (or both) when, with an impatient toot of the horn, the driver of a white minivan swept past me.

I exhaled with relief as its rear lights disappeared into the distance. I gripped the gear lever, to stop my hand from trembling, while edging the Fiesta forward again. After about a kilometre, I spotted a narrow dirt track. I turned into it, hoping that I wasn't making a terrible mistake. The satnav's directional arrow showed that I was driving through the middle of a field. It certainly felt like it.

I was beginning to doubt the wisdom of my actions when I suddenly saw two white pillars looming in the distance. Between them was an enormous iron gate. A metal arc over it had been fashioned into the words 'Villa Naranja'. To one side of the pillars was a smaller pedestrian gate. I sighed with relief and stopped the car. Then I took out the fob that Pilar had given me, pointed it at the gate and pressed. Nothing happened. I pointed and pressed again, more firmly this time, and then a yellow light on the top of the left-hand pillar began to blink and the gate rolled slowly back.

I drove through, stopping to press the fob for a third time. The gates closed behind me. The scrap of moon, which had appeared from behind a cloud for an instant, disappeared again. I shivered slightly. No matter how dismissive I wanted to be about ghosts and spirits, the general spookiness of the situation was beginning to get to me.

I followed the gravel driveway to the house, which was partly hidden by a couple of tall pine trees. Then I brought the car to a gentle halt in front of the whitewashed building.

Even though Pilar had shown me some photos, her grandmother's house was bigger than I'd expected. It was two-storeyed and rectangular, with a terracotta roof and a chimney at either end. There were three full-length windows on the first floor and two smaller windows on either side of a wide door that led to a narrow balcony running along the entire width of the house. The downstairs windows were protected by grilles and the upstairs ones were shuttered. In the car's headlights I could see pink and purple blossoms against textured walls that flaked in patches, while the dried petals of an unruly bougainvillea had fallen from a pergola that sheltered a wide tiled patio.

As Pilar had said, it looked neglected, although that might

15

have been as much to do with the eerie lighting from the car headlights as anything else. I switched off the engine but left the lights on as I picked up the fob. There were a number of metal keys attached to it as well as the electronic device for the gate.

I selected the correct key (a splash of bright-pink nail varnish identified it) and, feeling like a jailer, put it into the keyhole of the grille that also protected the front door. Once that was opened I unlocked the main door, which creaked slightly as it swung inwards. A warm fugue of air hit me and my mind was once again flooded with images of ghosts, spectres and the plots of old horror movies where awful things happened to stupid girls on their own in the dark. For someone who was always accused of not being in the slightest bit imaginative, I was being incredibly silly. I needed to wise up, I thought, as I allowed my eyes to adjust to the dim light. I needed to take control.

Pilar had told me that the master switch for the house electricity was in a panel just inside the door. I waited for my vision to adjust to the light inside the house and then saw the plastic cover. I pulled at it and it came away in my hand, which made me cry out in surprise. The sound echoed around me. I took a deep breath, put the cover on a nearby shelf and then looked at the switches. I flipped the bright-yellow one and a low hum filled the room. I identified the source as the huge fridge in the corner of the room. At least that meant there was power. I looked around for a light switch and saw one on the opposite wall. When I pressed it, a fluorescent bulb in the ceiling buzzed and flickered and then came on properly. The harsh light didn't make things more welcoming, but being able to see properly definitely made it less eerie.

I went outside and switched off the car lights. The last thing I wanted was to drain the battery and end up in total isolation without any form of transport. I opened the boot, took out my case and bumped it up the step into the house before closing the door behind me. After that, I looked around.

I was standing in a room that ran the length of the house. On one side was the kitchen and on the other a dining area. The kitchen was basic – comprising the fridge (which was now gurgling alarmingly), a gas hob and a separate electric oven that I reckoned had been installed sometime in the eighties. There was also a Belfast sink and a range of cupboards that seemed to date back even further. At floor level, the storage was simply shelves with blue gingham curtains in front of them, and the walls were covered in blue-and-white tiles with an intricate Moorish design.

The dining room was equally dated, and the walls here were painted a rather dull mustard. There was an open fireplace in the end wall which was stained black with soot. The table was pine and so were the chairs, the seats of which were straw. A wooden standard lamp was positioned in one corner, the cream lampshade slightly askew.

The floor was covered in rustic tiles – terracotta, like the roof. But it was clean, if dusty.

I moved in further. Between the kitchen/dining area and the back of the house was a square hallway with a staircase. I left my case at the bottom of the staircase and walked into the next room. It too ran the length of the house and was obviously the living room. Back in the day, when the farmhouse had been a family home, it had undoubtedly been fully furnished, but all that was there when I arrived was a three-seater sofa covered in a fairly hideous neon-orange fabric (which clashed with the mustard walls), two armchairs with the same fabric, only this time in faded yellow, and a rectangular coffee table on which had been left some Spanish newspapers and magazines as well as a couple of unused ashtrays and – bizarrely – an empty glass. The newspapers were two months old and the magazines were gossip magazines from the previous Christmas.

The fireplace in this room was at the opposite end to the one in the kitchen/dining area and was equally marked by soot, although this one had a basket of logs on the floor beside it, as well as unused logs in the grate itself. A faded print of a coastal view hung at an angle on the wall.

There was a double door leading out of the house from the living room but I didn't bother opening it. Nor did I look out of the windows. Stupidly, I was feeling spooked again. Despite the total silence, I felt as though someone was inside the house, watching me. I told myself not to be ridiculous as I straightened the crooked print on the wall; then I went back to the kitchen door and made sure it was securely locked from the inside and that the bolt was in place. I opened one of the windows to allow some air in and switched off the harsh fluorescent light, before turning on the standard lamp instead. The glow was softer and more relaxing, but I still couldn't quite get over the feeling of being watched. As I made my way upstairs I felt the need to remind myself yet again that I didn't believe in spirits or ghosts or things that went bump in the night. And it didn't matter that I was alone in the house in the middle of nowhere, because being alone was perfectly safe. After all, being alone couldn't hurt you. Other people could.

There were six rooms upstairs. Four bedrooms. Two bath-rooms. And a cupboard for bedlinen, which also contained a motley selection of old, but clean, oversized T-shirts and cotton shorts. The first doors I opened led into unfurnished rooms, but the next contained two unmade single beds and the fourth had a king-sized bed with bedlinen neatly folded and placed on the mattress. When I turned on the light a ceiling fan began to rotate slowly, although it didn't actually cool the warm air, just moved it around.

I was suddenly overcome by tiredness. I put my handbag on the small dressing table and opened the window. I left the shutters closed and slipped out of my skinny jeans, which I threw on to the tub chair in the corner. I unfolded the bedlinen. It was crisp and clean, with a faint scent of lavender. I made the bed and fiddled with the ceiling fan so that it stayed working when I turned off the light. Then I lay down and closed my eyes.

But even though I was exhausted, I couldn't sleep. I tossed and turned and finally reached for my phone again. This time accessed my voice messages. It was the only one he'd ever left for me.

I wish I was there with you. His voice was clear and strong. *I wish I had my arms around you right now.*

I wished he had too.

Chapter 2

The last time I'd had a decent night's sleep was the last time I'd slept with Brad, a week before he'd gone on holiday. He'd stayed with me at the apartment I shared with Saoirse. She was in Galway for the weekend and I had the place to myself. Even though Saoirse is a brilliant flatmate, I enjoyed the times she went home to visit her family. Whenever she was away I'd imagine what it would be like to be the owner of the apartment, able to do whatever I wanted with it. I'd paint the walls prettier colours than magnolia, that was for sure. And there'd be no ceramic frogs anywhere. Saoirse collected them and kept them in her room so they really shouldn't have bothered me, but they freaked me out with their bug eyes and green faces. If I owned the apartment the walls would be colourful, the frogs would go and, of course, Brad would stay over as much as possible. He might even move in. I realised that would mean I'd no longer be living on my own, but living with Brad would be wonderful because I loved him. And I was glad, back then, that Sean had broken off our engagement – because if he hadn't, I would never have known a love like this.

That night, as Brad joined me in my double bed, I was

wondering if I could introduce the topic of living together into the conversation. It would be complicated in a whole heap of ways. We lived and worked in different cities, for starters. Our relationship was still in the early stages. It was a big step and I wasn't sure he was ready to take it, though I certainly was. Even with Sean, whom I'd been so sure I loved and who'd hurt me so deeply, the thought of moving in together so quickly hadn't crossed my mind. Yet when I was with Brad I felt complete, as though we'd always been destined for each other. And I didn't ever want to lose that feeling. I didn't want to let him go.

I met him exactly one year and five days after Sean and I had split up, and six months after our scheduled wedding day. I hadn't been out with anyone since. I'd felt too bruised and too broken to make the effort. I hadn't entirely accepted that I was still Juno Ryan not Juno Harris. That none of the things I'd expected to be true about my life by now had actually happened. That I didn't wake up every morning with the man I loved beside me. That I'd had to move out of the Malahide town house we'd shared together – the one whose walls I *had* painted in shades of saffron and amber. That instead of sharing everything about my day with him at night, I was sleeping on my own again.

Sean had said, when he delivered his crushing blow, that he wasn't ready for the commitment. It was ten days before his thirty-second birthday. (I'd bought him tickets for a track day at Mondello Park to celebrate. In the end, I gave them to Saoirse's brother.) It took me a while to think of anything to say in reply to his statement, but when I did, I reminded him that my dad had been married with children at thirty-two. He'd said times were different back then. That if you weren't

21

married you were talked about, and not in a good way. He was right, of course. I knew that, despite their bohemian lifestyle by the standards of their day, my parents would have no more dreamed of living together without getting married than flying to the moon. Yet Mum had actively encouraged me to move in with Sean before marrying him.

'You have to find out if you work together in every department,' she'd told me. 'In bed, out of bed, day to day – everything.'

I'd shuddered when she'd said that. She was right, of course, but I get very uncomfortable when she starts to talk to me as though I'm her friend and not her daughter. That's most of the time, to be honest. Yet I prefer it when she's more of a mum, not that she would ever have been one in the more traditional sense. Mum is all for equality between parents and children, and everyone being open with everyone else. Which just doesn't work for me.

I remember her sitting me down when I was thirteen or so and giving me the talk about sex. It was excruciating.

'I know it already,' I said as I squirmed in the high-backed chair. 'You told me when I asked you where babies came from.'

'I gave you the factual information, yes,' said Mum. 'But I didn't tell you that sex is actually something very wonderful for a man and a woman, and when you're older it's important you enjoy it. Like Dad and I enjoy it.'

I winced.

'It's important that he satisfies you, Juno,' she told me. 'It won't work if your needs are different.'

She was giving me way too much information. I wanted to throw up.

Of course she was right about the sex. (Are mothers really

always right? Even mothers like Thea?) After some initial disappointments, I got the hang of it and realised that some men were better than others. Sean and I had been pretty good together. Even though it had all gone so horribly wrong in the end, it had been great at the start.

We'd met at a wedding and bonded over the fact that neither of us particularly wanted to be there. He was a cousin of the bride. I'd gone to college with the groom. Both of us agreed that extravagant weddings, like this, were a waste of money.

'My plan is to nip into a registry office in my lunchtime,' I said. 'No fuss.'

'I like that in a woman,' said Sean. 'I like you.'

I liked him too. I was happy to spend the rest of the evening with him, and that night too. The wedding had been in a castle in Donegal. Everyone had stayed over. Some of them even in their own rooms. I felt comfortable with Sean and I couldn't help thinking that maybe, this time, I'd found the right man for me. I wanted to make it work with him. I wanted to be hopelessly in love, to be carried away on an emotional tide of passion. Perhaps that was because I wanted to fit in with everyone else in my family.

Because there was no doubt that when it came to emotional stuff, I was very definitely the odd one out. The practical one among people who lived by feelings, not reason. The one who needed scientific proof before I could believe anything I was told. The one for whom my mother's airy 'just because' was never enough. I put this perceived flaw in my character down to the fact that I was a drunken mistake. The drunken mistake is factually accurate, as Mum confirmed during our sex education talk. I'd been conceived in her dressing room after a post-show celebration fuelled by champagne. She told me that it was a mistake I should take every effort to avoid myself, although in her case she'd been fooled by thinking she was menopausal. She did add, during our conversation, that being a mistake didn't mean I was unwanted or unloved. Just unexpected. I knew I wasn't unloved – the Ryans are a huggy, kissy, tactile bunch, and Mum frequently declares her undying devotion to all of us. But a mistake is still a mistake, and I'd arrived long after she'd imagined her family was complete. And even though she loved me, I knew I exasperated the hell out of her because I refused to believe a word she told me without proof. I needed to know the reason for everything around me.

'Oh my God, Juno!' she exclaimed theatrically after a day at the beach when I'd asked about the timings of high and low tides, and how they were affected by the phases of the moon. 'Why don't you ever stop with the questions? Can't you simply look at the sea and think how beautiful it is and how lucky we are to be alive?'

'Yes,' I said. 'But I have to know why—'

'You don't!' Dad was the playwright to Mum's actress. 'You need to feel it.'

'Right,' I said, and looked up tidal forces in the school library.

My parents, Desmond and Thea Ryan, are an institution on the Irish theatrical scene. Even when I was a child Mum was already being referred to as a National Treasure, while Dad was usually referred to as One of Ireland's Greatest Living Playwrights. Both of them had won multiple awards for their work. Mum and Dad are all-or-nothing sort of people, either at the pinnacle of excitement or in the depths of despair. When

I lived at home, their peaks and troughs of emotion exhausted me and drove me to my books. Unfortunately for my credibility within the family, they weren't poetry books or great works of literature. They were books about physics and science. I might as well have brought Satan's manual for Hell into the house. Which, now that I think about it, would probably have been welcomed a lot more than *A Brief History of Time*. I was as much of a mystery to my mother and father as they were to me and – leaving aside the long gap before my arrival – that was also why they were closer to my brother and sister. They'd been a secure, stable unit before I arrived. I'd messed that up.

Butler, my brother, works as a secondary school teacher to pay the bills, but is a published poet of note. 'Intimate and intelligent' according to the review of his last collection, *Pause for Paternity*, which won the Patrick Kavanagh Award. I was the only one in the family who wondered how a writer like Kavanagh (whose poems generally rhymed) would feel about Butler's win, because as far as I could see my brother's poetry was basically just paragraphs of prose with line breaks in the middle of sentences that didn't actually finish properly. (I only ever read poetry that rhymes. At least that way I understand the system.)

I mentioned this one evening to Gonne, who was horrified.

'Can't you see how clever he is?' my sister demanded. 'Can't you hear the music in the way he uses the words?'

I shrugged. Gonne plays the harp and her husband the fiddle in a traditional Irish band. She hears music in everything.

I like music. But I don't hear it in everything. I like beauty. But I like form and function more. There's nothing wrong with that – at least, that's what I keep telling myself.

That's why I was so sure Sean was the one for me. He's

a digital designer, which I suppose brings form and function together. He understood my work. I understood his. There were loads of reasons why we made a great couple and loads of reasons why I wanted him to be the love of my life. And although I didn't stalk him on social media or anything like that after our split, I couldn't help seeing photos of him on friends' timelines. About six weeks later there was a picture of him with another girl. Her name was Suki. He was sitting at a table and she was standing behind him, her hands resting on his shoulders in a very possessive way.

Despite not being a deranged stalker, I had to find out about her. She was a make-up artist. I saw the Facebook post about their engagement the day Brad went on holiday. I was more shocked than I'd expected. After all, Sean had said he wasn't ready for commitment with me, and here he was, committing to someone else. It hurt.

Saoirse said that Sean was a serial fiancé and that there was no guarantee he'd last the pace with Suki either. She had a point. It was his third attempt, after all. He'd been engaged before he proposed to me. I felt sorry for Suki then. Because I thought I was the luckier one.

I thought I had Brad.

Eventually, as always happened over the last few weeks, I drifted into an uneasy doze. My dreams were scrappy, fragments of people and places that disappeared like smoke each time I woke up. With the shutters tightly closed, the bedroom was in complete darkness and it was impossible to know what time it was.

But when finally my eyes snapped open and I was totally alert, I knew something had definitely jolted me out of my fretful sleep. I looked around the unfamiliar room with rising panic, but eventually remembered where I was and my heart rate slowed down. I remained sitting on the bed, listening for the sounds of someone in the house. But everything was silent and it seemed like nobody had broken in to murder me. So I got up and began to open the shutters. They creaked alarmingly and tilted on their hinges but I managed to secure them against the wall.

To my astonishment, because I'd been sure it was still night-time, the sky outside was periwinkle blue and dotted with high fluffy clouds. The warm air carried the scent of orange blossom. A nearby jacaranda tree rustled gently in the breeze.

I looked at my watch. It was almost eight o'clock. I hadn't stayed in bed much after six for weeks, so even if my sleep had been as restless as always, it had still been longer than usual. I told myself that this was a positive sign.

I looked around the room. All my things were where I'd left them – suitcase against the wall, handbag on the dressing table, jeans slung across the faded pink tub chair. It was already too warm for jeans. I hauled the suitcase on to the bed and unpacked. I left a white cotton top and a pair of denim shorts on the bed. Then I put my dozen T-shirts and three additional pairs of shorts into a drawer in the dressing table, hung up the jeans that were probably going to spend the next three months in the wardrobe anyway, and finally slid my summer dresses on to hangers beside them.

I grabbed a towel from the linen cupboard on my way to the bathroom at the end of the house. To my surprise, it had a clear window with a view towards the mountains. From it I could see a cluster of houses in the distance that I assumed was the town of Beniflor. Unless somebody there was using binoculars to look into the bathroom, it was private enough despite the clear glass. And there was something exhilarating about standing under the surprisingly powerful rain shower, soaping myself while looking out at the spectacular view.

Twenty minutes later, wearing the cotton top and shorts, my dark hair still damp, I walked downstairs. I'd forgotten to switch off the standard lamp and it glowed in the corner of the kitchen/dining room. I hit the switch, then looked around. I hadn't noticed the previous night, but the kitchen windows had roll-up bamboo curtains behind the grilles. I rolled each one up, then went into the living room to open the shutters there.

When the sunlight streamed through, I stopped and stared.

The empty glass that had been on the coffee table was now on the floor. It was chipped but not broken. But it must have been the sound of it falling that had woken me earlier.

I inhaled sharply. What had made it fall? Had I picked it up when I was looking at the magazines and left it precariously placed at the edge of the table? I didn't think so, but I supposed it was possible. I'd been so exhausted the previous night that I'd hardly known what I was doing. But even if it had been unsteady on the table, what had tipped it on to the floor? It was another spooky thing about the Villa Naranja, I thought, as I picked it up and brought it into the kitchen. No matter what Pilar had said, and no matter how little I believed in ghosts, perhaps her grandmother was around after all. Maybe the older woman didn't want anyone living in her house. Maybe she wanted to scare me away. Or perhaps it was someone else. Someone who wanted to get my attention. Perhaps here, away from the noise and the bustle of my other life, I was the sort of person who could believe in another plane of existence. Who would allow the possibility, however slight, of some kind of other-worldly communication. But if I did . . . if I did . . . was it possible that—

'Don't be a bloody fool, Juno.' I spoke out loud and my words echoed around the room.

It was pointless telling myself not to be a fool.

Anyone who knew anything about me already knew I was the biggest fool in the world.

I unlocked the door and went outside. The sun was pleasantly warm as I sauntered a little way down the flagstone path before turning to look back at the house.

In the daylight, the flaking paint and sun-bleached shutters were more obvious, but so was the vividness of the purple-and-pink bougainvillea and the multicoloured hibiscus plants, which I hadn't noticed in the darkness. The house might have needed maintenance, but it seemed perfectly happy in its neglect. It was a settled part of the landscape, not trying too hard to be lovely. And it *was* lovely, despite its faded glory. Set among the orange trees and a garden that was part tiled and part gravelled, there was a stately look about it. That stateliness extended to the outside, where there was a small fountain (not working) and – to my enormous surprise – a decent-sized swimming pool. The water was slightly cloudy but not green or slimy, so I reckoned someone must come in on a regular basis to maintain it.

I continued on my walk around the garden and the orange groves, where many of the trees were heavy with fruit. It hadn't simply been blossom I'd scented earlier, but the zesty tang of the oranges themselves. I wondered if it would be

OK to pick some and make fresh juice in the mornings. I would have to ask Pilar.

Closer to the house and away from the orange grove was a spreading jacaranda tree, smothered in a cloud of purple flowers. Beneath it was a large flat stone which, from its faded markings, looked like it might have been a sundial.

They'd been right, I thought. Cleo and Saoirse and Pilar, who'd all persuaded me to come away. They'd been absolutely right. Even though my heart was still smashed into a million pieces, the heat of the sun and the beauty of the orange groves was balm to my soul.

I suddenly remembered that I'd promised Pilar I'd let her know that I'd arrived and that everything at the villa was OK. I hurried indoors again and found my mobile, which had a mere ten per cent of battery remaining. I plugged it into one of the adaptors I'd brought and shoved it into a wall socket. Straight away, the power cut out.

I swore softly under my breath. I went to the fuse box, pushed up the trip switch, and then chose a different socket for the phone. This time it began to charge and almost immediately pinged with a message. It was from Pilar.

Everything all right? she asked. *I'm guessing you found it OK as I didn't get any panicked phone calls in the middle of the night.*

All well, I texted in reply. *The house is lovely. So is the weather.*

Damp and grey today, came her instant response. *Glad you're well. Don't forget there is Wi-Fi in the house. It's the one subscription Mama didn't cancel – she needs it herself when she stays there. Keep in touch. Have a great time. Px. PS: If the oranges are out, feel free to pick them.*

I smiled at her last comment and then felt a lump rise in

my throat. So many people wanted me to have a good time. So many people wanted me to be better. Yet even though time is supposed to be a great healer, and even though months had passed, I knew I wasn't healed at all. Nowhere near it. And it would be a long time, if ever, before I was. No matter where I went and what I did.

Chapter 3

'Have a great time.'

Those were the last words I'd said to Brad when I said goodbye to him before he went on holiday. I'd repeated it after he'd kissed me goodbye – a warm, passionate kiss in the car park of the hotel where he'd stayed the previous night. Brad divided his time between the hospital in Belfast where he was employed and a private clinic in Dublin in which he had a share. He was more ambitious and more successful than me. Well, of course he was. As a consultant radiologist he was also a fully qualified doctor. Despite my additional qualification in emergency medicine, I'm not.

'I'll miss you,' he said. 'I wish I didn't have to go.'

'I wish you didn't have to go either.'

'I'll text when I can. The bloody signal isn't great there but I'll do my best.'

'I'm sure we'll get the chance to go on holiday together soon,' I said.

'Of course.'

He sounded wistful. I was feeling a bit wistful myself. I didn't want him to go to Italy without me but the holiday had already been planned. He had family there, he told me.

He couldn't not go. And he was sorry but he couldn't ask me to come. Not until I'd met them in different circumstances.

I'd said that I was fine with it – although, to be honest, I thought meeting the Italian side of his family in their Umbrian villa would have been perfect. I don't know Italy well, but even saying Italian names makes me feel sexier. I said this to him, and he laughed and kissed me again and told me that I was the hottest Irish woman he'd ever met and that I didn't need to be in Italy to be sexy. And then he said '*ti amo*' in a way that made my knees buckle with desire.

I couldn't help thinking that, if I had Italian relatives, I wouldn't be working in Ireland at all, but Brad reminded me that he'd been born and bred in Carrickfergus, a short drive from Belfast, and that Italy was lovely but it wasn't his home. Then he murmured that he was wondering if Dublin, not Belfast, should be his home in the future, and my knees buckled even more.

When he got into his car and rolled down the window I told him to have a great time, because I didn't want him to think that I was a clinging girlfriend – even though I was dreaming of us living together, and he'd given me hope when he'd talked about Dublin as a place where we might do just that. But after Sean, I was playing things very easy. All the same, when I got back to the apartment that evening I had to get into the shower to cool off because I was still a hot mass of quivering desire.

I thought about him every day for the next few days, and although I was too busy to have hot quivering thoughts at work, I was missing him more than ever at night. He sent me regular WhatsApp messages with photos of the stunning

Italian countryside and the medieval town of San Alessio, which looked like something out of a history book. I couldn't quite believe people actually lived there, but Brad assured me that they did.

The final message I got from him was on the fourth day of his holiday, the message that had nearly caused me to collapse in the queue for the rental car.

Tonight's dinner location. Joining them shortly. Love you. Miss you. Bxx

The photo showed a burnt-sienna building with some lattice tables and green sun umbrellas outside. It looked perfect. I wished I'd persuaded him to take me with him. I sent a message with the same words I'd spoken when I'd said goodbye.

Have a great time.

And then I'd gone to the pub with Saoirse and Cleo and had a good time myself.

It wasn't until the following evening that I heard the news. It had been a busy day at the hospital and I'd been far too occupied to fret over the fact that I hadn't got a text from him that morning. In fact, I didn't really think about him at all until I got home and was making myself some beans on toast. I realised then that he hadn't been in touch, so I sent him a message, asking if he had another achingly gorgeous location for that night's dinner and attaching a pic of my single-portion can of beans. I was hurt that he didn't reply straight away and resented the fact that he was probably lounging around somewhere with a glass of Chianti, living the life and ignoring his phone – and me.

And then I switched on the TV.

'The earthquake measured 5.9 on the Richter scale,' a news reporter was saying. 'Buildings have been severely damaged, many are destroyed and there are reports of multiple casualties.' The reporter was standing in front of a building which looked like it had been demolished by a wrecking ball.

'There are a dozen confirmed dead but the death toll is expected to rise.'

Then, in the scrolling headline below him, the words: *Earthquake strikes Italian region of Umbria.*

'Residents of the small Italian town of San Alessio, closest to the epicentre, are in shock,' continued the reporter.

I dropped my toast on the floor.

Brad was in San Alessio.

I ignored the toast on the floor and took out my phone.

Heard news. Are you all right? I texted. *Call me.*

There was no reply. But, I reasoned, in a place where the mobile signal was already patchy, there could be even worse problems with communications after such a terrible event. Masts could be damaged. The network might be overloaded. It wasn't an ominous sign that he hadn't got in touch. Besides, Brad was a doctor. His first instinct would be to help people, not to call me. All the same, I would've liked a text to put my mind at rest. But perhaps he'd sent his first text to his parents. That's what Irish people did. They called home. And I wasn't part of Brad's home. Not yet.

I picked up the toast and threw it in the bin. The microwave was beeping to tell me the beans were done. I left them in the bowl and sat in front of the TV.

Saoirse came home at about eleven to find me obsessively switching between news channels.

35

'Oh my God, Juno!' she said when I told her. 'Are you OK?'

'I'm fine, of course I'm fine. It's Brad I'm worried about.'

'I'm sure he's OK too.' She put her arm around me and gave me a hug. 'He's probably helping out at one of the shelters.'

I nodded.

'That's what I thought.'

'He'll message you when he can,' Saoirse assured me.

'I know.'

'But it's still a concern,' she conceded.

'Yes,' I said and switched channels again.

I couldn't help but worry. But I was also sure that I'd have sensed it if something had happened to him. Which was a bloody stupid thought for someone who needs proof to believe in anything.

It was lucky that I didn't have work the next day, because I spent all night in front of the TV. The faint light of dawn was creeping over the horizon when the report finally came in.

'A Northern Ireland family has been confirmed as being among those caught up in the earthquake which struck central Italy yesterday.'

The male reporter was standing at the edge of a street that had been reduced to rubble.

'The family has been named as Brad and Alessandra McIntyre and their three-year-old son, Dylan.'

The photograph flashed up on the screen, and I stared at it soundlessly.

'Brad and Alessandra have been confirmed as dead, while

36

Dylan has been brought to a local hospital for treatment to his injuries, which are not life threatening.' The reporter glanced at his notes, then continued. 'The McIntyres have been described locally as a well-liked family who visit the town every year. Alessandra's grandparents come from this area, although they moved to Belfast to open a restaurant there in the 1960s. The restaurant is now run by Alessandra's father and is very popular.'

He kept talking but I didn't hear him. I was transfixed by the photograph that showed Brad – my Brad, tall and blond and beautiful – standing behind a stunningly attractive woman wearing a bright-red dress, her dark hair curling around her heart-shaped face. He had one arm around her shoulder and was holding a small boy in the other.

I was struggling to process what I was seeing. Something was horribly wrong. It had to be. Brad wasn't married with a family. He was my boyfriend. The man I'd hoped to marry one day. There'd been some kind of mistake. They'd confused him with someone else. And then it registered with me that the reporter had said the man in the photograph was dead. So if the photo was real, it meant my Brad was dead. That simply wasn't possible. My head was spinning. I couldn't think straight. I was in complete and total shock.

I could still hear the reporter speaking – he'd moved on to someone else's story now – and I could see the images on the TV, but I seemed disconnected from everything around me. Nothing was real, nothing was solid. I couldn't move. My legs weren't working. My body seemed to be separate from the rest of me. I was stuck to the sofa, hardly able to breathe.

About fifteen minutes later, they returned to the story of

the earthquake. They showed the photo of Brad and Alessandra again. They repeated that they had both died. I still couldn't process it. But this time it seemed more real. I started to cry.

I was still crying when Saoirse came out of her bedroom shortly afterwards. She'd stayed up with me until about half past one, but had been falling asleep by then. I'd told her that I'd be fine on my own and that I was sure Brad would call in the middle of the night. Now she was looking at me, concern etched on her face.

'Juno?' she said uncertainly.

'He . . . he . . .'

'Oh, Juno!'

She was beside me in an instant, her arms around me. The report had moved on to other people's stories – a miraculous escape for a teenage girl, a dog freed from beneath the rubble, a woman who was still trapped in the ruins of her home, a missing father of three. Stories of triumph and of tragedy. All meaningless to me.

Saoirse was telling me that she was so, so sorry but she didn't yet know that there was more to it than she thought. She had no idea about Brad's . . . well, what? What, I asked myself, had happened? What was the truth? Was it possible that there were two Brad McIntyres in Italy? One with a wife and son, and the other the man I loved? It was highly unlikely, but unlikely things did happen. I knew that from my work at the hospital. And then I remembered that they'd put up an actual picture of Brad with another woman and a young boy. And that the adults were dead, while the boy was in a serious but stable condition. There was no other family. Only this one.

'Did you get a message?' Saoirse asked. 'Or did you see something on the news?'

38

I didn't reply. Now that I'd started crying I couldn't stop. I knew that I was getting hysterical but there was nothing I could do about it.

'Juno!' She began to shake me by the shoulders. 'Come on. Snap out of it. I realise something awful has happened, but you need to get a grip on yourself or you'll make yourself sick.'

'I . . . I know.' I hiccoughed. 'But it's so . . . so . . .' And I dissolved into tears again.

It wasn't me who told her what had happened in the end but the news reporter, whose clip from in front of the ruined building was on a loop. I heard his words, I knew the photo was being flashed on screen, but my head was buried in my hands and I didn't look up.

'Oh my God,' she said, after he'd finished. 'What the hell, Juno?'

I looked up. Her expression was concerned and bewildered all at once.

'I don't know.' They were the first coherent words I'd uttered since she'd come into the room. 'I don't know what it's all about. I don't know what to think. But he's dead, Saoirse. Dead. He went on holiday and he died.'

She nodded slowly.

'They're saying a Northern Ireland family,' she said. 'Did he—'

'No!' I cried before she could finish. 'No, of course he didn't say anything about a family.'

'He must be separated,' she said. 'Or divorced.'

Why hadn't I thought of either of these options? Relief, mingled with even greater grief, flooded through me.

'Of course,' I breathed. 'Of course he was divorced. They

went on holiday because of their little boy. He didn't tell me because he didn't want to hurt me. Or because he was afraid I wouldn't understand. But I would've understood because I loved him. And now . . . now . . .' I started to cry again.

Saoirse allowed me to weep for a while and then she went into the galley kitchen, where she made me a cup of tea and insisted I drink it.

'Have you heard anything from anybody?' she asked.

I sipped the tea, even though I didn't want it, and then shook my head.

'Do you have a number for anyone close to him?' she asked.

I shook my head again.

'I'm so sorry,' she said. 'I know how much you loved him.'

'And he loved me.' My voice was shaky. 'He said so, Saoirse. Loads of times. He loved me, and it's all become complicated because of his first marriage and . . .' I knew the shock of knowing he'd been married was somehow distracting me from the fact that he was actually dead. It was as though thinking about his family meant I couldn't think about how he might have died. What might have happened to him.

'Maybe one of the staff at his hospital will get in touch with you,' said Saoirse. 'I know you went to Belfast once or twice. Where did he live?'

'We never actually stayed in Belfast itself,' I said. 'We went to a hotel outside the city.'

She said nothing.

'He wanted to treat me!' I cried. 'He wasn't keeping me a secret or anything.'

40

But even as I said the words I couldn't help thinking that I'd never met any of his friends. Or his family. And that we'd never gone out as a couple in Belfast. In Dublin we'd gone to the cinema and eaten out, but never with any of my friends either. The only person who'd actually met him was Saoirse, and that only briefly when we'd arrived back at the apartment before she'd gone out herself. People at work knew I had a boyfriend, but that was it. I'd never even mentioned his name.

'I liked him,' she said. 'He seemed a pretty straightforward guy to me. But . . .'

'But what?' I demanded.

'But nothing.' She looked at me with sympathy. 'It's awful, Juno. Absolutely awful.'

I turned my eyes to the TV screen again. The pictures were heartbreaking. Ruined homes, ruined buildings, a ruined city. And ruined lives.

Including mine.

Twenty-four-hour news with its scrolling headlines and repeated stories had always irritated me before, but I spent the rest of the day in front of the TV watching the same reporters say the same things, over and over again, in the hope that I'd get more information about Brad. However, it wasn't until I turned on the RTÉ news that evening that I did.

'Brad McIntyre was a consultant radiologist who, as well as working in Belfast, had a stake in a private clinic in south County Dublin,' said the newsreader. 'He was popular with his colleagues and everyone speaks highly of him.'

The report cut to a picture of the Belfast hospital where a clinician was talking to camera.

'Brad McIntyre was a brilliant radiologist,' he said. 'He was wonderful with staff and patients alike and had a warm manner that endeared him to everyone.'

And then a piece outside the Dublin clinic.

'I can't believe it,' a young nurse was saying. 'He was here last week talking about new equipment and . . .' She shook her head. 'It's a terrible tragedy. And his beautiful wife too – that poor boy. To lose his parents like that.'

Finally, another piece from Belfast.

'Our family has lost a treasured member in Brad.' The man speaking was tall and well built, with fair hair and slate-grey eyes, his accent a little more southern than Brad's. He was wearing a black suit and his voice was steady as he spoke. 'He was always part of everything we did, along with his amazing wife, Alessandra, and their beautiful boy, Dylan. We have been broken by what has happened and we pray with all our hearts that Dylan will make a full recovery. Brad and Alessandra had gone to San Alessio with their son, as they always did around this time of the year, to be with her extended family. Brad really connected with the town, where he was well known and liked. He regarded his visits to San Alessio as an essential part of his life. I want to pay tribute on his behalf, and on behalf of Alessandra, to the actions of the first responders in Italy who tried so hard to save them. I would also like to thank them for their prompt treatment of Dylan. Our thoughts and prayers go out to them and to the other people who have suffered in this appalling tragedy.'

I stared at the screen long after the news had moved on to something else.

Brad was dead.

So was his wife.

His son was critically injured.

And I was still here. The woman nobody knew anything about. The woman he hadn't told anybody about. Because he wasn't divorced. He was married.

I wasn't a girlfriend. I was a mistress. And I hadn't known that either.

Chapter 4

I finished my circuit of the Villa Naranja and walked back inside through the kitchen door. As I'd walked around I'd noticed, even though my head was somewhere else entirely, that there was an entrance on the other side of the house too, through double doors which led directly into the living room. Walking into it now from the inside and opening the shutters (proper wooden ones, like those upstairs, and equally creaky), I realised that it had probably been the main entrance at one point. I opened the door and allowed the ever warmer air to circulate through the room.

Behind me, I heard a faint noise and I whirled around. I'd left the kitchen door open and I suddenly felt very vulnerable. There was a scurrying sound and I rushed into the kitchen just in time to see a silver-grey tail disappearing outside. I followed it. Sitting beside the empty fountain, a plump cat observed me from amber-flecked eyes.

'You scared the living daylights out of me,' I told it as I approached it slowly. 'Were you in the house last night? Did you knock over the glass?'

The cat ignored me and began washing its face with its paw.

'What's your name?' I asked.

The cat continued to wash its face. I came a little closer. I've always liked cats, although my mother hates them and refused to allow me to adopt the skinny stray that used to frequent our house when I was smaller, even though I begged her like I'd never begged her before.

'But it's black and it's lucky,' I protested. 'You said that a black cat in the house makes a play successful.'

'In the audience on opening night,' she told me. 'Not in my house. Arrogant, wilful creatures.'

So I wasn't allowed to put out food for the black cat, and eventually he gave us up as a lost cause and moved on to more fruitful pastures (Mrs Jacobs, three houses down). But I still liked cats precisely because they were arrogant. Because they behaved as though they didn't need anyone. And sometimes I wanted to feel that way too.

'Are you hungry?' I asked the silver-grey cat now. 'Would you like something to eat?'

I realised almost at once that I was being silly. I had nothing to offer him other than one of the soggy Danish pastries that I'd taken from the plane. There was no food inside. It hadn't bothered me earlier because I wasn't hungry. But now, to my surprise, I was.

The Danish pastries, when I retrieved them, were even soggier and less appetising than they'd been the previous day. The only foodstuff in the kitchen cupboard was pasta and coffee. I made myself a cup of black coffee and drank it sitting on the doorstep watching the cat, which had now stretched itself out to its full length and was lying in the shade of the fountain. I wondered if it came by every day. I hoped so. Although I'd wanted nothing but seclusion

45

and isolation, I was already beginning to wonder if I'd be able to stick the total emptiness of Villa Naranja for very long.

I finished the coffee and stood up. The cat got to its feet too and shot off into the orange groves. I thought about following it and told myself not to be silly. But I went as far as the first tree and picked up an orange that was lying on the ground beneath it. I peeled the fruit and then popped a segment into my mouth. It was sweet and juicy and quite unlike anything I'd ever bought from the supermarket or the convenience store around the corner from the apartment.

But I wouldn't survive on windfall oranges, I told myself, even as I wondered if 'windfall' was the term when there wasn't even the slightest hint of a breeze. I needed to buy some food, no matter how uninterested I was in eating. And I needed to settle myself into the house so that I would be able to stay for a few weeks. I needed those few weeks. I needed to find myself again. I'd been failing miserably in Dublin, and everyone knew it. At least here I could be a failure on my own.

I went back upstairs and stood in front of the mirror. Until the previous year my nut-brown hair had been long and wavy, but as part of the annual fund-raiser for the hospital I'd shaved my head. Now, although my hair had grown again, it was cut in a bob just below my ears – an in-between length where it was going in all directions. I brushed it and used a tortoiseshell hairband to keep it in place. It needed the hair-band in order not to look as though I couldn't be bothered to brush it at all. The other rather scary thing about the regrowth was that more than a few greys had started to appear. At the moment I was pulling them out whenever I saw them, but I had a horrible feeling that one day I'd need to take more drastic measures. Except for a brief flirtation with pink streaks in my early twenties, I'd never bothered colouring it because I'd inherited the rich brown from my mother, who was famed for her luxurious, shiny locks. She wears it in a sophisticated silver now, carefully tinted to enhance its sheen, but I was a long way from wanting to be silver.

After fixing my hair and putting sunscreen on my face (something Mum had drummed into me from a young age – I always listened to her about beauty, even if I sometimes ignored her more time-consuming advice) I closed up the house and got into the car. Driving along the country road in daylight was a much less fraught experience than it had been the previous night, and I realised that the Villa Naranja wasn't as isolated as it had seemed either. There were more houses than I'd previously thought dotted among the orange, lemon and olive groves – although, like the Villa Naranja, most of them were set back from the road and behind big iron gates.

Five minutes brought me to the town of Beniflor. Again, I had to correct my preconceptions. I'd imagined a small, backward town, but the main street, which forked two-thirds of the way along, had a varied mix of shops including a couple of mobile phone stores, three café bars, a pharmacy and a florist.

I took the left-hand fork in the street, which led to a mid-sized supermarket with some empty parking spaces outside. I pulled in and stopped the car. There were lots of signs in the store showing prices having been cut for various items – although, as I had only about five words of Spanish, I had no idea what *cerezas, remolacha* or *pulpo* were, or if they were anything I'd possibly need regardless of the discounts.

I got out of the car and walked inside to find out.

Cerezas, it turned out, were cherries and there was an enormous punnet of them on sale for a little over €1, so I put it into the plastic shopping basket I'd taken from inside the door. Half a melon at an equally low price was added to the basket as well. Maybe I'd turn into a fruit and veg freak while I was here, I thought, as I spotted green beans for a few cents. Maybe something good would come of it all.

I swallowed the lump in my throat. Of course nothing good could come of the fact that I'd had my heart broken by a man who'd died in tragic circumstances along with 250 others, including the wife I hadn't known existed, and whose son had been dragged injured from the rubble.

I was glad that nobody knew about my relationship with him. At work they knew that my boyfriend had died in an accident but nobody linked it to an earthquake in another country. Of course there was talk about my personal 'tragedy', with people coming up to me and saying that they were sorry for my loss, even though most of them hadn't known I was going out with anyone at all. But it faded, as things do, except in the radiology department, where the staff knew that I was devastated and Drina might have guessed more than she ever let on.

I continued to walk around the supermarket, which was actually quite big inside and had a decent meat and deli counter along with a well-stocked fish counter. I discovered that *remolacha* was beetroot and *pulpo* was octopus, so neither of them found their way into my basket. I picked up other items at random – filtered coffee because I'd seen a machine in the kitchen and I'm not a big fan of instant, a large bottle of water, croissants, bread rolls, ham from the deli counter, some salad and tomatoes and then a variety of sauces in jars. I'd never have made it as a potential contestant on *MasterChef*. Most of my culinary efforts came from jars or frozen ready meals and, given that my hours could be erratic, my food often ended up being from a takeaway. But there were no ready meals in the supermarket's chiller cabinet and I ended up adding some pre-packed chicken breasts and some rice to my basket. The rice came in a little bag with the word *arroz* printed across it in blue. I identified it because of the picture of steaming grains on the front.

Given that I'd only had half a cup of flavourless coffee and an orange for my breakfast, I was beginning to feel peckish. I'd often felt hungry over the weeks since the earth-quake, although as soon as food passed my mouth I was unable to eat another bite. But since I was here, I decided to check out the town and find a place to have a coffee. I bought a freezer bag at the checkout and placed the chicken and ham into it, then put my bags in the boot of the car which was, fortunately, already in the shade.

I walked back down the street. After I'd passed the fork in the road again, I followed one of the side streets, which twisted in all sorts of directions before opening into a diamond-shaped plaza. The plaza was paved with smooth tiles and dotted with tubs of red and yellow flowers, which mirrored the flag hanging from what was clearly an official building on one of the diamond's diagonals. On the opposite side was a whitewashed church with a domed steeple covered in navy-blue tiles. There were a couple of clothes shops on another side and, on the last, a bar and a *pastelería* named the Café Flor.

I sat down beneath the dark blue umbrella of one of the outside tables and picked up the menu. Almost at once a pretty red-haired girl in skimpy shorts and a cropped T-shirt walked out and smiled at me. She hesitated for a nanosecond and then, in English, asked what I'd like.

'A coffee,' I replied.

'With milk? And would you like anything to eat?'

I looked at the menu again. Even reading it had taken the edge off my hunger but I knew I had to have something.

'A slice of cherry pie,' I said.

'Would you like cream or ice cream with the pie?' she asked.

When I didn't reply immediately she suggested the ice cream.

'Our cream comes out of an aerosol,' she said. 'The Spanish love it but it's sweetened and it sort of dissolves after a few minutes. On the other hand, the ice cream is from a local family and it's gorgeous. Although it's fifty cents extra.'

Even though I was on a strict budget (I didn't have a huge amount of savings and, of course, I wasn't being paid for my time off), I thought I could stretch to the extra fifty cents for the ice cream, and said so. The waitress grinned at me and disappeared back inside while I sat and observed the bustle of the plaza.

Most of the activity seemed to be taking place around the building with the flag, as a steady stream of people entered and left. The bar on the corner was filling up with elderly men who were mainly drinking coffee and small glasses of spirits. The women either went into the clothes shops or headed off to do other things – although, a few minutes after I had sat down, a group of young women in their twenties sat down at the table next to me, took out iPads and started talking animatedly about whatever they were sharing. Meanwhile, some young boys, all aged around ten, began racing each other. It took me a while to realise that they were actually trying to get around the plaza without touching the ground. They were attempting this feat by running along a tiled wall, jumping on to marble seats set into the ground, and using some raised planters as platforms to leap from. When they got as far as the bar, one of the old men shouted at them and they shouted back before running away, laughing.

The red-haired girl brought me my coffee and pie.

'Enjoy,' she said, putting it down beside me and then going to take the order from the young women at the other table.

The coffee was silky smooth and the cherry pie delicious. As for the ice cream – it was out of this world! Without even noticing it, I managed to eat everything in front of me.

'All OK?' asked the waitress when I signalled for the bill.

'Wonderful,' I said. 'I can't believe I've found a café like this in such an out-of-the-way place.'

The girl smiled. 'We're not that out of the way,' she told me. 'It's only a twenty-minute drive to Benidorm, you know.'

'Do you get many visitors?' I looked at her doubtfully, not thinking the little town of Beniflor had much to offer anyone who was looking for a traditional sun holiday.

'You'd be surprised,' she replied. 'Lots of people prefer to be in the mountains, rather than at the coast, and Beniflor has some old Arab baths which are quite an attraction. I'd recommend checking them out if you're here for a few days. My mum and dad run the hotel a little further outside town. It's always busy.'

'Is that the small and chic one?' I asked. 'I've forgotten the name.'

'La Higuera.' She smiled again. 'It means the Fig Tree – there's a really old one in the garden. My parents like to think of it as a boutique offering. The hotel used to be an old hunting lodge, and when the opportunity came up they decided to renovate it.'

'A big undertaking,' I observed.

'Mum and Dad ran a hotel in Benidorm for ten years,' said the waitress. 'They know what they're doing.'

'And it's going well?' I asked.

'So far so good,' she replied. 'Are you staying nearby? You should visit.'

'I'm at the Villa Naranja,' I said. 'It's—'

'Oh! Old Doña Carmen's place.' She nodded and her curls bobbed around her face. 'How nice.'

'You know it?'

'Everybody knows everybody in Beniflor,' she said. 'And they'll find out all about you too, so I hope you don't have any dark secrets.'

None worth talking about, I thought to myself, as I asked her if she lived here or if she was just working in the café for the summer.

'Mum and Dad moved here before I was born,' she replied. 'So I'm Spanish born but, I guess, English bred. I watch *Strictly* and *Corrie* with my mum in the evenings but I support Spain in every big sporting event, and I'm going to university in Alicante.'

'What are you studying?'

I realised, as I asked the question, that this was the most I'd spoken to anybody in weeks.

'Psychology,' she said. 'There are good prospects for psychologists here, and it's something that interests me.'

'And working in the café for the holidays?'

She nodded.

'Not the hotel?'

'Better all round for me not to work with Mum and Dad,' she said. 'But the café is owned by the mother of their pastry chef. I know you liked the cherry pie but I promise you her almond tarts are to die for.'

'Maybe next time,' I said as I put what seemed to be a paltry sum on the table.

'I hope we see you again soon.'

'I'll be back,' I promised. 'Thank you for all the local information . . . um . . . what's your name?'

'Rosa,' she said. 'Rosa Johnson.'

'I'm Juno Ryan. It was lovely to meet you.'

'You too.'

She flashed me another brilliant smile, then cleared my empty cup and plate from the table and brought them indoors.

I was feeling unexpectedly lighthearted as I arrived back at the Villa Naranja. Beniflor was a pretty town, and Rosa's cheerfulness was almost infectious. Besides, it was hard not to feel a little brighter beneath the warmth of the sun and the clear blue skies. Maybe I was getting over it, I told myself. Maybe I was getting to the point where I could see the sun and the skies and not have to ask myself if I was OK.

The moment was fleeting. I felt the pain stab me again, a

deep thrust in the very centre of my being. And I heard him say my name, the northern lilt in his voice. *Juno. How are ye, Juno?* I whirled around but there was nobody there. My heart was thumping and I stood immobile for at least a minute before I could walk into the kitchen to put the food away.

I understand the stages of grief. I learned about them. I'm familiar with the principles of denial, anger, bargaining, depression and acceptance. I know it's not a linear process, that you can go back and forward through them. But I'd no idea where I could place myself. I'd gone through denial and anger over the last few weeks. I wanted to leave both of them behind. But I didn't know what bargain I could make. There was nothing that could bring Brad back. And if there was – what could I say to him? What could he say to me? There was no explanation for his lies. Nothing to make me feel better. If I was anywhere in the five stages now, I was probably at depression, because it was hard not to feel the weight of despair that my unwitting relationship had left me with. Yet I don't like to think of myself as the kind of person who gets depressed. I'm usually a glass-half-full kind of person. But nobody tells you how overwhelming grief can be. How it can sneak up on you and take you over when you least expect it. How it can take you from the place you think you are and leave you somewhere entirely different. And it's even worse when you don't really know what you're grieving for. Was I more broken-hearted because Brad had lied to me than because he'd been killed? Was I devastated at his treachery or the fact that I'd never see him again? I couldn't answer my own question, and I didn't want to keep asking it.

I needed to keep busy, to block out the unwelcome thoughts that found their way into my head. I'd tried hard in Dublin but my success had been limited. Now I was here, alone, and I knew I'd have to find something to do or I'd go mad. Although I hadn't said anything to the girls, who'd urged me to occupy myself with something new and different, I'd planned on using my time here to study. I'd been thinking of adding to my specialisations for a while, and this was my opportunity. So I'd downloaded the latest books on nuclear medicine to read about other aspects of radiology before making choices. But I didn't have the heart to open them.

I took out my phone, accessed my voicemail and listened to his voice again.

I wish I was there with you. I wish I had my arms around you right now.

I wanted it so much. Just one more minute with him. With his arms around me. And I wouldn't waste it in asking him why he hadn't told me the truth. I didn't care. All I wanted was to be with him. If I'd been the one to have gone on the holiday with him, I would've been there when he died. I would have died myself. But it wouldn't have mattered. Because right now I was dead inside, anyway.

I shoved the phone into the pocket of my shorts, angry with myself. I worked in a hospital. I knew all about life and death. And the hope that keeps us going. I should be hopeful. I needed to be hopeful. That was why I was here. So no more listening to messages. No more wishing that things had been different. They weren't.

With a renewed sense of determination I pulled the phone out again and accessed voicemail once more. But when it came down to it, I wasn't able to delete his last words to me. Nor could I delete his final text. But at least I'd thought about it. I'd made a gesture. And now I needed to think about something else. Something to take my mind off him completely.

I looked around me critically.

Housework was as low on my scale of priorities as cooking but the Villa Naranja would definitely benefit from a bit of a clean. Being active helped to keep the darker thoughts away. I knew this, even though being active at work hadn't banished my despair.

I rummaged around the shelves beneath the sink and found bleach, surface cleaners and furniture polish as well as microfibre cloths. A tall cupboard held a bucket, mop and vacuum cleaner. And behind the gingham curtains I also found a light stepladder, which allowed me to reach the wall cupboards.

I opened them, one by one, including the cupboard where I'd just stacked the coffee, rice and sauces. The shelves were covered with old newspapers, which I took down and put in a cardboard box beside the kitchen door. I didn't know the original purpose of the box but I reckoned it could do for recycling. Judging by the dates and the sticky residues from old bottles and jars, the papers had been lining the cupboards for years. I didn't have anything to replace them with but I'd never bothered lining shelves before, and I didn't see the need to start now.

I began to wipe them all down and then sprayed the old wooden doors with the furniture polish to shine them up. I abandoned that idea after the first attempt, though, because the doors were greasy and the dust was sticking to them. So I used soapy water to clean them instead.

It took ages, and I was lathered in sweat by the time I was finished. My hair was damp and so were my clothes.

I looked at my watch and realised that it was mid-afternoon, the traditional time for a siesta. Pilar had told me that Spain was as much a 24/7 country as anywhere else in the world, these days, but that people took the opportunity for a siesta if they could. 'After all,' she'd pointed out, 'we stay up late. We need a few zzzs in the middle of the day.'

I'd laughed at her then, but a siesta seemed like a great idea to me now. I was sure I wouldn't sleep, but maybe a twenty-minute break would be good for me. I locked the door but left the windows open, secure behind the iron grilles. Talking to Rosa earlier had left me less paranoid about being on my own. This was a nice town. A safe place. There was no reason to be worried. And, of course, ghosts (if I believed in them) wouldn't appear in daylight.

I went upstairs and lay on the bed. Despite my promises to myself I couldn't help thinking of Brad as soon as I closed my eyes. I wished I could wipe him from my memory but I couldn't forget that I'd loved him. And that I thought he'd loved me. Yet what troubled me most, what I couldn't stop thinking about, was that I'd never know if what we had was a brief affair or if he'd expected it to be something else.

I wished he'd given me the choice about that.

Chapter 5

The earthquake had been headline news for nearly a week. The Irish newspapers focused in on Brad and his family, as they were the only local people caught up in it. The stories all described him as a devoted family man, a brilliant radiologist, a pillar of the community. Alessandra, they said, was a bright, popular woman who'd given up her job in the health service to be a full-time mum while continuing her voluntary work for a local children's charity.

I pored over every story, particularly any that mentioned Alessandra. Nothing gave the impression that their marriage had been anything other than happy. There was no sense that they'd come to San Alessio to resolve issues. And yet everything couldn't have been perfect if he'd been cheating on her with me. But maybe they wouldn't say anything negative in the newspaper reports? Maybe they wanted to paint a happy picture? It was more newsworthy that way. I wanted to know the truth about their relationship but I couldn't see any way of finding it out. Certainly not from the papers, which were portraying them as practically perfect.

Brad and Alessandra's bodies were eventually flown back

to Belfast. I told Cleo and Saoirse that I needed to go to the funeral service.

'Are you nuts?' demanded Cleo. 'Why would you put yourself through all that?'

'I need it to be real,' I replied. 'I need to hear people talking about him in the past tense. And if there's any information, any talk . . . well, I need to hear that too.'

'Juno, sweetheart, it's going to be madly emotional,' Saoirse told me. 'Plus it's going to be all about his family. There won't be any talk. You can't possibly be there.'

'I have to,' I said. 'Unless I see it, I won't truly believe it.'

I was still in denial and I needed proof.

I wasn't scheduled to be off work but I managed to swap a shift with one of the other radiographers, even though swapping shifts was frowned upon at the hospital. I caught the Enterprise train from Connolly Station and then took a cab from Belfast Central to the crematorium where the service was to be held. Although I was early, a large crowd had already gathered. Seating in the crematorium itself had been restricted to close family, but speakers had been rigged up so that everyone else could hear what was going on. The building was set in a surprisingly large and well-tended garden filled with shrubs and trees, which meant that the crowd could be accommodated. Somewhat inappropriately, it was a warm spring day, and the garden was a beautiful place to be.

I leaned against the trunk of a spreading beech tree, trying to keep my distance, but by the time the cortège pulled up even more people had arrived and I was surrounded by mourners who, from their murmured words, all seemed to be neighbours of the family.

There was a hushed silence as the undertakers slid the coffins from the hearse, and then people began to cry. I think if I hadn't been practically wedged against the tree trunk at that point I probably would have collapsed. It was so unbelievably tragic and so unutterably sad.

Over the loudspeakers came the sound of an unaccompanied female voice singing 'Amazing Grace'.

'The poor wee pet, left without his Mammy and Daddy,' murmured a woman behind me. 'Please God he'll recover.'

'A lovely family,' said her companion. 'So devoted to each other. Why are the best taken so young?'

'I heard she was pregnant,' whispered the first woman. 'Another life lost.'

I felt my head spin. Alessandra was pregnant? Pregnant? And I felt a spasm of disgust that I even allowed myself to wonder for a nanosecond if the baby was Brad's.

Silence fell again as the last notes of 'Amazing Grace' faded. I leaned against the tree trunk, grateful for the support as a wave of self-loathing engulfed me. My friends were right. I shouldn't have come here. It had been selfish and hypocritical. I didn't deserve to be among people who'd loved them, listening to the minister soothe the congregation, praise the lives of Brad and Alessandra and mourn their passing as well as leading prayers for the recovery of their beautiful son. I'd been in love with a completely different Brad, and I hadn't really known him at all.

I shivered despite the balmy breeze and the heat of the crowds around me. I pulled my jacket tighter and concentrated on staying upright as the minister told us that someone called Max would be giving the eulogy.

'I was five years old when I first met Brad McIntyre.' The

man's voice, calm and gentle, carried over the crowd. I recognised it. He was the man who'd spoken on TV. Holding it together then, solemn and steady. Holding it together now too, his voice even and measured. 'I walked into the house clutching my teddy bear who went everywhere with me. Brad came over to me and said hello. Then he looked at my teddy bear, who was missing an eye. "I can fix that for you," were his first words to me. And he's been fixing things ever since, because that's the sort of person Brad McIntyre was.'

Max continued speaking but I was lost in my own memories and the tears that were now flooding down my face.

'I loved my brother,' said Max in conclusion. 'I will always love him.'

His brother? I looked up as I blew my nose on my already sodden tissue. Brad hadn't said anything about a brother either. And how could he be his brother if he first met him when he was five? I realised that Brad hadn't told me anything about his life. I'd thought I'd known everything I needed to know, but I was wrong.

Brad and Alessandra hadn't been on a break. They were a married couple with a child, and possibly expecting another one. He'd lied by omission about everything in his life while he'd conducted his affair with me. I'd meant nothing at all to him. How could I have been so stupid?

The service concluded and the mourners began to drift away, still murmuring about how awful it all was, what a wonderful family they'd been and how eloquently Max had spoken. I moved along with the swell of people, although my legs were trembling and I felt as though I could keel over at any minute. Then I spotted a wooden bench in the corner of the garden and made my way towards it.

I collapsed on to it and closed my eyes. I tried to imagine what it had been like for Brad and Alessandra in those terrifying last moments. The house shaking, the walls crumbling, knowing that there was nothing they could do. The noise. The dust. The darkness. The panic. The fear that both Brad and Alessandra must have had for their son, and for their unborn child too. She'd been found beside Dylan. Brad had been a little further away. Had he been killed trying to get help? Or trying to reach them himself? I felt the tears roll down my face and I pulled another tissue from my bag.

'Are you OK?'

The man who came over to me was wearing a black suit and tie. I recognised his voice from earlier and I recognised his face from the TV. It was Max. The brother I hadn't known about. It was hard to tell if he was older or younger because his grief was etched on his face, giving him a pale, drawn appearance.

'Yes,' I said. 'Yes, I'm fine. I just . . .'

'It's difficult for everyone.' He was comforting me, even though I should have been the one with the words of comfort. 'Were you a friend of Allie's? Or Brad?'

'I . . . worked with Brad occasionally,' I replied.

'He was a great doctor.'

'Yes,' I said. 'He was.'

'Well, nice to meet you.' His grey eyes were serious in his angular face. 'Thank you for coming.'

'I had to come.'

He nodded. And then, as I thought he was going to say something else, he spotted someone walking along the gravel pathway and murmured a brief goodbye. He strode across the garden, tall and lean, holding himself with a certain dignity. I wished I could be more dignified myself but I was crying again and rubbing my eyes with yet another balled-up tissue.

It was about twenty minutes later before I left the crematorium. The next train to Dublin wasn't for an hour but I got a cab back to the station and had a watery coffee while I waited for it. I texted Cleo and Saoirse to say I was on the way back and that I hadn't made a show of myself.

But I hadn't achieved what I'd wanted either.

To say goodbye.

To have closure.

To leapfrog over anger, bargaining and depression straight into acceptance.

Because I was still struggling to accept what had happened.

I didn't know if I ever would.

This time it was a definite crash downstairs that jolted me out of my thoughts. I reminded myself I'd locked the door and there were grilles over the windows so nobody could be in the house. But there were no grilles on the bedroom windows, I recalled, as I slid off the bed. Someone could have climbed up – and God only knew what they were planning.

I peeped out of the window. There was nothing to see.

I tiptoed downstairs in my bare feet, holding my flip-flops in my hand. I've always been scathing about women in movies who investigate unexplained noises. I scream at them to lock themselves in the bedroom or phone for help. But there was no lock on the bedroom door, and I'd left my phone charging in the kitchen socket.

I held my breath as I stepped off the bottom stair. Everything was silent. If there were marauders in the house they were doing their marauding very quietly. I walked gingerly into the kitchen and immediately saw what had caused the noise. My phone was on the floor. It had clearly fallen from the counter on to the tiles, and that had been the crash I'd heard. I picked it up, hoping against hope that the screen wasn't broken.

A hairline crack snaked across it but the phone itself was working. I looked around me. Nothing else had been disturbed, and the door was firmly closed and locked. There was nobody here. The house was a marauder-free zone. So who – or what – had knocked over the phone? Was Doña Carmen's spirit still in the house and was she outraged at the wanton hussy who'd come to stay? Or was it Brad, trying to connect with me, to explain to me how things had turned out the way they had?

'You're losing it,' I muttered as I stood in the centre of the room. 'You know these are nonsense thoughts. You've finally tipped yourself over the edge.'

Then I saw the tiniest of movements out of the corner of my eye and heard a scrabbling sound. I went to the recycling box and looked inside. Slanted amber-flecked eyes looked back at me. The silver-grey cat was curled up inside, apparently having decided that the newspapers made an excellent bed.

'You again!' I exclaimed. 'You're quite determined to give me a heart attack before the week is out, aren't you?'

The cat yawned.

'Are you a ghost or a marauder?' I asked.

He licked his paw and began washing his face.

'I wish I knew your name.'

The cat finished his ablutions, stretched out in the box and then curled up again.

'I suppose you only speak Spanish.'
He closed his eyes.
'Do you live here?' I asked.
The cat ignored me.
But he'd clearly moved in.

I finished cleaning the kitchen while the cat snoozed content-edly in the recycling box. He didn't even open his eyes when I accidentally threw some used kitchen towel on top of him, simply rolled over and continued to sleep. Having a living creature in the house made it feel different. It made me feel different too. Less alone, obviously. But somehow calmer.

And hungry, I realised. I didn't think I'd be hungry again today, certainly not after the cherry pie and coffee earlier. I know that's hardly what you'd call a substantial meal, nor a healthy food choice for the day, but I'd felt full afterwards and thought it was more than enough to keep me going. It would have been, back in Dublin. But here, today, I was hungry.

So despite having scrubbed the gas hob until it was spark-ling, I took out a pan, added some oil and then chopped one of the chicken breasts I'd bought earlier. I put some mixed salad and tomatoes on one of the bright-blue plates from the cupboard and then filled a glass with the wine I'd added to my basket in the supermarket at the last minute. It had been chilling in the fridge since I'd got home. I hadn't planned to drink it tonight. I'd bought it 'in case' – without even knowing what 'in case' actually would be.

I took my phone and my mini wireless speakers from my bag and brought them out to the stone table on the patio area behind the house. I set up one of my favourite playlists then went inside and returned with the glass of wine, my chicken salad and a large cushion. The cushion was because the only seating around the table was a stone bench, and I couldn't see me lasting on that for any length of time.

The music was soothing. The wine was smooth. And the chicken salad – despite my lack of anything other than salt to season it – was tasty. The tomatoes were sweet and juicy, and the chicken itself was bursting with flavour. I was astonished. As well as not being a great cook I'm not a real foodie either. To be honest, I regard it as fuel. Some fuel is better than others (I have a fondness for Maltesers that is borderline fanatical) but I'm not one to go into raptures about anything. And yet this meal, sitting alone in the sun in a place I didn't even know, was one of the best I'd ever eaten.

It would have been so wonderful to be here with Brad. It would have been magical to share the moment with him. I couldn't help having those thoughts, even as I tried to push them to the furthest recesses of my mind. I wasn't allowed to think like that. I wasn't allowed to miss him. I should never have known him. I should never have loved him.

He'd been in love with someone else and I'd been nothing more than the other woman.

Chapter 6

The cat joined me, settling on to the bench with his head beside the cushion, then stealthily taking over more and more until he was stretched across the cushion and I was on the hard stone. I scratched him idly behind the ears as Imelda May sang of love and loss. I tried not to listen to the words and just let the music flow around me.

There were no other sounds in the garden. Just Imelda's voice and the cat's regular purr. I stopped rubbing him and he opened an eye, as if to complain, so I started again. It was restful. Peaceful.

Had it been peaceful in the Italian sunshine as they got ready to go to dinner that night? Had they sat in a garden as I was doing now? Had Dylan been running around in excitement? Had they been a happy family unit?

Had Alessandra believed that to be the case? Or had she suspected? Had she quizzed Brad about some throwaway remark, some careless comment? Had she seen his last text to me: *Tonight's dinner location. Joining them shortly. Love you. Miss you. Bxx.* Had she yelled at him that he'd betrayed her, even though she was going to have his baby? Or had she simply trusted him, as I'd trusted him, never thinking to look at his texts, simply looking forward to their romantic evening together.

Why hadn't I guessed? That was the question that I couldn't stop asking myself. Why hadn't I ever wondered about the fact that I'd never met any of his family or his close friends in the few months we'd been together? Why had I simply accepted that it was because we were long-distance lovers – even if the journey from Belfast to Dublin can be made in under two hours?

Apart from the couple of occasions I'd gone to Belfast (and when we hadn't ventured out of the luxury hotel he'd booked), he was the one who travelled every second week to visit the clinic he had a share in. Which meant that it was easy for him to see me in places where he wouldn't expect to bump into anyone he knew. Of course he had colleagues in the clinic, but I'd never been there or met any of them. He knew one of the senior registrars at my own hospital, but I'd only ever exchanged brief words with Jeff McCarthy in the lift once or twice and was hardly going to start talking about Brad with him. No, seeing me in Dublin was a safe bet for a man who had a secret lover.

I'd been easy pickings for him. Still a bit vulnerable after Sean but ready to dip my toe back in the water and fall for someone who was charming and intelligent and warm and compassionate. Because he was all of those things. I don't fall for bastards. At least . . . not the sort you know are already heartbreakers. Brad wasn't. He just wasn't. He was the most wonderful person I'd ever gone out with. We did that thing, you know, where we knew what the other person was going to say before they said it. We were on the same wavelength. We wanted the same things from life.

68

At least, that's what I'd thought. But I hadn't been on Brad's wavelength at all, had I? When I'd assumed he was in the moment with me, he could just as easily have been thinking about Alessandra. Or his beautiful son. Or the baby they were going to have. I'd been so sure of him. I'd been so wrong.

I stood up abruptly and the cat gave a mew of disapproval before scurrying into the orange grove, a flash of silver among the green and gold. I went into the house and picked up the phone that I'd left on the kitchen counter. I had a number of messages from Cleo, Saoirse and Pilar and a couple from my sister, Gonne. I didn't want to look at them yet. Instead I opened my photo stream and scrolled back to the last one I'd taken. It had been a selfie. Brad hadn't wanted me to take it and he'd looked away at the last minute so his face was blurred.

'I'll have to do it again!' I wailed as I looked at it. 'That's hopeless.'

'I hate having my photo taken,' he told me. 'I don't like looking at pictures of myself.'

'This isn't for you.' I grinned at him. 'It's for me. So that when you're in Belfast and I'm here pining for you I can look at it and feel close to you.'

'Don't be an idiot, Juno,' he said.

'Maybe I should X-ray you instead,' I teased. 'I could put a picture of your femur on my wall.'

'Didn't you hear my words about being an idiot?' But his eyes were twinkling.

I tried to take another selfie but he grabbed the phone and took photos of me instead. In them I'm laughing, my hair tousled, my eyes bright with the knowledge of loving him. In our selfie I'm laughing too, even though the only part of him that's in focus is his ear.

Why had he pretended?

Why had he lied?

And why had he gone on that damn holiday and got himself killed?

I went into the house as soon as I started to scratch my arm and realised the mozzies were biting. I hadn't thought of mozzies and didn't have any repellent to spray on my skin. There were some dusty citronella tea lights in the house, though, so I lit a few of them before going into the living room.

The cat was in the armchair. I had no idea how he'd got from the orange grove into the house without being seen, but he'd managed it.

'Out, cat!' I ordered. 'You're not meant to be in here. And you're especially not meant to be on the furniture.'

He ignored me.

'Come on.' I nudged him gently. 'You can't stay here.'

He took no notice as I watched him delicately wash his face. I was perfectly well aware that cats felt themselves to be pretty much above the inane requests of humans and that this cat had no intention of doing anything I asked.

'Maybe it's because you're Spanish,' I said out loud. 'Maybe I have to talk to you in Spanish. In which case – *vamos!*' I used one of my five words.

The cat continued with his toilette as though I wasn't there.

'Do you have a name?' I repeated my earlier question.

His ears flickered slightly.

'Does it matter if you have a name?'

He yawned and then moved to washing his behind.

'Oh, please!' I yelped. 'That's disgusting. Stop!'

He gave me a disdainful look, gave himself another lick and then leaped gracefully from the chair and walked into the kitchen, where he jumped into the recycling box.

'I guess you've decided this is home,' I said. 'Which is fine, you're very welcome. But I'm the boss here. To start off, I'm going to give you a name, and it's going to be English.'

I stood over him as he made himself more comfortable in the box. Along with his chunky girth he was a determined-looking creature, very sure of himself and his place at the Villa Naranja. And – despite knocking things over – he was as stealthy as the ghosts I didn't want to believe in.

'Banquo,' I told him. 'It's appropriate.'

Banquo was my first introduction to ghosts, thanks to my mother, who had played the part of Lady Macbeth a number of times. I'd walked in on her reading through the play with my godfather, another leading actor of his generation. She was giving the 'out, damned spot' speech, and the ferocity of it made me cry. Afterwards she explained to me that it was all pretend and I looked at her in surprise and asked her why she had to pretend to be someone else at all.

'You pretend, don't you?' she'd asked. 'When you're being a doctor or a teacher or an astronaut?' (I'd wanted to be an astronaut when I was smaller. I wanted to go to the stars.)

'I'm a child,' I'd replied to her. 'I'm supposed to pretend. You're a grown-up. You don't have to.'

I didn't realise then that grown-ups pretend a lot more than children. And we're a good deal less honest about it.

When I was a little older and she was once again playing the part, she explained to me about Lady Macbeth's descent into madness and the character of Banquo, who haunts the king. Gonne brought me to the opening night at the Abbey Theatre. I remember her poking me in the ribs when Mum first appeared. In character, she was even more imposing than she'd been when I'd walked in on her reading, and I was completely caught up in her performance. I knew she was still my mother, the woman who made my breakfast in the morning and yelled at me for leaving my clothes on my bedroom floor, but she'd turned into somebody else too, someone I didn't know.

Banquo, played by my godfather, was just as much of a revelation. I totally believed in him as a haunting presence, and it took a lot of reading of my favourite picture science books to dislodge the feeling that it might be possible for ghosts to exist, after all – despite the complete lack of proof.

Regardless of the intensity of the play, though, I was more taken with the stage set and the changing scenery and the way the cauldron of the three witches bubbled and belched out smoke than with the brilliance of the acting. When, afterwards, I asked my mother about all the backstage activity she'd looked at me in despair. 'You're not supposed to think about it,' she said. 'You're supposed to be transported.'

Because of my questions about the practicalities, Mum never really understood how much I'd loved her performance. And even though I'd gone to many of her opening nights after that, I always felt that she'd given me up as a lost cause. I suppose to her I was. But perhaps not entirely. Not if I could name a cat after Banquo's ghost.

Banquo himself had now curled up in a ball in the box

and was purring happily again. I headed back to the living room and looked at my phone.

The messages from my friends were all hoping that I was enjoying Spain and that everything was OK. I got the feeling that Saoirse was particularly anxious about me. She'd been the one who'd seen me at my worst, after all, and I suppose she was afraid I'd go into some terrible decline on my own.

The one from Gonne was long and rambling, just like her usual conversation, but the gist of it was that she was stuck for a babysitter for Cian on Saturday night and asking if I was free. Cian, my youngest nephew, had just turned thirteen. His sister, Alannah, is sixteen. Both of them are as dreamy and musical as their parents, but I would've thought Alannah, who is a leading light in her school choir, was perfectly capable of keeping an eye on her brother for an evening. I said as much in my reply and then added that I was in Spain.

Whaaattt! Gonne's message arrived with the appropriate harp sound as an alert. *When did u go?*

Yesterday.

You said nothing.

Was spur of moment.

Anywhere nice?

Place called Beniflor. Somewhere between Alicante and Valencia.

Oh! With who?

Alone.

There was a text silence as my sister digested this. Being alone to channel the creative muse is part and parcel of the Ryan family but it's not a part that I usually embrace.

Are you all right?

Of course.

73

She didn't know anything about Brad. Why should she? We don't talk much.

OK. Well, give me a shout when you're home. We could meet for coffee.

Sure.

I didn't say that I planned to be away for a few months. That would have caused a barrage of questions. Mum might even have got involved. After all, this was completely out of character for me. The serious one. The sensible one. The one with the boring life.

The one who'd fallen in love with a married man who'd died in an earthquake.

We'd met at a workshop during a seminar on diagnostic imaging, which was being held at the National Convention Centre. We'd starting chatting as we queued for coffee after the session and discovered we'd both been to the Bruce Springsteen concert earlier in the year – Brad had been in the row directly behind me.

'You weren't the one with the *River* baseball cap, were you?' he asked. 'Leppin' up and down like a mad thing.'

I grinned.

'No, that was my friend Cleo,' I told him. 'I was the one with the home-made knitted scarf.'

'I remember!' he exclaimed. 'It had his song titles knitted into it.'

'Only some of them,' I protested. 'I knit in the winter evenings. It keeps me calm.'

'We all need things to keep us calm,' he said, and the tone of his voice was suddenly softer and more intimate. 'Would you like to have a calming drink with me when this is over?'

Of course I said yes. We'd only spoken a few words but I think I'd fallen for him already.

I fell for him properly on our first real date, a couple of weeks later. We met at the National Gallery (Sean wouldn't have been seen dead wandering around an art gallery but I like it, and it has a brilliant café) and then headed to one of Dublin's newest and most fashionable restaurants off Grafton Street. After that, Brad insisted on a nightcap at the Shelbourne Hotel, where we both had cocktails.

I felt very sophisticated as I sat in a window seat with my gin sling, watching people hurrying along the street outside while I half listened to Brad talking about the new developments in diagnostic imaging they'd featured at the seminar.

Suddenly he stopped talking and laughed.

'I'm so sorry,' he said. 'I'm giving you the lecture I give my staff. And you're so very much not my staff, Juno Ryan.'

'I should hope not.' I grinned at him. 'It wouldn't do to be quaffing cocktails with the boss at all.'

'It's just that it's so nice to be with someone who knows exactly what I'm talking about,' he said.

'After a few of these you could be talking about anything on earth and I wouldn't have a clue.' I raised the cocktail glass.

'They're lovely, aren't they?' He raised his in return. We clinked glasses. And then he told me that I was beautiful.

I'm not beautiful. I'm not trying to be self-deprecating or overly modest when I say that. I'm being as factual as ever. My mother is beautiful, even now. She was a total stunner in her twenties. She has the sort of delicate bone structure that never ages. She just becomes more and more elegant with age. When I look at old photographs of her I can't understand why she wasn't snapped up for movies. Even in un-posed, off-the-cuff photos, she looks amazing. Gonne is beautiful too, although without the arresting quality Mum possesses. But she has the same golden-brown eyes, which always look fab in photos. My eyes are mid-brown with no exceptionally beautiful qualities. And my hair at that time was even more troublesome than it is now – too long to keep tidy, but too short to do anything clever with it. I still hadn't got used to it, to be honest. When I caught sight of myself in mirrors I was always surprised at how I looked.

So when Brad told me I was beautiful, I smiled and said nothing. He repeated his words and I came out with my usual blather of having grown up with really beautiful women in my family and that I was the runt of the litter, but he stopped me mid-sentence, took the cocktail from my hand, and kissed me. Then he told me that I was the most beautiful girl he'd ever met and that it wasn't just because my beauty came from being smart and intelligent, it was that I was lovely to look at too. Who wouldn't have fallen for that? Who?

He insisted on more cocktails and I said yes, simply because I didn't want to go home. He said that if he'd been staying anywhere less posh than the Shelbourne he might have tried sneaking me up to his room – always provided I wanted to be sneaked up to his room – but that he didn't have the nerve to try it in one of Dublin's finest hotels. And I said that I didn't allow myself to be sneaked into rooms on first dates, but if I did, I'd certainly have been happy to join him, and we both laughed and I stood up and he put his arm around me to steady me as we walked outside to find me a taxi. Which wasn't hard, because there's a rank outside the hotel and they were lined up.

'I wish I could see you before I go back tomorrow,' he said.

'What time are you leaving?'

'Early,' he told me. 'I've to be at the train station by nine.'

'I could meet you for coffee at seven,' I suggested.

'Would you?'

'Of course.'

He kissed me goodnight and I went home in a cloud of happiness. I was still on the cloud the following morning as we had coffee and pastries, again in the Shelbourne.

'Are you working today too?' he asked as he signed the bill, and I said yes, but that I was on the evening shift.

'Better go home and get a bit more shut-eye in that case,' he said.

I nodded but I was too awake and feeling too elated to go home. I walked down Grafton Street humming 'Dublin Can Be Heaven' under my breath and wondering how it was that a few weeks ago I'd been in the depths of despair over Sean, and now . . . now, even if Sean had called and told me he'd made a terrible mistake and that he really and truly loved me and he should never have broken up with me, I'd have said 'Sean who?' and put the phone down.

Sean was my past. Brad was my present. And I hoped that he'd be my future too.

Obviously, having only had three months together and that time curtailed because of living in two different cities – as well as timing difficulties because of the nature of hospital work – we didn't see each other as often as we might other-wise have done. In fact, I think we went out together about eight times, although we FaceTimed almost every day. I slept with him after the third date. He was, without doubt, a better lover than Sean. He was perfect.

Or he would have been, if he hadn't already been married to Alessandra.

Chapter 7

I didn't jump out of my bed in fright a couple of mornings later when yet another clatter from downstairs woke me up. After a few days at the Villa Naranja I'd got used to the fact that it was probably Banquo either coming home from a night on the tiles, or leaving by the window for a morning stroll. Because of the grilles, I'd decided it was OK to leave the kitchen window and shutters open at night, but while my imagined marauders couldn't get in, Banquo was happy to use the open window as his personal entrance.

I got out of bed and carefully opened the creaky bedroom shutters. There was a small white van parked outside the house. I ducked back inside because I wasn't wearing a stitch of clothing and didn't want to put on a show for whoever had turned up. I got dressed hastily, wondering if it had been a knock on the door that had woken me. Then I ran a brush through my hair and went downstairs.

Banquo had clearly gone out during the night because there was no sign of him, although the paper in the recycling box now bore the indent of his body and a little mound of silver-grey hairs. I unlocked the kitchen door and stepped

79

into the warm air. I couldn't see anyone but I could hear sounds coming from the side of the house.

Maybe the local farmer had come to pick the oranges, I thought, as their scent wafted towards me, but if that was the case he should've let me know. I walked cautiously around the house to see who was there.

The answer was a Greek god.

He was the most perfect man I'd ever seen. Tall and well built, he was wearing faded blue shorts that reached his knees, and no top. His torso, honey brown and glistening with a sheen of sweat, was perfectly toned. I caught my breath. It was impossible not to stare.

He was cleaning the swimming pool, and he didn't look up as I approached. I realised that he hadn't heard me because he was wearing ear buds in his ears. I stared at him, hardly able to believe that such a man existed.

'Hello.'

My voice was croaky from lack of use. I hadn't spoken properly to anyone since Rosa at the café, although obviously I'd shared a few exchanges with Banquo.

'Hello,' I repeated, more loudly.

He looked up. His eyes were the colour of bitter chocolate. His chin had the traces of dark stubble. He was heart-meltingly gorgeous. I reckoned he was in his early twenties.

'Hello,' I said again. 'I'm Juno. I'm staying here.'

He took the buds out of his ears and put them in the pocket of his shorts.

'Hello,' he said in accented English. 'I am here for to clean the pool.'

'So I see.'

He pushed the hose across the base of the pool. The water was a lot clearer than it had been when I'd first arrived.

'Do you come every day?' I asked.

He hesitated as he processed my words.

'Only one time a week,' he told me. 'Today. This day every week.'

'OK,' I said.

'She . . . the pool . . . had not been cleaned for a time,' he added. 'So I came two times last week. There is a . . . a . . .' he searched for the right word but eventually gave up, '. . . a piece that must be changed in the . . . the pump but I cannot do that today. It is a simple thing. There is no problem to use the pool. She . . . it is good.'

'Great. Thank you.'

'You like to swim?'

I hadn't really thought about it.

'Yes.'

'Is nice to have pool in the summer,' he said. 'Now is not very hot. But later, yes. There is very much heat here in next weeks.'

It mightn't have seemed very hot to him but it was hot enough for me. I felt a trickle of perspiration slide from my neck and down my back.

'Um . . . would you like something to drink?' I asked. 'Water? Juice?'

'No, thank you,' he replied, his English suddenly becoming a little more fluent, as though he'd got all of the difficult stuff out of the way. 'I have bottle of water with me.'

'OK.'

'I finish soon,' he said. 'You will be able to swim.'

'Thanks,' I said.

'They told me someone was coming to stay. You are friend of the family?'

'I work with Pilar,' I replied.

'I know her.' He nodded. 'She come . . . came . . . here many times with her *mamá*. She is nice girl.'

'Very nice,' I agreed.

He hauled the large blue hose out of the pool and curled it up. Then he took a squeegee-type brush and began to clean the tops of the tiles.

'She will come here, Pilar?' he asked. 'While you are here?'

'I don't know,' I replied.

'I have not seen her for a long time. She is working in England with you?'

'Ireland,' I corrected him.

'Ah.' His eyes suddenly lightened. 'Not the same place, no? Very different.'

'Very.' I grinned.

'Guinness,' he said.

There is a sad inevitability about people mentioning Guinness when you say you're Irish.

I nodded.

'I have drinked . . . drunk . . . it once,' he said. 'I am sorry, I did not like it very much.'

'I don't like it very much either,' I confessed. 'I'm more of a wine person.'

'Lots of good wines here,' he said. 'You must try them.'

'I will.'

'My family makes wines,' he told me. 'I will bring some for you next time.'

'You don't have to . . .' And then I realised I was being rude. 'That would be lovely. Thank you.'

82

He finished the tiles and then lifted the cover to what I realised was the pump for the pool.

'I have set times for it to come on and off,' he said. 'Is necessary to keep water clean.'

'OK,' I said.

'Is good for swimming now.'

'Great,' I said.

He closed the lid and hefted the hose over his shoulder.

'I will see you next week. You are here for many weeks, yes?'

'I'm not sure how long,' I said. 'But I'll definitely be here next week.'

'I see you then,' he assured me. 'I will have wine.'

'Thank you. Do you need me to close the gate behind you?'

He thought about it for a moment then shook his head.

'I have the button.' He reached into his shorts and took out a remote control. 'Is OK.'

'In that case, see you next week.'

'*Hasta luego*,' he said and went to the van.

I was a woman devastated by the death of her secret lover in a tragic accident. A woman who'd discovered that he'd betrayed both her and the wife she'd known nothing about. I'd kept my sorrow and my grief balled up inside me. I was on leave of absence from my job because I'd totally lost it. I hadn't slept for months. I'd come away to try to find myself again, even though I knew I'd never be the same person as I was before. And, out of nowhere, I was lusting after the pool cleaner.

'You are a total slut, Juno Ryan,' I said to myself as I

returned to the kitchen. 'You haven't a decent bone in your body. How could you possibly be imagining . . .' I didn't even let myself think of what images could easily fill my head if I allowed them to. Instead, I made myself some coffee and took it out to the stone table with one of the croissants I'd bought in the mini-market.

As I licked the last crumbs of the croissant from my fingers, Banquo appeared and jumped on the bench beside me. He pushed his head into my lap and purred happily.

What is it about the purring of a cat that instantly relaxes you? Banquo's presence soothed me and stopped me from working myself into another frenzy of self-loathing. You can't have ugly thoughts when you're stroking a cat behind the ears. It's impossible. Even though I was uncomfortable on the hard stone bench by now, I didn't want to get up and disturb him.

'Not that you'd give a toss about disturbing me,' I remarked as I began to lose the feeling in my legs. 'It's true that cats still think they're gods.' Which made me think of the pool cleaner again.

My phone vibrated with a message from Cleo. She hoped that I was having a lovely relaxing time. I replied to say that I was. I didn't mention the pool cleaner. But I did say that I'd been joined by a cat.

You've become a single woman living alone with a cat, she responded. *Maybe I need to visit.*

You're very welcome, I replied.

Will do my best, she texted back. *But you know what it's like here. Manically busy. BTW new radiographer started today. Very competent.*

That's good, I said.

We exchanged a few more texts and then Cleo said that her break was over and she had to get back to work. I pictured her in the ground-floor room of the hospital, talking to the patients, being as kind and as gentle with them as possible, trying to allay any anxieties they had. People sometimes ask us if we can see anything on the scans or X-rays. It's not us but people like Brad McIntyre who make the diagnosis and tell the patient. But, of course, there are times when a tumour is very evident and you know that someone is in for a hard road ahead. Those are the times when the job is difficult.

I was feeling guilty as I continued to rub Banquo's head. Cleo was still at the coalface of the hospital, having to cover some of my work and having to familiarise the new radiographer with our procedures, while the most taxing thing in my day would be deciding what was for lunch.

It wasn't right. I shouldn't have crumbled. I shouldn't have let my personal life interfere with my work. I should have been able to cope.

I thought of the Greek god again. I supposed I must at least be moving on now if I had what the nuns at my convent school would have called 'impure thoughts' about him. But that's all they were. Thoughts. It was nice to know I could still have them, but I wasn't going to act on them. I didn't actually want to have mad passionate sex with someone I hardly knew. I wanted . . . and here I stood up abruptly. I didn't know what I wanted.

Banquo gave me a reproachful look as he jumped delicately from the stone bench to the ground.

'Sorry,' I said.

He stalked off towards the orange grove, his tail high.

I liked the fact that he didn't care about me. I didn't want people to care about me. To be honest, *I* didn't care about me.

I began to walk around the outside of the house, dragging my feet through the pink and white stones. I tried to empty my mind completely. When I'd completed a circuit, I stood back and looked at the Villa Naranja. As I gazed at the shutters, I realised they badly needed attention. If they were varnished and hung properly, I thought, the house would look far less tumbledown and maybe a good deal more appealing to the buyers Pilar's mother needed to attract. Of course painting the outside would help too, but that was a big job. The shutters, on the other hand . . .

I went inside and examined them up close. The wood, once dark, had been bleached to a pale tint by the sun, and the hinges were loose as well as being rusty. I might not be creative but I'm definitely good at practical tasks. I once told Sean that I'd love a hammer-action drill as a birthday present. He gave me perfume. Beautiful expensive perfume. But I would have preferred the drill. Now, as I looked thoughtfully at them, I knew I could fix the shutters. It was a job that I wanted to do. And it would be better than sitting around with the medical books that would only remind me of Brad. Much better to embark on something useful while I was here. That's what I needed in order to move on.

I sent a message to Pilar asking if her mum would mind if I did some maintenance work around the house.

Are you crazy? she replied. *You're on a break. Mamá doesn't expect you to do anything.*

But I'd like to, I sent in return. *It won't be much.*

A few minutes later she responded with a *No problem – you mad thing!* which made me laugh.

I did a bit of a search and eventually found some DIY equipment, as well as a pair of wickerwork outdoor chairs and a striped parasol, in an outside shed. Much to my delight, among the hammers, hoes, rakes and saws was a small electric sander, which would be perfect for working on the shutters. I carried the chairs and their cushions to the patio and placed them in the shade. I erected the parasol over the stone table. Then I went indoors again, took a quick shower and got dressed in a T-shirt and shorts. After that, feeling rather pleased with myself, I locked up the house and drove to Beniflor.

Chapter 8

I parked in the same spot outside the supermarket and walked back along the main street. The town houses, which shared the street with the shops, were painted in shades of yellow and cream. Many of the deep window sills contained flower boxes and baskets, and their blossoms spilled through the wrought-iron grilles in a cascade of colour.

I was walking in the direction of the plaza, although this time along a narrower street with more houses on one side and a plot of arid land on the other. At the end of it, much to my delight, was a large store with a sign that said *Bricolaje* and *DIY*.

I'd expected to have to struggle with the shopkeeper to explain that I needed sanding paper, hinges, screws and varnish, but when I went inside I saw that it was a self-service store where I could walk happily along the aisles and pick up the supplies I needed. I like DIY stores. I like the woody smell of them, and the bare bones of what are going to be home projects – the doors, the floorboards, the power tools . . . I like the power tools most of all. I picked up a new bit for the drill that I'd found at the Villa Naranja, as well as some face protectors to save me from the dust. Then I brought all of my purchases to the till where the assistant, behind a white counter, was cutting keys for another customer. Both assistant and customer – men in their mid-fifties, I reckoned – stared at me as I put my basket of purchases on the counter. I knew I looked like the complete tourist in my gaudy green shorts, striped T-shirt and jewelled sandals. And even though I have the imagination of a newt, I couldn't help wondering if either of them had read *Fifty Shades of Grey* and were questioning my motives in having a large roll of masking tape in the basket.

The customer said something to the assistant and both of them laughed while I felt my face flush. Then the customer left with the keys and the assistant turned to me with a friendly *hola*.

I said *hola* in return and then he scanned my purchases and told me the amount, which obviously I didn't understand. I craned my neck to peer at the cash register, and he then repeated the amount in slow, careful English.

'Thank you,' I said as I handed over the money. 'I mean, *gracias.*'

'You are welcome.' He passed over my purchases.

The plaza was only a short walk away so I decided to call into the Café Flor for a coffee again. With my plastic bag full of non-tourist things, I was suddenly beginning to feel part of the place. I was finding my feet, finding my way around. I wasn't a tourist. I was living here. Even if it was only for a short time.

'Hello!' Rosa beamed at me as I sat down beneath one of the big parasols. 'Nice to see you again. How are you getting on?'

'Not bad,' I told her. 'Settling in.'

'Running repairs?' she asked with a brief nod towards the plastic bag bearing the name of the DIY store. 'Is everything OK up there?'

'Oh yes,' I replied. 'I'm just doing a few little jobs around the house.'

'Señora Perez will be pleased,' said Rosa. 'Eduardo is supposed to look after it, but he doesn't have a huge amount of time either.'

'Eduardo?'

'Her son,' said Rosa. 'He's a lawyer. He has an office in Beniflor Costa but he's been in Madrid for the past couple of months.'

'Beniflor Costa?'

'If you take the road to the coast you'll reach it,' said Rosa. 'We're the rural cousin of the hipper costal hangout. It has the original influx of expats, we get the ones who can't afford the sea-view prices.'

I grinned.

'Are there many non-Spanish residents around here?'

'Not in the town itself but in some of the nearby *urbanizaciones*,' said Rosa. 'Many of them came to Beniflor in the seventies and the communities expanded. There used to be a lot of Brits, but these days the buyers are coming from northern Europe.'

'I was thinking it'd be a struggle for me without a word of Spanish, but everyone seems to have some English,' I said.

'Well, for some, especially the older generation, it's just basic stuff,' she told me. 'But most of the younger people have learned it since school – and nearly everyone has worked in the hospitality industry at some point, so they're not bad.'

'They make me feel ashamed,' I admitted.

'Oh, once you've been here for a couple of weeks you'll pick up some words,' said Rosa. 'And it's not as though you need it to get by in Beniflor.'

'I guess not.' I picked up the menu and scanned it. 'What do you recommend today?'

'The lemon tart,' she told me.

'I'll have that – and a cappuccino,' I said.

She nodded and went to get my order while I sat back and luxuriated in the warmth of the sun on my legs. I reminded myself that I was on a longer break than a fortnight's holiday. That I didn't have to plan on going back to work yet. That, even if I had left them in the lurch, the radiology department was getting on fine without me and my replacement was competent. It was hard to believe that such a big part of my life now seemed distant and remote. Everyone likes to think that they're indispensable – but none of us are, really. Not me. And not Brad either. Because the team in Belfast were getting on without him too. It was just me who was struggling.

I wasn't going to think about Brad. I was here to forget him. I picked up the menu again and studied it without taking in a word.

'Here you go.' Rosa put my coffee and cake in front of me.

'Thanks.'

She bustled off and I took out my phone. The café had free Wi-Fi and so I logged on and checked my various social accounts, something I hadn't bothered to do at the villa. I don't post very much myself, but I like seeing what other people are up to. Facebook doesn't make me feel inadequate or hopeless, like some people claim. I like seeing my friends' happy status updates. I like wasting time on trivia. There are so many horrible things going on in the world that it's nice to lose yourself in a cat obsessively flushing a toilet from time to time. I thought then about Banquo and wondered what his real name was and who his real owners were. He hadn't seemed feral to me. He'd been perfectly comfortable in the house.

A couple of pickup trucks drove into the square and began unloading yellow crash barriers. A few minutes later, a bright-yellow cherry picker trundled in too. The men from the trucks and the cherry picker started a loud and animated conversation. Rosa came out of the café.

'They're getting ready for the fiesta,' she told me.

'What fiesta?'

'The Beniflor fiesta, of course. It's in honour of San Bernardo, our patron saint.'

'Is it a religious festival?'

I'm not religious. I can't get my head around a God who created a world where so many awful things happen to good people. Like incurable diseases, or abject poverty, or earthquakes.

'There's a religious aspect,' Rosa said. 'But it's not really a religious event. It starts with a Mass and a parade of San Bernardo's statue. Then there's the crowning of the fiesta queens followed by a big community dinner in the plaza. All of the streets have their own tables. There's lots of events the following week, and the bars and restaurants do special deals. Then we finish off with a firework display in front of the town hall at midnight. That's the town hall,' she added, pointing to the official-looking building which now had three flags hanging from the upper balcony. I recognised one as the Spanish flag.

The red-and-yellow striped one, Rosa told me, was the flag of Valencia, which was the regional community we were in, and the third – blue and white with a picture in the middle – was the town's flag. The picture was of San Bernardo.

'You have to come, it'll be great fun,' she promised. 'It's the highlight of the summer. Of course, every town has its own festival – and some are much bigger affairs – but ours is the best fun.'

I laughed.

'Seriously,' she said. 'We pack more in than anyone else.'

'I thought I'd come to a quiet backwater,' I remarked. 'But it seems like it's all go.'

'The summer season is about having fun,' Rosa told me. 'Which is why people come here.' She looked at me curiously. 'Why did you come?'

I drained my coffee cup.

'Oh, just getting away from it all.'

She paused before speaking.

'Getting away from it all is great,' she told me. 'But it's nice to be involved too. So I hope we see you at the fiesta. It kicks off next week. There'll be dancing and all sorts. And, of course, we choose the Fiesta Queen. This year it's Beatriz Navarro. Her father owns the finca next to the Villa Naranja.'

'I guess it'd be nice to meet the neighbours,' I said.

'Beatriz is gorgeous,' Rosa told me. 'The whole family is. Miguel Navarro married a beauty queen, and their kids are all heartbreakers.'

'Any good-looking men?' I spoke before even realising what I was saying, and my words shocked me. I wasn't looking for a man. Even if I'd had lustful thoughts about the pool cleaner, my heart wasn't ready for it.

'Three sons,' Rosa said. 'The second, Carlos, is married and lives in Argentina. But Luis might suit you. He's the eldest and works on the finca. He's about thirty-five, very handsome.'

'It's OK,' I said. 'I won't be chasing after him.'

She grinned.

'You'd be the only one.'

'Honestly,' I said. 'I'm here for a rest, not . . . not anything else.' I took my purse out of my bag. 'How much do I owe you?'

I handed over the paltry sum and left another euro on the table as a tip.

'Good luck with the DIY,' she said as I stood up.

'I'll let you know how I get on,' I promised.

I called into the supermarket before going back to the villa and stocked up on essentials. I also bought a large bag of dried cat food. I wasn't sure who was feeding Banquo but I thought I'd better get in on the act, just in case.

In true cat fashion, though, there was no sign of him when I got home.

Although I was still struggling to sleep at night, the sultry heat of the early afternoon had made me feel lethargic. I didn't bother to take my purchases out of the bag, but simply left them in the kitchen and flopped down in one of the newly discovered wicker chairs. I hadn't expected to nod off but it was an hour later before I came to, and that was only because Banquo had jumped on to my lap and was kneading my stomach viciously.

'Ow!' I cried as I sat up. And then called, 'You wretch!' after him as he fled into the orange grove.

I got up and poured him some water, then shook some of the dried cat food into a yellow ceramic bowl, which I put down for him. Almost at once, he reappeared and rubbed up against my legs, purring noisily before sticking his nose into the bowl and sniffing a few times. He turned to me and gave me a reproachful look, which seemed to say, 'Dried food? Really? I have better taste than this.' But when he realised it was all that was on offer, he tucked in.

While he ate I wandered over to the swimming pool. It was clear and inviting, and for the first time I realised that, despite the fact the Villa Naranja had seen better days, I was staying at a private house with a swimming pool of its own. Which meant that I could swim whenever I liked. However I liked.

I peeled off my shorts and T-shirt and dived in.

The water was fresh but not freezing, and as I surfaced I felt a sudden explosion of well-being. A sense that life was worth living. That there was joy in the simple things. Yet even as all these emotions coursed through me, I couldn't help remembering that the only reason I was here was because of something truly awful.

And I felt guilty for my moment of pure delight.

Chapter 9

I spent the next few days alone in the house – except for Banquo, who divided his time between the recycling box and one of the wicker chairs on the patio. Although it had taken longer than I'd expected, I'd eventually managed to unscrew the shutters and bring them downstairs, where I propped them in the shade of the patio. (I'd managed to catch my index finger in one of the rusty hinges, and I had to remove a splinter from my thumb when a shutter slid from my grasp on the terracotta stairs, but I'd coped without a major disaster.) I sanded them during the day, and at night I sat outside in the balmy air with my iPad and read until it was dark. I was eating mainly fruit and salad, which meant that my body was currently a shrine to healthy living – if I ignored the glass or two of wine that accompanied the salads.

But the best part of being alone was not having to put on a game face, to pretend everything was all right when it wasn't. It was also good to get up at whatever time I felt like and not be ruled by my alarm clock – although I was usually up early because, without the shutters on the windows, the sun flooded into the bedroom. Most nights, I went to bed late because I dreaded lying in the dark not sleeping, yet I dreaded sleeping even more because I was afraid of what my dreams might be. But even though my sleep was still erratic, the nightmares that had plagued me in Dublin had eased, and while I saw Brad in some of my dreams, others were the usual confusion of jumbled events. There were even some blissful moments when I wasn't dreaming at all. So staying at the Villa Naranja had made me healthier and more rested, that was certain.

Yet no matter how much I wanted it to be different, I was still stuck in 'if only'. If only I'd asked Brad more about his family. If only I'd asked about his life in Belfast. About his friends. If only I hadn't been so damn accepting of everything he said and did. If only I'd questioned him about his family holiday, about why it was so important to him. If only . . . if only . . . if only I hadn't been dazzled by love, he might have admitted the truth to me and I'd still have been shocked at the tragedy of the earthquake but I wouldn't have been so completely and utterly steamrollered by what had happened.

Because if I'd known the truth, I would have broken it off with him as soon as I knew he was married. Of course I would. Wouldn't I? I had no interest in having a relationship with a married man. I wouldn't have accepted his invitation to dinner if he'd mentioned he had a wife. Unless, perhaps, I'd had a reason to believe that his relationship had irretrievably broken down. If he'd told me that Alessandra didn't understand him. Or that he didn't understand her. Or that they were staying together for Dylan's sake. Would I have gone out with him then? Would I have decided that their marriage was over and that it was OK to be with him? But if that was the case, would he still be sleeping with her? And would she have wanted to get pregnant?

The trouble was, I simply didn't know, and it was eating me up inside. I'd told him all about Sean, yet he hadn't said a word about previous – or current – relationships, even though it would have been the perfect opportunity. So why had he kept his secrets from me? Why hadn't he been the person I so badly wanted him to be?

Despite the balmy days at the Villa Naranja, despite the great food and the lazy evenings, I was still trapped in a kind of limbo. Of not being able to let go. Of not knowing how I was supposed to feel. Of searching for answers to questions I'd never dreamed of asking and would never know how to answer.

There were a dozen shutters on the house altogether, eight full length and four smaller. I'd divided the work into two separate projects – the upstairs and the downstairs – beginning upstairs. My plan was to sand and varnish all of the upstairs shutters before starting on the downstairs ones, just in case it took longer than I expected. At least this way, half of them would be done. I was doing all the sanding first so that there was no chance of dust settling in the varnish.

I fitted a new sheet of sandpaper to the sander and plugged it in. Then I pulled the mask over my face and started work on the final shutter of the upstairs batch. Because I was totally engrossed in what I was doing, I nearly had a heart attack when I saw the shadow of a figure behind me.

I whirled around, the sander still going.

'Oh,' I gasped. 'I didn't hear you.'

'I'm sorry.' The Greek god looked at me apologetically.

I switched off the sander and removed my mask. The Greek god looked at the shutters.

'You are doing all this work yourself?'

A sexist Greek god, I thought, as I replied a little tartly that I was perfectly capable of doing some sanding or painting or whatever else needed doing around the house. Even pool cleaning, I added, if somebody showed me how.

He grinned at me.

'It is clear that you know what you do,' he said. 'I am surprised that you are doing it, that is all. You are on holiday, no? Most people on holiday do not start *reformas*.'

'I'm not exactly on holiday,' I told him, my tone slightly abashed. 'I'm staying here for a few weeks and I could see that the shutters needed some attention so I thought . . . well, I like being useful. I'm not good at sitting around doing nothing.'

'You like doing this?' He looked at me appraisingly.

'I like practical things,' I told him.

'Me, too.' He nodded. 'That is why I am cleaning the pool.'

'Do you work full time at it?' I asked.

He frowned. 'Full time?'

'Is it your job?'

His face brightened.

'For the summer,' he said. 'Because we – my family – are close to Doña Carmen's family, and my father made the offer to Señora Perez. The offer of me,' he added. 'But I do not mind. I spent a lot of time here when I was younger. Anyway, I am sorry to have frightened you. I came to clean the pool and to fix the seal.' He said the last word with a triumphant smile.

'You startled me, not frightened me,' I said.

'Startled is not frightened?' he asked.

'Not exactly.' I tried to explain the difference but he threw up his hands in despair.

'So many words in English for the same thing,' he said.

'Nearly the same thing,' I corrected him.

'I studied it in school,' he said. 'And I worked in England for some months. But I have not spoken very much for some time and it is hard to remember.'

'Actually, you're getting better by the second,' I said. 'I guess it comes back to you.'

'I think that is true.' He smiled again.

I was trying to think of a man in the whole world who was better-looking than him. But I couldn't. Not one. Not a singer, not a Hollywood star, not an athlete . . . nobody. As a Greek god, even a Spanish Greek god, he was out on his own.

'It is OK that I start now?' he asked.

'Of course.'

I deliberately didn't watch him. I concentrated on sanding the wood in front of me, although I was conscious that the heat I was feeling had nothing at all to do with the warmth of the sun.

It seemed to take him forever, but eventually he finished. He showed me the old seal, as if he needed to prove there really had been a problem with it.

'Would you like a drink of water this time?' I asked. I wanted something to drink myself. My throat was parched.

He nodded, and I went inside. I filled two glasses from the five-litre bottle I'd bought at the supermarket and handed one to him.

'Thank you,' he said. 'Do you need any help?'

'I'm doing all right so far,' I told him.

'Yes,' he agreed as he examined the shutters. 'But putting them back will be more difficult, no? You need new . . . new . . .'

'*Bisagras.*' I beamed at him and picked up the packet on the ground beside me. 'Hinges.'

'Hinges.' He nodded. 'You need to put them in the wall also.'

'I'm sure I can manage.'

'If you need help, ask for me,' he said. 'It's not a problem.'

'That's kind of you.'

He took a phone out of his pocket. 'You have WhatsApp? For message.'

A fleeting sense of foreboding gripped me at the idea of sharing contact information with a man I didn't know. Whose name I still didn't know, I realised, as he looked at me expectantly. I could be getting myself into a messy situation. He could be married. He could . . . And then I told myself that I was being stupid, he was a local guy, and he wasn't trying to date me by pretending he was a free agent. He was just being nice.

I reached for my own phone.

'I'm Pep,' he told me. 'Pep Navarro.'

Navarro. Navarro. It sounded familiar. Then I remembered my conversation with Rosa at the café. The family of beautiful women and handsome men. Of course. He must be the youngest son. We shared contact information, and then he went to his van. He returned with three bottles of wine: one red, one white and one rosé. 'These are from our bodega,' he said as he put them on the stone table. 'Let me know what you think.'

'Thank you for bringing them.' I looked at the bottles. 'I'm not a wine expert. I just drink what I like.'

'It will be good to have the opinion of someone who is not an expert,' he said. 'I hope you enjoy them.'

'I'll let you know.'

'Will you be at the fiesta?' he asked. 'It begins on Friday.'

'Possibly.'

'Then I also hope to see you there.'

'You, too.'

He drained the water and waved goodbye. I didn't return to sanding the shutters right away. Instead, I cooled off in the crystal-clear pool.

Rosa gave me a fuller description of the upcoming fiesta when I went into town for coffee and pecan pie.

'The opening ceremony on Friday is always great,' she said. 'Then on Saturday there's a huge fancy-dress parade around the town. Obviously, there's a competition for the best – and the participants take it very, very seriously.'

'Are you in it?' I asked.

She looked a little embarrassed.

'Well, yes. I've taken part every year since I was a teenager. I've never won, though.'

'Does everybody take part?'

'No, but a good crowd do,' she said. 'I'm going as Snow White this year. I realise I don't have the look but I have a lovely costume.'

'Do people line the streets to watch?' I asked.

'Oh yes. And they shout encouragement at us. It's fun. It starts at half eight,' she added, 'and it finishes here in the plaza. The Fiesta Queen hands out the prizes.'

'And is that it?'

'Are you mad?' She grinned at me. 'A one-day fiesta! Whoever heard of such a thing. On Sunday there's a paella competition in the square and later there's another parade, although this time it's the statue of San Bernardo from the church and around the town. On Monday there's music and a flamenco show.'

'Action-packed,' I said.

'Oh, that's only the start of it,' Rosa told me. 'Like I said before, there's stuff on every day. There's a concert on Tuesday, a bullfight on Thursday—' She stopped when she saw the look of unadulterated horror on my face. 'Not a real bullfight,' she assured me. 'It's a mock one in the square, but the guys get dressed up in all the gear and they really go for it. There's a flower-offering parade on Friday, that's mainly for the children. The final fiesta day is on Saturday. That starts with bell ringing and firecrackers in the morning, a parade of the Fiesta Queen and town dignitaries, another Mass, another parade of the statue and another concert. It ends with music and a firework display in the plaza.'

'Wow.' I was gobsmacked. 'Does anybody do any work during the fiesta?'

'Of course,' she said. 'But it fits around the celebrations.'

'And does everybody attend every event?'

'Some people do,' she replied. 'You can't miss the crowning of the Fiesta Queens on the first night and the fireworks on the last, but the rest is optional. There are three Queens, by the way. Beatriz is the main one, but there's the Fiesta Queen *abuela* and the young Fiesta Queen too.'

I stared blankly at her.

'The Fiesta Queen *abuela* is a senior citizen,' Rosa explained. '*Abuela* means "granny" in Spanish – and the grannies rule the roost here, absolutely. The young queen is from the batch of girls who made their Communion this year. We have all the age groups covered.'

My mother would have been perfect in the role of the senior citizen Fiesta Queen. I could see her standing there looking regal. Not grandmotherly. Thea Ryan only looks like a grandmother when she's acting.

'I'll have a think about how much partying I can do,' I said.

'It's a good way to meet people,' said Rosa. 'If you're going to be here for a while, you need to mingle. You can't hole up at Doña Carmen's the whole time.'

'I've met people there,' I said. 'Pep Navarro is the pool cleaner. I'm guessing he's the Fiesta Queen's brother.'

'Oh.' She was taken aback. 'I thought he was working at the finca this summer, not pool cleaning.'

'I think he's doing the Villa Naranja as a favour,' I said. 'He said that he spent a lot of time there when he was younger.'

'The Perez and the Navarros are good friends.' Rosa sounded a little strained, and I looked at her curiously as she wiped a few imaginary crumbs from the table.

'I'm sure Ana's pleased,' she said when she'd finished.
'Ana?'
'Mrs Perez. Doña Carmen's daughter.'
'Pilar's mother,' I said.
'Yes.'
'I'm starting to get a handle on who's who,' I said.
'By the end of the fiesta you'll be totally up to speed.'

Rosa had regained her equilibrium and her sunny smile. 'You'll know everyone.'

She went to serve more customers while I ate my pie and watched the boys race around the plaza. They were playing the game of getting around the square without touching the ground again, leaping from tubs to the benches set into the tiled surface of the plaza, and swinging around the small orange trees. They were laughing and shouting and generally having a good time, and as they got closer to the café I wondered how they'd bridge the gap between the nearest tub and the bench. There was an orange tree between them, but I couldn't see how they'd manage to grab it and swing across. The first boy who tried very nearly succeeded, though. He leaped from the tub and tried to grasp the branch of the tree to propel himself forward. But somehow gravity took hold, he wasn't able to swing enough, and he tumbled to the ground amid good-natured laughter. The second boy tried for a higher branch. He couldn't quite reach it and made an attempt to grab a lower one as he fell. It was all so quick, it was impossible to see exactly what happened, but suddenly he was lying on the ground and shrieking loudly. The cry was one of pain as well as fright. I was up from my seat in an instant and over to him. The other boys crowded round, trying to get close to the action. The boy himself was screaming and I didn't need my radiographer's skills to see why. He'd managed to dislocate his shoulder.

'I'm sure it hurts a lot,' I said in English as I ran my fingers gently over the injury to see if I could detect any further damage.

The boy screamed louder and my heart went out to him.

A dislocated shoulder is one of the most painful traumas that can happen to you.

Rosa turned up at that moment and I quickly explained what had happened.

'Honestly,' she muttered. 'It's a wonder that child is still alive. Xavi's only eight but he's already broken his arm and his ankle.'

'And now his shoulder,' I told her. 'I'm pretty confident he hasn't fractured his arm too, but we need to ice it as quickly as we can and get him to A&E.'

'Are you a doctor?' she asked.

'No, but I have emergency response training, and I've X-rayed lots of dislocated shoulders,' I said. 'Is there a hospital nearby?'

'Benidorm,' she said. 'He knows it well, don't you, Xavi?'

The boy's screams had reached hysteria level at this point and the other children were starting to get upset. A woman came hurrying across the plaza and kneeled down beside him, trying to comfort him.

'Get ice,' I said to Rosa. 'And some plastic bags to put it in. And towels or pillowcases or some kind of fabric. I'll strap it up for him and that'll make it easier to get him to hospital.'

I hunkered down beside Xavi.

'You're OK.' I hoped he'd be comforted by my tone even if he didn't understand my words. 'Honestly you are. I'm going to help you.'

Rosa said something to both the woman and the boy and then disappeared into the café. She returned with a basin full of ice, a couple of plastic bags and a selection of towels.

'You're very brave,' I told him as I put the ice into one

of the bags and then placed it on his shoulder. 'This will help.'

Rosa translated while I looked at the towels. None of them would make a decent sling but I really needed to immobilise Xavi's arm. It would help lessen his pain as well as the damage to the surrounding tissue. I looked at Rosa again.

'Would you have a spare T-shirt?' I asked.

She hesitated for a moment, before going back into the café and returning with a neon-pink cropped top. I looked at it speculatively for a moment then, in one fluid motion, pulled my own T-shirt over my head and replaced it with the one Rosa had brought. The top was tight and tiny and it just about covered my bra. Then, to a collective gasp from the assembled crowd, I ripped my own T-shirt along the seam.

'Yours was too small,' I said as I fashioned a sling for the little boy. 'Better this way.'

Rosa's mouth was open in surprise. It wasn't the only one. But I ignored the crowd around us.

'You're doing great,' I said as I positioned Xavi's arm across his body and secured it with my improvised sling. 'We'll soon have you fixed, and then we'll get you to the hospital.'

His screams died down and the woman, who'd been stroking his hair, took out her phone and made a call.

'She can't get hold of Xavi's mum,' Rosa told me when the woman ended the call and spoke to her. 'the woman is his next-door neighbour. Catalina, his mum, is a security guard at the airport, so she probably can't take the call at the moment.'

'If someone can come with me to give me directions, I'll

drive him to the hospital myself,' I said. 'It's no problem.'

'Would you?' Rosa looked relieved and spoke to Maribel again. The other woman nodded, and Rosa told me that Maribel would accompany me.

'Can you give me directions in English?' I asked her. 'I'm sorry, I don't speak Spanish.'

'Yes. A little in English,' she said.

I lifted Xavi up, taking care to guard his damaged shoulder, and brought him to the car.

The drive to the hospital wasn't too difficult, although the road twisted and turned through the hillside and I knew the occasional bumps were painful for the little boy. When we arrived at A&E, we only had to wait about fifteen minutes before he was seen. Xavi, courtesy of having broken bones before, wasn't frightened by the hospital or the equipment when he was X-rayed, although he was still white with pain. The radiographer, a pleasant man in his thirties, showed us the film, where I could clearly see Xavi's anterior dislocation but, fortunately, no other breaks or injuries.

I smiled encouragingly at him as the doctor gave him a sedative and then worked the shoulder back into place. A couple of hours after arriving, with Xavi a little woozy but no longer in pain, we were ready to leave.

Maribel directed me back to her house, which was near the town and just two doors down from Xavi. On the way she finally got to speak with his mum. I didn't know what she was saying but I knew she mentioned me because I saw her glance at me a couple of times as she spoke – and I also heard the word *inglesa*, which I knew meant English. The distinction between English and Irish was irrelevant to the people of Beniflor so I didn't try to correct her.

'You like coffee?' Maribel asked as we pulled up outside the small single-storey house.

I shook my head.

'Thanks, but I'll go home now,' I said.

'Or tea? I have tea.'

'Honestly, no,' I assured her. 'But thank you very much for the offer. And for your directions.'

'It is not a trouble. The trouble is yours,' she said.

'It was no trouble at all,' I said. 'I was happy to do it.'

Then I told a sleepy Xavi to take care of himself, allowed Maribel to kiss me on the cheek, and drove back to the Villa Naranja, thinking that I'd taken a step towards being a part of the community today, even if it would only be for a short time.

Chapter 10

I was varnishing the first of the newly sanded shutters the following morning when I was disturbed by a loud electronic buzz. It took me a couple of seconds to realise that it was the bell at the Villa Naranja's gate. It was the first time that anyone had rung it. The only person to have visited since my arrival was Pep Navarro, and he had a fob. I balanced my paintbrush carefully on the tin of varnish and then walked towards the entrance.

A small green car had stopped outside and a woman of around my own age was standing beside it. She was wearing jeans and a T-shirt, and her butter-blonde hair was pulled back into a pert ponytail.

'Hello,' I said. 'Can I help you?'

'You are Juno?' she asked in English. 'I am Catalina, the mother of Xavi.'

'Oh, Xavi's mum.' I beamed at her as I pressed the release button and the gate slid open. 'How is he?'

'He is well,' she said. 'I came to thank you for bringing him to the hospital.'

'No problem.'

She didn't bother to get back into the car, but simply

walked inside and followed me to the back of the house.

'He was unlucky,' I added. 'I guess reaching for the branch wrenched his shoulder and then when he fell . . .'

'He was not unlucky.' She made a face. 'He was very disobedient. He has been told – they have all been told – that the plaza is not a playground for their silly game.'

'Kids think everywhere is a playground,' I said.

'You are right.' She shrugged. 'But boys do not listen. They are so much harder work than girls.'

'I don't know,' I said. 'I don't have any children myself. Would you like a coffee?' I added. 'Or water? Maybe juice?'

'Water would be nice,' she replied.

I went into the kitchen and got water for both of us. When I returned, she was sitting at the stone table in the shade of the striped umbrella.

'Thank you,' she said as she accepted the water. 'I came also to give you this.' She opened her bag and took out two lemon-scented candles in jars. 'I make them myself,' she said when I'd sniffed them and told her they were beautiful. 'I thought you might like them.'

'You didn't have to give me anything,' I said. 'It was no trouble to bring him.'

'Maribel told me how you tied up his arm.' She looked at me, suddenly doubtful. 'Is that the right word? Tied up? It sounds odd.'

'Strapped up is what we'd say,' I told her. 'I'm impressed by your English!'

'I worked in London for three years, and my husband lived there for even longer,' she said. 'I have forgotten a lot, though.'

'Everyone here seems to have worked abroad,' I said. 'And

111

you all speak fantastic English. Maybe I'll improve from *gracias* and *por favor* after a few more weeks. Though I doubt it.'

She smiled. 'I am sure you will learn. How long will you spend here?'

'I haven't decided yet,' I replied. 'It's a lovely place and I like it very much. But even if I wanted to, I couldn't afford to stay for a long time.'

'It would be nice to do only the things we want to do,' said Catalina. 'I am fortunate that you are here now. And so is Xavi. My other reason for coming was to say that we would be honoured if you would join us at our table in the plaza on Friday night.' She looked at me earnestly. 'I hope you say yes.'

'Oh . . . that's very kind of you . . .' I was about to add that I hadn't decided on whether or not I was even going to go to the fiesta, but her words had been so genuine that I couldn't say no. And so I told her I'd be delighted.

'My husband, José, will come for you in the car,' she said. 'He will bring you home. You do not have to worry about a thing.'

'Thank you,' I said.

'You will have fun. The fiesta is always fun. And,' she added with a shrewd glance at me, 'I think you need more fun while you are here than painting Doña Carmen's shutters and bringing my son to the hospital.'

Put like that, she had a point.

The sunny weather meant that I was able to wash and return Rosa's cropped top to her the following day.

'You could've kept it,' she said as I handed it over.

'I'm slim, but I think my cropped-top days are behind

me.' I grinned. 'The doctors in the hospital were giving me some very funny looks.'

'They were probably just awed by your sling,' she told me with a laugh. 'Anyhow, thanks for bringing it back. Everyone's dead impressed by how you dealt with Xavi.'

'No problem,' I told her. 'I was glad to help. His mum has asked me to join them for the fiesta on Friday, which is really kind.'

'You'll be on their Christmas card list forever.'

I smiled goodbye and then walked around to the DIY store, where I bought another pot of varnish. My fame as a first-aider had reached there too, and the owner, Sergio, praised me for my quick thinking.

'It wasn't really quick thinking,' I said as I handed over the money. 'It's my job to know how to deal with stuff like that.'

'Xavi was very lucky you were there,' he told me. 'Maybe in the future he will be more careful. But I doubt it. He is *loco*, that one.'

The Greek god, Pep Navarro, had heard about my exploits too.

'They said you took off your clothes,' he told me when he turned up to clean the pool. 'In the middle of the square!'

'I did not!' I felt myself go bright red. 'I changed my T-shirt because Rosa's was too small to make a sling.'

'I would have liked to see that,' he said with a grin, and then returned to his pool cleaning.

I bathed in the warm glow of the town's acceptance, and by Friday afternoon I was looking forward to the fiesta. Even though I'd come to Beniflor to be alone, I wasn't used to spending so much time not talking to anyone. The hospital is always busy with lots of talk going on. Obviously my one-sided chats with Banquo didn't count as conversation.

Nevertheless, the idea of being in a crowd of people was a little unnerving. This was partly because of the language barrier and partly because – outside of an emergency situation like Xavi's – I didn't entirely trust myself not to burst into tears at exactly the wrong moment. However, I hadn't burst into tears in ages, and I couldn't imagine how anyone here was going to do or say anything that might provoke them. As I got ready that evening, I wondered if I'd skipped over the fourth stage of grief, which is depression. Because at that moment I wasn't feeling depressed. I was feeling excited. All the same, I very definitely hadn't moved on to the fifth stage. Acceptance. I still wasn't ready to accept that Brad was gone. I wasn't ready to accept that I couldn't challenge him about how he'd cheated on both Alessandra and me.

I made myself forget about Brad as I looked at myself in the full-length mirror in my bedroom. I was wearing a pale lilac sundress with a border of yellow flowers around the hem, and my favourite wedge sandals. I still needed the tortoiseshell hairband to keep my hair in place but I suddenly realised that, despite the lashings of sunscreen, my face was lightly tinted by the sun, and my arms and legs sported a healthy glow. I looked better than when I'd first arrived. A lot better. Almost normal.

My phone pinged with a message from Cleo.

Having drinks in town. Thinking of you. Hoping you're well.

I took my bag from the bed and went downstairs. Then, with the orange trees behind me, I took a selfie and sent it to her.

You wagon! The reply came instantly. *You look amazing.*

I kind of did. All summery and holiday-ish and carefree. Which wasn't really how I felt inside. But it was how I appeared at that exact moment. So perhaps I was moving on towards acceptance, after all. No matter how remote that option still seemed to be.

The plaza was buzzing with life. Coloured lights had been strung around the square and the adjoining streets, and music blared from speakers on the balcony of the town hall – or *ayuntamiento*, as Catalina called it. In front of the *ayuntamiento*, three large red velvet thrones awaited the Fiesta Queens on a stage decorated with masses of flowers. Meantime, the trestle tables, which had been placed in the plaza earlier, were nearly all occupied by the townspeople who'd brought their own food and drink and were happily tucking in.

Catalina, José and I, along with Xavi and his baby sister, Agata, were at one corner of the plaza with quite a good view of the stage. Agata was asleep in her pram – she was less than a year old but that hadn't stopped her parents bringing her out for the night, and I could see that there were plenty of other babies in prams at the fiesta, apparently untroubled by the light and the noise. There were lots of other children too, some running around but many sitting at the tables with their families and neighbours. Xavi's arm was still supported by a sling and he wasn't doing any running about. But he was having a heated conversation with one of his friends, which I gathered had something to do with football. Xavi was wearing a Barcelona shirt. His friend's – according to José – was Real Madrid.

José and Catalina were being very attentive towards me

– having introduced me to their neighbours, they made sure that I wasn't stuck behind my language barrier and kept up a running commentary on everything that was going on, including the parading of San Bernardo's statue and the arrival of the Fiesta Queens.

By the time the crowning ceremony took place I'd already downed a couple of glasses of Catalina's home-made sangria, which was cold, refreshing and very fruity.

'Made with wine from the Navarro bodega,' she told me. 'They produce the best wines in the region.'

I still hadn't tried the ones Pep Navarro had left me. But I promised myself that I would.

Catalina had just poured more sangria for everyone when the crowning ceremony began. Beatriz was every bit as beautiful as people had said – a stunning girl with a tumble of dark hair, and equally dark, seductive eyes. The older Fiesta Queen, Señora Sotomayor, looked younger than her seventy years, although not in the glamorous way that my own mother did, but simply because of her beaming smile and outgoing nature. The young Queen, a little girl named Linda, was petite and pretty and equally smiley. Actually, the delightful thing about the whole Fiesta Queen scenario was that it wasn't like a beauty contest at all, despite Beatriz's undoubted glamour, it was all just family fun.

The three Queens presided over some speechifying, which naturally I didn't understand. Then some firecrackers were set off in an unbelievable cacophony of noise. Little Agata slept through it all.

I was finding it difficult to keep any kind of conversation going because, although Catalina and José spoke excellent English, it was harder for them and for me over the gabble of other people talking as well as the hip-hop music that was now playing. I was sure they were exhausted with looking after me and so during a lull in the conversation I excused myself from the table. They immediately began talking to their neighbours while I started to stroll around the plaza.

'Is fun for you?'

I whirled around at the touch on my shoulder and found myself facing Pep Navarro. He was wearing a plain white shirt and blue jeans and, quite honestly, looked even more like a Greek god than ever.

'Yes.' I smiled easily at him, even though my heart had skipped a beat. 'I've never been to anything like this before.'

'You have fiesta in Ireland,' he said. 'St Patrick's Day?'

'You know about St Patrick's Day?'

'There is an Irish pub in Beniflor Costa,' he said. 'Every year they have green beer.'

'I've never actually drunk green beer,' I admitted. 'I'm not sure I'd want to.'

'I do not think it would taste very good.' Pep laughed. 'I have not tried it myself. But I have been in this pub and seen the dancing. *Riverdance*.'

I nodded. There's probably nobody in the world who hasn't seen or heard of *Riverdance*, the musical production that took Irish dancing to a whole new level.

Fired up by the sangria, I boasted that I was an Irish dancer.

'Really?'

You'd think that I wouldn't be any good at any sort of dancing, what with the lack of creativity and artistry in my make-up, but the thing about Irish dancing is that it's quite technical – and, of course, that's exactly what I *am* good at.

It was a big relief to my mother when she realised I could manage a reel and a jig. It made her feel I had some connection with my traditional roots. I started going to classes pre-*Riverdance*, when the dancers were ramrod straight and totally expressionless, and the outfits were usually sludge green or a miserable fawn. Afterwards, when the show toured the world, it went madly in the other direction as the costumes became more and more extravagant and glittery, and the traditional ringlets of the female dancers morphed into a mophead of curly hair pretty much only achievable by wearing a wig. My own hair had a slight wave back then, but it wasn't enough to satisfy Mrs McConnell, our teacher, who wanted us all to look like Jean Butler.

So Mum bought me a curly wig in what she fondly imagined was an alluring shade of Titian, but which was undoubtedly orange. I absolutely refused to wear it – which meant that I never got the leading dance roles, even though I was probably good enough. Truthfully, though, I wouldn't have wanted to be the one on my own in front of everyone. Unlike the rest of my family, I was happier in the background. Anyhow, the bottom line is that I can put on a decent performance if someone starts with the fiddle and the bodhrán.

'You will have to show me,' said Pep.

'On St Patrick's Day,' I joked.

'You will still be here then?' He looked surprised.

'Well, no,' I admitted. 'But maybe I'll come back for a visit.'

'I hope so.' His dark brown eyes bored into me, and I felt my heart pick up the pace as though I'd just danced a series of double jigs.

As I tried to think of something to say, Beatriz, the Fiesta

Queen, came to join us. Close up she was even more gorgeous. The Navarros were a stunning family. I wondered about Luis, the brother Rosa had suggested would be perfect for me. And then I dismissed him from my mind. Nobody in Beniflor was perfect for me. I didn't want anyone to be perfect for me. I didn't want to get involved ever again.

Pep and Beatriz were talking intently and I sidled away from them. I was beginning to feel tired, as much from the effort of trying to understand what was being said around me as for any other reason. I realised I was also a little drunk. Catalina's sangria had been so lovely that I'd forgotten there was alcohol in it. I glanced at my watch. It was nearly one in the morning but nobody showed any signs of wanting to go home. The babies were still sleeping happily in their prams. The younger children were running around the square. The teenagers were dancing. The adults were talking.

'You disappeared.' Pep turned up at my side again. 'Is everything all right?'

'Of course,' I replied. 'I was just wondering about going home.'

'But . . .' he looked at me in surprise, 'it is early.'

'For you, perhaps,' I said. 'I'm used to different hours.'

'Even the tourists do not go to bed before midnight,' he said.

'It's after midnight,' I pointed out.

'You truly wish to leave?'

'It's nothing against the fiesta,' I assured him. 'I just . . .'

'I will bring you home,' he said.

'Oh no,' I told him. 'Xavi's dad will . . .'

He shrugged dismissively. 'José is with his family. I will do it.'

119

'But you want to stay here,' I said.

'I can come back.'

'Are you sure?'

'Of course.'

So I went back to Catalina and José's table and told them I was leaving. They were equally aghast at the idea of me going home so early, but after a brief conversation with Pep they nodded their agreement and said goodnight.

'And please, anything we can ever do for you, just ask,' said José. 'We are very grateful to you for how you looked after Xavi.'

'I was glad to help,' I said.

After another flurry of hugs and kisses goodbye, I followed Pep out of the square and along the street to where he'd parked the little van.

I hadn't noticed before that the lettering on the side said *Bodegas Navarro.*

I clambered into the passenger seat, then Pep put the van into gear and we rattled down the main street and back to the Villa Naranja. He opened the gates with his fob, drove in and pulled up outside the house.

'Thank you,' I said.

'*De nada.*'

I didn't know if I should ask him in for a coffee. It seemed polite. And yet it was probably also laden with expectation.

So I asked him.

I was sure he'd say yes.

He said no.

Chapter 11

'I must get back to the fiesta,' he told me. 'I am helping with the sound system. I am sorry.'

In the depths of my disappointment, I also felt relief. I was lusting after Pep Navarro, that was for certain, but sleeping with him would be a complication I could do without. Although, the devil voice said in my head, what complications could possibly arise from a one-night stand with a gorgeous man you'll never see again after the summer?

I'd thought there'd be no complications with Brad too, though, hadn't I? And see how that had turned out.

'Another time?' Pep said. 'I would like coffee with you. Very much.'

I think he emphasised the word coffee. I didn't know if that meant he was underlining its meaning or adding the meaning that I'd ascribed to it myself.

'That would be nice,' I said. 'Thanks again for driving me home.'

'You are welcome.'

'Have fun at the fiesta.'

He grinned. 'We will be there until morning. Are you sure you do not wish to return with me?'

'I'm exhausted,' I said.

'Then you must sleep.'

'Yes,' I said. 'I must.'

I felt like we were characters in a play. But maybe that was because English wasn't his natural language. Or because, like an actor, I was being another person. For the first time ever I wondered how my mother felt when she was playing a role. Did she immerse herself totally in the character and become that person? Or did she feel, as I did now, like someone observing herself from a distance?

'I will see you when I come to clean the pool,' he said.

'Of course.'

He leaned forward and I stayed standing straight, very prim and proper, as he kissed me on the cheek.

'*Hasta pronto*,' he said.

I knew that meant something like 'See you soon' and I wondered how soon it might be.

I was aching with desire for him. I didn't want to feel it. But I did.

I was having breakfast (a chocolate muffin and aromatic coffee) the following morning when my phone rang. For a heart-stopping moment I thought it was Pep, and then I saw the caller ID.

'Hello, Mum,' I said as I answered it.

'Where the hell are you?' she demanded. 'I talked to Gonne and she said you were in Spain, and the ringtone definitely makes it sound like you're abroad, but you didn't say you were going on holiday. I really don't understand why you'd simply take off without a word. It's not as though we're in constant contact but it would have been nice to have been told. I'm hoping you'll come to a charity lunch I'm hosting. I'm counting on you, in fact, to save the date.'

That's the way my mum talks. She takes a deep breath and keeps going until she needs to breathe again. The best thing is to let her finish, because she doesn't even notice an interruption.

'I had the chance to stay in a private villa,' I told her. 'I thought I'd take it.'

'A private what? Where? Why? With whom?'

'A private villa,' I repeated. 'It's owned by the family of one of the girls I work with.'

'But . . . but why would you head off without saying anything to anybody? Is it anything to do with that man? Are you back together? Are you with him?'

My mother knew I'd been going out with someone and that he was my first boyfriend since Sean, that it was over and I was upset about it. She has a way of worming at least the basic information out of me that I can never quite resist. But I hadn't told her anything else. Not about him being married, not about the earthquake, not about going to his funeral, nothing. I didn't want her to make a drama out of my crisis. And she would have, because that's what she does. She can't help herself.

She'd gone into high-drama mode when Sean had broken our engagement. I'd had to move back home for a short while and, grateful though I was to have a place to go, Mum had organised a family dinner 'to cheer me up' on my very first evening there. I'm not sure why she thought having Butler, Gonne and their happy families over could possibly cheer me up. All their arrival did was emphasise my rejected state. I know they felt they were being supportive by calling him a shit and telling me that there were plenty more fish in the sea, but the more they dissed Sean, the more idiotic I felt for having fallen in love with him in the first place. The thought of them picking over the ruins of my unknowingly illicit relationship with Brad was more than I could bear. And they would have done. Because there was no point in telling Mum and swearing her to secrecy. I love her dearly, I truly do, but the woman is incapable of keeping her mouth shut about anything. I'd always been the sensible one in a family of passionate people. I didn't want to be the one whose emotional life had crumbled around her. Again.

'We're not back together.' I felt my fingers tighten around the phone. 'I simply wanted to be on my own for a bit.'

'What did he do to you?' she demanded. 'Why have you run away? You weren't like this even after the Dolt.'

She always referred to Sean as the Dolt. Even when I was engaged to him. She thought it was funny.

'I haven't run away,' I said. 'I'm just chilling out.'

'You don't chill out, Juno,' said my mother. 'You've never chilled out in your entire life.'

'Sometimes I do.'

'Are you coming home soon?' she asked. 'Will you be able to come to the lunch? It's for osteoporosis. I thought it would interest you.'

Osteoporosis is a cause close to Mum's heart. After she broke a bone in her wrist from a fall, I was the one who made her get a DXA scan and then told her that she was in the moderate osteoporosis category. In one of life's little coincidences, a close theatrical friend of hers tripped a few days after her and fractured her hip. Until then, Marnie Mulcahy had been an active woman. The fall aged her overnight. Mum is paranoid about her own condition worsening. It's the only thing she listens to me about. (Well, she doesn't actually listen any more. She's the one who lectures me now. She thinks she knows more about it than I do. Sometimes I think she might.)

'It's a great cause and I'd be happy to go, but I'm staying here for a few more weeks,' I told her.

'A few more weeks! How can you possibly do that? You're always complaining that you don't have enough time off, so how could you have enough holidays to spend in private villas in Spain? How can you even afford it? What the hell is going on with you?'

'Nothing's going on. And I have some savings . . . the money I didn't spend on my wedding, remember? Is it so impossible to believe that I'd like some time out for once?'

'I thought you said you weren't still upset about the Dolt!' cried my mother. 'But here you are, talking about your wedding – your great escape, if you ask me.'

'I'm not talking about my wedding.' I sighed with exasperation. 'I'm simply trying to—'

'Gonne said she thought there was something odd about your messages,' said Mum before I could finish.

'There wasn't.'

'There's something not right with you. A mother can always tell.'

'I was feeling a bit down before I came,' I told her. 'But I'm fine now. I really am. You don't have to worry.'

'I worry about you more than the other two combined. There's been something wrong with you for ages. But instead of sharing it with us, like a normal person, you insist on doing your own thing. Now you've fled the country and you're holing up somewhere in Spain.'

'I haven't fled the country,' I protested. 'Nor am I holing up. You're being silly.'

Although she wasn't, really. I *had* fled the country. I *was* holing up. It was just that she made it sound a million times more dramatic than it was.

'I could come and see you,' she said. 'Maybe you'll be a bit more forthcoming face to face.'

'Please don't, Mum,' I said. 'Not that I want to deprive you of a holiday or anything, but . . . but maybe you could come later. Right now I really need time to myself.'

'And you have the nerve to say there's nothing wrong!' she exclaimed. 'If it was Butler I could accept it. He needs solitude for his poetry, even though Larry doesn't always see it that way. But you – you're a Duracell bunny, Juno Ryan, always on the go. You don't do well on your own.'

'I'm doing perfectly well on my own,' I assured her, ignoring the slight directed at my brother's very understanding husband. 'Besides, Saoirse or Cleo might come out for a few days.'

'Oh.'

'So you don't have to worry about me. You really don't.'

I'd been surprised when she said she worried about me more than Gonne and Butler. I'd rather thought that she mostly despaired of me.

'Mothers are programmed to worry about their children,' said Mum. 'It's what we do. And we're programmed to know when they're lying their little asses off too.'

'I'm not lying to you,' I lied. 'I'm fine.'

'I'm not going to force myself on you,' said Mum. 'But if you need me, call.'

My eyes welled with tears. Just because my mother hadn't

wanted me didn't mean she didn't love me. I knew that. But I allowed myself to forget it sometimes. I was a terrible daughter. A terrible person.

'I'll call, I promise,' I said.

'Good.'

'Are you working on anything right now?' I asked.

She's seventy years old and she still likes acting more than anything. In the last few years she's reprised her role on an Irish soap opera as a guest star, returning as a woman who'd disappeared and who everyone thought had been murdered. The storyline had kept the nation on tenterhooks for months, but it had shifted focus and she hadn't appeared in the most recent episodes.

'I'll be back on *Clarendon Park* soon,' she said with a note of satisfaction. 'They know I bring in the viewers.'

Her character, Imelda, was a total battleaxe. Everyone loved to hate her, and Mum was totally brilliant in the role although, as she occasionally muttered darkly, to have a decent role as an older woman it's almost obligatory to play a hardcore bitch. Someone deranged or vengeful, she said, or else cold-hearted and frigid. Imelda slotted into the vengeful mode, and even though Mum said she was fun to play, she bemoaned the fact that nobody over thirty-five was allowed to be a love interest. Unless it was part of some complicated affair.

'Older women are sexual beings too,' she told me. 'I wish we were allowed to portray that on screen more regularly. But of course only the male ideal of beauty and allure is ever shown. It does a terrible disservice to the rest of us. You'd think no woman past the menopause had a sex life. Which is patently untrue.'

She had a point, I knew she had. But it was lost in my attempts not to think of my mother as someone with a sex life.

I told her I was delighted that Imelda was making a comeback on *Clarendon Park*.

'The schedule is very manageable for the first episodes. But if you don't come home after a few weeks I'm coming to see for myself that you're OK.'

'I'm fine,' I assured her.

'I love you,' said Mum.

'I love you too,' I told her in return.

Her words echoed in my ears even after she'd ended the call.

Chapter 12

It had clouded over while I was talking to Mum; the first grey clouds I'd seen since I'd arrived at the Villa Naranja. But it was still warm, and I spent the rest of the morning varnishing another set of shutters while wondering if Pep Navarro, who had to be at least eight years younger than me, thought of me as a sexual being or a battleaxe. I'd fondly imagined that my early thirties were my prime years, but after my conversation with Mum I couldn't help thinking that I was deluding myself. Yes, I was young, even if most women of my mother's generation had been married with children at my age. Yes, I could be considered attractive, notwithstanding the grey hairs that were beginning to make their appearance on my head more and more regularly. But was I young enough or attractive enough for a man in his twenties? Did I fit into his picture of an ideal woman?

Probably not, I concluded as I put the lid on my tin of varnish. Pep Navarro undoubtedly had his pick of fresh-faced girls. My ridiculous desire for him was encouraging me to make a fool of myself. And I'd had enough of making a fool of myself. I wasn't going to do it again.

I put away the varnish and the brushes and changed into my

swimsuit. Then I dived into the pool and flipped on to my back so that I was floating gently on the surface. I closed my eyes and emptied my mind. I'd had enough soul-searching for one day.

I was still floating when I heard the sound of the gates sliding open and a car pulling up outside the house. A treacherous frisson of excitement ran through me. Pep had come back. Perhaps he saw me as a sexual being after all.

I hauled myself out of the water and pulled in my stomach as I stood dripping on the edge of the pool. If the Greek god was going to see me in a bikini for the first time, I wanted to look my best. I didn't care how superficial that made me.

I heard footsteps on the gravel and then the woman appeared.

She was tall and elegant, her long legs encased in skinny jeans, and bright-red high-heeled sandals on her feet. She wore a loose white blouse over the jeans, and her dark hair was tied back. Her eyes were hidden by a pair of Ray-Bans. She could have been anywhere from thirty-five to fifty-five, and I had no idea who she was or how she'd got past the gate.

'*Hola*,' she said. 'You must be Juno. I am Ana Perez Moralles.'

I stared at her.

'Pilar's mother,' she added.

'Oh!' I was still holding in my stomach. Ana Perez was so startlingly chic that it was the only way I could feel even vaguely adequate in her company. I hadn't imagined that Pilar's mother would be as poised as a fashion model. If I'd thought of her at all, it would have been as a nondescript motherly figure. I was annoyed at myself for falling into the kind of stereotyping that I'd actually been irritated by just a few moments earlier.

'It's good to meet you.' She held out a perfectly manicured hand but didn't try the customary kiss on the cheek. I was too wet for that. 'Pilar has talked of you a lot.'

'Nice things, I hope.' I picked up the towel, which I'd draped over the stone bench, and wrapped it around me.

'But of course,' said Ana Perez. 'She says that you and your colleagues have been very helpful to her. That you are kind and generous with your time and your knowledge. She is happy working with you.'

'I'm glad to hear it,' I said.

'I, too.' Ana smiled. 'She is my only daughter and I want very much that she be happy.'

'She's good at her job,' I told her. 'She gets on well with the patients.'

'Excellent,' said Ana.

I shifted a little uncomfortably. I was conscious that I was still wet and dripping beneath the towel.

'I'm sorry,' I said. 'I was swimming and . . .'

'Would you like to change?'

I nodded, then hurried into the house and up the stairs, where I dried off and put on a bright-pink sundress and my jewelled flip-flops. Nothing in my wardrobe could possibly make me feel equal to Ana Perez but at least now I was wearing clothes. I came downstairs again. She was sitting at the stone table.

'I must apologise to you,' she said as I joined her. 'I should have phoned to say I was coming.'

'It's your house,' I said. 'You can come any time you like.'

'Not while you're renting it,' she said. 'But this was my first free day since you arrived, and I wanted to welcome you. I believe you have already settled into life in Beniflor and have even given first aid to Xavi Ruiz.'

'Anyone would have done the same,' I said.

'Nevertheless, you were very kind. As for Elena Navarro – she has spoken of the work you are doing to the house.' She glanced towards the villa, where this morning's shutters were still drying. 'Pilar did not tell me you would do so much. I must pay you for it.'

'Oh, no!' I cried. 'I didn't do it to be paid. I did it because I wanted to. It's not like I had anything else to keep me busy.'

'Nevertheless, you are a radiographer not a carpenter,' said Ana. 'And I'm very grateful.'

I laughed. 'I can do both.'

'And you are happy here at the Villa Naranja?' she asked. 'You are enjoying your stay? You are not too lonely?'

'How can I be? I'm taking children to hospital and varnishing the shutters.'

She smiled.

'Well, if it gets too boring for you, you could come to Valencia for a few days,' she said. 'I would be delighted to have you stay with me. You should see something more of the country while you are here.'

'I couldn't possibly impose on you like that,' I said.

'Nonsense,' retorted Ana. 'Beniflor is my home town and very beautiful, but it would be a shame not to come to the city too. To be truthful . . .' her voice dropped and she looked around as though we could be overheard, 'although I like to visit Beniflor, this house . . . well, it will always be

132

my mother's house to me, even though I lived here. It has more of her presence than mine or my brother's.'

'I understand,' I said. 'All the same, as a weekend retreat or somewhere for the summer it must be nice.'

'It is good to have somewhere different,' she agreed. 'But as you have seen yourself, the villa is a little too much for us to manage. It needs more maintenance than we have time for. Better to sell it and buy an apartment in Beniflor Costa for weekends. That is what I hope to do. At the same time . . .' she looked around again, 'I feel guilty about it. Because it has been in our family for a long time, and it's hard to let it go.'

'How long have you lived here?' I was genuinely interested in the history of the villa. I felt an ownership, after all.

She glanced at her watch. 'Let us have something to eat,' she said. 'Then we can talk.'

'Um . . . I only have salad in the fridge,' I told her. 'I'm sorry, I—'

'I do not expect you to prepare food for me,' she said. 'We will go to Beniflor Costa. There is a nice restaurant overlooking the sea.'

'Oh, but—'

'Come along.' Her voice was firm. 'I will drive.'

She wasn't the kind of person you could say no to.

So I nodded in agreement and fetched my bag.

Ana's car was a silver-grey Mercedes cabriolet. The soft top was down, and when I got into the passenger's seat I couldn't help feeling a little chic and glamorous. At least until she gunned the car down the twisting road to the coast and I didn't feel glamorous at all, just scared.

So I was relieved when we turned the last corner and stretched out in front of us was a small bay of golden sand and the blue waters of the Mediterranean. Despite the cloudy day, the beach was still dotted with multicoloured sunshades, and there were plenty of people swimming in the sea and lying out on loungers.

Beniflor Costa was much bigger than Beniflor itself. There were lots of apartment buildings and villas overlooking the sea, and I could easily imagine Ana spending her summer weekends in one of them. I wondered suddenly about the rest of her family. Would they like a holiday apartment or would they prefer to keep the villa in the hills? Did Mr Perez – if there was a Mr Perez – agree with the idea of selling the family home? Rosa had mentioned a brother who actually lived in Beniflor Costa too, so perhaps Ana wanted to be closer to him.

She turned the car towards the wide promenade that encompassed almost the entirety of the bay. It was crammed with restaurants, bars and the kind of shops that sell all things beach related, from inflatable balls to bikinis. She drove past them and eventually pulled up outside a small wooden building, a few hundred metres after the prom.

'Lucky to find a space,' she remarked as she killed the engine.

We both got out of the car and walked into the restaurant. I'd been expecting something equally small inside but it opened out on to a wide wooden deck, which overlooked the sea. About half the tables were already occupied and others had a reserved notice on them. I wasn't surprised, because it was clear that the view had to be one of the best in the town.

'How lovely!' I said as I turned to Ana. 'I'd never have guessed this was here.'

Ana grinned. 'It's my favourite place. Ah, Iker, *buenos días. Qué tal?*'

The restaurant owner, a man with curly grey hair and an extravagant moustache, had come to greet us. He and Ana exchanged the customary kisses and then Iker led us to the best table in the place – at the corner of the deck, with uninterrupted views of the sea.

'Iker and I were at school together,' Ana told me. 'We hated each other then. But we grew up and now we're good friends. I've asked him to bring the tapas menu, is that OK for you?'

'Perfect,' I said.

Apart from at the fiesta, the only eating out I'd done in the last couple of weeks was coffee and pie in the Café Flor, so I was looking forward to the opportunity of sampling some tapas. After studying the menu for a while we ordered patatas bravas, calamari, olives and mussels. Iker then brought us a large jug of water, infused with lime.

'This is lovely,' I said. 'It really is. Thank you for bringing me here.'

'It's the nicest place on the Costa,' said Ana. 'Iker is a great chef. The food is good but simple. I hope you like the *mejillones.*'

The *mejillones* were the mussels. I'm not a big shellfish eater, but Iker recommended them and so I thought I should give them a try.

'Not bad,' I said, after I'd doused one with lemon and popped it into my mouth. 'I don't think I'd order them on a regular basis, but maybe from time to time.'

'By the time you go home you will be accustomed to all of our wonderful seafood,' she assured me. 'You must visit some more of our good restaurants while you are here.'

'Oh, I'm living the simple life,' I said. 'My eating out is usually coffee and cake at the Café Flor. It's in Beniflor.'

'I know it,' she said.'The owner is another person I went to school with.'

'I suppose everyone knows everyone around here,' I said as I helped myself to some spicy potato.

'In the past, yes,' she agreed. 'Of course the town has grown and changed over the years, and there are lots of new people we don't know. But the Beniflorencos all know each other.'

'Has your family lived in the Villa Naranja all your lives?' I asked. 'It's a much grander house than a lot of them around here seem to be.'

'That's because it's not a finca. It was originally built as a country home for a Valencian nobleman,' she told me. 'In 1931, after a new government was elected and the King went into exile, Don Fernando and his family left Spain too. My grandfather supported the new government, but not everyone in Beniflor did, and there was a lot of civil unrest in Spain at that time. The country moved closer and closer to civil war, and when that broke out the house was taken over by nationalists and my grandparents moved in. It became a safe house for those who opposed Franco's forces.' She sighed. 'My family was very involved in the war, and they paid the price.'

'What price?'

'My grandfather was executed,' she said. 'He was hanged from a tree in the garden.'

136

I stared at her in disbelief.

'It was a turbulent and difficult time in our history,' she told me. 'The fascists tried to take my grandmother too, but she was prepared. She shot the local leader and became a bit of a heroine.'

'Ana!'

'I know. It sounds so unlikely and unbelievable now, doesn't it? But the scars are still there, although the tree is not. My mother chopped it down. She was a baby when it happened, so she didn't remember it, but her mother kept the stories alive. When she died, my mother decided that it was time for the tree to go too. She didn't like to talk about it, but she often said that it was important to get rid of the symbols while keeping the memories of the people alive. However, she marked the spot where it happened and she planted a jacaranda there instead of the olive tree they hanged him from.'

'Oh!' I exclaimed. 'I've seen the jacaranda. There's a stone beneath it.'

Ana nodded. 'It was an old sundial. It would probably still be effective at telling the time, but of course it's in the shade of the tree now. We weren't allowed near it when we were children, but over time, it just became part of the garden.'

'Does Pilar know?' I asked. 'She never said a thing about it to me.'

'Of course. But to her it's just an old story that means very little. And we tend not to talk about those times very much.'

'I suppose we need to learn from them.' I was still coming to terms with the Villa Naranja's violent past, so at odds with its tranquil present.

'That's true. Although somehow we seem to repeat the past, over and over, just in a slightly different way. Anyhow . . .' she filled my glass with more water, 'there is no need for us to be depressed about it now. The house was legally given to my family, and my brother and I grew up there. We didn't know anything about the politics, but whenever we were naughty my mother used to tell us that our grandfather was watching us, and that if we disobeyed her we'd see his ghost standing on the sundial.'

'That would have freaked me out!' I cried.

'It had its uncomfortable moments,' admitted Ana. 'My brother and I often spent nights peering out of the window hoping to see Grandfather's ghost. My brother, Pablo, insisted he had seen him once or twice – but that's nonsense, of course. He was only trying to scare me.'

Once again I had to remind myself that I didn't believe in ghosts. And yet I was recalling the noises I'd heard on the first night I arrived, and the broken glass and how I'd reassured myself that it had been caused by Banquo. If I'd been a believer in anything else, the fact that a man had been hanged only a few metres from the house could easily have accounted for a restless spirit!

'Have I scared you now?' asked Ana when I didn't speak. 'I'm sorry, I didn't mean to. It's just a house, and there was never a single day that I thought my grandfather haunted it. I never said that to my children – I wouldn't have dreamed of it. It's just that it's such a long time since I've spoken of it, I couldn't help myself.'

'It's fine,' I assured her. 'I'm fine. It's just hard to believe, that's all. The Villa Naranja is so peaceful and serene. I'm struggling to picture it as a hotbed of rebel activity.'

'It was called El Rincón then,' she told me. 'It means a corner, a little place, hidden away. My parents renamed it. They thought it was a good idea.'

I nodded. 'I don't know how you can possibly want to sell it,' I said. 'It has such history.'

'It's good to remember, but knowing when to move on is also part of life,' said Ana. 'My husband and I have our home in Valencia. My son has his own apartment here and divides his time between Beniflor Costa and Madrid. And Pilar is living in Ireland. The Villa Naranja is neglected, and that's not the legacy I want to leave.'

'Would the Navarros buy it?' I asked. 'After all, they own the finca next door.'

'We have talked about it,' said Ana. 'But when it comes to negotiations, Miguel Navarro is a total shark. He won't pay anything like what I want. We will see, though. You have already made it look more attractive to buyers. I have to thank you for that.'

'Actually I was wondering if I could do a little more,' I said.

'More! What have you got in mind?'

'Painting the inside,' I replied. 'Those mustard walls are so depressing.'

Anna laughed. 'I hate them too,' she said. 'My mother would have changed them, I think, but she felt they were her mother's choice and she couldn't do it.'

'If you'd prefer that I didn't . . .'

'If you want to spend your holiday doing up my house, you are welcome,' said Ana. 'I feel bad that you feel the need to do it.'

'It's not that,' I said. 'I'm just not good at lounging around. I like to keep active.'

139

'Allow me to give you money for paint.' She reached for her bag.

'Oh, no,' I protested. 'I want to do this. You mightn't like it, and then you'll have to pay to have it redone. So—'

'I will hardly dislike it more than I do already,' she said. She took out her purse and handed me a couple of hundred euros. 'Buy what you need. If there is any money left, you can treat yourself to a nice bottle of wine.'

'I don't think I'll spend that much on paint,' I said.

'But there may be other things,' said Ana. 'Brushes and . . . and . . . well, whatever. I appreciate you doing it.'

'I want to,' I said. 'I was thinking an off-white.'

I smiled inside as I said it. Back in Dublin I'd dreamed of changing the walls from a neutral colour to something more vibrant. But here, the vibrancy was all around. The walls needed to be a focal point of calm, not call attention to themselves.

'I will leave it to you,' she said. 'You seem to know what you are doing.'

'I hope you find the right buyer,' I said.

'So do I,' said Ana. 'It's a nuisance having to travel backwards and forwards from Valencia to look after it, especially since I do it so badly!'

'Do you work in Valencia?' I asked.

'I'm a curator at the City of Arts and Sciences,' she said. I'd seen pictures of the futuristic buildings, designed by Santiago Calatrava, in the city's reclaimed river bed. They looked amazing, and I said so.

'Our current exhibition is about the body as a machine,' said Ana. 'You might find that interesting.'

'I probably would.'

140

'So come to Valencia,' she suggested again. 'We would love to have you stay.'

'That's very kind of you. But—'

'Let's exchange numbers,' said Ana. 'And if you want to visit, just let me know.'

'OK,' I said. 'Thank you.'

'It's my pleasure,' said Ana.

She signalled for the bill and I picked up my bag. But she refused to allow me to pay or even to pay my share.

'You're a guest in my country,' she said. 'When I come to Ireland you can pay. Besides, you're working for me as my decorator now, so this is a business lunch.'

'Hardly,' I said. 'I'm doing something I enjoy.'

'And I've enjoyed chatting to you,' Ana told me. 'Now, accept lunch as my gift and let's go.'

It was late in the afternoon by the time Ana left for Valencia again. I waved goodbye and then walked through the garden, stopping at the sundial beneath the jacaranda. Some of the purple blossoms had fallen from the tree on to the stone. Suddenly I *could* visualise Ana's grandfather being dragged from the house by factions baying for his blood. His wife and children shrieking in terror. And then the moment he was strung up – it was a truly horrific scene. And it had happened less than a hundred years earlier.

Banquo appeared and rubbed against my ankles.

'What about your ancestors?' I asked. 'Which side were they on in the Civil War?'

The cat ignored this patently ridiculous question (cats don't take sides, they only look out for themselves) and strode through the open kitchen door. I followed him and shook some dried food into his bowl. Then I sat on the terrace and thought about the heartbreak that the family had suffered. And I felt ashamed of my self-inflicted problems, which paled into insignificance beside the atrocities of the past.

The clouds were heavier and darker the next day and the air was close and sultry. Having received Ana's blessing to paint the inside of the house, I drove into Beniflor and visited the DIY store. Sergio greeted me with a casual '*buenas*' and then helped me carry my purchases to the car. Then I wandered down to the plaza to see how that day's preparations for the fiesta were coming along. The entire town square had been taken over by trestle tables where huge paella pans were being watched over by a variety of townspeople.

I stood in front of one of them and almost immediately felt my mouth water at the rich, complex aromas coming from the pan.

'Hi, Juno.' Rosa came up behind me. 'I didn't expect you to come to the paella competition.'

'I didn't realise it would be on in the middle of the day,' I said.

'Paella is always eaten in the middle of the day,' she told me. 'My money is on Roberto Bertana. He's won it a couple of times. Or Ronaldo Marcean.'

'What about the women?' I asked. 'It's all men behind those pans.'

Rosa grinned. 'It's like barbecues,' she told me. 'The men like to think of themselves as the experts.'

I laughed and then the mayor got up and announced that Roberto was the winner, and everyone clapped and then joined the queue to taste the different offerings. I tried not to look at the snails, which seemed to be a component of most of them. I was thinking that the authentic paella was quite a bit different to what was served at the tapas bars back in Dublin.

The weather was beginning to deteriorate as we ate. The sky grew even darker and there were mutterings about an imminent storm. I hadn't heard anything about a storm because, owing to the generally sunny skies, I never bothered to check the weather app on my phone. But Rosa said it had been forecast for that evening and that festivities were being curtailed as a result. And indeed, most people were beginning to leave the square – which, I reckoned, wouldn't have happened if the skies had stayed blue and cloud-free.

I said goodbye to Rosa and hopped into my car. By the time I got back to the Villa Naranja an occasional drop of rain was plopping on to the tiled part of the garden. It was still warm and muggy, so after I'd unloaded my paint I sat in the wicker chair on the patio and took out my iPad.

I suddenly felt as though I could look at the medical books I'd downloaded. But even as I opened the app, my time as a radiographer seemed like another life, another me, and the titles of the books were almost meaningless.

Then I saw the PDF document. I'd downloaded it a few months earlier. It was a paper on methods for renal segmentation from MRI imaging and had been co-authored by Brad. Just seeing his name, seeing the words he'd written, brought it all back again.

I put the iPad to one side and stared towards the mountains. I couldn't study. I wasn't ready.

The tears slid down my face.

It didn't matter that my grief was less worthy than that

of the Perez family. It was still very real. And we all hurt in different ways.

It started to rain more heavily. At first it was lazier rain than Ireland's needle-sharp version. The fat, laden drops seemed to slump from the clouds in an exhausted fall, as though they were simply too heavy to stay above the earth. But slowly and surely they gathered pace until they were pummelling into the ground, turning the ungravelled and untiled areas of the garden into puddles of sticky yellow mud.

I liked the no-nonsense way the rain seemed to be going about its business. The earth needs water, it said. Well, here it is. Lots of it. A relentless torrent. There was an enthusiasm to it that was almost infectious, although I felt sorry the fiesta had turned into a complete washout for the evening.

Even though it normally didn't get dark until well after eight thirty, it was already gloomy. The incessant rain had drawn a veil over the valley and it was now impossible to see further than the orange grove. I went inside and made myself a coffee. Banquo, who'd appeared at the first heavy drops, wound his way around my legs and mewed plaintively.

A sudden roll of distant thunder startled both of us and I almost tripped over him as he spun around with fright. I enjoy a good storm, and this promised to be one, so I took my coffee and a Magdalena cake on to the terrace with me. It was still dry there, apart from some splashes around the steps. Banquo didn't join me. He burrowed into the recycling box and covered his ears with his paws.

I took out the iPad again. I ignored the books on nuclear medicine and selected something light and frothy instead. But I was conscious that Brad's paper on MRI imaging was just a couple of clicks away, even as I stayed resolutely focused on the page in front of me. All the same, I read it half a dozen times and still didn't know what the hell was going on.

The next crash of thunder was still distant, but louder and a good deal more violent. Almost unbelievably, the rain began falling even harder. As I moved into the house my phone buzzed.

Are you OK?

Pep had sent a WhatsApp message. A warm glow enveloped me.

Of course, I responded.

No problem with rain?

I'm from Ireland, I typed. *I'm good with rain.*

He sent back a laughing emoji.

I poured myself a glass of Navarro wine and went back to my iPad.

Two hours later, the rain was still falling and the once-distant thunder was now almost overhead. Spectacular flashes of lightning ripped across the dark skies as I stood at the door and watched in delight. The force of the storm was energising me and I'd abandoned the iPad to concentrate on it.

Banquo, however, was clearly miserable and had forsaken the recycling box to disappear upstairs. Normally I'd shoo him down again but I decided that, if he was happier up there, he was better off. But, I thought, as the loudest roll of thunder so far and the brightest flash of lightning illuminated the room, I should go and check on him.

I couldn't find him anywhere. What I did discover, however, was that the roof of the Villa Naranja had a leak. A steady drip of water was coming in about a foot away from the base of my bed. And when I went to the bathroom to get something to mop it up with, I was met by an assortment of leaks there too.

'Crap,' I muttered and went to check the rest of the rooms. 'This isn't good.'

I'd noticed on one of my walks around the house that a couple of the roof tiles seemed damaged, but the fact that the skies had remained clear and blue for the duration of my stay so far had put them out of my mind. Actually, I hadn't even considered that they might be broken or cracked enough to allow water in. But unless I did something right now, the bathroom would soon be a lake and my bedroom wouldn't be much better.

I went back to the kitchen and brought a selection of pots and saucepans upstairs. I also had two fairly large buckets and was hopeful they'd contain the worst of the rain. I took a couple of large towels from the cupboard on the landing and used them to mop the bathroom floor. Then I placed the biggest bucket under the most persistent leak and arranged the pots strategically around the room. Tinny sounds rang out as the raindrops fell into them.

After the bathroom was relatively protected, I went to my bedroom and placed the second bucket at the foot of the bed. I was pretty confident that it would do the job, but I worried that if the rain didn't let up the buckets and pots would all be full before morning. In fact, I mused, when I went back to the bathroom again, it would only take a few hours to fill some of them.

But there was nothing more I could do. I'd have to hope for the best. Meantime, I decided I'd watch TV. What with all the thunder and lightning, and the deluge of rain, the

Villa Naranja was beginning to regain its formerly spooky atmosphere. And even though I didn't believe the ghost of Ana's grandfather roamed the house, I felt that a little bit of light-hearted entertainment would help to put any ideas of restless spirits out of my head completely.

It was the first time I'd switched the TV on. Every other evening had been far too warm and beautiful to waste it sitting in the rather dingy living room watching telly. Rather stupidly, though, I'd forgotten that there wouldn't be any English TV in the Villa Naranja. All the channels that I could access seemed to either be news stations, or showing children's cartoons. From the news, I could see that there was some political-type crisis going on, thanks to the pictures of serious-faced people in suits clustering around an important-looking building, but I hadn't the faintest idea of what was actually happening. However, before abandoning it for one of the apps on my iPad (and I suddenly remembered I'd have to renew my Netflix subscription if I wanted to watch anything half-decent), I decided to stick with the news channel on the basis that it might give me a more detailed weather forecast than I was getting on my phone. I was hoping for something a little more cheery than the row of grey clouds, lightning flashes and one hundred per cent chance of rain the weather app was showing. Not that there was much I could do about it anyhow, but it would be nice to know.

About thirty minutes after I'd turned the TV on, the weather forecast began. The presenter spent a lot of time showing different weather conditions over various parts of the country before focusing on Valencia and the *'tormentas'* that were currently afflicting the region. The report switched to people's home videos of rainwater swirling down streets, in some cases taking parked cars with it, while the presenter was clearly urging people to stay at home. She was getting no argument from me there. You'd want to be nuts to even step outside.

I got up from the chair and walked on to the patio, hoping that Beniflor was safe from flooding. The garden was in darkness, but looking towards the pool it seemed to me that the water level was extremely high. I grabbed a towel from the kitchen counter, forgot that I'd thought going outside was nuts, and used the towel to protect my hair as I scurried towards the pool. Clearly the pool itself wouldn't flood – it was capturing the rainwater as much as it could – but such a quantity of rain had fallen that the level was now up to the very edge. If this kept on, the garden would be under water; although I comforted myself with the fact that it sloped away from the house, and so the Villa Naranja itself was very unlikely to be flooded.

I was still comforting myself with this assessment when everything suddenly went dark. The lights of the house and the only visible lights further down the valley had all disappeared.

The power was off and I was on my own.

Chapter 13

No matter how little you believe in ghosts or spirits, I'd defy anyone not to have found the total darkness unnerving.

I hurried back to the house and stumbled around the living room trying to locate my phone so that I could use the torch app, but I couldn't remember where I'd put it. My early-generation iPad didn't have a torch but at least opening it would give a little light. I felt my way to the table where I'd left it and flicked it open. The simplest thing to do, I thought, would be to send myself a message and I'd hear it arrive at the phone. But of course the Wi-Fi was off, and my iPad didn't have a SIM card, so that idea didn't work. However, I used it to light my way to the kitchen, where I found the lemon-scented candles Catalina had given me, and lit them thankfully.

But even though the scent was lovely, their flickering light made the house creepier rather than cosier. I continued an increasingly frantic search for my phone and eventually found it on the mantelpiece in the living room. I switched on the torch and went upstairs, where Banquo almost gave me heart failure by scurrying out of my bedroom and doing his best to trip me up again.

'It's a real house of horrors tonight, isn't it?' I asked him when my heartbeat had settled down. 'Are you going to come into the bathroom with me?'

Somewhat surprisingly, he did. He watched me empty the half-full pots of water down the sink and replace them beneath the leaks. And then my phone died.

'Fuckity-fuck,' I cried, annoyed by the fact that I hadn't bothered to charge it overnight.

I made my way cautiously downstairs again. Banquo was following me closely.

When I got to the kitchen, I felt around for the phone charger and plugged it in, forgetting that no power meant no charge. I told myself that it didn't matter – I wasn't likely to be getting calls from anyone, anyhow – but no matter how little I sometimes use it, I feel like someone's cut off my arm when I don't have a working phone. And, of course, I felt more cut off than ever in a deserted house in the hills where a man had once been hanged in the garden.

'I guess we just have to curl up and ride it out,' I told Banquo as I sat on the sofa. 'And we won't talk about the atrocities of the Civil War and men being strung up in the garden.'

He mewed and jumped on to my lap. I scratched his head and picked up the iPad, glad of its light. This time I couldn't stop myself from opening Brad's paper. It was full of jargon but it was jargon I was familiar with, so understanding it wasn't a problem; the problem was hearing his voice as I read the words. It was as though he was beside me, talking to me. When I looked around, I expected to see him sitting on the sofa, an earnest expression on his face as he discussed MRI and segmentation of internal renal structures.

150

A flash of lightning lit up the room and the loudest crash of thunder yet broke overhead. Any minute now, I thought, the ubiquitous marauder (or zombie) would appear.

'You're totally losing it, Juno Ryan,' I muttered to myself. 'You need help.'

And then I heard a different noise. The loud, insistent parping of a car horn being continually pressed. It was close by. Maybe even just outside.

The everyday sound snapped me back to reality. My first concern was that there'd been a road accident. The track to the Villa Naranja was twisting and narrow, and heaven only knew what it was like in the rain. But as I hurried out of the house and into the deluge I realised that nobody should be coming down the track in the first place, and I hesitated. Then I saw the lights of a car and ran towards the gate.

There was a figure standing outside, lit by the car's headlights. I held up my arm to shield my eyes from the glare.

'Juno!' he cried. 'It is me. Pep Navarro.'

'Pep.' I felt a surge of relief. 'What on earth are you doing here?'

'My mother sent me to check if you are OK.' He peered at me through his wet hair. 'There is no power in the valley. There is much water everywhere. She was worried for you. I was worried for you too. Your phone did not receive my message.'

His words warmed me. It didn't matter that I was a couple of thousand kilometres from home. People I hardly knew were concerned for me. Pep was concerned about me. It was a good feeling.

'I'm fine,' I said. 'The battery on my phone died, and obviously I can't charge it. Why didn't you come in – oh!'

151

I realised that without power, the electric gates wouldn't work.

'My mother suggests that you come to us,' Pep said. 'We have a . . . a . . . we have our own machine for the light.'

'A generator?'

'Yes.' He nodded.

'Even if I could open the gates, I can't leave the house,' I told him. 'The roof is leaking.'

'The roof is what?'

'Leaking,' I said. 'Water is coming in.'

'I will come in to you,' he said.

'You're not going to try and climb over, are you?' I looked at him in disbelief.

'There is a key for the gate,' he told me.

'Where?'

'In the box. On the wall.'

I looked around, and then I saw it. A little structure attached to the boundary wall. I'd thought it was some kind of mail box and hadn't dreamed of opening it.

'It is key to . . . to little gate,' said Pep.

I'd completely forgotten about the pedestrian gate, which I'd never needed to use.

I opened the box and took the large key from its hook. The rain was dripping down my face as I inserted the key into the lock. It was too stiff to turn. I looked at Pep in frustration.

'It doesn't matter,' I said as another crack of thunder rolled overhead and a dazzling flash of lightning lit up the sky. 'You can see that I'm fine.'

'Give her to me,' he said.

I passed the key through the gate and he put it in the lock and turned it firmly. The gate creaked open.

'Oh, well done!' I cried.

'*No problema.*'

He went back to the car and took out a large torch before he switched off the engine.

'It is bad this water in the house?' he asked when he returned.

'I'm not sure.'

It was nice not to be alone. And it was even nicer to have some light. Pep's torch was a lot brighter than the one on my dead iPhone had been. He flashed it around the living room. Banquo, sprawled along the sofa, opened eyes that now gleamed emerald green in the beam.

'Not down here, upstairs,' I told Pep.

He went ahead of me, lighting the way. I showed him into the bathroom. The pots and saucepans were half full again.

'*Mierda,*' he murmured.

'Hopefully, it'll stop raining soon.' I shivered involuntarily.

'You are wet,' said Pep unnecessarily.

'So are you.'

We exchanged looks and he grinned suddenly.

'Perhaps to change your clothes?' he said. 'You do not want to be ill, no?'

I nodded and went into the bedroom.

'There's a leak here too,' I said before closing the door and changing into a dry T-shirt and shorts.

'I will phone my home,' said Pep when I emerged again. I will tell them of the . . . leaks.'

He took his mobile from his pocket. His conversation was rapid and intense.

'My mother wishes that you come to us,' he said.

'I can't, Pep. Really I can't. I have to stay and make sure

that the house doesn't flood completely. You can see that yourself.'

He spoke on the phone again and finally ended the call.

'She says I am to stay to . . . to take care of you.'

'I can manage.'

'You cannot be alone here with no power and a roof that . . . that . . .'

'Leaks,' I supplied.

'Exactly.'

'In that case you'll have to get out of your own wet things,' I told him as the rain dripped from his shorts.

He slipped his feet out of his trainers and smiled at me.

'That's not quite what I meant.'

'I know.'

I laughed, suddenly exhilarated and no longer worried by the storm.

'There are some old clothes in the cupboard on the landing,' I told him.

He opened it, then looked at the threadbare T-shirts and grey cotton shorts. 'These are not your clothes?'

'They were here when I arrived.'

'Possible they are Eduardo's,' he said as he took a white T-shirt from the pile and shook it out. 'He is a big man.'

He peeled off his T-shirt, and I felt a shiver down my spine.

'I'll leave you in privacy.' I hurried downstairs.

Banquo greeted me with a knowing look.

'I can't help it,' I hissed at the cat. 'He's very sexy.'

A few minutes later, Pep followed me. He was wearing the T-shirt and a pair of grey cotton shorts. It didn't matter that both were clearly too big for him. He looked amazing.

154

'I have left the wet clothes in the bathroom,' he said.

'Right.'

'I am not sure about these shorts.' He pulled the draw-string tighter. 'I am afraid they might fall off.'

I couldn't speak. It was probably just as well.

He sat down beside Banquo and began rubbing his back. The cat rolled over and started to purr.

'Coffee?' I'd found my voice. 'I can make it on the gas hob.'

'Thank you.'

I think I just meant coffee. I can't honestly be sure.

Sitting in the candlelit living room with Pep wasn't exactly relaxing. At least, not until I remembered the bottle of red wine on the kitchen counter. I fetched it and poured us both a generous measure. It was very smooth and tasted very faintly of raspberries.

'*Frambuesa*.' Pep nodded when I said this to him, and when I looked surprised he laughed. 'My English is good for fruit and things about wine,' he told me. 'Not so good for . . .' he gave an annoyed shrug and gazed upwards, 'water coming in.'

'Leaks,' I reminded him.

'I do not know why I cannot remember that word,' he said in exasperation. 'It is not difficult.'

'Teach me some Spanish,' I said. 'What's a leak?'

'*Una gotera*,' he said.

'*Gotera*.' I repeated the word a couple of times. 'And what about red wine?'

'*Vino tinto*.'

'And . . . rain?'

'*Lluvia.*'

'How do you say it's lashing rain?'

'I do not understand lashing,' he said.

'Raining a lot. Like now.'

'*Está lloviendo a cántaros.*'

It sounded impossibly seductive when he said it, not at all like he was describing a downpour.

'I wonder when it will stop this *lloviendo a cántaros*,' I said, trying to mimic his accent.

'Tomorrow morning,' he said. 'That is what they say.' He smiled at me. 'You speak Spanish very well.'

'I don't speak it at all,' I reminded him.

'But when you say the words, they sound very good. And you learned *bisagra* before. I do not remember the English for it.'

'Hinge,' I reminded him.

'Ah, yes. Hinge.' He nodded. 'I will teach you more, if you like.'

'I should learn,' I agreed. 'But I won't be here long enough for it to really matter. All I need is "yes" and "no" and "please" and "thank you" and "have a nice day".'

'*Qué tengas un buen día,*' he said.

'That's "have a nice day"?'

He nodded.

I repeated that too.

'I will make you into a Spanish girl,' he teased. 'Word by word.'

He was looking straight into my eyes. And I was looking into his. We both leaned towards each other. And then he kissed me.

'What's a kiss?' I gasped.

'*Un beso.*'

He kissed me again. His kiss was passionate and demanding, and I kissed him back in exactly the same way. And then he was sliding the strings of my top from my shoulders and I was pulling the too big T-shirt from him, and he pulled me to him even as I wrapped my arms around him. I was shaking with desire. I wanted nothing more than to make love to him on the old and very unromantic sofa of Doña Carmen's living room, but Pep suddenly scooped me up in his arms – at the same time grabbing the torch, which he'd left on the floor beside us – and carried me up the stairs to the bedroom, where he dropped me gently on to the bed.

It gave me a moment to think.

'And the Spanish for condom?' I asked.

'*Condón,*' he said, without a moment's hesitation.

'In the bathroom. In the bag beside the sink.'

He walked out of the bedroom. I had a couple of moments to ponder on the fact that I was going to have sex with the hot young Greek god, after all. And that I was really, really excited about it.

Pep returned with the packet of Durex that had been in my toilet bag ever since I first went to Belfast to be with Brad. I'd gone back on the pill when I'd started seeing him but hadn't been on it long enough to be one hundred per cent sure of its effectiveness, so I'd brought the condoms with me. There were three left.

'Just the right number.' He grinned as he took one out of its wrapper.

I wondered if he thought I was some wanton Irish hussy who'd arrived prepared for a sexual adventure with a Spanish hunk. I didn't care. There's a bit of an assumption that every woman wants to be in a proper loving relationship before she sleeps with someone, but of course that's not strictly true. The first time I slept with Sean I didn't know I'd end up engaged to him. It had been a spur-of-the-moment decision. But the first time I'd slept with Brad . . . that had been very special. To me. Clearly not to him.

I put my past lovers out of my head. In the present, Pep Navarro knew exactly what he was doing, and I lost myself completely in the pleasure of it all. Then we did it all over again before he rolled on to the bed beside me and sighed deeply.

'That was good,' he said in a voice replete with satisfaction.

'Not bad,' I agreed.

He laughed. 'Better than not bad. Wonderful. For me. I hope for you too.'

'Oh, yes,' I said. 'For me too.'

And then, even though there was one condom left, I closed my eyes, leaned my head against his shoulder and fell asleep.

I was once told that we always dream when we're asleep, it's just that sometimes we don't remember. I certainly remembered nothing when I opened my eyes again. As always, the effectiveness of the shutters meant that I'd no idea what time it was, but I doubted that I'd been asleep for too long, even if I couldn't recall a dream. After all, that was what I was used to. Asleep for fifteen minutes. Awake for an hour. Repeated over and over, throughout the night, so that I was always tired when I got up. But I didn't feel tired now. In fact, I felt wide awake.

I realised that the constant drip, drip of the water into the saucepan at the end of the bed had stopped, and I wondered if it was the silence that had disturbed me.

I sat up and stretched my arms over my head, then got out of the bed and opened the shutters. Bright sunlight poured into the room and I blinked in surprise. After the violence of the previous day's weather, I couldn't quite believe that the sky had returned to its former cloudless blue state, and that the sun was as hot as ever. And then I remembered Pep Navarro. And that I must have been asleep all night with a man I hardly knew in the bed beside me.

But I was awake now.

And he was gone.

Chapter 14

I got dressed and went downstairs. As soon as I walked into the kitchen, Banquo jumped delicately from the recycling box and headbutted me on the legs.

'So was it a dream?' I asked as I scratched him under the chin. 'Did I sleep with Pep Navarro last night? Or am I going crazy?'

Banquo purred loudly. I opened the kitchen door and he went outside, immediately sitting in front of his empty food bowl. His needs came before everything, so I took the bag of dried cat food from the cupboard and filled the bowl. Then I filled another with water from the outside tap.

I saw the note when I went back inside. It was beneath a glass on the drainer beside the sink.

I have to leave at this moment, Pep had written in a bold, decisive script. *I do not want to wake you. You look very tired. But very beautiful. Will return later with man to fix roofs.*

OK, I told myself. It wasn't a dream. I'd had sex for the first time since Brad's death. And, from what I could remember, it had been pretty sensational sex. In fact, possibly the best sex I'd ever had. I liked Pep, I really did. But I didn't want to get involved with him. I wasn't ready for that.

And it would be so damn complicated . . . and then I reminded myself that I was done with involvement and complications, and that Pep and I didn't have to be anything more than fun in the sun.

I was relieved to see that the power had been restored, so I made myself a cup of coffee and took it outside. Banquo watched me as I sipped it. I wondered if he was making a moral judgement on me and my desire to have uncomplicated sex.

'It's none of your business,' I said while he continued to stare at me. 'You don't have any say in the matter.'

I finished the coffee, had a quick swim in the pool and was getting dressed again when I heard the bell at the gate ring. I hurried to the front of the house. There was a small van outside. But it wasn't Pep's. Two older men got out and started talking in unbelievably fast Spanish at me.

I looked at them helplessly for a moment and then one of them said, in very broken English, that they were here for the tiles. I realised they were the people Pep had arranged to come and repair the roof, and I was impressed by the speed of their arrival. He could only have called them earlier in the morning, yet here they were already.

I buzzed them in, and after the older of the two had parked the van I showed them upstairs. It occurred to me, as we stood in the bedroom, that I hadn't asked for any ID and that I hadn't a clue who they were, but they weren't paying any attention to me. They looked at the pots and then at the water-stained ceiling and nodded a few times. Then they went back to their van and took out some ladders. Less than fifteen minutes after I'd let them in, they were scrambling around on the roof.

It was about ten minutes later that Pep himself arrived,

161

this time accompanied by an older man and a woman around the same age as Ana Perez. He introduced them to me as his parents, Elena and Miguel.

'It's nice to meet you,' said Elena as she leaned forward and gave me a continental double kiss. 'The storm was terrible. I'm glad Pep stayed with you and that you did not have to face it alone.'

I felt my face redden and hoped she'd put it down to the fact that we were standing in the full sun, not because I was remembering what Pep and I had done together.

'The Jimenez brothers are good builders,' said Miguel. 'They will fix it for you.'

'Um . . . there's just one thing,' I said. 'I'm not sure how much it will cost and—'

'Oh, don't worry about that,' said Elena. 'I phoned Ana Perez earlier and she was horrified to think that you were stuck in a house with the rain coming inside. She was very distressed that she'd been here with you and hadn't noticed a problem.'

'I was fine,' I assured her. 'And Pep was . . . very comforting.'

Pep grinned and Elena turned to her husband. She said something to him in Spanish and he walked over to the house and began talking to one of the men on the ladder.

'You should come to eat with us tonight,' Elena said to me. 'It is not good to be too much on your own.'

'I don't—'

'You must,' Pep said. 'I will collect you.'

'We will eat early,' said Elena. 'Half past eight?'

'Well . . .'

'Excellent,' she said.

162

Her husband rejoined us and spoke to her again, then Elena said that the builders would be finished with the repair work in a couple of hours.

'Thank you,' I said.

'It is no problem,' she said. 'Ana would not allow me to leave you in a house that is open to the skies.'

Which was a bit of an exaggeration, but I smiled at her, anyhow.

'I will see you at eight,' said Pep.

'Your mum said eight thirty,' I reminded him.

'For eating,' he said. 'I will collect you before then.'

'OK.'

He kissed me then. Very chastely on each of my still hot cheeks.

Pep arrived at eight o'clock exactly. I'd changed into my only non-sundress dress – a multicoloured Ted Baker sheath, which had once been a little tight but was now a perfect fit.

'*Guapísima*,' he said when he saw me, and I didn't need him to translate the word.

This time his kiss wasn't in the slightest bit chaste, and neither was my response. We moved from the garden to the bedroom in a few seconds, and the sex was quick and frantic and absolutely brilliant.

'Your mother will be wondering where we are,' I said as I got dressed again.

Pep shrugged and ran his fingers through his hair. I brushed mine and reapplied my lipgloss.

'Even more beautiful now,' said Pep. 'You have colour in your face.'

I felt myself blush, which probably turned it even redder.

163

I'd expected Elena and Miguel to be waiting for us to arrive, but when we walked around the house – a large, well-maintained finca – there was already quite a gathering in the garden, and Pep's parents were laughing and joking with them.

'My family,' said Pep.

'I thought you only had a brother and a sister here!' I exclaimed.

'And aunts. And uncles. And cousins. And their children.' Pep grinned. 'This dinner was arranged a long time ago. We are honoured you could join us.'

I counted a dozen people, excluding me and a group of children whose ages ranged from about four to ten.

When Elena spotted me, she hurried over, did the kissing thing and then asked if the work had been finished on the roof.

'It didn't take long,' I said. 'They were great.'

'Good,' said Elena. 'I didn't want to think of you in the house on your own when it might rain again.'

I glanced up at the cloudless sky, and she laughed.

'It may rain,' she said. 'It does sometimes. Now come and meet the rest of the family.'

Suddenly I was in a whirl of introductions and kisses and good wishes. It was entirely stereotypical, I thought, everything I imagined a Mediterranean family gathering would be. Everyone was talking loudly and at the same time, and although I didn't understand most of it, I could tell it was good-natured and cheerful.

Then Elena led us around a corner, and my heart stopped. Because although the table was long enough to cater for everyone, the setting – with its green parasols and pergolas and tiled terrace – was achingly similar to the last photo Brad had sent me. Of the dinner he'd been going to with Alessandra and Dylan. The dinner I'd thought had been with family and friends, but not a wife and son. It was as though I'd been jerked back into a place I thought I'd left behind. And it was like a hammer blow.

'Are you all right?' Pep looked at me curiously.

'I . . .'

'Is something wrong?'

I took a deep breath.

'No,' I said. 'Nothing's wrong.'

But all during dinner, even as I fixed a smile on to my face and reminded myself that I had moved on enough to have sex with someone new, I was as hollow as ever inside.

It was after midnight when I got back to the Villa Naranja. This time, because we'd all had wine at dinner, I walked. I hadn't realised that it was possible to access the Navarro finca from Doña Carmen's house, but there was a narrow trail through the orange groves. It wasn't used much, Pep told me as he unlocked the gate in the boundary fence so that we could pass through, but it had been useful in the past.

As we walked past the jacaranda tree I thought of that past, when Pilar's great-grandfather had been hanged in the garden, and I shivered.

'You are cold?' Pep sounded surprised.

I shook my head and scratched the mozzie bites that I'd suffered in the walk through the trees.

'Was it too . . . too . . . too many people for you at dinner?' he asked. 'You are tired?'

'No,' I replied.

'Because we try to speak English but not always, and this is a little rude,' he added.

'You were all lovely,' I assured him. 'And I think I'm starting to understand some Spanish.'

'You seemed sad,' he told me. 'I do not want that you are sad.'

'I'm not . . . well, yes, I am a bit sad,' I said. 'Before I came here, things went wrong for me. And sometimes I still feel . . .' I shrugged. I didn't really know what I felt.

Pep put his arm around my shoulder and didn't say anything else until we were outside the door of the house.

'You want that I come in?' he asked.

I shook my head. 'I wouldn't be good company.'

'That is OK. Another time.'

This time I nodded. 'Another time.'

He didn't try to give me any type of kiss, simply squeezed my hand and walked away.

I put some cream on my bites, then sat on the wicker chair on the patio and stared up at the sky. There was no moon but the stars were bright. When I was very small, my mother had told me that the stars were the souls of everyone who'd ever lived.

'Like heaven?' I'd asked.

'Exactly,' she'd replied.

And I'd thought about it for a long time because I couldn't make sense of it. How could a living, breathing person turn into a star? How could that possibly happen? When I was old enough, I looked up stars in the library. And learned that they were objects that sent out their own light, producing energy by nuclear fusion. That didn't sound much like a dead person to me. Or what a dead person might become. And

166

so I studied more and learned more and decided that my mum had, as usual, been talking complete nonsense.

Only I wished she hadn't. I wished it was true, that when people died they lit up the sky.

Banquo jumped on to my lap and began to purr contentedly.

When I'd asked about getting a cat as a child and Mum had refused, on account of them being arrogant and wilful, she'd also snapped that they were demons. Or spirits. I'd ignored her, because by then I knew she said stuff like that all the time. And yet sitting there, with Banquo purring loudly even as his claws dug into my stomach, I couldn't help but feel that he was communicating with me on another level. Trying to tell me something. Which I knew was complete nonsense.

Spain was having a weird effect on me. All the things I didn't believe in – ghosts and spirits and stuff that you can't see and prove – seemed to be insinuating themselves into my life and my thoughts. And I was powerless to stop them.

'Bat-shit crazy,' I said out loud as I stood up, and Banquo gave me a disappointed look. 'This is what I've become. And this is why women shouldn't ever live alone with their cats.'

Chapter 15

The following morning, I seriously considered going home. Somehow the thought of staying on at the Villa Naranja, with its turbulent history and occasionally spooky vibe, as well as its devastatingly sexy neighbour, was less appealing than before. I'd taken time out, I'd moved on enough to shag the pool cleaner, and even if I hadn't completely reached acceptance in the five levels of grief I could hardly classify myself as depressed.

But then I received an excited text from Cleo.

Coming to Spain, it said. *Arrive Friday, depart Sunday. Woohoo!*

I texted her back for more information. Cleo is a great woman for deals and special offers, and she subscribes to a multitude of bargain-hunting sites and apps – in this case, she'd seen a flash seat sale for flights to Alicante and had booked them for herself and Saoirse in the short window of opportunity before they sold out. They would be arriving on Friday morning, she told me, departing on Sunday night. As Cleo had the Friday and Saturday off, it wasn't a problem for the radiology department, and Saoirse herself was simply taking a day's annual leave.

Can't wait to see you, my flatmate texted. *Miss having you around*.

No harm in having them stay for a few days before I went home myself, I thought. And it would be fun to indulge in some holiday-making stuff. It would totally get rid of the unwanted and unaccustomed thoughts I'd been having lately. Saoirse, Cleo and I always had a good time when we went away together. We would have fun this time too.

I told Pep about their imminent arrival, when he called around later that day. Not to clean the pool. Just to be with me.

'I am glad you will have friends here,' he said. 'It is not good to be alone.'

'But sometimes it's necessary,' I told him.

He rolled over in the bed. Whatever I'd been thinking about reclaiming my life, it had only taken the merest of touches from Pep's fingers on my arm to reduce me to a puddle of desire. I wanted nothing more than to make love with him again. Now he regarded me thoughtfully from his mocha-brown eyes.

'It is better to have people,' he said seriously. 'Better for everyone.'

'I have you,' I said.

'Yes. But I am not yet your people.'

Not yet? I didn't know if his words had been deliberate or accidental. Did he think he could be in my future? Did he want to be? Did I want him to be?

He pulled me towards him and kissed me.

I kissed him back.

Whatever I felt about the future, I thought as his hand

slid slowly along my thigh, I was completely undone by his part in my present.

Cleo and Saoirse's flight arrived into Alicante at eleven o'clock on Friday morning. I stood among the crowd at the terminal building and waited impatiently for them to appear. I hadn't realised just how homesick I'd been starting to feel until I saw Saoirse waving at me, a broad beam on her face.

'You'd swear it'd been years since we'd seen each other!' I cried as I embraced them both and then wiped a happy tear from my eye. 'I don't know what I'm getting so emotional about.'

'It's a bit mad, isn't it?' agreed Saoirse, who had her arm around my waist. 'It's good to be here, Juno.'

'And it's good to have you.'

The journey to the Villa Naranja was very different to my night-time drive a few weeks earlier. The sun was shining, the sky was blue, and the occasional glimpses of the aquamarine sea were enough to send my friends into raptures.

'It's a pity Pilar couldn't come,' I remarked. 'I bet she would've loved to be home.'

'Maybe she'll get here sometime before you come back,' said Cleo. 'It's manically busy at the hospital right now, though.'

I glanced at her. 'How's the temp getting on?'

'Great,' she said. 'Like I told you, very experienced. But it's not the same as having you there.'

'That's nice to know.'

I took the motorway exit and then the twisting road through the mountains to Beniflor.

'You did this at night!' Cleo cried as I turned on to the

narrow track to the house. 'On your own! Weren't you freaked out?'

'Juno doesn't freak out,' Saoirse reminded her. 'Remember when we all went to see that *Cloverfield* movie? I thought I was going to have a heart attack but Juno kept on eating popcorn.'

'Because it wasn't real,' I said.

'It seemed real enough to me,' muttered Cleo. 'I don't know what persuaded us that it'd be a good idea to see it.'

'Danny Shaw in phlebotomy,' I said. 'It was a bet.'

'Oh, yeah.' She snorted. 'Those guys and their flippin' blood samples. They think they're so cool. Whereas the radiology department really is cool.'

I laughed. 'They look at blood. We see right through people.'

'Like ghosts,' said Saoirse.

I said nothing. I was remembering how uncool I actually had been when I'd been on my own on this road, thinking about ghosts and marauders myself.

'Oh, how pretty!' cried Cleo as I pulled up in front of the gates and clicked the fob. 'It's like a proper country house.'

'It *is* a proper country house,' I said. 'Not a huge amount of furniture, but amazing rooms. Actually,' I added, remembering what Pilar's mum had told me, 'it was built for a Spanish nobleman, back in the day.'

'Wow,' said Saoirse. 'How amazing is that.'

'I thought Pilar said it was neglected,' Cleo said. 'It could do with a lick of paint maybe, but those shutters are fabulous.'

I told them about my sanding and varnishing efforts, and they laughed at me. Then, as we got out of the car, they spotted the pool and shrieked with delight.

'This is even better than I expected!' cried Saoirse. 'Why didn't you say anything about the pool?'

Because I hadn't thought to, at first. And then because the pool was tied up in my mind with the man who cleaned it. And I hadn't told them about Pep Navarro either.

I showed them the rooms upstairs, and there were more appreciative comments. It was lovely to hear chatter and laughter echoing around the house, and I was feeling de-mob happy as I popped open the bottle of Freixenet that I'd bought at the supermarket the day before.

'How posh!' Cleo grinned as I handed her a glass with a strawberry perched on the side. 'Have you been doing this every day?'

'Not quite every day,' I told her. 'I've rolled out the big guns for you.'

There were only two wicker chairs on the patio but I dragged one of the indoor ones outside and we toasted each other with cava. My two best friends kept up a steady stream of anecdotes and conversation, which carefully avoided the reason why I was here in the first place.

'Beniflor is in fiesta at the moment,' I told them as I refilled the glasses. 'There have been events going on in the town since last week. This evening there's a flower parade.'

'What does that entail?'

'I haven't a clue,' I admitted. 'But it sounds lovely.'

'What time?'

'Around six,' I said. 'Every fiesta event seems to involve parading around a few streets, then ending up in the main square for a bit of a party. Most of it also takes place later at night – tomorrow there's another parade and fireworks – but I thought this might be a fun thing to do.'

'Sounds good to me,' said Saoirse. 'And in the meantime . . . we can just sit out by the pool and chill?'

'Absolutely,' I said. 'Chill time it is.'

Which is what we did. And it was lovely.

Cleo had bought a couple of books in the buy-one-get-one-half-price promotion at the airport and so she gave me the latest Michael Connelly to read. I'm more into crime and thrillers than either literary novels or romance, so I enjoyed it immensely. Much better to be caught up in crime and murder in LA than my own messy thoughts.

We were all stretched out on the sunloungers when we heard footsteps on the gravel. I looked up and saw Pep Navarro striding towards the pool, the big blue cleaning hose coiled over his arm.

'Oh. My. God,' murmured Saoirse. 'Who the hell is that?'

'The pool cleaner.' I cleared my throat. '*Hola*, Pep.'

He'd said that he'd try to clean the pool while I was at the airport, so that he wouldn't be in the way. I'd told him to clean it whenever it suited him. Clearly, he'd decided that this was a more suitable time.

'*Hola*, Juno,' he said. 'I am sorry. I could not come earlier, as I had planned. I had to do some things for my father.'

'That's OK,' I said.

'I will not be long.'

'Take as long as you like,' murmured Cleo.

'You never mentioned him.' Saoirse swung her legs over the side of the lounger so that she was facing me accusingly. 'You never said a word about a desirable hunk making visits to the house.'

'Didn't I?' I tried to sound nonchalant.

173

'I know you've been stressed,' said Saoirse. 'But how could you not have noticed him?'

'If he was coming around every day to clean the pool, I wouldn't leave,' said Cleo. 'Bloody hell, Juno. You've hit the jackpot.'

I didn't trust myself to speak, especially with Pep only a few metres away, so I shrugged again.

'Oh, sweetheart, I'm sorry!' Cleo gave me an anguished look as she totally misinterpreted my shrug. 'I was being insensitive. I know you're still . . . well . . . it's been hard. And we're making inappropriate comments.'

'It's fine. But could we not talk about it right now?'

'Of course.'

The two girls lay back on the loungers.

I felt bad about misleading them, but I couldn't say anything about me and Pep while he was nearby. I couldn't tell them that last night, after sex in the bedroom, we'd done it again in the kitchen. He'd walked into the room behind me and put his arms around me, and I'd completely forgotten that I was supposed to be making a cup of tea. It had been hot and steamy, and Banquo – who'd been in the recycling box – had clearly found it all a bit much because he'd gone out and hadn't returned until the morning.

'*Hasta luego*,' called Pep when he'd finished cleaning the pool.

'*Hasta luego*,' I said.

Three pairs of eyes watched him walk to his van.

And I sighed with relief when he finally drove away.

Chapter 16

After Pep had gone, I went into the house and returned with chilled bottles of water for everyone.

'Actually, I was planning to get into the lovely clean pool to cool down,' said Saoirse. 'That was one seriously hot guy.'

'I know,' I said.

And this time they could tell from the tone of my voice there was more.

'Juno Ryan! You didn't!' It was Cleo who spoke first.

I think my expression was a mixture of guilt and glee.

'But that's fantastic!' cried Saoirse. 'Although I can't believe you didn't tell us before now. How on earth could you sit there so calm and collected and not say a word? And he just kept on working – as though nothing had happened either.'

'I hadn't intended to . . . to . . .'

'Hey, nobody in the world would pass up the opportunity to get closer to a man like that!' said Cleo. 'Nobody.'

'He's a nice person,' I said.

The two of them snorted with laughter.

'He is.'

I'd already told them a bit about the night of the storm

and the leak and the blackout, but this time I detailed Pep's role in events.

'That is *soooo* romantic,' breathed Cleo. 'Thunder. Lightning. Naked in the rain. Oh, Juno. You lucky, lucky thing.'

'We weren't naked in the rain!' I cried. 'And it wasn't romantic. It was . . . it was . . .'

'It was what?' asked Saoirse. 'Is this going somewhere, Juno?'

'I'm not sure,' I replied. 'I like him. But I don't speak Spanish – and although his English is pretty good, it's not conversational, so . . .'

'So it's all about the sex?' finished Cleo.

'I guess.'

'It's a good start,' Saoirse insisted. 'I mean, remember me and Stan McCrae? On paper we were totally compatible, but in bed . . . it was a disaster. And there was no way it was going to work. At least you wouldn't have to worry about that part of it, Juno.'

'I'm not at the stage of worrying about any part of it,' I said. 'I'm . . . oh, look, I still don't know where I am, to be honest. No matter how hard I try, I can't get Brad and what happened out of my head, and . . . and . . .'

Then, to my horror, I burst into tears.

I hate women who cry at the drop of a hat, I really do. I'd been one of them over the last few months but I thought I'd come out the other side. So I couldn't understand why I was suddenly sobbing as though my heart would break, while my two friends did their best to comfort me.

'I'm sorry.' I sniffed. 'It seems that I've spent more than my fair share of time snivelling on your shoulders lately.'

'It's OK,' said Saoirse. 'It really is.'

'It's not.' I sniffed again, a bit more vigorously this time. 'It's been months. I should be at acceptance, not bawling like a baby.'

'You went through a terrible time,' said Cleo. 'You're entitled to cry.'

I scrubbed at my eyes. 'I was going out with a cheat. He lied to me. He lied to his wife too. Dammit, if he hadn't been killed I would've killed him myself.'

They looked at me sympathetically. I'd said this before. More than once. But this was the first time I'd said it with a real spark of anger. Until now, it had been in bewilderment.

'More cava?' suggested Saoirse, looking at the almost empty bottle.

I shook my head. 'I'll be driving you into town later. I've had enough.'

'Maybe—'

'Honestly.' My voice was firm and my eyes dry. 'I'm fine now, really. And I have accepted it, I truly have.'

They smiled at me. But I could see in their eyes that they didn't really believe me. And how could I blame them, when it wasn't hard to see that I didn't entirely believe myself?

We arrived at the town square just after six o'clock. Additional planters filled with multicoloured hibiscus, vibrant hypericum and spiky yuccas had been dotted around it, and a heady floral scent filled the air. Young girls in white dresses, with garlands in their hair, were lined up near the stage. Their excited chatter would have made magpies jealous.

'The flower parade is for the children,' explained Rosa when we sat down at the last available table outside the Café

177

Flor. 'They all get a posy to carry, and they walk around the town singing.'

'It's all so . . . so communal,' said Saoirse. 'I wish we did stuff like this at home.'

'In the lashing rain?' Cleo raised an eyebrow.

'It doesn't always rain,' objected Saoirse.

'And of course it lashed rain here the other day. It was . . . it was . . . *lloviendo a cántaros!*' I finished triumphantly as I remembered the expression.

They continued to joke about the weather and what they called my colloquial Spanish while I watched the little girls, who – at the arrival of an adult – had stopped chattering and were now standing solemnly in front of the stage. They'd been joined by boys dressed in white shirts and trousers, who looked equally solemn. I pointed out Xavi Ruiz, his arm now out of the sling, to the girls.

'You've really got involved, haven't you?' said Cleo. 'Bonking the pool guy, acting as an ambulance service for that kid, renovating the house, speaking Spanish – plus you're clearly a regular here, because the waitress seems to know you very well.'

'It was the first place I came,' I said. 'And she's English, so it made things easier.'

The parade set off, led by what I assumed was a local brass band playing loudly and cheerfully. The adults who'd congregated in the plaza applauded as the boys and girls waved to them. I couldn't help thinking of Brad and Alessandra's son, Dylan, and I wondered how he was recovering from his injuries. The physical ones, anyway. It was impossible to know what emotional scars he'd been left with. Even though I checked the papers online every day, I hadn't seen any news stories about him. But, of course, the earthquake had vanished from the news, replaced by other people's tragedies. Meanwhile, Dylan's utterly changed life would carry on outside the glare of the media.

I love you. I could suddenly hear Brad's voice in my ear and feel his breath warm on the back of my neck, just as it had been the day before he left. *I love you, Juno Ryan.*

I flinched. The words seemed so real, so vivid. As though Brad really was close by. Instinctively, I turned around. But the only person behind me was Rosa, carrying a tray of drinks.

'*Granizado,*' she said. 'A special flavour for today. Multifruit.'

I took one of the crushed ice drinks from her and focused my attention on the real people around me, not the phantom voices in my head.

'Lovely,' I said after I'd tasted it. 'Very refreshing.'

The square began to fill up with even more people, mainly younger parents who clearly had children in the parade. Many of them were also pushing prams or had smaller children in their arms. The hubbub of good-natured conversation grew louder and louder. After a while, the marching band appeared again, followed by the children, who'd lost the solemnity and were laughing and waving. They marched up the steps of the stage and, led by a teacher, organised themselves into rows and began to sing.

'It's the song of the town,' Rosa explained when she returned with more *granizado* for me and a couple of glasses of wine for the girls. 'About how strong and determined we all are, and how we all support each other.'

'It's great. And the kids are fantastic.' Saoirse was totally into the spirit of it all.

'This is their day,' said Rosa.

'Though it's not like they don't join in everything else,' I observed. 'There were as many children as adults the first night.'

'People tend to do more things as a family group here,' agreed Rosa.

I used to think I'd have a family by the time I reached my thirties. I hadn't wanted to wait until it was too late. I'd talked it over with Sean, and he'd agreed with me. Two kids, he'd said. One of each. And he'd smiled at me.

I hadn't got around to thinking about Brad and babies. We were still too new as a couple. But it would have been there, in the back of my mind, sooner rather than later.

How did I get it so wrong?

Twice.

There was no sign of Pep, or any of the Navarros, at the flower parade. I realised, as the sun set and the marching band was replaced with a local group, that I'd been looking out for him. But the Navarros didn't have small children, at least not in the immediate family. There had been younger cousins and nieces and nephews at the dinner the other evening. But I doubted I would have recognised them, anyhow.

The girls ordered more wine. I switched from *granizado* to sparkling water. The music seemed to grow louder. The crowd grew bigger. People started dancing. Cleo and Saoirse got up and dragged me with them. It felt weird to be hopping around as though I hadn't a care in the world. But the truth was – I hadn't. I was a single woman with no ties, living in Spain. I should be able to lose myself in the dance as much as I liked.

And then I felt a tap on my shoulder. I spun around.

Pep was smiling. He held out his hand. Saoirse and Cleo pushed me towards him.

The music was too fast for an old-fashioned smooch, but he continued to hold me by the hand, twisting me, turning me this way and that until I was breathless and begging to stop. But when I sat down I saw that both Cleo and Saoirse were now dancing with men themselves and weren't paying any attention to me.

'You are happy to have your friends here?' asked Pep as he sat down beside me.

'Yes.'

He nodded. 'There is less sadness in your eyes.'

'My eyes are sad?'

'Yes,' he said.

I wished he hadn't said that. I didn't want people looking at me and feeling sorry for me. Really I didn't. I wanted to keep my misery inside. Actually, that wasn't true. I wanted to let it go. I couldn't believe Pep had seen it. After all, it was patently obviously that I wasn't miserable when I was with him.

'Now I have made you sad again,' said Pep. 'I am sorry.'

'I'm not sad,' I assured him. 'I was before. But I'm not now.'

'That is good.' And he put his arm around me.

Suddenly the music had a very Celtic tone to it.

'*Riverdance!*' cried Pep, even though it wasn't actually *Riverdance*.

'G'wan, Juno.' Cleo flopped down at the table, accompanied by her dance partner, a man I didn't know. She grinned at me. 'Give us an aul' reel there.'

'I can't,' I protested.

'But you said you could,' Pep reminded me.

My objections were overruled. I took off my shoes so that I was dancing barefoot and, because it was in time to the music, danced the simplest of slip jigs. At first just Cleo and Saoirse, as well as Pep and his friends, were watching, but suddenly I realised that everyone in the plaza had gathered and were cheering me on. And when I'd finished the applause was as loud and generous as Michael Flatley and Jean Butler had ever experienced.

'But that was amazing!' said Pep, who then placed the lightest of kisses on my lips. 'You are a proper dancer.'

'I'm not that good, honestly.' I was embarrassed at all the back-slapping I was getting. As well as the public kiss, no matter how fleeting it had been.

'You won a medal at the Feis Ceoil,' Saoirse teased.

'When I was ten!'

As far as the people of Beniflor were concerned, I was talented beyond belief, and they made me dance again. After another slip jig and a reel, I collapsed on to a chair, protesting that I couldn't do any more.

'*Estupendo*,' said José Ruiz, which seemed to be the general opinion on my efforts. Then some of the local girls danced flamenco, which, with all its foot-stamping and fan-fluttering, was a good deal sexier than Irish dancing. After that, the music reverted to more general stuff. By this point Saoirse had to admit that she was exhausted, and Cleo chimed in that she wasn't much better, so we got up to go.

'*Hasta luego*,' said Pep, who hugged us all.

'See you soon,' I told him.

*   *   *

'That was brilliant,' said Cleo when we flopped down in the living room. 'I haven't had as much fun in ages. Your dancing was great, Juno. Everyone loved it.'

'I guess it's nice to bring a bit of Irish culture abroad with us,' I said.

'The guys were good fun too,' said Saoirse. 'None of them as sexy as your Pep, though.'

'He's not my Pep,' I protested, even as they sniggered.

'The town seems to think he is,' said Cleo.

'The town!' I cried. 'The whole town?'

'You're a hot topic of conversation.' Saoirse winked at me.

'In what way?'

'A pretty girl living in a house on her own,' she said. 'They're intrigued by it. And the fact that you did an emergency dash to the hospital with that little boy only enhanced their interest.'

'What are they saying?' I demanded.

'That you're some kind of artist looking for solitude.' She grinned at me. 'I told them your mum was a famous Irish actress and that you came from a well-known Irish family.'

'Saoirse!'

'And Andres said that there was a lot of talk about how you're single-handedly renovating the Villa Naranja.'

'I did the shutters, that's all.'

'And, of course, there's the gossip about you and Pep.'

'Please tell me you're pulling my leg about that.'

She laughed. 'What did you expect? You can't spend your days shagging one of the town's most eligible bachelors without people talking.'

'They're not saying that I'm spending my days shagging him. Are they?'

183

'Well . . .'

'No!'

'Ah, they just say he's besotted with you,' she told me. 'That you've enchanted him. And that he's at the house more than is strictly necessary for maintaining the pool.'

'My poor reputation,' I said.

'Good on you,' said Cleo. 'Put yourself out there. Fly the flag for sexy Irish women.'

'I'm not . . .' And then I laughed. There were worse things to do than fly the flag. I knew that already.

Chapter 17

I could hear Saoirse snoring through the bedroom wall. She doesn't snore all the time, only when she's had a few drinks. It was a rhythmic sound, a long, deep rattle as she inhaled, then a loud sigh when she released her breath. It drove me mad back in Dublin but here it was familiar and companionable

I was wide awake and her snoring was keeping me that way. So I put on my shorts and T-shirt and went downstairs. I let myself out of the house and sat on one of the patio chairs, overlooking the valley. There was no sign of the moon, but the stars were as bright as ever.

Like the ghost I'd named him after, Banquo suddenly appeared and jumped on to my lap. In the play, Lady Macbeth can't see Banquo's ghost, but my mum said that she always interpreted her as though she could. Yet despite the evidence of her own eyes, Mum's Lady Macbeth ignored Banquo's spirit because she wouldn't let herself believe in ghosts.

'Do you?' I'd asked.

'There are more things in heaven and earth, Horatio, than are dreamt of in your philosophy,' she told me. And when I looked at her in bewilderment she said it was another Shakespearean quote, and it meant that we couldn't explain

185

everything. So there might be ghosts, or there might not. It was important to have an open mind.

As a practical person who believes in scientific research, I always have an open mind. Just because something is unexplained now, it doesn't mean it can't be explained eventually. All it means is we haven't found out how. Which is why I don't believe in ghosts – and never will.

And yet, sitting on the patio in the middle of the night, with Banquo purring on my lap, I was overcome with the feelings I'd had so many times since Brad had died. The feeling of being watched. The feeling that he had something to say to me. And a longing to say something to him in return.

Eventually, I went back to bed. Saoirse had stopped snoring, and I fell into an unsettled sleep.

I was up before the girls the following morning. By the time they arrived downstairs, I'd picked and squeezed oranges so that there was fresh juice for them to go with the fruit bowl I'd prepared. I wasn't feeling watched now. And I'd shoved my shame and jealousy to the back of my mind.

'This is the life,' said Cleo after we'd finished with the fruit and moved on to coffee. 'How could Pilar abandon it and move to Dublin?'

'Better job opportunities,' I said. 'Also, Pilar didn't live here. She was brought up in Valencia, remember? That's where her parents still live. But there's a lot of history to this house.'

I told them about the visit of Ana Perez and what she'd told me about Pilar's great-grandfather.

'That'd totally freak me out.' Cleo glanced in the direction of the jacaranda tree. 'I'd be terrified he was haunting the place.'

186

Now that I was over my uneasiness of the night before, I was able to tell her not to be so bloody silly.

'I can't help how I feel – ow!' Cleo winced as Saoirse dug her in the ribs.

'Juno has to stay here after we're gone,' she said. 'You don't want to have her worrying about ghosts while she's stuck here in the middle of nowhere.'

'I'm not worried about ghosts!' I said in exasperation. 'I shouldn't have opened my mouth.'

Cleo shrugged.

'Anyway.' I got up and began to clear away the breakfast things. 'I was thinking the beach might be nice today. The only thing we need to worry about there is having enough sunscreen.'

'Sounds like a plan,' said Saoirse and went off to change.

The beach was fun. We lay around on the loungers in the sunshine, then swam in the sea for a while, then Cleo insisted we have a game of beach volleyball before having anything to eat. There were nets on the beach and we bought a ball at the beach bar, which seemed to sell everything, so we spent an hour throwing ourselves about on the sand enthusiastically if not very expertly. After that, we had burgers and chips. It was so long since a chip had passed my lips that it felt almost sinful eating it. I wondered if I'd turned into the kind of person who regards her body as a shrine but then remembered that I was knocking back a glass of the Navarro finest most evenings, so decided probably not.

By the time we got back to the Villa Naranja we were all exhausted, and I suggested that perhaps we might give the last night of the fiesta a miss. But the girls insisted that we had to go into town again and scurried off to wash their hair and beautify themselves. I headed for the shower too and scrubbed the sand from my body, thinking that it made a great exfoliator.

Eventually, we were ready. We assembled in the kitchen, all wearing light sundresses – mine was yellow, Saoirse's pink and Cleo's an almost neon orange.

'Looking hot, if I say so myself,' said Saoirse as she made us pose for a selfie. 'Come on, ladies. Let's show this town what we've got.'

If Beniflor had been buzzing on the previous nights, the atmosphere now was electric. The entire population seemed to have gathered in the square where, once again, there was live music and lots of food.

'We picked the right time to come,' Cleo said over the general hubbub. 'Honestly, Juno, we might only be here for a couple of days but it's as good as a fortnight!'

I grinned at her as I elbowed my way to one of the bars to get something to drink. I'd stayed on alcohol-free beer at the beach so that I'd been able to drive, and I was still on the alcohol-free stuff, but to be honest the whole ambience was so much fun that I didn't mind in the least. The girls were drinking San Miguel, despite Saoirse having muttered earlier about not wanting a hangover two days in a row.

The first people we met were Catalina and her husband, José. There was no sign of Xavi, but Catalina was holding baby Agata in her arms. We chatted for a while and then Elena Navarro joined us. Catalina complimented her on how well Beatriz had carried out her duties as the Fiesta Queen and Elena said that it had been an honour for Beatriz and that the whole family was very proud of her. Beatriz would be lighting the first rocket for the fireworks later, she said. It would be a great show. In the meantime, there was another parade to get through (Beatriz and the other Fiesta Queens were at the head of that) and lots more music, food and dance.

'I don't know how anyone here does any work at all,' said Saoirse after we'd found ourselves some seats in the corner of the square. 'It's party central the whole time.'

'I guess it goes back to normal tomorrow,' I said. 'Oh, look, there's Pep.'

He was walking over to me, accompanied by his older brother, Luis. I'd met Luis at the family dinner, although I hadn't spoken to him very much. He was as handsome as Pep, with the same smouldering eyes and dark hair, although Luis had some strands of grey.

'Wow,' murmured Saoirse. 'Another fine thing. What a family!'

I gave her ankle a kick.

We all said hello to each other, and the two men dragged over a couple of chairs to join us.

Cleo asked Pep a question about the fiesta, which he began answering in detail, while Luis asked me if everything was now OK at the Villa Naranja.

'It was always OK,' I said.

'I meant the leak in the roof.'

I smiled. 'Hard to tell. The weather has been glorious ever since.'

'If you need anything, anything at all, you must ask.' Luis's tone was polite but his voice lacked Pep's warmth. 'We are happy to help.'

'Pep and your family have been really lovely to me,' I told him. 'I appreciate all the concern you've shown.'

189

'We have always been friends and good neighbours to the Perez family,' Luis said. 'It matters to us that you are well looked after.'

'I'm fine,' I said.

'And Pep is kind to you?'

'Yes, he's great.' I wondered how much Luis knew about my relationship with his younger brother.

'He does a good job with the pool?'

'Very.'

'And he has helped you out at other times, not just when it rained?'

'Well . . . he's called to the house, yes. And he drove me home after the first night of the fiesta.'

'He is a kind-hearted boy, Pep. A little . . . impulsive sometimes, perhaps.'

Was I being overly sensitive or could I detect an edge to Luis's voice?

'Only in a good way,' I told him.

'I am glad to hear it.'

I said nothing. I felt as though Luis might be warning me as far as Pep was concerned. But what would he need to warn me about? I'd decided to have an uncomplicated relationship with the youngest Navarro boy, hadn't I? It didn't matter to me whether he was impulsive or not.

Yet as I danced with him later that night, I wondered how much of life is really uncomplicated. And I couldn't help thinking that seemingly straightforward things can sometimes carry intricacies that take a long time to discover.

Chapter 18

Although I'd suggested a trip to the Arab baths for Sunday (I still hadn't seen them, and I thought that perhaps the girls might like to do something cultural), there was a general agreement that we needed to recover from the night before, and so we didn't make it any further than the pool. Banquo had decided that the girls were acceptable company and joined us for a while, curling up in the shade beneath my lounger while we lazed away the afternoon.

'He's a nice cat,' Cleo remarked as she reapplied Factor 30 to her legs. 'I was worried when you said you were alone with him that you might have tipped over the line into madwoman territory. But now that I've met Pep I have no fears for you at all.'

'I'm glad to hear it,' I said.

'I'll be thinking of you tomorrow when I'm propping my eyes open with matchsticks,' she added. 'I'll be picturing you eating fresh oranges and drinking glasses of local wine.'

We'd shared a bottle after we'd arrived back from the fiesta, at about three o'clock that morning. (The fiesta would end at six with the ringing of the church bells, Pep had said, but I'd told him there wasn't a hope in hell we could've stayed awake till then. Though, as it turned out, it was after four by the time we'd finished the wine and gone to bed, which is probably why the Arab baths idea was never going to be a runner.) The girls were complimentary about the wine and very impressed that I had it delivered.

'Gran complains that we don't even get milk delivered any more,' observed Saoirse. 'She'd be gobsmacked at wine!'

'It's a bit decadent all right,' I agreed.

'You deserve a bit of decadence,' said Saoirse. 'And even though I'm looking forward to you coming home, I'm glad that you're having fun.'

'I bet you're having just as much fun at home,' I said. 'The flat to yourself every night!'

'Which is nice, but I miss you,' she said.

'Don't you have Conal over?'

'Not every night,' she said. 'He's got his own place, and I like my space.'

I frowned. 'That doesn't sound like you're taking it to the next level.'

'Oh, who cares about levels?' said Saoirse. 'I love being with Conal but I also love being on my own. And I love being with my girlfriends.'

'I thought you guys were long-term,' I said.

'We might be.' She shrugged. 'I don't know. It's like . . . when he's not around I miss him, but when he's with me I'm also happy to see him go.'

'Wow,' said Cleo. 'I thought you were in line for the engagement ring, Saoirse. I thought it was what you wanted.'

'For a while I did,' she admitted. 'And then . . . well . . .'

'What?' I asked.

'I saw how broken up Juno was about Brad.' She turned

192

to look at me directly. 'I wondered how I'd feel if it had been Conal who'd been killed. And, of course, I would have been devastated and heart-broken, but I wouldn't have gone to pieces the way you did.'

'I went to pieces because he was a lying bastard,' I told her. 'Not because he was dead.'

The three of us stared at each other.

'God,' I said. 'That sounded terrible. I mean, I was distraught about him being killed. I shouldn't even have to say that. I loved him. I was sure I had a future with him. But he was a liar and a cheat, and if he'd lived I would have dumped him.' I stared at my friends. 'I would have dumped him. Definitely.'

They were still staring at me. And at that moment I knew I truly had meant what I said. I would have left him. It would have been over and I would have moved on. Which meant that right there, and right then, I had. I'd reached acceptance. Just like that. All of a sudden.

So, to celebrate, they threw me into the pool.

It was good to feel good again. Good to feel able to laugh as I hauled myself out of the water. Good to joke with my friends. Good to be alive. We spent the rest of the afternoon gossiping like mad things and had dinner on the patio – my almost staple warm chicken salad.

'I definitely should come home,' I remarked to Cleo as I dropped them off outside the airport that evening. 'If I'm OK again, there's no good reason to stay.'

'Are you out of your mind?' she demanded. 'You're on a break. Take it. Use the time. Why on earth would you rush back?'

'I feel bad . . .' I began, but she told me to shut up and smell the roses.

'Besides, there's Pep to consider,' said Saoirse.

'Well, yes,' I agreed. 'But really, girls, you're absolutely right and I'm just using him for sex. Which, I suppose, makes me a total harlot.'

They laughed and I grinned, and then Saoirse gave me a more serious look.

'Are you sure?' she asked. 'Every time I've seen you two together, you seem pretty loved up – and not just in a can't-keep-your-hands-off-each-other sort of way.'

'I'm not ready to rebound by jumping out of the frying pan and into the fire,' I said. 'Especially such a hot fire.'

'Give it a chance, though,' argued Saoirse. 'You never know.'

'Besides, the intern is with us till the end of the summer,' Cleo said.

'You don't want me back?' I asked.

'Don't be silly,' she said. 'You know we miss you. And even though Anji is good, she's not half as good as you. But she needs the work.'

I hadn't been thinking of my replacement. I'd only been thinking of myself. I might have moved on to acceptance but I was still horribly self-absorbed.

'I don't know what'll happen if I stay,' I said.

'Think of it as an extended holiday romance,' advised Saoirse. 'If it turns into something else, great. If it doesn't, at least you've had a fantastic time. And he's helped you move on from Brad.'

But as I waved goodbye to them and drove away from the airport I couldn't help thinking that I'd needed Brad to forget about Sean, and Pep to forget about Brad. Was I the kind of woman who couldn't make it on her own? Who needed a man in her life to feel OK about herself? That wasn't the person I wanted to be. It wasn't the person I thought I was. And it wasn't the person I would allow myself to become.

Darkness had fallen by the time I reached the exit from the motorway. I was using the satnav again, because although I now knew the local roads around Beniflor, I still wasn't one hundred per cent sure about the exit. But with Jane guiding me I moved into the correct lane and on to the country roads again.

There was a sliver of moon but it wasn't bright enough to light the way. Unlike the night I'd first arrived, though, I knew the lights in the distance were indeed the lights of the various fincas dotted around the countryside, and I knew too that Beniflor wasn't far away, even though it wasn't yet visible. I smiled to myself as I remembered stopping on the road, unsure of where I was going, and being terrified by the headlights of the van behind me. But I was relaxed about it now.

I was relaxed with myself too, I realised. At peace with who I was and where I was in my life. Broken relationships happened, I thought, as I stopped in front of the villa's gates. They happened to everyone. And even though the earthquake and the subsequent revelations had been a shock, there was nothing to blame myself for. Brad's tragedy wasn't my tragedy. His life hadn't been my life. I was over him.

The gates slid open. I caught sight of Banquo's eyes reflected in the headlights of the car. I edged forward and parked outside the house.

Chapter 19

I hadn't been in Beniflor since the last night of the fiesta, so the following Saturday, still feeling good after another night with Pep, I drove into town and went for a coffee in the Café Flor. The plaza was as busy as always, and I spent the time people-watching while I waited for Rosa to take my order. Mum is a great people-watcher – she sees someone and instantly makes up a story about their life – but I tend to take what I see at face value. However, it wasn't hard to separate the locals (who, despite the climbing temperatures, hadn't completely abandoned their jeans and long-sleeved shirts) from the tourists and the expats, who'd switched to full summer mode.

'Hello.' Rosa stood in front of me with her notebook and pencil, and her tone was unusually grumpy. 'What can I get you?'

'What do you recommend?' I asked.

'You should know what we have by now,' she replied. 'It's all on the menu.'

I ordered coffee and a slice of apple pie, wondering what on earth was the matter with her.

She returned with the coffee and cake a few minutes later and put them silently on the table in front of me.

'Are you all right?' I looked at her with concern 'You seem very . . . distracted. Is it because the fiesta is over?'

'I suppose I'm tired.' She hesitated for a moment before adding that I seemed to have enjoyed the fiesta, and so had my friends. But particularly me.

'The star of the show,' she said, and there was no mistaking the sourness in her voice.

'I'm sorry?'

'You took over, didn't you? Dancing in front of everyone like you did. It was very show-offy.'

'I . . . They asked,' I said.

'Pep asked. But then what Pep wants you give him, don't you?'

'What?'

'Oh, come on.' She gave me a disdainful look. 'You and Pep. You were all over each other like the plague. I'd heard rumours but until then I didn't believe them. But when I saw you together, I knew.'

'I . . .'

'If you had to throw yourself at someone, it should've been Luis. He's the right age for you, after all. But Pep! I can't believe you and Pep. He's not for you. He was never for you.' She shook her head and walked away from me.

I stared after her retreating back as the realisation hit me. Rosa had some kind of past with Pep. And here I was, suddenly caught in another person's relationship again. It didn't matter how tenuous it might have been. It didn't matter that I hadn't known. Or that I hadn't meant it.

Somehow, I'd become the other woman.

It was getting to be a bad habit.

I drank my coffee but I wasn't hungry any more. I left

enough money to cover the pie and the coffee, as well as a tip, then hurried out of the square without seeing Rosa again. There was nothing I could do about her feelings for Pep Navarro, but I wished I'd known about them before now. I recalled the tightness in her voice the very first time she'd spoken to me about him. I should've guessed. But I'd been oblivious.

Complete disregard for other people's feelings was clearly a fatal flaw in my character. My mother had told me, more than once, that I was totally lacking in empathy. That wasn't strictly true. I was very empathic when it came to the patients who presented themselves at the radiology department. I was good with them. I knew how to talk to them, to ease their very real fears. But maybe I was only good in a hospital environment. And the real world was still a mystery to me.

Mum rang me again later that night.

'You're still in Spain, then,' she said when I answered. 'I knew by the dialling tone. Have you been doing anything interesting?'

Mum hardly ever speaks in less than entire paragraphs. But she was clearly still bemused by my recent actions and was trying to get to the bottom of them. I wondered where on her scale of 'interesting' having amazing sex with a Spanish Greek god would be. But obviously I wasn't going to tell her about the sex. So instead I told her about Saoirse and Cleo coming to visit and the fun we'd had at the fiesta and the fact that I'd danced for the entire town.

'Goodness!' She sounded taken aback. 'You danced? For everybody?'

'It was that kind of night,' I said.

'Maybe you were right.' She still sounded a little bemused. 'Maybe you did need a bit of time out to find yourself properly. And that's a good thing, Juno. Because you've never really embraced mindfulness before.'

'I'm not embracing it now!' I exclaimed. 'I danced because everyone was dancing.'

'Of course, if you're away to find yourself, you must find yourself completely.' Mum continued as though I hadn't spoken. 'There's a wonderful website – I can't remember the name of it now, but I have it saved on my computer – and it helps you with ways of reaching deep inside your psyche. I'll send you a link after we finish talking.'

'Thank you.' I'd no intention of checking out the website. That sort of claptrap is totally not me.

'So have you made any friends?' asked Mum. 'That's something else you're not good at.'

'Did you ring specifically to lecture me on the things I'm not good at?' I demanded. 'Because that's what it sounds like.'

'Don't be silly,' she said. 'I'm just trying to take care of you from a distance. I'm happy that you finally seem to be learning to enjoy life, though I'm not convinced you really know how to go about it. I'm going to send you a link to another website that is really good with chakras. I've never been truly convinced that your root chakra is properly balanced, and I worry about your third eye.'

'My what?'

'Oh, come on, Juno. You must know about chakras. It's important to be centred and secure in the world. If your root is unbalanced, you won't be. And your third eye helps you to see the big picture. It looks after your intuition, it makes everything work together and helps you to make the right decisions.'

'Well, they must both be fine because I made the decision to come here and everything's working out OK.' Although I wasn't sure about that. Not now, not after speaking to Rosa.

'Have you met a man? Are you getting some sex?'

'Mum!' I was outraged. 'That's *so* not an appropriate question to ask me.'

'Allow yourself to love,' she told me, as though I hadn't spoken. 'Lose yourself to it. That's what you're not good at, Juno. You think about it too much. You over-analyse. You did with the Dolt, you know. I could see it in your eyes.'

Maybe I had overthought it with Sean. But not with Brad. With him it had been all heart and no head – and it had been the worst mistake of my life.

'Nothing to say?' she asked.

'Trying to figure out which one of your gems of wisdom is most appropriate,' I told her.

'Did I tell you that I'm going to play Lady Bracknell again?'

Her change of topic threw me for a moment. She does it all the time. I think it's to check you've been listening to her. When I gathered my thoughts, I remembered that she'd played the role about ten years previously in a stage production of *The Importance of Being Earnest*. It was an award-winning role for her and she uses the rather gaudy trophy she received as a doorstop. Of all her plays I've ever gone to, it's the one I've genuinely enjoyed the most; though when I first said this to her, she sniffed and told me that it was probably because it was a comedy. And it didn't really have soul. 'But it's witty,' I'd replied. 'And I love Lady Bracknell.' Which pleased her.

'A short run at the Gate,' she told me when I asked about it now. 'I hope you'll be back for that.'

'It's hardly in the next few weeks, is it?'

'The end of November,' she told me.

'I'll be home well before then!' I cried. 'I have to go back to work, you know. I can't afford to swan around forever.'

'Perhaps I'll see you sooner,' she said. 'If I come to stay.'

'You'd be more than welcome, but it's getting hotter by the day, and you don't like the heat,' I reminded her. 'You said it drains your soul.' Nevertheless, I felt I'd be more able to cope with a visit from her now than a few weeks ago. Because I'd found acceptance. And Pep.

'I could do with warming my bones,' she said. 'It's rained for the past three days. I hate it when the sky is grey.'

I glanced up at the midnight blue of the night sky.

'So do I,' I said. 'I'd be happy to see you. Truly.'

'I'll see about it,' she said. 'But in the meantime, take care of yourself.' There was real affection in her voice as she spoke. 'Look after those chakras. I mean it.'

'I will,' I said.

She ended the call.

I stayed where I was, still looking up at the sky. It had been a different type of conversation with my mother.

Maybe we were moving on too.

Chapter 20

I stayed away from Beniflor for a while because I didn't want to bump into Rosa again. Instead, I finally made the trip to the Arab baths, which were amazingly well preserved. I sat on one of the stone benches, imagining what life had been like in the thirteenth century, when people would spend several hours in the various hot and cold rooms, chatting about their day. According to the information leaflet, a trip to the baths was a social outing, and I thought to myself that the old walls had probably heard plenty of gossip over the years. I supposed that a lot of the conversation was very different to now, but there was no reason to think that there weren't just as many broken hearts and deceptions eight hundred years ago. What had happened in my life was really nothing out of the ordinary. And just as it had happened in the past, it would, unfortunately, happen in the future too. But not to me. Never again to me.

Eventually, having exhausted Beniflor's history and cultural offerings and spent more time on some minor repairs to the Villa Naranja, I had no option but to go into the town for some shopping. After picking up my supply of fresh fruit and vegetables, I made a decision to go to the Café Flor for my usual coffee. It was ridiculous to feel unable to sit in the plaza, which was the focal point of everything, and equally ridiculous to feel intimidated by Rosa for something that wasn't my fault.

As I walked out of the supermarket, I bumped into Catalina Ruiz. Xavi was with her, dressed in his Barça gear.

'*Hola*,' she said. 'How are you, Juno?'

'I'm great,' I replied. 'And you, Xavi? Your shoulder is OK?' I hunkered down to his level and felt it experimentally.

'Is good,' he said. 'Is better.'

'I'm glad to hear it.'

'He has promised not to jump around stupidly again,' said Catalina.

Even as both of us smiled, I knew we were having the same thought. That Xavi wasn't the sort of boy not to do stupid things. But kids had to experience life. It was something I often said to parents when they turned up at the hospital with their bloodied offspring in tow. Arms and legs break. But they can be fixed. It's the other things in life that are more difficult to repair.

In work, I have a reputation for being the kind of person who never shies away from the difficult stuff. Interacting with Rosa might be hard, but I had to do it. Even though we weren't exactly friends, she had been friendly towards me. And despite the fact that her relationship with Pep must have been in the past, I might have been rattled too in the same circumstances. I didn't want to feel that my history was repeating itself, however tenuously. And I didn't want to feel guilty either. I was done with guilt.

Maybe I was getting in touch my chakras after all, I thought, as I sat down at the table nearest the door. Maybe

I was following Mum's advice and looking after myself a bit more. I glanced around. It was a quiet time of the day and only one other table was occupied. There was no sign of Rosa, so I picked up a Spanish gossip magazine that someone had left behind and flicked through it as I waited for her to appear. It wasn't my imagination that she was still cooler and more offhand than she'd ever been before when she took my order. So when she returned to put the coffee and cake in front of me, I asked her if she had a moment to sit down.

'Why?' she asked.

'I wanted to talk to you,' I said.

'I'm busy.'

I looked around. The occupants of the other table had two full glasses of Coke in front of them. I raised an eyebrow, and she shrugged before sitting opposite me.

'I wanted to talk about Pep Navarro,' I said.

'Pep?'

'Yes. The last time I was here you were obviously upset by the fact that he and I have become friends.' I wasn't going to say lovers. That sounded far too dramatic for a sunny afternoon.

'Oh, that's nothing.' She tossed her head and her auburn curls glinted in the sunlight.

'Really?' I asked. 'It didn't seem nothing to me. And so I thought perhaps you and he might have had a relationship before, and you're bothered that he and I are seeing each other now.'

'Why would you think that? Why are you even asking me about it? It's none of your business.'

'You sort of made it my business by being rude to me,' I said.

'Oh, all right.' She didn't look at me as she spoke. 'We had a thing for a while. But it wasn't serious. I apologise if you got the impression I was rude to you.'

'Your thing with Pep is over, but you don't like to think of him being with me?'

'Why should you care what I think?' This time she looked at me directly. Her eyes were dark and angry, regardless of her words.

'I just do,' I said.

'He's a free agent. We all are.'

'I know,' I said. 'But you've been nice to me and I don't want to . . .'

'Don't want to what?' she demanded. 'It's too late. Everyone knows he's completely under your spell.'

'I'm not sure if—'

'That's the trouble with all you outsiders!' she interrupted. 'People who come to the town for a few weeks and think you're part of it. Well, you're not. You never will be.'

'I know,' I said. 'I do know. I'm not trying to be part of anything, Rosa. I'm just trying to . . . to get over something myself.'

I'd felt part of it, though. When I'd gone to the DIY store to buy varnish and paint. When I'd taken Xavi to the hospital. When I'd met Ana Perez. When the men had come to fix the roof. When I'd started work on the house. When I'd gone to dinner at the Navarros'. And most of all when I'd made love to Pep. I'd felt more than a tourist. I felt as though I belonged. But I didn't. And I never would, no matter how long I stayed. I was kidding myself if I thought any differently.

'I'm sorry.' Her shoulders slumped suddenly and she looked at me with eyes that now held resignation rather than anger.

'I'm taking it out on you, and I shouldn't. It's just that, for a time, I thought Pep and I might . . . that we were . . .' She shrugged. 'I was wrong.'

'You're very young,' I said. 'And there are plenty of men.'

'That's what my mum says.' She made a face. 'It doesn't matter how right people are when they tell you stuff like that. About there being more fish in the sea. It's how you feel inside that counts.'

'How do you feel?' I asked.

'I know it's over but I can't get him out of my mind,' she told me.

I could empathise with that.

'How long is it since you were seeing him?' I asked.

'Eleven months, three days.'

'Oh.'

'I only remember it that accurately because we split up on my mum's birthday.' She smiled faintly. 'Dad had organised a family dinner at the hotel, and when I invited Pep he . . . well, basically he said he wasn't my family and that I shouldn't think like that about him.'

'Ouch.' I was taken aback at Pep's harshness.

'Maybe he was right,' she said. 'Like you said, we were very young. We're still young. It's just that when you think you've found the right person . . . well, you don't care about anything else.'

I knew exactly how she felt.

'But if you want to go out with him, that's entirely up to you,' said Rosa, and her tone, while not warm, had lost some of its chill. 'Even though he's a lot younger than you. I'm fine with it, and I shouldn't have given you a different impression.'

'I don't know what I want.' I ignored the crack about my age. 'My track history of relationships isn't great, and before I came here . . . well . . . like you, I thought I'd found someone – but I hadn't.'

'What happened?' She looked at me with undisguised interest, her voice suddenly a good deal warmer.

'He was married,' I said.

'Oh.'

'I didn't know at the time.'

'How did you find out?'

'That doesn't matter. What matters is, I did.'

'And what about his wife? Did he have a family?'

I couldn't tell her everything. Despite acceptance, it was still too hard and it still hurt too much. And I didn't want her to have a worse opinion of me than she already had.

'None of it is important,' I said. 'But I came here to get over it. And Pep . . .'

'Was available to help.'

'He was coming to the house to do the pool, and he's very attractive.' I sighed. 'I didn't realise there was anyone else.'

'There isn't,' she said. 'At least, I'm not the "anyone else". Not after nearly a year. I should have realised that by now.'

'I'm sorry,' I said.

'Are you in love with him?'

'I like him a lot,' I replied. 'But I don't want to be in love with anyone right now. As for him, he's young – and, as he said before, he's not ready for commitment.'

'All the same, he's crazy about you,' said Rosa. 'It's perfectly obvious. Everyone's noticed.'

'Hardly everyone—'

208

'What did you expect?' She stared at me. 'You're very pretty, and people can't help being interested in how you're living at Doña Carmen's all on your own. You're . . . well, you're older and more experienced than most of the other girls in Beniflor. It's no wonder he's interested in you. After you did that Irish dancing stuff at the fiesta and he kissed you . . . well, that was that.'

'It wasn't much of a kiss,' I protested. Then I thought about the rest of it, what we'd done in the Villa Naranja afterwards and what we continued to do, and I sighed. I'd basically turned into the cougar who comes into town and has an affair with its most eligible bachelor. I was a walking cliché. And the idea of being gossip fodder chilled me. 'You're right,' I added. 'I'm too old for him.'

'You're not that old,' conceded Rosa. 'I mean, yes, you're older than me. And him. But you're not ancient.'

Deliberately or not, she'd succeeded in making me feel it.

Some more people arrived and sat down at a nearby table. Rosa got up to serve them and I picked up the magazine again. But I was looking at the pictures, rather than trying to understand the stories, when she returned and sat down again.

'Are you thinking of consulting one?' she asked as I put the magazine on the table.

I looked at her in surprise and she nodded at the Classified Ads page, which was open. Most of the notices were for fortune tellers, and I didn't need to be able to understand Spanish to know what they were offering.

'To find out if you and Pep are the real deal?'

I shook my head. 'I don't know how people can be persuaded to spend money on these charlatans. I mean, look at the cost per minute. And they don't tell you anything you don't already know. It's a complete con.'

'I'd never ring a premium line,' said Rosa. 'But a few of us go to Magda once a month. She'd change your mind about it. She's brilliant. It might be a good idea for you to consult her.'

'Who on earth is Magda?' I asked.

'She's a psychic.' Rosa's tone was respectful. 'She knows stuff that she couldn't possibly find out unless she was in touch with some kind of spirit. She has a guide, of course. An Egyptian cat called Tetu.'

I couldn't believe that the modern young woman in front of me truly believed this drivel. And I wondered what it was about Beniflor that kept pushing me in the direction of the kind of other-worldliness I knew was utter nonsense. Feeling watched at the Villa Naranja. Imagining that Brad wanted to communicate with me from beyond the grave. And now this psychic rubbish.

'I can tell you think it's silly,' said Rosa. 'But I swear that after a session with her you'll change your mind. She helped me a lot after the split with Pep. She told me there were good things on the horizon for me, and there were. I did well in my end-of-year exams. I got the job in the café, even though lots of people were after it.'

But she clearly hadn't told Rosa that I was going to show up and throw a spanner in the works, or that she'd be wracked with jealousy when Pep moved on to someone new. So not that much help, really. Rosa would have done well in her exams anyway. She'd have got her waitressing job too. Magda telling her that there were good things out there for her hadn't changed anything.

210

'Even if you don't believe in it, it's a great evening out,' said Rosa when I remained silent. 'We're going to her the day after tomorrow. Why don't you come?'

In less than an hour we'd gone from her hating me to wanting me to come with her to see a psychic. I supposed that was progress.

'Why would I, when I don't believe a word of it?' I asked. 'I'd only ruin it for you.'

'Because you're uncertain about your future,' Rosa said. 'You need to know how you feel about Pep. And Magda will help you. She's good like that.'

I laughed dismissively as she got up to serve more customers. Then I flicked through the magazine again before stopping at the horoscopes. Obviously, I couldn't understand a word of them either, but it suddenly occurred to me that I often read my horoscope in magazines, even though I think astrology is about as scientific as reading the tea leaves. I never remember what it says, of course. But I do know that my sign, Virgo, means that I'm supposed to be methodical and analytical, which was is obviously true for me. I'd once read that Virgos are often misunderstood, and I remembered feeling a little self-satisfied at that, because my most frequent refrain at home when I was small had been, 'You just don't understand me!' But you can make your zodiac sign fit your personality in the same way as you can make your horoscope fit what you expect from the week ahead.

'So?' asked Rosa when she returned to collect my empty plate and cup. 'Are you going to come?'

I didn't want to upset her any more than I already had, and I was concerned she'd take offence if I said no. So I smothered my reservations and said yes instead.

'Who else will be there?' I asked.

'Me, my mum, Carola from the TV shop, Esther from the pizzeria and Catalina Ruiz,' she replied.

'I just met Catalina in the street,' I remarked. 'She had Xavi with her.'

'You see.' Rosa gave me a knowing look. 'You meeting her and now coming to see Magda with us. It was meant to be.'

I shook my head as I got up to leave.

I had no idea what my future was going to be. But I did know that it was going to be on my terms and my terms only, no matter what some charlatan might predict.

Pep arrived at nine in the evening, when I was sitting on the patio reading the last of the novels that the girls had bought at the airport. It was partly set in Andalucia during the war, which made reading it now doubly atmospheric. Every so often I thought about Pilar's great-grandfather and the tragedy that had befallen him right here, in this garden. But it didn't spook me. Nor was it making me feel as though I was being watched. It was just interesting.

Pep had brought some more of the Navarro wine with him and he poured me a glass.

'What do you think?'

'Lovely,' I said.

'Nearly as lovely as you.' His English, especially his flattery, was coming on in leaps and bounds. My Spanish – despite the occasional phrases he'd taught me – was still pretty terrible. 'You are thinking of your friends?' he asked when I didn't speak.

'No.' I turned to him. 'I was thinking about Rosa Johnson.'

'Rosa? Why?' he asked.

'Because I had coffee with her today.'

He said nothing.

'We talked about you.'

'I am sure I am not very exciting to talk about,' said Pep.

'Actually, it was very interesting. I didn't know you'd gone out with her before.'

'When we were younger,' he said.

'Until a year ago. So not that much younger.'

'It was a big romance,' he admitted, 'but it was too much for me. She . . . she is a lovely person but she wanted it to be forever, and I am not ready for forever.'

He was still too young for forever. I said so.

'I am young, but good for a mature woman,' he told me.

'I'm the mature woman?'

'But yes. You are very mature. Mature women have more wisdom than younger women, no?'

It was a long time since I'd felt wise, and certainly not mature. And I wasn't even sure I wanted him to think of me as mature. It was another way of saying old, wasn't it?

'I am sorry it did not go the way Rosa wanted,' he remarked after a moment's silence. 'I still like her very much. But she was angry with me so we do not talk.'

'From what she says you were quite harsh with her.'

'Harsh?'

I picked up my phone and opened the dictionary app I'd downloaded.

'*Duro*,' I said. 'You told her you weren't her family.'

'I did not intend to be harsh,' he said. 'I did not want to hurt her. I was just saying the truth.'

'I think she's over it now,' I told him with a hint of satisfaction.

'I am glad.' His tone was relaxed. 'And you?'

'Me?'

'Are you over what made you come to Spain and fall into my arms?'

'I don't know,' I replied. 'It's complicated.'

'Complicated I understand,' said Pep. 'But it is people who make things complicated, no? They do not have to be.'

'You might be young but you have a way with words,' I said. 'Even in a foreign language.'

'You have helped me a lot with my English,' he said as he put his arm around me and pulled me towards him. 'As well as other things.'

And the rest of the night wasn't complicated at all.

Chapter 21

If I believed in psychic coincidence, I'd have found significance in the fact that an email from my mother with links to her mindfulness and chakra sites arrived just before I headed out for the trip to Magda. (Rosa had utterly forbidden me to call her a fortune teller. She'd got quite snippy about it when I'd messaged her at the café to check what time we were meeting up.) Anyhow, whatever I felt about the concept of meditation – something I've tried from time to time but singularly failed to accomplish, as I simply can't control the thoughts in my head – I was having none of Mum's assertion that I should think of my chakras as internal batteries constantly recharged by cosmic forces. But I didn't say that in my reply. I just thanked her for the links and then left my iPad charging its own internal batteries on the table.

Rosa's mum, Bridget, was already at the café when I arrived, along with Carola, who was about the same age as me. They were chatting about the last visit, at which Bridget had been told that patience would be its own reward.

'And so,' she told us triumphantly, 'I didn't get on the decorator's case but left him to it – and he came back with a much better proposal for the spa, which we'll be going ahead with at the end of the season. Magda was right, as always.'

I kept my mouth shut. I wasn't going to offend Rosa's mother by saying that the running of a business shouldn't be dependent on the advice of a bloody fortune teller.

The others arrived and we set off for the psychic's apartment. I'd expected her to live in an isolated country house – perhaps one of the pinpricks of light that I'd seen when I was first driving to the Villa Naranja – but her home was on the top floor of a four-storey modern block at the edge of the town. The conversation as we walked to it was a mixture of English and Spanish, depending on who was talking – and although I didn't understand everything they said, I got the drift, which was that Magda Burnaia had a real gift. A gift for conning people, I thought, even as I was getting slightly caught up in the general excitement. I warned myself not to leave my critical faculties at the door.

Everyone seemed to have a question they wanted answered by her. Catalina was eager to know if she would get pregnant again by the end of the year. Apparently, Magda had predicted her previous two pregnancies, and Catalina's plan was to have her third (and final) child as soon as possible, even though Agata was only a year old.

'There was too much of a gap between her and Xavi,' Catalina explained. 'We didn't want that. I hope it will be different this time.'

Carola, who worked in the TV shop, had applied for a job at an IT company in Alicante and wanted to know what her chances were. Esther, a bright and bubbly student in the same year as Rosa, was worried about her grandmother, who'd had a bad fall a few weeks previously. Her gran's recovery was slow and Esther wanted to know if the older woman would get better soon. When she told me that Sara was sixty, and normally an active, healthy woman, I assured her that she would. But apparently my medical knowledge wasn't as important as the nod from Magda.

Bridget was anxious about some new programmes the hotel was going to run, and Rosa herself simply wanted to know if there was romance on the horizon. I hoped she meant with someone other than Pep Navarro.

'And you?' they asked as we approached the apartment block. 'What about you?'

'Oh, I'm just interested in what she has to say.'

'But you must have a question,' said Esther. 'You have to have a question for her.'

Had Brad loved me?

That was my question. No matter how over him I now was, I still needed to know the answer. Had he loved me? Or was I just a notch on his bedpost? Had he loved his wife? Was she pregnant? Why had he cheated on her? Why had he cheated on me? Six questions I wanted to ask. Six questions that nobody, least of all a con artist, could answer.

'I don't have a question,' I said.

Rosa rang the bell in the entrance hall and we were buzzed in. I'd assumed an assistant would let us into the apartment, but as soon as the door was opened everyone greeted the young woman with cries of 'Magda!' so I realised that it was the psychic herself. And that was another surprise, because she wasn't wearing any kind of traditional 'psychic' attire; she was dressed in a T-shirt and a pair of shorts. Admittedly, the T-shirt had a picture of the moon on it, but it didn't look like a very psychic moon. Magda's dark hair was cropped short, and behind her black-rimmed glasses her blue eyes were warm and cheerful.

The living room, into which we were shown, was simply

decorated, with cream walls and pale floor tiles. The colour came from the autumnal shades of the green sofa and russet cushions. It was a comfortable room, and somehow comforting too. I'd expected pictures of pentacles on the walls, and a decor of purple and gold. But even if Magda's apartment wasn't a shrine to my prejudices, I still wasn't about to be suckered in.

There was a large jug of water and six glasses on a small table. We sat down and helped ourselves. Carola was the first to enter the inner sanctum, but not before placing some money in a carved box on the sideboard.

'Magda doesn't take the money directly,' Rosa explained.

Clearly she liked to pretend she wasn't doing it for the money. But the bottom line was that that was probably what it was all about for her. Easy money too, I reckoned. No having to spend years of your life studying at college. No exams to pass. No technical knowledge to master. No responsibility to get it right. No performance targets to meet. All Magda had to do was make up stuff and feed it to gullible people. I was suddenly feeling stupidly gullible myself. I wished I hadn't come. This was so not my thing.

The others continued their Spanglish conversation about the things they wanted to find out. I listened without contributing, thinking that they were all strong-minded women and wondering why they felt the need to have someone else tell them what to do.

'She doesn't,' said Rosa, when I eventually couldn't hold back and said this. 'She just shows a possible future.'

But couldn't anyone do that? I wondered, still at a loss to understand.

'Magda is gifted,' insisted Esther. 'You'll see.'

Carola returned, beaming. Magda had assured her that her future career was on track.

'But did she say you'll get the job?' I asked.

'She said I'll get the job I deserve,' Carola replied.

I refrained from snorting.

As the others returned from their sessions they all spoke positively about the experience. Magda was confident about the future of the hotel, about Esther's grandmother, about Catalina's pregnancy (within twelve months, Catalina said, which wasn't exactly what she'd wanted to know but which seemed to satisfy her all the same) and about Rosa's love life.

'In the next few weeks.' She beamed at me. 'There's a man for me. We're already close. We know each other.'

'Any idea who that is?' I asked.

'Well . . .' Rosa looked a little anxious. 'It might be someone I've already gone out with.'

I opened my mouth to speak, then closed it again.

A bell tinkled. It was to summon me to Magda's presence.

She was sitting behind a glass table in an almost spartan room. A roller blind was pulled down over the window so that it was in semi-darkness. A single candle, with a faint scent of lavender, burned on a ledge. It was less 'spiritual' than I'd anticipated but she'd still succeeded in creating an other-worldly atmosphere.

'Hello,' she said. 'Welcome.'

Her English was perfect. According to Rosa she also spoke Spanish, German and French. Handy, I supposed, if you were plying your trade near a tourist resort.

'You are a doubter,' she said as I sat down in front of her. 'But that's OK.'

Her voice was soft and calming.

219

'You have a strong aura,' she said. 'The aura of a perfectionist. One who likes clarity. Who likes details. But,' she added, 'you fear loss. You have experienced it.'

An accurate assessment, I supposed. But anyone could think of themselves as a perfectionist – even a person who clearly wasn't. All of us have experienced loss. And all of us fear it.

'You are a healer,' she said. 'But you cannot heal yourself.'

I'm not a healer. I find out if people need to be healed. But I don't heal them. Other people do that.

'You are a practical person. You like physical things,' said Magda. 'I think you would do best with a tarot reading.'

'Whatever you think.'

It made no difference to me what she chose. I wasn't going to believe any of it.

She picked up a worn deck of cards and handed them to me. The deck was heavy and the cards themselves had intricate gold-and-silver patterns embossed on the back.

'Shuffle them,' she said.

I did.

She fanned them out in front of me.

'Pick seven.'

I placed seven cards, face down, on the table.

She turned the first one over. It showed eight silver cups on a table.

'There was sadness,' she said. 'And even though it is lifting, it is still the backdrop to your life at the moment.'

She turned over another. This was a picture of a long, narrow tower being hit by lightning. I thought of the storm and the flooded house. But that was the past, not the future. Magda looked at me and then the card again.

'There has been an unwanted change, a great loss,' she said.

220

I kept my eyes fixed on the cards as she turned over the next.

Two rows of five swords, their ends overlapping.

'There has been treachery. A stab in the back. People you trusted were found wanting.'

The next was another ten. This time the silver cups again.

'You have a warm and loving family who cherish you. But you feel distant from them, even though they are proud of you.'

And then a King, richly dressed, holding one of those silver cups.

I felt her look at me again.

'A man is coming to you,' she said. 'He will travel some distance. He is important. He has a message for you. Something you will want to hear.'

For the first time I looked directly at her. Her eyes, behind her glasses, were regarding me thoughtfully. I frowned. Everything else she'd told me had been generic. Great losses, unhappiness, feeling isolated – nobody came to a psychic because they were feeling great. Nobody came without wanting to be told things were going to get better. So it was reasonable to suggest that there was unhappiness or dissatisfaction in the background. Reasonable to sympathise.

But a man coming to me with a message. That was a definite statement. So was travelling some distance. Although perhaps that was subjective too. Ten kilometres was some distance if you were walking. Nothing if you were in a car. I was allowing myself to be swayed by her gentleness and the rhythmic cadences of her voice. And the fact that, no matter how generic, everything she'd said applied to me. The loss. The treachery. The distant family.

I said nothing.

The next card made her smile. It was the Lovers. She closed her eyes and tilted her head back so that it was facing the ceiling.

'A new relationship for you,' she said. 'A deep, meaningful relationship from an unexpected place.'

It would certainly be unexpected if Pep and I ended up being deep and meaningful, I thought. Especially as I was determined we wouldn't be. But could she be right? Was it long-term after all? Would I leave my life in Dublin and move to Beniflor? How would that work? What would I do here? Where would I get a job? Given my non-existent Spanish, my options would be very limited. Even as the questions raced through my head, I gave myself a mental kick for trying to make her words fit what was going on in my life.

'There is a renewal here,' she continued. 'But it is not clear to me how. I am sorry.'

She turned over another card.

It doesn't matter how much total nonsense you believe it is, nobody wants to see Death in a card.

'I am sorry that there was loss in your life,' said Magda. 'But this does not mean loss now. This means something new. The death of the old. A time for change.'

Oh, please! I thought.

'There will be a transformation,' she said. 'You have been in a dark place. You are moving forward. People love you, and you will find love.'

And that was that, I thought, as I came to my senses again. Fortune telling always ends up with the reassurance that you'll overcome the sadness of your past, or even of your present, and that there's someone out there for you. That you'll find love and happiness, probably when you least expect it. Magda hadn't said a single thing that couldn't have applied just as much to Cleo or Saoirse. Or Rosa. Or anyone else I knew. It had been complete nonsense, just as I'd expected.

'Thanks,' I said.

'You still have doubts.'

'Yes.' There was no point in pretending otherwise.

'You only believe in things you can see.'

'More or less.'

'And yet there is much that we do not see. Even physical things. You must be more open. More receptive.'

I shrugged and thought of my chakras. Obviously, they were sealed shut and totally unbalanced. I intended to keep them that way – no matter how disappointed my mother might be.

Magda picked up the cards and shuffled them. Then she fanned them out again.

'Choose one.'

I selected one from the middle.

It was the Fool.

I laughed. I couldn't help myself.

'You are at a moment of new beginnings,' said Magda. 'You must leave much behind you and move forward with optimism. There is a reason to be optimistic. I see it. I feel it. You must take a leap of faith and trust in the universe. You will find what you are looking for.'

I looked at her sceptically.

She took a deep breath, then reached out and put her hands on mine. I flinched but she didn't move. She stared into my eyes for a moment, then closed her own, keeping her hands on mine.

'Tetu,' she said. 'Can you help?'

Her spirit guide, I remembered. An Egyptian cat. Despite myself I was starting to feel drawn in to her. I felt as though she was in my head, in my mind. I wasn't going to let that happen. I thought of Banquo. I was pretty sure he'd be a worthy adversary for any Egyptian moggy.

Magda released my hands. She took off her glasses and polished them with a white cloth that had been on the desk. She didn't replace them but looked directly at me again.

'You are mourning a man who treated you badly,' she said calmly. 'He did not do this out of malice. He regretted his actions. He still has a hold over you. You are not a weak person. You must put him behind you and embrace the new possibilities ahead of you. He wants this for you too.'

She was reading me, not the cards, I told myself. That was what psychics did. They studied your body language. They were experts at it. They did *not* contact either dead people or dead cats. Nobody did. Nobody could. I had to remember that.

'When will all this happen?' I asked. 'When will I meet this man who's travelled a distance? When will I find the man I'm supposed to love? When will the man who treated me badly no longer be a part of my life?'

She waited for a moment and then smiled at me.

'When you choose,' she said. 'You are the one with the power over your own life. It is important that you remember this.'

And then the reading was over.

'You were ages,' said Rosa when I finally left Magda's room. 'What did she tell you?'

'That I'm going to meet a tall, dark, handsome stranger and fall madly in love,' I said.

They all looked at each other and I didn't need to be a psychic to know they were thinking of Pep Navarro.

'Anything else?' asked Esther.

'That was the gist of it,' I told her. 'Lots of stuff about getting over myself and moving on. But a man on the horizon. I suppose there's always men on the horizon.'

'She foretold my break with Pep,' said Rosa. 'She doesn't always say there's a man in your future.'

'My track record in the past hasn't been too good,' I said. 'So quite honestly, I'm not holding out much hope for the future either.'

'But you've been doing well in Beniflor so far,' said Rosa.

I was afraid for a moment that she was getting at me again. But then she grinned. Clearly the news that there was someone new on the horizon had changed her attitude towards me even more.

There was a general agreement to go to the bar in the town square for tapas and beer and talk about Magda's predictions, but I honestly couldn't listen to more mumbo-jumbo, so I told them that I was tired and would prefer to head home.

'Are you sure?' asked Rosa. 'You're very welcome to join us.'

'Certain.' I smiled at her. 'I have to think about my future, apparently, and I do that best when I'm on my own.'

'See you soon,' she said.

I nodded, then we all embraced.

I got into the car and left them to it.

Chapter 22

I didn't mention to Pep that I'd been to a fortune teller. It wasn't the sort of thing I'd want to talk to him about, and anyhow, I was too embarrassed to admit I'd gone, even to myself. I put everything Magda had said out of my head and instead considered my actual future. The real-life one that I was going to face for myself. How was I going to move on from here? Should I stay in Spain for the rest of my sabbatical from work, or should I go home and get back to my real life? Did I want to stay or leave? And what influence would Pep have over my decision?

As for Magda's comments about my future – if she was right (which she wasn't), how likely was it that I could ever be deep and meaningful with Pep Navarro when, just a year ago, he'd told Rosa Johnson that he was too young for commitment? All the same, the sex was still great and I didn't want to finish with that. Which presumably meant I was far more shallow than deep and meaningful myself!

I was looking forward to seeing him the next morning, his usual day for cleaning the pool. Often he was already at work when I came downstairs, but this morning there was no sign of him so I assumed he'd been delayed at the finca.

The Hideaway

I squeezed a couple of oranges for some fresh juice, chopped some of the fruit I'd bought during the week, and took my breakfast to the patio. Banquo joined me, stretching out in the shade of the table, close to my feet.

'Do you commune with psychic cats?' I asked him as I rubbed him with my toes. 'Have you heard of an Egyptian moggy called Tetu?'

Banquo purred.

'According to him, I'm going to fall madly in love,' I added. 'But my fortune teller hasn't told me when exactly my handsome prince will show up.'

I heard the sound of the gates open and the van drove up to the house. I grinned. Coming by the twisty road from his family's finca, Pep had to travel a long distance. And one psychic's deep and meaningful was another person's good time. I put Magda Burnaia and her predictions out of my mind and went to meet my handsome prince.

But it wasn't Pep who got out of the van. It was his brother, Luis.

'*Hola*,' he said.

'*Hola*.' I looked at him in surprise. 'Where's Pep?'

'He is in Mallorca, of course,' said Luis.

'Mallorca!' Pep hadn't said anything about going to Mallorca. 'Why? When did he go?'

'This morning,' said Luis. 'Early. He has gone to assist my aunt.'

'Assist your aunt? Doing what?'

'Tía Almudena has a boat hire business in Soller,' Luis replied. 'One of her staff left unexpectedly. Pep has gone to fill the space for a time.'

227

'How long a time?' I asked.

'A couple of weeks.'

I stared at him. The thought going through my head at that moment was that the Navarro family had sent Pep away. Because of his relationship with me. The blow-in *extranjera*. The foreigner. Who wasn't part of it at all, just like Rosa had said. But who was trying to muscle her way in anyhow.

'He has helped her out before,' said Luis as he took the bright-blue hose from the back of the van. 'He is good with boats. That is why she asked for him.'

'He seems to be good with everything. And to spend a lot of time helping people out,' I said. 'He told me that he was doing the pool as a favour to the Perez family, because you're neighbours and friends.'

'He's a hard worker,' said Luis. 'But you have seen that already, no?'

Was there a double meaning to what he was saying? Or was I being silly?

'I'm surprised he didn't say anything to me.' I frowned. 'He knew I'd be expecting him today.'

'But he did,' said Luis. 'I saw him. He sent you a message last night.'

I hadn't looked at my phone that morning. Since I'd come to Spain I'd got out of the habit of checking it every few minutes, mainly because I didn't carry it around with me all the time as I did in Dublin. There was no need. I wasn't at anyone's beck and call, or getting frequent texts about hospital issues. Besides, after the night of the storm, when it had died on me, I tended to leave it charging in the living room unless I was actually using it.

228

I went into the house to fetch it. The first message had arrived at eleven the previous night.

I am sorry, Pep had written. *I must go to help my aunt. I will be on early flight. I will send text later.*

And this morning I'd been having breakfast outside when his text had arrived, and so hadn't heard the alert. It was a photo message of a small house in the hills.

My aunt's house. Home for next week or two. I miss you.

I immediately replied with a *Miss you too* message, and went outside again.

Luis was cleaning the pool. Unlike Pep, he was wearing his T-shirt while he worked. He wasn't a Greek god, but he was still an attractive man. Closer to my age. And therefore, at least according to Rosa Johnson, more suitable.

'You have got on well with my brother, no?' He glanced at me as he continued to clean the pool, and I wondered again if there had been some family conspiracy to send Pep away. A sudden breeze, strong and unexpected, rustled through the orange groves. I looked away, towards the jacaranda tree, and then back at Luis again.

'Oh, let's cut to the chase,' I said abruptly. 'I'm sleeping with Pep and you're perfectly well aware of that. If you have an issue with it, just say so.'

He stopped his rhythmic pushing of the hose along the bottom of the pool and looked at me thoughtfully from his dark eyes.

'Of course I do not have an issue with who my brother sleeps with,' he said. 'It is his business.'

'So why are you making it yours?' I demanded.

'He is my family. My younger brother. And I look after him,' said Luis.

229

'You sound like some kind of Mafia Don!' I exclaimed. 'For heaven's sake, this is the twenty-first century.' Even as I said the words, I remembered the history of the Villa Naranja and I shivered. The Navarros and the Perez had been neighbours for a long time. Perhaps Luis's family had been involved in the death of Pilar's great-grandfather. Maybe there was bad blood between them and I was in the middle of something I didn't understand.

'It is not just Pep,' said Luis. 'Nobody knows why you are here. Why you are working so hard on Doña Carmen's house. What your plans are. I am curious, that is all.'

'I thought the whole damn town knew,' I said. 'I'm on a break, that's all. I'm doing up the house because I need to be busy.'

'And being busy includes Pep?'

'Pep just happened. Look,' I said, 'I'm sure he's already told you I'll be going back to Dublin at the end of the summer. I have a life there. And a job. I've no interest in staying in Beniflor. I've no ulterior motive for working on the house . . .' I broke off at the expression on his face. Was that it? Did everyone in Beniflor suspect me of being some kind of fraudster, ready to steal the Villa Naranja from under the noses of the Perez family? And somehow adding Pep Navarro to the mix?

'I have a job,' I repeated as I decided that I was allowing myself to be swept up in melodrama. 'I'm going back to it.'

'You are a medical person?' said Luis. 'I asked Pep before. He said you were a nurse but not a nurse.'

I clearly hadn't explained radiographer properly to him. I tried with Luis, whose English was a lot better than Pep's. He nodded.

'And I'm not trying to rob Ana's house from her,' I added.

'Why would I think that?'

'You suspect me of something,' I said. 'You're treating me like some kind of criminal.'

'But no.' He shook his head. 'Pep says you are a good person. My mother thinks so. Catalina thinks so too.'

'And you?'

'I think you are an interesting person,' he said.

Interesting didn't mean good, though. I said nothing.

'Why did you come to Beniflor?' he asked.

I wasn't going to go through it all again. I was tired of going through it.

'For a holiday,' I told him.

'But it is not a holiday to renovate Doña Carmen's house.'

'It's not a renovation. Just a few bits and pieces,' I said. 'Are you nearly finished with the pool?'

'I'm not as quick as Pep,' said Luis.

OK, that remark definitely had a double meaning. I said nothing but walked away and sat in the shade of the patio again. There was no sign of Banquo. I picked up my iPad and checked my social media.

'I'm sorry if I seemed rude.' He came up to me about ten minutes later, the blue hose coiled over his shoulder.

'No, you're not,' I said.

He looked startled.

'I am,' he protested. 'I was curious about you, that's all. I've never met anyone like you before.'

'What's so different about me?' I asked sharply. 'Other than I'm an *extranjera* and so obviously a suspicious character!'

'You're not suspicious,' said Luis. 'You're independent.'

'Isn't everyone?'

'This is a small town,' said Luis. 'And although it is in the modern world, we sometimes live our lives in a more traditional ways. You are different.'

'And that's bad?'

'I do not know.'

'Actually, I don't care what you think,' I said. 'Have you quite finished?'

'Perhaps you are good for Pep,' said Luis as he walked towards the van. 'Perhaps you will break his heart and not the other way around.' His sudden smile was unexpectedly warm and open.

'You never know,' I said, thinking that perhaps I'd been reading things into his words that really weren't there.

'It would be good for him,' said Luis.

And then he left.

Everyone seemed far too interested in me and how I was living my life, I thought, as I got into the pool and swam a few lengths. I didn't know why. Despite Luis's assertion that it was traditional, it wasn't as though Beniflor was such a small place, or so backward, that one new person should be the object of everyone's attention. But it seemed to me that I was.

Although maybe that was simply my self-obsession again. After all, one of the less endearing traits in Virgos, I remember being told, is that we can be self-pitying and uptight, which leads us down the road of analysing everyone's motives, including our own. Given my dismissal of all things astrological, it was annoying that this description had stuck with me. Especially because it was true.

I dived beneath the water and stayed down until my lungs

were bursting. I was losing it altogether, I thought, as I surfaced and gasped for air. I should never have gone to that damn psychic.

Or perhaps the problem was that I should never have come here.

Chapter 23

And yet, when I sat on the patio that night after my almost compulsory salad for dinner, my irritation with Luis and with myself dissipated. I watched the lights of the valley twinkle in the distance and I forgot all about Magda and her silly predictions. I forgot about Luis's intrusive questioning, and – after Pep had sent me a WhatsApp message once again telling me how much he missed me – I forgot about him too. Instead, I lost myself in the stillness of the night where the only noises were the steady chirping of a cricket and Banquo's satisfied purring.

It wasn't only my anger that left me. It was everything. Like shedding a skin, I could feel the tensions and stresses of the last few months almost physically slide away from me. A few days earlier, I'd reached acceptance. But I still hadn't let go of the other stuff. The jealousy and the shame and the guilt. But now I suddenly did. And I felt like me again.

Juno Ryan. Back to her best. An independent woman, just like Luis had said.

It was liberating.

I finished my wine, closed up the house, and went to bed.

*　　*　　*

I slept like a baby. I didn't dream, didn't wake up to use the bathroom, didn't open my eyes, as had so often happened in recent times, simply because I'd turned over in the bed. It was the ringing of my mobile that eventually woke me, and by the time I realised what it was, it had stopped.

I got up and opened the shutters, allowing the unfiltered sunlight to pour into the room. I pulled on my sundress and went downstairs. Banquo was sitting in the middle of the living room, his ears twitching. I gave him a quick rub and unplugged the phone.

I dismissed my initial thought that it was Pep who'd called when I realised that it had actually been the ringtone of the phone itself and not a WhatsApp alert. I tapped the screen and caught my breath. My hand started to shake. Because the call I'd missed was from Brad McIntyre. I stared at the notification, utterly unable to move.

Banquo mewed a few times, anxious to go outside and urging me to open the door, unwilling to exert himself to jump up on the sink and exit via the open window. But I was – quite literally – rooted to the spot, unable to take my eyes from the screen, staring at the name in front of me.

Missed call.

Brad McIntyre.

And his number.

And suddenly, like the tarot card that had showed the tower being hit by lightning, it all came crashing down around me again.

I knew, of course I knew, that Brad couldn't have called me. Brad was dead. He'd been killed in an earthquake along with his probably pregnant wife. I'd gone to the funeral and seen his coffin. I'd heard the minister talk about what a wonderful man he was. I'd heard his friends and neighbours say the same thing. I knew he was gone.

Yet my phone was telling me that I had a missed call from him.

I felt exactly as I had on the night when I'd first heard the news. I could hardly breathe, was totally unable to process the information in front of me. Back then, it was because I'd learned Brad had died. Now, it was because he'd phoned me. So either he wasn't dead at all, or . . . or it was his spirit contacting me from beyond the grave. Perhaps I'd been wrong to dismiss the spirit world so easily. There was something mystical about Beniflor, about the Villa Naranja and about Magda herself. Perhaps Mum was right about auras and chakras and all of her favourite mumbo-jumbo. Perhaps it wasn't mumbo-jumbo at all.

Was Brad's spirit watching over me? Was it the reason I'd so often felt as though there was someone with me in the house? Did it explain the unexpected noises, the broken glass, the other moments when I'd felt stuff going on that I didn't understand? Was he here, now? Could he see me? Hear me?

I looked up from the phone. Banquo was staring at me silently, his amber eyes thoughtful and considering. Was it him? I wondered wildly. Was his spirit in the cat? Was that why he'd adopted me? Was that why he was always around?

Banquo turned away and walked to the door. He waited by it until I opened it. Then sunlight flooded the room and the spell was broken.

'What the hell is wrong with me?' I said the words out loud. 'What am I thinking?'

Brad hadn't called, of course he hadn't. He was neither

alive, nor an attentive spirit inhabiting an overweight cat. His body was in the ground and his spirit was . . . well . . . there were no spirits. My belief that done is done was right. What lives on is how people have touched our lives. How they've made us feel. That's their everlasting spirit, nothing else.

But if that was the case, I asked myself, who on earth was using Brad's phone? Had it been found in Italy, beneath the rubble? Had whoever had found it decided to keep it for themselves? But why hadn't they simply restored it? Why had they called a number from his contact list? Why had they called me? Why? Why? Why?

Banquo walked back into the kitchen and headbutted my ankles.

'OK, OK,' I said. I got some dried food from the cupboard and filled his empty bowl for him. He set to the task of having his breakfast while I put the kettle on for a cup of tea. I usually drank coffee first thing, but I was still in shock, and tea was better than coffee for shock.

I made the tea, then opened the umbrella over the stone table and sat down. I wrapped my hands around the mug as I stared at the phone in front of me. The caller – not Brad and not Brad's spirit, I reminded myself once again – hadn't left a message. He, or she, had simply hung up. Were they working their way through people on Brad's contact list? Trying to talk to his friends? Or had someone simply made a mistake in dialling my number from Brad's phone?

Who had it? Who?

A warm gust of wind rattled the parasol and sent bougain-villea petals skittering across the garden. And I thought that

I heard his voice. I thought I heard him say *It's me*. But I knew I hadn't.

Because the dead can't talk.

The sensible thing to do would have been to call back straight away, but I couldn't make myself do it. I didn't know who might answer and what I could possibly say. I knew it wouldn't be Brad. And I didn't want to speak to whoever had acquired his phone. Besides . . . I shivered in the morning heat – no matter who answered, it would be an awkward conversation.

I recalled, with a sense of unease, that they would have seen his message stream. We messaged all the time. They would have seen his last text to me: *Tonight's dinner location. Joining them shortly. Love you. Miss you. Bxx.* They would have seen my messages to him. The ones telling him how much I loved him. The ones wishing I was with him. The ones wishing he was with me. The ones where I talked about what I wanted to do with him. What I liked to do with him.

Whoever had his phone would see my heart laid bare.

I had to ring. I had to find out who it was. But I didn't want to.

I took a deep breath and I hit 'dial'.

It took an age for the phone to connect.

'Hi. This is Brad. I can't take your call. Please leave a message.'

The sound of his voice, a voice I hadn't heard in months, was overwhelming. I burst into tears and ended the call without saying a word.

I was still crying when the Bodega Navarro van pulled up outside the house.

'What is the matter? Are you all right?' Luis Navarro was beside me in an instant.

'I'm fine,' I said as I wiped my eyes with the back of my hand. 'I got a shock, that's all.'

'What shocked you? Not me, I hope.'

'Nothing like that.' I smiled weakly. 'I'm fine.'

'Can I help?' There was no edge to his voice now. No undercurrent. Just concern.

I shook my head. 'Something unexpected happened and I've reacted like a baby. Please don't worry about me.' I sniffed inelegantly. 'Why are you here?'

He put a bottle of wine on the table.

'I brought this to apologise,' he said. 'I was rude to you yesterday. I treated you without consideration, and I shouldn't have.'

'It's OK. Don't worry about it.' I wiped the traces of tears from my eyes. 'You didn't have to bring anything, but it's very kind of you.'

'It is one of our best wines,' he said.

'Thank you.'

'Are you sure you're all right?'

I nodded. 'A friend of mine died a few months ago. And someone seems to have his phone now. They called my number. It was a shock.'

'Oh,' he said. 'I am sorry for your loss. And a phone call . . . that would be hard. Who has the phone?'

'I don't know,' I replied. 'I was asleep when it rang and I didn't answer. There was no message.'

'It must be a friend. Or someone in the family. You will call them back, no?'

'Yes,' I said. 'But not now. I . . . I can't.'

'I will do it for you.' He held out his hand for the phone.

'No.' The word came more sharply from my lips than I'd intended. 'No,' I repeated less harshly. 'I don't want to call. It's not important. I don't need to speak to anyone.'

He was looking at me with a thoughtful expression and I wondered if he was still suspicious about me and my reasons for being here. But he'd apologised for being rude and he'd brought wine . . . I suddenly thought of Magda again and her prediction that a man would come some distance with a message. Would wine be considered a message – even if Luis had only come from the finca next door? I took a deep breath. I knew I was close to losing it.

'Are you sure you would not like me to make this call for you?' he asked.

'Certain,' I said. 'I was close to my friend. I don't need to talk to whoever has his phone, no matter who it might be.'

His dark eyes were puzzled. 'A friend of your friend would not also be a friend?'

'I don't know who the friend of my friend is,' I told him. 'I don't know . . . well . . . I only knew him. That's all. I don't want to talk to anyone else about him.' Very deliberately, I switched off the phone. 'I'm fine now,' I said firmly. 'And this doesn't matter.'

But of course it did.

Luis didn't stay long. He told me he'd drop by the next day if I liked, but I said that I was absolutely fine and there was no need. I said that I planned to be out all day.

'Where?' he asked.

My mind went blank as he waited for my reply.

'Valencia,' I said eventually.

'Valencia?'

'Yes.' I was speaking with more confidence now. 'Ana Perez invited me there, and I want to see the City of Arts and Sciences.'

Even as I spoke I realised that this was actually an excellent plan. Visiting a place dedicated to science and not airy-fairy thoughts would be good for me. Going there would be going to a place that would anchor me in my beliefs.

'Oh.'

'So I'll be fine,' I repeated.

'Call me if you need anything,' said Luis. 'I would be happy to help you, Juno.'

'I can manage,' I said. 'No need for you to worry about me.'

'What are you going to do for the rest of today?'

I hadn't thought much about it and blurted out that I'd be spending time in the garden. I'd finished painting, I said. Now it was time to turn my attention to outside the house. Plants needed to be cut back. Weeds needed to be killed. He didn't look convinced but he nodded and said goodbye.

When he was gone, I switched on the phone again. And my heart tumbled.

Because there'd been another call from Brad's number.

But still no message.

Chapter 24

I couldn't make myself call back. I wasn't prepared to talk to whoever was on the other end. I needed to keep busy. To do other things. I'd told Luis I was going to work on the garden, so that's what I would do.

My decision made, I switched off the phone again and went to investigate the shed for garden products.

There was a large shears but no weedkiller, so I got into the car and drove to Beniflor to buy some. But no matter how hard I tried to ignore it, my mind was firmly on the phone in my bag. Part of me wanted to leave it switched off, but I knew I couldn't do that forever. Yet I'd no idea how I'd feel – or what I'd do – if it rang again and I actually saw Brad's name on the screen.

Once I'd bought everything I needed, I put the weedkiller and plant food in the car and walked slowly to the plaza, where I sat at my usual table in the Café Flor.

Rosa, back to her cheerful self, took my order and then asked if I'd thought any more about Magda's predictions.

'Not really.' I didn't want to muddy the waters by talking about phone calls from a dead man. Back from the dead with a message is a long way to come, I thought suddenly, even though I knew I was being silly.

'I have a date tonight,' she told me, and I realised that she was more bubbly than usual. 'With an old friend.'

'Who?' I asked.

'His name is Tom Deasy,' she replied. 'His parents own the Irish pub in Beniflor Costa. I've known him for years, we went to school together.'

'And he just suddenly asked you out?'

'I bumped into him at the hotel last night.' Rosa and her parents lived in a small cottage in the grounds of La Higuera. 'He was having dinner with his family. And he went for a walk in the grounds at the same time as me. We got talking. And he asked me out. So Magda was right, you see. A new romance with someone I already know.'

'Well, maybe,' I said. 'It's just a date.'

'It's my first date since Pep Navarro,' she told me. 'I hear he's gone to Mallorca.'

The town grapevine worked quickly.

I nodded.

'Missing him?'

This time I shook my head.

'Really?' asked Rosa. 'Not even a little bit?'

I was too preoccupied to miss Pep. But I couldn't tell her that. So in the end I said that I was keeping myself busy at the house and hadn't had time to miss him. She gave me an unbelieving look, then went off to serve some other customers. I finished my coffee and left the money on the table.

When I got back to the Villa Naranja, I switched the phone

on once more. There were two messages from Pep, but nothing from Brad's number.

I released the breath I hadn't realised I'd been holding, and went for a swim.

I'd been expecting the phone to ring when I was in the pool, because that's how life usually works out, but it didn't. Nor did it ring while I sat in the shade and finished the book set in Andalucia. Feeling slightly demented, I checked my social media accounts – although, as Brad hadn't used social media, I've no idea why. In any event, they only contained the usual notifications about new postings by people I didn't really know that well. There was nothing from Saoirse or Cleo, either as a message to me or an update on their own statuses.

I might as well not have existed.

It was much later that night when I looked at my recent calls list again. It still contained all of Brad's to me and mine to him. We rarely phoned each other, preferring to text – although, given that he'd been having an affair with me, the texts were damning evidence against him. I felt a shiver as I thought again of whoever had his phone reading them. Could it have been one of the rescue workers who discovered it beneath the rubble? Or on Brad's body? Had they returned it to someone in his family? Or had it been found by someone who had no idea who owned it and had kept it for themselves?

No matter who had it, I still wondered how they'd unlocked it without erasing all his data. Unless, of course, it was a family member who already knew his PIN number. But Brad had been extremely protective of it. I certainly didn't know what it was. We'd talked once about the ridiculous quantity of passwords you had to have in modern life, and he'd said that he had one code that he used for his most important devices. When I'd asked what it was, he'd winked and told me it was a memorable number to him.

'You're always advised against using memorable numbers,' I warned him. 'Because somebody else might guess it.'

'Nobody would guess mine,' he said.

'Are you sure?'

'Positive.'

Despite Brad's certainty, I supposed someone might have unlocked his phone thanks to a monumentally lucky guess. Nevertheless, the most likely situation was that the new owner of the phone already knew it. Yet surely the only person who might have had any idea what it was was Alessandra.

Would Brad have deleted our explicit messages? Certainly, if she knew his PIN number, he would. Yet I remembered him scrolling through them with me, smiling at me, remembering receiving them. They were still on the phone. I knew they were. He hadn't deleted them, because he was confident that no one else would read them. But someone had. I shuddered to think of it being Alessandra. I couldn't imagine what she would feel. But, I reminded myself, she wouldn't be feeling anything, because she couldn't be the person reading them. After all, Alessandra, like Brad, was dead.

It was four in the morning. The house was still, and when I got up and opened the shutters, the full moon cast a silver light on the garden towards the jacaranda tree. In my mind I could see Pilar's great-grandfather being hauled from the house and hanged in that exact spot. I shivered, even though the warm air was like a blanket in the room.

Four in the morning in Spain was three in the morning in Dublin. It was a bad time to call anyone. But I didn't care. I dialled Brad's number.

The message was in Spanish. But I could guess what the automated voice was telling me. The number I'd dialled wasn't in service. Somehow, between the first time the call had been made to me and now, the phone had stopped working. So maybe whoever had cracked the PIN had wiped the data after all. Or maybe . . . maybe Brad's spirit had moved on and he wasn't able to access his phone any more.

I needed to stop thinking about spirits. There were none. Not of Brad. Not of Alessandra. Not of Pilar's great-grandparents. Not of anyone. The question of the phone was entirely practical. And, in a practical way, I would eventually work out who had it and how they'd accessed it. Not that it mattered to me at all.

I didn't go back to sleep. Instead, I made myself coffee (guaranteed to keep me awake, anyhow) and drank it at the stone table in the garden to the sound of the gentle rustle of the orange trees and the continued chirruping of the crickets.

Then I got into the car. I drove to Beniflor Costa, where the sky was beginning to brighten and the sea lapped gently on to the shore. It was just after six thirty when the sun rose over the Mediterranean, drenching the landscape in a vibrant rose-gold light. A flock of the flamingos who fed in the nearby salt lakes wheeled overhead in a flash of shocking pink. A solitary white cloud drifted across the horizon.

Another magical sunrise. Another day when the earth kept

turning. I knew that, globally, our current life expectancy is around seventy-one years. That's 25,915 days. 25,915 sunrises. Some of which might be as spectacularly beautiful as this morning's. Some of which would be hidden behind dark clouds and rain. No matter what was going on in the lives of the people below, the sun rose every single day. Brad had been nearly thirty-five when he died. So he was missing out on at least 13,000 sunrises and sunsets. I felt sad at the thought. But the sadness didn't grip me in the way it had before. It didn't nearly knock me over. It was a quiet sadness for someone who would never again experience the serenity of daybreak, or the rustle of a gentle breeze through the trees, or the awesomeness of a night sky. But I would. And that made me the lucky one.

I sat on the beach and watched as the sun continued its ascent and the town began to shake itself awake. As the last traces of pink and gold were replaced by another azure-blue sky, I got up and dusted the sand from my clothes. Then I drove back to the Villa Naranja.

The house, with its freshly painted shutters and newly tidied garden, looked serene in the morning sun, its turbulent past only vaguely remembered. The people who'd lived here had moved on too. Just as I had when I realised I would've left Brad McIntyre because he was married. My problem then had been that I hadn't got over my sense of loss. That was why the phantom phone call had been such a shock. But now, as I let myself into the house, I realised I'd got over that too. I remembered that life is about finding and losing and finding and losing, over and over again. I'd lost Sean and found Brad. I'd lost Brad and found Pep. And if – when – I lost Pep too, there would be someone else. Maybe not

Chapter 25

Because I'd told Luis I was going to Valencia, I decided that was exactly what I'd do. The coastal city was about an hour and a half away, and I reckoned it would be good for me to get in the car and drive. I'd always intended to go to its famous City of Arts and Sciences while I was in Spain. Constructed on the dry bed of the diverted river Túria, the complex contains a concert hall, a science exhibition centre and an enormous aquarium. The three main buildings, all glass and metal and surrounded by water, look like something from a sci-fi movie. In all honesty, their stark modernity is far more appealing to me than cute towns like Beniflor.

I reserved a ticket for the Prince Felipe Science Museum online, then set Jane, the satnav, to bring me to a nearby shopping centre with parking. I was fully confident in her ability to find it. What I was less confident in, I realised, was my own ability to arrive unscathed – whatever my driving skills on the motorway, the city traffic was unbelievably scary, and there were a few times when I was blasted out of my lane by an impatient Valenciano with no time for tourists in hire cars clogging up the streets. But eventually, nearly two hours after I set off, I parked the car in the El Saler Centre and made my way to the museum.

There were queues at the entrance but they weren't as long as the one I'd encountered at Alicante airport on the night I'd arrived, and I got to the desk without too much of a delay. After I'd collected my ticket, I asked the girl who'd served me if Ana Perez was around.

'Ana?' She looked at me curiously. 'You know her?'

'Yes,' I said. 'My name is Juno Ryan.'

She hesitated for a moment then made a phone call, stumbling a little over my name. She looked rather surprised as she hung up and told me that Ana would be down to see me shortly.

I stood to one side and waited for Pilar's mother to arrive. The reception area was a cool haven after the scorching sun outside, but I was hot and thirsty after the short walk from the commercial centre, and I bought myself a bottle of juice from a machine while I waited.

'Juno!'

I hadn't seen her arrive but she looked at me with an expression of surprise and pleasure. 'How are you? Why didn't you tell me you were coming sooner?'

'Because I only decided on the spur of the moment,' I admitted. 'I thought it would be a fun thing to do.'

'You are all right?' Her eyes scanned my face. 'There is no problem at the house?'

'Not at all,' I said. 'It just seemed a good idea to come here today. I didn't want to go home without having seen it.'

'Of course you shouldn't go without seeing it,' she agreed. 'And it will be my pleasure to show you around.'

'Oh, you don't have to do that!' I exclaimed. 'I just couldn't come without saying hello, that's all.'

'I cannot be with you the whole time,' she said. 'It can take a few hours to look at everything in the museum, but perhaps you would like to start with the science of the human body? And after that the electrical exhibition?'

She knew exactly the things that appealed to me most, I thought, as we began the tour. My own mother would have been bored after five minutes, but Ana Perez laughed and joked with me as I measured my body strength and tried to beat various agility tests designed to demonstrate the complexity of the human body.

When we got to the electrical exhibition she left me to my own devices. She had a meeting, she explained, but she could see me again in about an hour. She suggested a small café just outside the entrance to the museum as a meeting point, and when I nodded, she hurried away.

I stood in front of an experiment showing how alternating and direct currents work, and I thought of how powerful and frightening electricity must have seemed to people who were experiencing it for the first time. It would be almost supernatural. And, as I thought about my phone, still switched off in my bag, I reminded myself once again that there was nothing supernatural in our world, that there were simply phenomena we hadn't yet managed to explain.

The fact that I'd been up literally since the crack of dawn was beginning to tell, and by the time I met Ana again I was feeling tired. When she produced tickets for all of the different exhibitions, I felt myself tense up. I'd never manage to see them all in a day and get home. I'd fall asleep at the wheel of the car.

'You can stay with Alonso and me,' she said. 'Our apartment isn't very far.'

'I couldn't possibly,' I told her. 'You've been kind enough already – and besides, I didn't bring anything for an overnight stay.'

'Do not worry about that,' said Ana. 'I have a robe you can borrow. Besides, you've been more than kind to me. What about all the work to the house? It's amazing.'

I'd sent her photos of the painted rooms and she'd sent back ecstatic replies. Perhaps a little too ecstatic. She was just being very nice about it. But sitting in front of her now, I realised that she meant it, that she liked the facelift I'd given to the house.

'I couldn't have done it myself,' she admitted. 'It would have felt disrespectful to my mother.'

'Ana!' I stared at her, aghast. 'I thought you were OK with me doing it. You said it was all right to go ahead. I wouldn't have—'

'No, no,' she interrupted me. 'It had to be done. It was simply that I didn't have the heart to do it. I'm happy to let the house go, but I couldn't make the changes it needed. I realise that sounds silly.'

'I understand,' I said.

And I did.

I spent the rest of the day at the City of Arts and Sciences (although I fell asleep during the show at the Planetarium) and then retrieved my car and drove Ana home. Her husband hadn't yet arrived but she phoned him and told him to meet us at a nearby tapas bar, which he did. Alonso was a genial man in his fifties who, like Ana, spoke impeccable English.

While we picked at Serrano ham and prawns in garlic, he used the bar's Wi-Fi to FaceTime Pilar. I grinned and gave her the thumbs-up, telling her that I was loving her country and her city, and she said that she hoped to be home for a visit in September when the weather was cooler.

Then she and her parents spoke in Spanish while I sipped my glass of cold white wine and thought about my own mum – and realised, with a sense of guilt, that I hadn't spoken to her in a while. So I took my phone from my bag and switched it on.

One missed call. *Unknown Caller.* One message.

The noise of the bar and the chatter of Ana and her husband with Pilar receded into the distance. One missed call. One message. From an unknown caller. It could be from anyone, of course, but as I stared at the screen I knew it wasn't just anyone. I was certain it was the person who had Brad's phone. I wanted to listen to the message straight away but I couldn't, not here and now, surrounded by people. I stared at the notification and, even though I could feel the rapid beat of my heart, I very deliberately dismissed it.

Instead, I made my own video call to Mum. She was delighted to see me – and also to see Ana and Alonso, and know that there were people looking after me.

'I don't need looking after,' I told her. 'I can take care of myself. But,' I added before she could speak, 'it's lovely to have people I can count on here.'

'Be well, sweetheart,' she said. 'Your aura is still a bit shot. But at least you've got some colour in your cheeks.'

Then she ended the call and I resolutely switched off the phone again.

*　　*　　*

When we got back to the apartment I gave in to the absolute exhaustion that had come over me and (rather shamefacedly, because it wasn't even eleven) said that I had to go to bed. Ana made sure I had everything I needed and then I got between the sheets and, without switching on my phone again, immediately conked out.

I switched it on the following morning but still couldn't bring myself to listen to the message. I would wait until I got back to Beniflor, I decided. It would be easier to deal with it then. Although I would've liked to spend more time in Valencia, I was anxious about leaving Banquo. And so, after an early breakfast with Ana and Alonso, I set off. The sky was a crystal-clear blue, the air conditioning kept me cool, and I turned on the radio, which was preset to a cheery pop channel.

My heart was light when I finally turned into the rutted road that led to the Villa Naranja.

But even when I was sitting down having a glass of freshly squeezed orange juice, I still didn't listen to my voicemail. I was in my very own Schrödinger's Cat experiment, I thought. And I wasn't ready to choose the outcome.

The theoretical experiment is very simple. You put a cat and a vial of poisonous gas in a sealed box. At some point the vial containing the gas will break and the cat will be poisoned. But until you open the box and see the dead cat, you don't know if the event has happened. The cat is, according to Schrödinger, in the state of being both dead and alive. It's only when you look at its body and fix it in time and space that you seal its fate. Obviously Schrödinger never had a cat, because none that I knew, especially Banquo, would allow itself to be put in a box containing a vial of poisonous gas. The so-called scientist trying it would have been scratched to ribbons in seconds. But I understood the basis of the theory. Right now, the message on my phone was both trivial and important. But when I listened to it, it would be one or the other forever. And I didn't want to listen.

Not yet.

Nevertheless, I was ready when the phone rang that evening and *Unknown Caller* flashed up on the screen. I took a deep breath and answered it as confidently as I could.

'Hello. Who's there?'

There was a silence at the other end.

'Hello,' I said again. 'Who is this? Why are you calling me? What do you want?'

'Who are you?' he asked in return.

'Um . . . you rang me, not the other way around. So I think you should answer the question first.'

'You're listed as a contact on a phone I used recently,' said the man. 'Am I speaking to Ms Paycock?'

I caught my breath. Paycock had been Brad's nickname for me. Which, to anyone who doesn't know much about Irish theatre, might sound odd. But the explanation is simple. Like my brother and sister, who were named after an Irish poet and his muse, my name has artistic links. Mum had called me after the title character in a famous Irish playwright's most noted work *Juno and the Paycock*. Juno is a strong female figure and her husband, Jack, is the Paycock of the play. (The name is a very Dublin pronunciation of peacock, and he's so called because he struts around making a lot of noise but doing very little.) When Brad first gave me the nickname I'd protested loudly, but he'd laughed and said

255

he'd studied the Seán O'Casey play at school and the two names were completely linked in his mind.

'Juno and Paycock,' he said. 'It's like fish and chips.'

I'd thought it was funny at the time.

'How did you get that phone?' I didn't answer the caller's question. 'It wasn't yours. So how did you access it and its contacts? And who the hell are you?'

There was a brief silence before he replied.

'My name is Max Hollander.'

I frowned. It sounded vaguely familiar but I couldn't remember where on earth I'd heard it before.

'Why did you call?' I asked. 'Why do you keep calling?'

'I wanted to know who you were. Who Paycock was. What it means.'

When the phone had rung with Brad's ID, I'd felt as though I was in the middle of a ghost story. Now it seemed more like a spy thriller with some sinister, shady organisation. Paycock. Headed up by a woman who hadn't got a clue.

'Paycock isn't my name,' I said, even as I realised that Brad had used the nickname to avoid ever using my real one.

'The texts say that they come from Paycock.'

'You shouldn't have been looking at them,' I said. 'You're breaching someone else's privacy.'

'The phone belonged to my brother,' he said, and I immediately remembered where I'd seen and heard him before. On the TV when he'd thanked people for their concern. And at the funeral. The tall, slightly gaunt man who'd spoken so movingly about Brad and Alessandra. Who'd taken time to comfort me too. The brother I hadn't known existed. But if he was Brad's brother, why wasn't he a McIntyre?

'I need to talk to you.' He didn't answer my unspoken question. 'We have to meet.'

'I don't want to meet you,' I said. 'I don't need to.'

'Please,' said Max Hollander. 'It's important.'

At the funeral, when he'd spoken so briefly to me, I'd have given anything to have talked to him for longer. But things had changed. I didn't need to meet any of Brad's family now. I didn't want to.

'I'm away,' I told him. 'I can't meet anyone.'

'I knew that from the ringtone. How long are you away for? Where are you?'

I thought about not answering him, but in the end I told him I was in Spain for the summer.

'The Costa Blanca,' I added. 'So, really and truly, there's no chance of us meeting up. And I'd appreciate it if you didn't call me again. In fact,' I said, 'I'm going to block this number, so there's no point in you calling me any more.'

'I'll get the next flight I can and meet you.' He was ignoring me completely. 'I'll call again when I get there, so please don't block me. Just one meeting. It won't take long. Which airport should I fly into?'

'Alicante. But I really don't think—'

'I'll see you soon, Ms Paycock.'

I didn't have time to correct him again. He'd ended the call.

His arrogance infuriated me. I realised that he'd probably gone through a hard time since Brad and Alessandra's deaths, but what made him think he could talk to me like that? It would have served him right if I'd blocked the number there and then. He would have wasted his money coming to Spain without any hope of finding me. But he'd said that it was important to talk – and even though I knew there was nothing he could say that would matter in my life any more, I couldn't help wanting to know what he intended.

I went as far as scrolling down to the 'block contact' option before realising I was utterly unable to do it.

Then I waited for him to phone back.

It was three days later before he rang again.

In that time I'd stayed as busy as I could. I'd begun pruning the bougainvillea on the patio. It was hard work, and hot work too, so that I ended each day in a lather of sweat, utterly exhausted and unable to concentrate on anything.

The mystery of the phone had been solved – despite Brad's certainty over his PIN number, his brother had obviously been able to guess what it was. As always, the answers to the questions I had were based in fact, not some weird kind of spiritual fantasy. So I tried to keep my mind focused entirely on the facts, and not think of what Max Hollander might have to say to me. I deliberately pushed the idea of him reading my private texts to Brad to the very back of my mind. Instead, I exchanged flirty messages with Pep, who was still in Mallorca, and went each day to the Café Flor, where Rosa was in high spirits and cheerier than ever.

The call came in the early afternoon, and because the ringing of the phone startled me – despite knowing that eventually it would come – I managed to cut my arm on a particularly vicious thorn. A snaking line of blood made its way towards my wrist as I answered the call.

'I'm in Alicante,' Max said. 'Where are you?'

'I told you there was no point in coming to see me,' I told him.

'Where are you?' Once again he was completely ignoring anything I said. 'We can meet somewhere public, if you're worried.'

Strangely enough, I hadn't been worried – at least, not in the way that Max was implying. I wasn't frightened of meeting him in private. How could I be? After all, I'd already met him briefly at the funeral, where I'd got the impression of a quiet, thoughtful person. Certainly not someone to fear. Although, I thought, my ability to judge people was so crap it was entirely possible Max was an axe murderer. However, I would meet him and see what he had to say, and close the chapter of my life that had anything to do with him or with Brad. Maybe it would be a good thing. Maybe it would bring complete and utter closure to a time I now wanted nothing more than to forget.

'I'm in a town called Beniflor,' I said. 'North of the airport.'

'Is there somewhere to stay?' he asked.

'A hotel called La Higuera,' I replied. 'But it's small and usually booked up. There are hotels in the nearest seaside town called Beniflor Costa, and we're not that far from Benidorm itself, which has tons of them.'

For someone who didn't want him to come, I thought, I sounded like a bloody tour guide.

'I'll call you again when I get there,' said Max.

He hung up before me.

He was good at that.

I went to put some salve on my injured arm.

He called again a couple of hours later.

'I'm here,' he said. 'In that Higuera hotel.'

259

Clearly, it wasn't as exclusive as everyone said if Max had managed to get a room just like that.

'Will you meet me here in an hour?' His tone was pleasant but his voice was firm.

It occurred to me that I'd always done what Brad had asked, met him when he'd wanted, where he'd wanted. And now I was falling in with his brother's demands too. But I agreed.

'I'll be waiting for you at reception,' he said. 'I'm wearing a blue shirt.'

He didn't know that we'd already met. He didn't know I'd recognise him, no matter what he was wearing.

'An hour,' I said.

I put away my gardening equipment and had a shower. Afterwards, I spent ages trying to decide what to wear. I wanted to look serious and thoughtful, as unlike a seductive mistress as possible. Not that mistresses have to look seductive. Not that I'd realised I was one. Not that, until that very moment, I'd even thought of the word to describe myself.

But I hadn't brought any serious and thoughtful clothes. My wardrobe still consisted of T-shirts, shorts, sundresses and jeans. I hadn't worn the jeans since the day I'd arrived; it was far too hot to even think about it. Shorts seemed too carefree. And my dresses were light and flighty. I tried on every single stitch of clothing I had before eventually selecting a white blouse, which I tied loosely over the lavender sundress. The blouse made me appear a little more formal, and the dress itself was the most elegant of them all. I added earrings to my ears, a couple of pretty necklaces around my neck and a selection of bangles to my wrist.

By the time I'd finally got myself ready, forty-five minutes had passed and I hurried to the car in a panic about being late.

Despite Rosa having said how pretty it was, I'd never visited La Higuera before. Past the town, the hotel was set high up in the mountains, with a spectacular view over the valley and towards the sea. When I got out of the car I gasped out loud with the beauty of it all. The hotel building was like a small country mansion, painted in the creamy yellow that seemed to be a favoured colour of the region, and with the same dark-wood shutters on the windows that I'd spent so much time restoring at the Villa Naranja. The gravel path from the car park wound its way through a garden filled with colourful scented flowers before opening on to a tiled square at the entrance to the building. The fig tree, ancient and all-knowing, was in the centre of the square. The setting was peaceful and relaxing, and if I hadn't been anxious about meeting Max Hollander I would have sat down on one of the cane chairs artfully placed around the garden and simply gazed out over the sea.

But I didn't have time for taking in views. I walked up the three steps that led to the entrance. The glass doors opened automatically.

I stepped inside.

The reception area of La Higuera was cool and elegant, with a small fountain in the centre of the marbled tiles. Beyond that, further glass doors led to a terrace with tables and chairs. I wondered where Max Hollander had meant us to meet. The only other people in the reception area were a blonde woman sitting opposite the reception desk – which was actually a large modern table – and the receptionist, who were chatting animatedly to each other.

There were two other chairs set back from the fountain. I chose one of them and sat down to wait.

I'd barely settled myself when Max Hollander walked into reception. The last time I'd seen him he'd been wearing a suitably funereal black suit and tie. Today his blue shirt was casual over a pair of pale linen trousers, but I recognised him instantly. He saw me too, and looked at me with a slightly puzzled expression.

'Ms Paycock,' he said.

I didn't bother to correct him about my name again.

'I've reserved a table for us outside,' he said. 'We can't talk privately here.'

I nodded and followed him through to the terrace, where we were shown to a table at one corner, overlooking more gardens, the swimming pool and the distant sea. It was very beautiful and also very hot. The waiter raised a red parasol over the table and then asked what we'd like to drink.

'Water,' I said, and then, to Max, 'I wasn't planning on eating anything.'

'Me neither,' said Max. 'I just reserved the table so we could talk. But,' he added to the waiter after he'd ordered a beer, 'you could bring some nuts, perhaps. Or olives.'

The waiter nodded and disappeared back inside.

I exhaled slowly.

'So.' Max looked at me speculatively from solemn grey eyes. 'What was the relationship between you and my brother, Ms Paycock?'

'First of all, as I told you on the phone, my name isn't Paycock. So please stop calling me that. It's Juno. Juno Ryan. And before we talk about anything else, how is Dylan?'

He looked startled at my question.

'The news reports said he was seriously injured but not critical,' I said.

'He's improving,' replied Max. 'Not that it's really any of your concern.'

'If you didn't want me to ask questions then you shouldn't have come here.' I kept my voice as steady as I could.

He looked startled again, then frowned.

'Why are you called Paycock on Brad's mobile?' he asked.

'How did you get hold of it?' I asked in return.

'There was an accident,' said Max.

I stared at him.

'I know about the accident, for heaven's sake,' I said. 'That's why I asked about Dylan. And I was at the funeral.'

'Of course!' Max exhaled slowly. 'I knew I'd seen you before. I just couldn't place you. You look different now.'

'Did you come all the way here because you were afraid I didn't know?' I asked. 'Is that what was so bloody important?'

'Partly,' he said. 'I guessed, of course, because there hadn't been any more messages from you, but I couldn't be certain.'

I relaxed a little too.

'But I also came because of the messages,' said Max. 'They were disturbing.'

'Disturbing?'

He took the phone out of his pocket and looked at it.

'I dream about you naked,' he read. 'I dream about being beside you. About moving my hand—'

'OK. OK,' I interrupted. 'I know what I wrote. And there's nothing disturbing about it. Not for two people in a relationship.'

'What kind of relationship did you have with him?' he asked. 'Was he paying you?'

'You think I'm a prostitute!' My words came out louder than I'd intended, and I glanced around, afraid some of the other guests might have heard me. But they were all engrossed in their own conversations. 'You think I'm a prostitute,' I repeated. 'How bloody dare you!'

'I don't know what to think,' he said.

I tried to keep my voice steady. 'Like I said, Brad and I were in a relationship.'

'My brother was already in a relationship,' said Max. 'He was married.'

'I know.' I took a sip of the water. 'I know now. I didn't know then.'

He stared at me.

'You think I'm lying?' I asked. 'Why would I lie?'

'Why does anyone lie?' he asked.

'Why did Brad?'

'What exactly did he lie about?'

'What didn't he lie about?' I retorted.

And then, fool that I was, I started to cry.

Max Hollander said nothing as he offered me one of the paper napkins on the table to dry my eyes. I pressed it against my face, hiding myself from him. I hadn't wanted to cry. I hadn't wanted to let myself down.

'Please stop,' he said after a couple of minutes. 'Can I get you something else to drink? A brandy perhaps?'

I shook my head, mopped my eyes again, sniffed and finally scrunched up the napkin.

Max poured me some more water.

'I'd like to know,' he said. 'About you and my brother.'

'He can't actually be your brother,' I said. 'Different surnames.'

'We're stepbrothers,' he told me. 'Brad's father married my mother. His parents were divorced when he was about four. My dad died shortly after I was born.'

'I'm so sorry,' I said.

'No need.' He shrugged. 'Obviously, it would have been nice to know him. But I don't remember him, so it doesn't hurt me. As far as I'm concerned, the man who raised me, Brad's dad, was my own dad too. And Brad and I were as close as any brothers could be.'

'You said . . .' I frowned as I tried to remember, '. . . you said at the funeral that you were about five when you first met him.'

'Yes, I was. Why did you come to the funeral?'

'I had to,' I said. 'I had to see for myself.'

'That he was dead?' Max's expression was troubled.

'Why are you here?' I asked without replying. 'It surely isn't because of a few explicit texts. And you can't really have cared what sort of woman I was.'

'I had to see who you were,' said Max. 'And why my brother sent those messages to you. I wanted to know what the hell was going on. I thought he was in love with Allie.'

Once again, my stomach contracted as I thought of anyone scrolling through our private texts. Max Hollander had no right to have done that. But I supposed that having read one, it would be hard to stop.

'I had to see who it was who'd caused him to put his whole life in jeopardy,' Max continued. 'I wanted to know what sort of person had made him do it.'

'It hardly matters, does it?' I shrugged. 'Your opinion of me is irrelevant – not that it was very high to start with, obviously. Nothing will change the fact that Brad is dead.

And you had his phone. Did you know his PIN number? He told me nobody did.'

'I guessed,' said Max.

'So he was wrong when he said nobody would ever guess it.'

'First attempt,' Max said. 'It was the date we met. Impossible for anyone else to know, but we used it for accessing our computer games and stuff like that.'

Brad had been closer to Max than anyone. Even Alessandra. And me.

'When did you start your relationship with him?' asked Max. 'And why?'

I took a sip of my water as I looked at my lover's brother. Stepbrother, I reminded myself. They'd been brought up together but they weren't blood relations. And yet there was something of Brad in Max, and something of Max in Brad. It was the way they both had of looking at you from those solemn eyes. I'd sometimes told Brad that he was X-raying me with them, and he'd laughed. But I'd meant it. His gaze seemed to see right through me. Max's was exactly the same. Grey eyes, not blue, but with an identical expression.

'I didn't know,' I said.

I wasn't sure that I wanted to talk to Max Hollander about his brother. And yet that quiet, watchful look of his meant I couldn't stay silent.

'I didn't know he was married. I didn't know about Alessandra. I didn't know about Dylan. And I didn't know about you.' Having started, my words tumbled over each other. 'I thought he loved me. I thought I loved him. I thought it was forever.'

'Bloody hell,' said Max.

And then I started to cry again.

He thrust another of the napkins at me without saying a word. I pressed it against my hot eyes and allowed the tears to be soaked up. Max stayed silent. He was probably looking at me in the horrified way men look at women when they start to cry. I didn't know if he was mortified to be in my company. I didn't know if he was still sitting opposite me – maybe, I thought, as the tears still fell, maybe he'd got up and walked away, regretting that he'd wasted his money by coming here in the first place. And I didn't care if he had. I hadn't wanted him to come.

But when I eventually removed the now sodden napkin, he was still sitting there, still watching me.

'Are you OK?' he asked.

'I'm sitting with the brother of the dead man I had an affair with,' I said. 'OK isn't quite the appropriate word.'

'I guess not,' said Max.

'How come his phone is still working?' I asked abruptly. 'Surely once he died the contract would've ended.'

'His phone was owned by the company he set up,' said Max. 'The one that owned his business shares. It kept paying the bill.'

I don't know why something so trivial had bugged me.

'Tell me about him.' I balled the napkin up and dropped it on to the table. 'Tell me about him and Alessandra and Dylan, and why the actual *fuck* he decided to cheat on them with me.'

'Brad was a great brother,' said Max slowly. 'He was compassionate and generous and loving. And being a couple of years older than me, he looked out for me and I looked up to him. Our respective parents were worried that we might not get on. You know, two boys suddenly having to be part of the one family. But even though we were different in lots of ways, we . . . well, I suppose we bonded, really.'

'At the funeral you said he mended your teddy bear.'

Max smiled.

'Bloo Ted,' he said. 'He came with me everywhere but he was losing his stuffing as well as missing an eye. Brad was only seven then, but he could sew. I would've thought it was a really sissy thing for a boy, except he did such a good job on my teddy.'

'Do you still have it?' I don't know why I asked the question. It wasn't relevant.

'No,' said Max. 'We moved house a couple of times, and in one of those moves Bloo Ted went AWOL. But he was only a teddy bear. I got over it.'

I smiled briefly.

'The thing about Brad was that he was kind. And he had charisma,' Max continued. 'Everyone liked him. He was good at sports, so he got on well with the guys. He was good-looking, so the girls fancied him. He had it made, really.'

'Alessandra?' I asked.

'He met her at a party,' said Max. 'She was smitten straight away.'

'And they got married?'

He nodded, suddenly more reticent.

'What?' I asked. 'What's the issue with Alessandra?'

'No issue,' said Max. 'She came to the party with me, that's all.'

'He pinched your girlfriend!' Had Brad been a serial womaniser? I wondered. Always moving on to someone new, no matter who she was.

'Not exactly,' admitted Max. 'It wasn't a date. I'd worked with Alessandra on a children's health project – I work in corporate branding, and my company specialises in helping not-for-profit organisations get their message across. So I asked if she'd like to come along with me that night, and she said yes. But not a date. Really not.'

'And she met Brad on your not-a-date?'

He nodded. 'Of course, they had lots in common with the whole health thing. So they got talking and stayed talking, and that was pretty much that.'

'You must have been pissed off with him.'

'Why?' asked Max. 'Like I said, she wasn't my girlfriend. And it was inevitable. Girls fell for him all the time. It would have been a surprise if she hadn't.'

I took another sip of water. It seemed that I'd been the notch on his bedpost, after all.

'Thing is,' Max said, 'he was really in love with Alessandra in a way that he hadn't been with anyone before. He made all the running.'

'I thought you said she was smitten?'

'Smitten but smart,' said Max. 'She didn't drop everything to be with him. She led him a bit of a dance. He couldn't wait to marry her.'

'And then when he married her, he reverted back to his playboy self?'

Max made a face. 'He wasn't a playboy. Not really. He just liked women.'

'Oh, please.'

'He loved Alessandra,' said Max. 'He really did. And he adored Dylan.'

'And yet he was shagging me.'

269

'Which is what I can't understand.'

'Neither can I,' I said grimly. 'She was so much more beautiful.'

'You're pretty enough.' Max damned my average looks with faint praise. 'I can see why he was attracted to you. But—'

'But I was just an affair,' I said. 'I meant nothing to him.'

'That's the thing,' said Max. 'I can't believe he would've put his family at risk for you.'

'Yet you're here.'

'Because he sent me a text too,' Max said.

'What? When?'

'The day he died.'

'What did it say?'

Max tapped the screen and showed it to me.

Hey Bro, Brad had written. *Need to talk when I get back. Seem to have dug myself a hole and jumped into it. Making a mess of my life. Not sure what to do. Advice?*

I stared at it. Brad had been troubled about something. He needed advice. Was it me? Had he wanted to talk to his brother about our relationship? Because it mattered to him? Enough to do what Max said he wouldn't, and risk his family? Or had Alessandra found out? Had she been issuing ultimatums? Was he afraid of being thrown out of the house, of losing her, losing his son and losing his unborn baby?

'I didn't see the message when he sent it,' Max told me. 'I was out, and when I got home all hell had broken loose because of the earthquake. So when I replied, asking if he was OK, it was about that, not his original message.'

'And, of course, he wasn't OK,' I said.

270

'No,' said Max. 'There was a suggestion that he was outside when the earthquake struck and that he ran back towards the house.'

'To save them,' I said.

He nodded.

'I wouldn't have expected him to do anything else,' I said.

'Alessandra was killed instantly,' Max told me. 'She was protecting Dylan. He was lucky because, although he had some internal injuries, they got to him quickly. Other than that, the worst of the damage was a broken arm and a pretty big bump to the head. Brad was hit by a falling beam. If he'd lived, he would have been paralysed.'

I could see it. The shuddering movement of the earth, the collapsing house and the clouds of dust. And I could hear the screams too, of Alessandra and Dylan and Brad. It was more real than the news reports had been. More visceral. And more shocking.

'Are you all right?' asked Max.

I wasn't.

I got up from the table and hurried to the Ladies, where I was sick in the first cubicle.

Max Hollander was still sitting at the table when I returned, having splashed water on my face and brushed my hair. I knew I looked awful.

'Everything OK?' He looked at me with concern.

'It will be.'

'I'm sorry,' he said. 'I truly didn't want to upset you, but it was important for me to come and see you, and to know what was going on in my brother's life. I needed to do it for Dylan's sake, as much as anything.'

I stared at him. 'You think that I would've made myself known to the family for some reason? To Dylan, who's only a child? Why on earth would I? Besides, if I'd wanted to contact them, I would've done it at the funeral.'

'I didn't know,' said Max. 'I didn't know the extent of Brad's relationship with you. I guessed the name was some kind of joke, but I didn't know the sort of person you were or what you thought your situation might be in the future. I didn't know what sort of hole he thought he'd dug for himself or what he was planning to ask my advice about. I needed to check for myself.'

'And now you do?'

'I think you're a good person,' said Max. 'I'm sorry for thinking the worst of you, and I'm very sorry that my brother—'

'Lied to me,' I said. 'That's what hurts the most, you know. When I realised he was dead, I felt a part of me had died too. But hearing about his wife and child on a TV news report was like someone having hit me over the head. I couldn't believe it. I thought it was a mistake.'

'I'm sorry,' he said again.

'Part of the reason I went to the funeral was to see if I could find out why,' I said. 'Not by questioning people, or anything like that – I just thought I might get an impression of his life with her. I thought perhaps they'd been living apart. But it seemed to be perfect.'

'I thought it was too,' said Max. 'I know she wasn't entirely happy about his involvement with the Dublin clinic, because it took him away from home so much, but—' He stopped suddenly and stared at me. 'Or was he with you? When he

272

told Alessandra he had a meeting at the clinic, was it really to see you?'

'How should I know!' I cried. 'I didn't know he was carrying on a bloody secret life.'

'Of course you didn't.' Max sighed. 'I have to keep apologising to you.'

'You're not the one who should be apologising,' I said. 'It's him. But he can't.' I rubbed my eyes. 'Anyway, the bottom line is that you can rest assured that I won't suddenly turn up trying to . . . well, I don't know what you thought I might do, but I won't be doing it.'

'I don't know what I thought, either,' admitted Max. 'I was worried about Dylan, you see. I'm his guardian and I wanted to do what was best for him. I wanted to make sure he was protected.'

'Is he out of hospital yet?' I asked.

'He came home two weeks ago,' said Max. 'He's doing surprisingly well. It's amazing how physically resilient children are. There may be a need for some minor plastic surgery to his face later, but he's healing fast.'

'How is he otherwise?'

'Still quiet and withdrawn,' Max replied. 'We're doing our best with him, and he's had some counselling, but it's an ongoing process. He's living with my parents at the moment, although that will only be a temporary measure. Alessandra has a cousin who has offered to take him, but she's in Italy and . . . well, I don't know yet what's best. Her parents would have loved to have him, but her mother has MS and Dylan would be too much for her.'

'The poor woman!' I cried. 'Her daughter killed, her

grandson badly injured, and she's got that to deal with too. Why is life so bloody shitty sometimes?'

Max didn't answer. He unlocked his phone and opened the photo app.

'This is Dylan in hospital in Italy.'

I grimaced as I looked at the little boy amid the plaster cast and the tubes and all the paraphernalia of trauma injuries.

'And this is when he came out.' Max scrolled to another photo.

It was clearer than the one they'd used on the TV news. Dressed in his proper clothes and with the cast removed, Brad and Alessandra's son was a good-looking boy. His dark hair had been shaved at the side of his head where he'd sustained the trauma injury, and there were still shadows under his eyes, but I could see both Brad's easy charm and Alessandra's Italian beauty in his face.

'I hope he'll do well,' I said as I returned the phone.

'I hope I don't mess it all up,' said Max. 'I have with you, I think. I honestly didn't mean to offend you.'

'I'm not offended.' I gave him a wry smile.

'Can I ask how you and Brad met?' He signalled the waiter and ordered another glass of beer for himself. He gave me an inquiring look and I asked for coffee. Then I told him about meeting Brad at the conference and how he'd seen me at the concert and how we'd clicked straight away.

'He wasn't wearing a wedding ring,' I said. 'I couldn't have guessed.'

'He didn't,' said Max. 'He was allergic to nickel. Even though he bought a platinum wedding ring, he wasn't used to having anything on his finger and it irritated him. He only wore it when they went out together.'

'Maybe he was lonely,' I suggested. 'After all, when I first met him he was in Dublin for work. And he did visit the clinic a lot.'

'I guess we'll never know,' said Max. 'Which is frustrating.'

'I'm sorry,' I said. 'You have your own grieving to do and it's got mixed up with me.'

'Oh, Brad never did things in a straightforward way,' said Max. 'He was always . . .' He sighed. 'I loved him, you know.'

I wanted to say that I loved him too, but I wasn't going to. Because I'd been an insignificant part of his life and because I knew that, no matter what I'd gone through, it had been a thousand times worse for Brad's close family. Including Max.

'You loved him,' he said suddenly. 'I can see that.'

'It doesn't matter how I felt.'

'It does, you know.'

'I've worked hard over the last while to get over him,' I told Max. 'I'd put him out of my mind.'

'And I'm making you remember,' he said.

'Maybe it's good for me to talk it over one more time,' I said. 'With someone who knew him. But I've got to the acceptance stage. Now I'm trying to move on.'

'The acceptance stage?'

I explained about the five stages of grief, and he nodded.

'Is that why you're here in Spain?' he asked.

'Sort of.' I mentioned Pilar's offer of the Villa Naranja and my decision to take it.

'It's a beautiful area,' he said as he glanced around at the vine-clad mountains.

'I'll be home soon,' I said. 'Coming here was an indulgence,

275

really. I can't afford not to work – and besides, I like being a radiographer.'

'It's good to do something else from time to time,' said Max.

'Was Alessandra pregnant?' I asked the question suddenly.

Max looked startled. 'How . . . ?'

'They said so at the funeral,' I told him.

'Who?'

'Some women standing nearby.'

'How the hell would they know about that?'

I shrugged.

'Yes,' he said.

I felt sick again. Somewhere, in the back of my head, I'd been hoping that Brad and Alessandra hadn't been sleeping together. That their marriage had been a sham. But that wasn't true. He'd cheated on both of us. And that was why he'd needed advice from his brother.

'How can someone who was so good have been so . . . so . . . so damn . . .' I couldn't finish the sentence. Max said nothing but I saw him eyeing up the napkins again. He was ready for a torrent of tears. I wasn't going to give them to him.

Neither of us spoke for at least five minutes. I allowed my churning emotions to settle, then I took a deep breath and looked at him as evenly as I could.

'Are you staying here for long?' I asked.

'Juno . . .' He reached across the table and covered my hand with his. I flinched but he kept his hand where it was. 'I'm truly, truly sorry,' he said. 'You need time and space, and I haven't given it to you.'

'I've had plenty of time and space.' I slid my hand away.

'I'm a bit shaken up by revisiting everything, but please don't worry about me. You should be giving all your time to your family.'

'He had feelings for you,' said Max. 'That's pretty clear.'

'He wasn't entitled to have feelings for me.' I could hear the steel in my own voice. 'He had a pregnant wife, and a son. They were the people he should have had feelings for.'

Max nodded.

'So,' I said, after another silence. 'To get back to my question. Are you staying long?'

'The weekend.' His tone was light again, as though we were casual friends and hadn't been speaking of anything more taxing than our plans for the next few days. 'The hotel would only take a reservation for a minimum of two nights.'

'I was surprised you got one at all.'

'Lucky, I guess.' He glanced around the terrace.

All the tables were full now, although it was the guests from overseas who were eating proper meals while the Spanish themselves were, like us, snacking on peanuts and olives.

'They don't eat much before nine,' I said when he remarked on this. 'It's too hot.'

'Would you like something to eat yourself?' asked Max.

I shook my head.

'I've succumbed to the timetable,' I said. 'I hardly ever eat before nine, either. Mostly I just graze. Anyhow, I'm not hungry.'

'Perhaps tomorrow?' He looked at me inquiringly. 'Lunch perhaps? I feel as though . . . well, I've come all this way to confront you and you're not the evil scheming bitch I'd half expected you to be. I need to apologise.'

'You think lunch will make me feel better?' I shook my head.

'Of course not. But . . . I'd like to . . . I feel I should . . .'

I couldn't have lunch with Brad's brother. It would be too hard. And too . . . too weird. But Max was looking at me with his solemn gaze, so like Brad's and yet so different, and I suddenly found myself nodding slowly.

'We could go to Beniflor Costa,' I said.

'Whatever you think.'

'It'll have a nice sea breeze.'

'OK.'

'I'll pick you up,' I told him.

'Oh, no. I'll drive,' he said. 'I can't possibly expect you to—'

'Why not?' I asked. 'I'm the one who's living here, after all.'

'Maybe. But it seems . . . I'd like to drive you. To be the one taking you to lunch.'

'You'd have to find the Villa Naranja,' I reminded him. 'Which isn't an easy task on an empty stomach.'

He laughed, and suddenly his eyes lightened and his face seemed ten years younger.

'I'm good at directions.'

'In that case . . .' I took a pen from my bag and sketched them out on one of the napkins.

'What time?' he asked.

'The Spanish usually eat around two p.m.,' I told him. 'But we'll never get a table if we wait till then. So if you get to me around twelve thirty, we can be in Beniflor Costa before one.'

'Whatever you say. You have my phone number, just in case.'

I saved his name against the Unknown Caller, then stood up.

So did he.

'Thank you for coming,' he said.

'I'll see you tomorrow.'

He held out his hand and shook mine. I'd almost moved forward for the casual cheek-to-cheek kisses that all the Spanish people took for granted. But this was different. Very different.

And then I walked through the hotel and drove home.

Chapter 26

Even though meeting Max Hollander had been traumatic, I was feeling a lot calmer by the time I returned to the house. Banquo greeted me with a gentle headbutt and followed me inside, where I got my priorities straight by taking the dried food out of the cupboard and refilling his bowl before pouring myself a glass of crisp Navarro white.

I was getting used to sitting on the patio with my glass of wine in the evenings. And it occurred to me, as I sat there once again, that there was an unrivalled peacefulness to the Villa Naranja that I'd miss back in Dublin. Despite my somewhat manic insistence on doing up the house and garden, I'd also learned to sit still as dusk fell, and to be comfortable in my own company. I'd never been able to do that before. I'd always had to have the TV on, or tap away at my iPad, or go out and meet people. But now I was accustomed to being on my own, doing nothing, calmed by the chirping of the crickets and Banquo's purrs as he lay across my feet.

My iPhone pinged with a WhatsApp from Pep. He said that he had nearly finished the work for his aunt and hoped to be back in Beniflor in a day or two. I sent him a happy-faced emoji in reply. And he sent one of two hearts to me.

I looked at it for a long time before sending the same to him in return.

Max arrived at exactly twelve thirty p.m. the following day. He rang the bell at the gates and I walked out to open them with the fob. He drove in and parked alongside the house.

'It's beautiful,' he said as he got out of the car and looked around. 'When you said you were staying in a villa, I never imagined anything like this.'

I glowed with a proprietorial pride. After all of my work, both inside and out, the Villa Naranja had lost its air of benign neglect and was looking more like a cared-for home. I was tempted to give him the villa's history, but he was holding the passenger door open for me so instead I just got into the car.

Max was a careful but competent driver as he followed my instructions to the coast, and when we pulled up outside the restaurant that Ana Perez had brought me to a couple of weeks earlier he parked the car in a tight space with practised ease.

Brad had hated driving, even though he practically commuted from Belfast to Dublin.

'It's stressful,' he'd said. 'And a waste of time. I'd much rather take the train and do something useful while I'm on the move.'

But then he was the sort of man who didn't waste a minute. He liked to pack things in. Including a wife and a mistress.

I hadn't made a reservation at the restaurant and panicked when I saw that it was already busy, but Iker, the owner, remembered me and smiled in welcome.

'You came with Ana,' he said. 'You're staying at Doña Carmen's house.'

It always amused me how everyone in Beniflor knew the house by the older woman's name. Somehow, Ana's mother – Pilar's grandmother – had left her mark on it, and that was how it was remembered. Not as the Perez house. Not as the Villa Naranja. But as Doña Carmen's.

'I have a good table for you,' Iker told us. 'Not the best but good.'

It was the last available table on the deck.

'Stunning,' said Max as we sat down facing the azure-blue sea. 'Really stunning.'

A young waiter brought us a large jug of iced water and Max asked if we could have some tapas. 'When in Spain,' he added. I suggested more or less the same as I'd had with Ana, although without the mussels. When I mentioned them, Max made a face and said they weren't exactly his thing. But he urged me to order them if I wanted, and I grinned and said that I was just trying to appear sophisticated about it but they weren't exactly my thing, either.

'This is living the dream,' he said as he helped himself instead to a slice of wafer-thin Serrano ham. 'What more could you ask for than good food in a stunning location?'

I said nothing.

'Oh God.' He grimaced. 'That was bloody insensitive. This isn't what you dreamed of at all, was it?'

'Not really,' I said. 'But . . . well, if I had to have a hide-away, Beniflor is certainly an excellent one.'

After that stumbling block our conversation flowed more easily. We became comfortable in each other's company, while keeping to topics that were safe – summer holidays, books we'd read and movies we'd seen.

'I prefer theatre to the movies,' Max remarked as the waiter brought us coffee. 'I like being close to the actors. But I'm also intrigued by everything that goes on offstage.'

'Me, too!' I looked at him in surprise. 'My mum despairs of me when I say that. She wants me to be lost in the world. Yet I get too distracted.'

'Is your mum a theatregoer, then?' he asked.

'She . . .' I hesitated. I rarely told people who Mum was. It always felt a bit boasty to talk about her, as though I was trying to bask in her reflected glory.

Max was looking at me expectantly.

'She's an actress,' I said. 'She did a lot of theatre work.'

'How exciting. Would I know her?'

'Her name is Thea Ryan.'

His eyes widened. 'Thea Ryan who played Lady Macbeth at the Abbey?' he asked, with an almost reverential hush to his voice. 'The Thea Ryan who won an award for her Lady Bracknell, and who gave an outstanding performance as Masha in *Three Sisters*?'

'That's Mum.' I nodded.

'She's amazing,' he said. 'Such a great presence onstage.'

'She'd be delighted to hear that,' I said.

'Is she working now?' he asked.

I told him about *Clarendon Park,* and then added that Mum would also be playing Lady Bracknell again soon.

'I'll definitely go and see that,' he said. 'As for *Clarendon Park*, I've heard of it but never watched it. I must tune in.'

'It's just a soap,' I reminded him. 'Not Chekhov.'

He laughed. 'I bet she's great anyway. And you have no desire to be onstage yourself?'

I shook my head. 'I'm a radiographer. I don't have an artistic bone in my body. No imagination, either.'

'That's not true,' he said. 'From what you've said you're single-handedly renovating the villa, and it looks fantastic – so that's artistic, in a way. And having a scientific background doesn't mean a lack of imagination. Far from it. Brad always said you had to think intuitively to work in medicine.'

'Intuition isn't imagination,' I pointed out.

'Of course it is,' he said. 'It's seeing things another way, and if that isn't imagination, I don't know what is.'

I looked at him in an almost stunned silence as the image of Magda Burnaia turning over the tarot card to reveal the tower being struck by lightning flashed in front of me. My entire relationship with my family had been built on their shared creative imaginations and my utter lack of one. My inadequacies as a daughter and a sister, as one of the artistic Ryans, all stemmed from the fact that I lived in a world very different to theirs, a world I would never be able to share. Yet Max Hollander had changed all that in a single sentence.

'Are you OK?' he asked when I didn't speak

'Yes . . . Yes. You just turned a lifetime of belief on its head, that's all.'

'And is that good or bad?'

'Good.' I smiled. 'Really good.'

And it was. Crazy as it sounds, I suddenly felt a connection with my parents and my brother and sister that I'd never had before. I wasn't imaginative. I wasn't creative. But I was intuitive, and that tapped into the same stuff. I was one of them, after all.

Unaware of the profound impact he'd had, Max started talking again, this time about the kind of work he did for the various clients of his company. To my surprise I recognised some of the names he spoke about.

'Do you work entirely with charities?' I asked.

'A not-for-profit isn't necessarily a charity,' he replied. 'Some of the organisations are state-funded bodies. And there are times I don't necessarily agree with their message. But mostly I do, and they're great clients to have.'

'So you're creative too,' I said. 'I always thought that being an artist was more noble than being a practical person. But today you're making me realise that the line between the two can be blurred. And that practical can have creative outcomes too.'

'Now I've got you talking in corporate-speak,' he said.

I laughed. 'Never!'

We ordered more coffee as we continued chatting, and then I realised that the restaurant was almost empty and only one other table was occupied.

'We'd better go,' I said.

Max waved for the bill and refused my attempt to split it, reminding me that he'd offered to take me to lunch. Then he drove back to the Villa Naranja.

'It really is picture-postcard perfect,' he said, as we sat outside the villa in the air-conditioned comfort of his hire car. 'Eternally traditional.'

'Would you like to have a look around?' I asked.

'If you don't mind.'

'Of course not.'

He switched off the engine.

Banquo came rushing through the orange trees and skidded to a stop in front of me. His slanted eyes looked between me and Max, then he languidly lifted a leg and started washing himself.

'Oh, please!' I cried. 'We've got visitors, Banquo. Be nice.'

'You're a child of the theatre, after all,' said Max. 'I don't know many cats named after a literary ghost.'

'It seemed apt,' I said. 'When I first came here I thought the house . . . well, I didn't think it was haunted exactly, but it was certainly spooky.' I explained how Banquo's nocturnal visits had scared me witless.

Max laughed.

'That's not very caring of you,' I remarked. 'I could've died of fright.'

'I can't see it, somehow,' said Max.

'That's because you haven't heard about the execution,' I said.

He looked at me, and I grinned. Then I led him to the sundial beneath the jacaranda tree and told him the story of Ana's grandfather.

'My God,' he said as he inspected the flagstone. 'That's chilling.'

'Obviously, I don't believe in ghosts or spirits,' I said. 'But I guess there might be a . . . a resonance still here. Although less so now that I've taken the house in hand.'

The two of us looked back at the Villa Naranja, majestic in the afternoon sun.

'I don't believe in them either,' said Max. 'But I can understand the need to connect with someone who's gone. I didn't feel that way about my dad, because I grew up without him. But it's taking time to accept that I'll never see Brad again.'

I remembered resenting the grief that Brad's family had been allowed to show. I was ashamed of myself.

'Can I see inside?' asked Max.

I hadn't intended to show him the interior of the Villa Naranja. But I nodded. 'Of course.'

I felt an enormous sense of pride as I stepped through the door. The downstairs interior walls were now white, with an almost imperceptible hint of blue, which made the space look bigger and brighter. I'd rummaged around in the airing cupboard and found a linen tablecloth with midnight-blue embroidery, which I'd ironed and put on the pine dining table. I'd also found a glass vase and filled it with flowers that I'd bought at the Beniflor market. The blue and white echoed the tiles in the kitchen and linked the two rooms far more effectively than before. Meanwhile, I'd bought some inexpensive white throws, which I'd placed over the armchairs and the living-room sofas, and added a couple of bright-blue cushions.

'This is lovely,' said Max. 'Really pretty.'

'I was trying to reflect the white walls and blue roof tiles that are typical of this area,' I explained. 'It doesn't entirely gel with the terracotta floors, but I didn't think Ana would be too keen on ripping them out.'

'You're sure you're a radiographer and not an interior designer?' he asked.

'It's just a lick of paint,' I said. 'But it does make a difference. You should've seen it before.'

'Have you done everywhere?' he asked.

'This is as far as I've got. Upstairs is still the way it was. You can take a look, if you like.'

We went up and I brought him into one of the unused bedrooms. It looked gloomy and unwelcoming after the brightness downstairs.

'It's sort of authentic, I suppose,' said Max. 'In a trapped-in-the-seventies kind of way.'

'But that's not a way most people want,' I said. 'When the family moved out they took their main pieces of furniture with them, and they didn't bother upgrading because they reckoned it didn't matter for rentals. They're wrong, though. Most people want to stay in a beautiful place with decent facilities and furniture.'

He nodded.

'But you can access the balcony from the bedrooms, and there's also a magnificent bathroom.'

I opened the French door that led to the balcony, and he exclaimed in delight at the mountain view.

'The problem, according to Ana, is that most people want views of the sea,' I explained. 'That's partly why she's had trouble selling it.'

'If she upgraded the bedrooms, like you've done downstairs, I bet she'd have no trouble,' declared Max. 'Can I see the bathroom?'

I recounted the exploits of the leaking roof as we went back inside – although, obviously, I omitted to mention that the night had ended up with me and Pep Navarro in bed together. Max was enthusiastic about the big bathroom and, like me, was taken with the novelty of being able to look across towards the town as you showered. He stumbled slightly as he turned away from the window and grimaced in pain.

'Are you OK?' I asked.

'Sore foot,' he said. 'It's fine some of the time, and then it starts to hurt.'

I'd noticed an almost imperceptible favouring of his left leg when he'd walked ahead of me earlier but hadn't said anything.

'Where?' I asked.

'Oh, just when I put pressure on it. I've probably pulled something.'

'Do you play sport?'

'Mostly I go to the gym,' he said. 'I've been doing some running over the last few weeks.'

'On the treadmill or the road?'

'Both.'

'You might have a stress fracture,' I said.

He made a face. 'I don't do enough to get injured.'

'If you've been training on a treadmill and then moved to the road, you could have done something,' I said. 'You should get it looked at when you go home.'

'It's happened before,' he said. 'It'll be fine.'

'Why are men so reluctant to get something seen to?' I demanded as we went downstairs again.

'Because we're afraid we'll be told it's something terrible.' Max grinned at me. 'And that we'll be given advice about our lives that we don't want to take.'

I laughed. We went into the kitchen, where Banquo had taken up a position at the door.

'Your guard cat.' Max scratched him behind the ears and Banquo purred with pleasure.

'He does a good job,' I said. 'But I don't know why he's taken such a shine to me. I'm sure he has a perfectly good home somewhere.'

'The cat from the other end of our road adopted us,' Max remarked as he continued to pet Banquo. 'We thought he was a stray. It was only when we saw the "Missing" notices on lamp posts that we realised he was using us for extra food.'

'You might be right about this one too,' I said as I refilled Banquo's bowl. 'He eats like an elephant, and I'm sure he's put on at least a kilo since I came.'

Despite the fact that it was late afternoon, the sun was still blazing down. I offered Max a glass of water, which he accepted, and the two of us sat in the shade of the umbrella.

'How long will you stay here?' he asked.

'I'm on a three-month leave of absence,' I said. 'So I'll be home before the end of the summer.'

'I feel bad that you needed it,' said Max.

'I won't lie.' I put my glass on the table and turned to him. 'I thought my life had ended when Brad's did, both because he'd died and because he'd lied. I wasn't holding it together at work, and that's why I came here. But I'm over it now. The scars are still there – and they will be for a while yet, I know. They're scars, though. That's all.'

'I think you're amazing,' said Max. 'I'm still coming to terms with it myself, and yet you . . .'

I caught my breath as I realised that, once again, I'd been monumentally self-centred. Most of my conversations with Max about Brad had focused on me. What had happened to me. How I'd felt. What I'd done. But we'd only barely scratched the surface of how he was feeling, and how he was getting over the loss of someone who'd been very close to him.

'I'm doing all right,' said Max when I put the question to him. 'It's hard, of course. Brad and I were very close. Not as close as I thought, obviously,' he added with a hint of bitterness. 'I didn't know about you, but perhaps that's why he texted looking for advice. He used to call on me – at least, when it was something practical . . .' He broke off and gave me a lopsided smile. 'Maybe that's what he always needed in his life. Someone practical. That's who you say you are, isn't it?'

'I'm sure his practical needs were well covered by you and his wife,' I said. 'I really don't know if he needed me at all. Maybe he just wanted me and I was available.'

'I didn't give much thought to how you were affected,' said Max. 'I guess I thought of you as the other woman and somebody who might need to be managed. I didn't think of you as a person who was grieving.'

'I didn't deserve to grieve,' I said. 'That should have been reserved for you and the rest of his family. I haven't thought about your feelings half enough, either. I've been too self-obsessed.'

'Not at all.' Max reached over to me and took my hand. 'You were in a relationship with him. You're entitled to be sad.' His grip was warm, and firm and comforting. We stayed like that for a moment, then I slid my hand free again.

'It was hard for a time,' I said. 'But I'm better now. I really am. And I'm glad I met you.'

'I'm glad I met you too,' said Max.

It seemed wrong to feel good at that moment, but I did. Previously, I thought I'd reached acceptance, but now I knew it had only been a halfway house. This time, I truly had. Not just the acceptance of Brad's death, difficult though that had been, but also of the type of relationship we'd had. I'd accepted that the life I'd hoped to live with him would never have happened. And I was OK with that. It still hurt. It would always hurt. But I knew that I would never again be almost poleaxed by grief and by missing him. I exhaled slowly and steadily. Then Banquo jumped up on my lap and started kneading my stomach with his claws.

The moment of serenity was broken and I shrieked. Banquo gave me an offended glare.

'You've punctured me in a thousand places,' I complained. 'You do it all the time and you don't care.'

'I'd better go.' Max stood up. 'I know the circumstances were difficult, but it was good of you to meet me and talk to me. And—'

He broke off as we both heard the sound of a car pulling up close to the house. I picked Banquo up from my lap and walked to the edge of the patio.

Luis Navarro got out of a white BMW. He was looking very smart in a dark suit and white shirt.

'*Hola*,' I said. 'I didn't expect you here today.'

'No.' His eyes flickered between me and Max. 'I came because my mother wished to invite you to lunch tomorrow. Catalina and José will also be there. Mamá thought that, as you were on your own, you might like to join us. But I see you are not alone, after all.'

'Luis, Max. Max, Luis,' I said.

'*Mucho gusto*,' said Luis.

'Pleased to meet you,' said Max.

As they shook hands they reminded me of two cats eyeing each other up. I could sense the tension between them. So could Banquo.

'Juno?' Luis gave me an inquiring look. 'You can come? Or no?'

I glanced at Max, who was gazing towards the jacaranda tree.

'It's a very kind invitation, thank you.'

'If your friend wishes to come, he would also be welcome,' said Luis blandly.

'I don't know if—'

'My flight is at midnight,' said Max. 'It would be lovely to join you all for lunch, if you don't mind, Juno. And if Luis's parents really want to include someone else in their generous offer.'

'Of course you must come,' said Luis. 'We will see you at two o'clock.'

'Perfect,' I said. 'Please thank your mother, Luis.'

He nodded and walked back to his car.

'The Navarros live in the adjoining finca,' I explained. 'They've been very welcoming.'

I felt my face redden as I recalled exactly how welcoming Pep Navarro had been.

Max misunderstood the blush.

'Oh,' he said. 'I didn't realise. You and Luis are clearly . . . Of course, I won't come to lunch if I'm in the way. I don't want to embarrass you.'

'No,' I said. 'It's not like that at all.'

'Isn't it?' Max gave me a quizzical look. 'It felt like there was something between you.'

'He doesn't trust me,' I said.

'Why?'

'I think he thinks I'm trying to muscle my way into the Perez family, somehow,' I said. 'He hates that I've done up the house.'

'That's daft.'

Max no longer thought I was some kind of marriage-wrecking floozy, so I wasn't going to tell him that Luis was also wary of me because I was sleeping with his younger brother. I didn't want him to revise his opinion of me. At least, not this quickly.

'But the rest of the family is lovely,' I said. 'And I'm sure you'll enjoy meeting them.'

'I'm looking forward to it,' said Max.

Then he got into his car and drove away.

I dived into the pool and swam five lengths under the water. When I surfaced again, Banquo was sitting by the steps, watching me intently.

'What?' I asked as I towelled myself dry. 'Why are you looking at me like that? Don't you dare be judgemental. Whatever it is you're being judgemental about.'

Banquo said nothing. Well, of course he said nothing. He's a cat. But he didn't need to be able to speak to somehow impart a general level of disapproval. I just had to figure out exactly what he was disapproving of. And then my phone beeped with a WhatsApp call from Pep.

I didn't generally use my phone for video calls, because the broadband connection at the Villa Naranja was slow. But I wrapped a towel around me and walked closer to the router to accept Pep's.

'Hey!' His pixellated face finally sharpened into focus. 'How are you?'

'Good,' I said.

'You have been swimming? I get you out of the pool?'

'I was out anyway,' I said. 'It's very hot today.'

'Here also,' said Pep. 'There is heatwave coming. The pool is OK? Luis is doing a good job?'

'Not as good as you,' I said. 'He was here a short time ago. Your mum has invited me to lunch tomorrow.'

'You will go?' asked Pep.

'Yes.'

'I hope you have fun.'

I wasn't entirely sure about that. I still felt a cloud of disapproval hanging over me whenever Luis Navarro was around.

'You miss me?' he asked.

'Yes,' I said.

'I am hoping to come home very soon. My aunt has new person to help her. Is good. I am working lots of hours with no time for anything else.'

I told him that I'd been working too.

'More painting?' he asked. 'Or garden?'

'I've finished painting downstairs,' I told him. 'And the garden is looking good too. Maybe I'll start painting upstairs now.'

'You are crazy Irish girl,' said Pep. 'Nobody comes to Spain in the summer to paint houses.'

'It wasn't my original plan,' I admitted.

'You have to learn not to be busy all the time,' he said. 'You have to learn to just sit.'

'I've been doing nothing but sitting every evening,' I protested.

'When I come home I will keep you active in the evening,' he said with a chuckle.

I missed what he said next as the connection worsened and his face pixellated again. When it refocused, the background behind him had changed. Previously he'd been indoors. Now he was on a balcony overlooking a port.

'Are you still at your aunt's house?' I asked. 'I thought it was in the country.'

'At her apartment,' he said. 'She has one near the coast. For the summer when she is very busy with the boats.'

'Does everyone in Spain have a house in the country and an apartment by the sea?' I asked. 'It's what Pilar's mother wants too.'

'An apartment by the sea is lovely,' said Pep. 'Especially now. The breeze is welcome.'

I knew what he meant. In the last few days the temperature at the Villa Naranja had gone up significantly, and this evening was the warmest and most sultry of my stay so far.

'Anyway, I look forward to seeing you soon,' he told me. 'I hope you have nice day tomorrow.'

'I'm sure I shall,' I said. 'Your parents are lovely.'

'They think you are lovely too,' he said.

We said nice things to each other for another couple of minutes. Then he kissed the screen and ended the conversation.

I dreamed about Brad that night for the first time in weeks. We were walking along Custom House Quay, hand in hand, the sunlight glinting off the gunmetal grey of the Liffey and the glass fronts of the buildings opposite. We had walked along the quays together many times. But this time he was telling me about Alessandra.

'She's my wife,' he said. 'So, obviously, you have to work around that. You can stay in the attic when she's in the house.'

'Who will be doing the cooking?' I asked.

'She will.' His response was swift. 'She's better at that sort of stuff.'

'What am I better at?' I stopped and turned to look at him.

'The sex, of course,' he replied.

And then I woke up.

I checked the time on my iPad. Almost six. Nearly daybreak. I lay in the bed staring up at the ceiling. Had I been better in bed? I wondered. Was that why Brad had kept seeing me? Was that why Pep was seeing me now? Was I some kind of total sex kitten who knew how to keep men satisfied? Was that my only appeal?

But Sean had left me, I remembered. So it couldn't be the sex.

I heard a thud downstairs, which I assumed was Banquo returning from a night on the tiles. His comings and goings didn't wake me any more but I got up to check, anyhow. When I walked into the kitchen he was sitting in the middle of the floor.

'Pre-dawn snack?' I asked.

Banquo never refused food. I unlocked the kitchen door and retrieved his bowl. I filled it and left it on the floor while I stood in the doorway and looked over the garden. It was still very warm and there wasn't a hint of a breeze. The moon was high in the sky, lighting up the garden. The sudden shriek of an animal startled me, and Banquo's ears pricked up. I looked towards the jacaranda and shivered.

There are no ghosts, but the things we do live on forever.

So doing the right thing is important.

I poured myself a glass of water and went back to bed.

Chapter 27

When Max arrived at the house just after one forty-five the following day, I was ready and waiting for him. I was wearing the purple sundress with the yellow floral border, and my wedge sandals again, and was thinking that it was just as well my social life was relatively limited in Spain because I was hauling the same clothes out of the wardrobe every time I went out. Max himself was wearing a rather gaudy pink shirt over a pair of chinos.

'It's a bit bright,' he admitted when I complimented him on looking very cheery. 'But it's the only holiday-type shirt I have with me. I'll be changing back into something duller before I head home. My bag's in the boot. I know my flight isn't until later tonight, but I don't mind getting there early.'

I nodded. I'm a bit anal when it comes to getting to the airport early myself, ever since I got stuck in traffic and missed a flight to London. I was going to a friend's wedding and it cost me a fortune to rebook, so I'm hopelessly paranoid now.

Before we left I put some food in Banquo's bowl, although he hadn't returned since our dawn encounter. I left the kitchen window open so that he could access the recycling box if he wanted, then locked the door and the grille of the Villa Naranja.

'I always thought the grilles were because of crime,' said Max when I explained why I'd left the window open. 'I didn't realise they were for cats!'

I laughed. 'If I closed up all the windows, the house would be stifling,' I said. 'That's the real reason.'

'Isn't there air conditioning?' he asked.

The Villa Naranja had two units: one in the living room, and another in the bedroom I was using. I hadn't bothered switching them on before now because, although it had been warm, the big celling fans were usually enough to keep the air reasonably comfortable. But if things continued like the last few days, I told him, I could see myself giving in.

'They have super-chilled air con in the hotel,' he remarked. 'It's actually quite nice to feel warm.'

We got into the car and I directed Max down the road to the Navarro house. I hopped out to ring the bell on their gate, which then swung gently inwards.

'I could get used to this,' said Max. 'Big detached houses with electric gates and driveways.'

'Where do you live?' I asked, surprised at myself that I hadn't asked the question before.

'Donnybrook,' he replied. 'I bought one of those little artisan cottages in the village a couple of years ago.'

'Oh.' I was still surprised. 'I thought you'd have been in Belfast.'

'I've lived in Dublin for years,' said Max. 'I went to college in Cork. I don't get back to Belfast that often, to be honest – though, obviously, over the last couple of months I've had to be there a lot.'

'I did wonder why your accent was so different to Brad's,' I told him.

'He used to tease me about it,' said Max as he brought the car to a stop. 'My mum is from Cork, and she never lost her accent. I was born there, so that's why I chose to go to college there too.'

We got out and walked around to the back of the house. Once again, the long table was set and the green umbrellas were open. But although it recalled the last photo Brad had sent, the sight wasn't the hammer blow it had been before. Beside me, though, I could feel Max's sharp intake of breath and I glanced at him.

'It looks like Italy,' he said. 'Brad—'

'I know.' I took his hand and squeezed it. 'He sent me the same photo.'

Elena Navarro was already walking towards us, smiling in welcome. She kissed me on both cheeks and ushered me towards the table where Miguel was pouring glasses of wine. Behind him, an enormous paella was already cooking on the fire.

'Men cook the paellas here.' I repeated the information Rosa had given me. 'Apparently, it's like barbecuing.'

Max laughed. I introduced him to Miguel, who shook his hand and offered him a glass of wine. Max refused, saying that he had to drive to the airport later, and it was Elena who bustled forward and gave him a glass of minted water. Meanwhile, Catalina and José arrived, this time without Xavi, although baby Agata was wriggling in her mother's arms.

'Xavi is at my sister's in Calpe,' she said.

I hadn't been to Calpe, which was another costal town about half an hour's drive from Beniflor. Catalina told us that her sister worked in a language school there. Every few weeks Xavi stayed with her for a sleepover. Liliana had a son of around the same age.

'Although no husband,' Catalina said to me while Max got into conversation with José and Miguel. 'Daniel's father lives in Bilbao, which is not very convenient.'

I knew Bilbao was on the northern coast, so it had to be a good distance.

'Nearly eight hundred kilometres,' said Catalina with a snort. 'He travelled a long way to evade his responsibilities.'

As Elena joined us there was a brief conversation about the fact that women were always left to look after the messes that men made, a conversation I happily participated in. But without the bitterness I would have felt even a couple of weeks ago. It was good to feel better. It really was.

Beatriz then joined us, looking as beautiful as ever, accompanied by an elderly woman, dressed in black.

'This is my grandmother,' she said. 'Rosario.'

I shook hands with the older woman, who took herself off to sit in the shade of a palm tree.

'Where's Luis?' I asked Beatriz.

'He will be here soon,' she said. 'He has gone to – oh, *abuela*, are you all right?'

Her grandmother had dropped a glass, and everyone rushed forward both to assure themselves that she was OK and to clear up the mess. Rosario herself was muttering under her breath, clearly unhurt but annoyed.

'She hates a fuss,' Elena told me as Beatriz brought a new glass for her grandmother. 'She's eighty-eight and her eyesight is failing – but she's as sharp as a tack and the person who holds the whole family together. She lived with Catalina for

301

a while in her seventies but she moved in with us a few years ago. She wasn't at the last lunch because she had to spend a couple of days in hospital. But she's fine now.'

'She lived with Catalina?' I glanced at the younger woman in surprise. 'Is she related to you too?'

'My cousin,' said Elena.

'Oh!' I was surprised. 'Then Max and I are the only non-family members here.'

'But you are practically family now, Juno.' Elena grinned. 'You're living in Doña Carmen's house. And we were related too, although it's not the strongest link. My grand-aunt was the second wife of Ana's grand-uncle.'

'Right.' I tried to get it all clear in my head.

'Which means I'm the only real outsider,' said Max. 'So thank you for including me in the invitation.'

'You are welcome, of course,' said Elena. 'We have been concerned for Juno, living alone. I am glad that another friend of hers has come to stay.'

'Oh, he's not . . .' I broke off. It would be wrong to say that Max wasn't a friend. He wasn't, of course. But I didn't want to insult him. Besides, he'd become – well, if not a friend, someone I liked.

'I'm just an acquaintance,' said Max. 'I wasn't staying with Juno. I was at La Higuera.'

Elena's glance flickered between us.

'Well, you are very welcome, in any event,' she said. 'And—' She broke off and her eyes lit up. Then she waved.

Max and I turned. Two men had walked around the side of the house.

One of them was Luis.

The other was Pep.

302

'Pep!' I looked at him in astonishment. 'When we were talking last night you didn't say you'd be back today.'

'Was going to. Then thought better to make it surprise for you,' he said as he stepped forward to kiss me on the cheek.

'It's lovely to see you.' I was very conscious of Max standing beside me.

'I come back from Mallorca this morning,' said Pep. 'Luis collects me at the airport. Early flight.'

Pep turned towards Max, who was looking very foreign in his pink top and chinos compared with the Navarro brothers' crisp white shirts and dark trousers. I introduced them.

'Luis tells me . . . told me . . . you have friend to stay?' Pep looked at me and then at Max again.

'Staying at the hotel. And just an acquaintance,' repeated Max. His words made me wince.

'An acquaintance is not a friend?' asked Pep. 'Is like startled and frightened?'

I smiled. 'You remember your English lessons.'

'You teach me well,' he said.

'You're giving him English lessons?' asked Max.

I shook my head.

'Pep has been practising his English with me,' I said. 'But only when he calls to the house. He . . . he . . . cleans the pool and has done other things for me.'

I sensed Max's thoughtful look at me but I kept my eyes firmly fixed on Pep and Luis.

And then our awkward tableau was broken up by José asking if Pep and Luis wanted beer, and grandmother Rosario requesting a glass of wine, and Beatriz putting an enormous bowl of mixed salad on the table.

Elena then told us to sit down. I found myself sitting between Max and Pep, with Luis opposite me and Beatriz beside him. There was a general hubbub of chat, mostly in Spanish, before Elena disappeared into the kitchen and returned with large plates of enormous prawns and mussels cooked in garlic.

The Navarro family divvied them up. I stuck with the prawns, but, despite his previous comments about mussels, Max piled his plate with everything. He also helped himself to some of the crusty bread on offer before then asking Luis about the bodega.

'Juno has told me a lot about it,' he said. 'It must be very interesting to work in a family business.'

Luis began to explain something about winemaking. I caught Pep's eyes as he looked at me across the table and then stifled a grin as I felt his bare foot graze my leg beneath the table. He winked at me and I nearly choked on my garlicky prawn.

'Did you enjoy your time in Mallorca?' I asked him.

'It is always fun to work on the boats with my aunt,' he replied. 'But I missed you and I wanted to come home.'

Once again, I sensed Max shooting a look in my direction. Once again, I studiously ignored it.

'I'm sure being on a boat is better fun than cleaning a pool,' I said to Pep.

'But I am not always cleaning the pool,' he reminded me.

I didn't say a word.

On the other side of me, Max was engaged in a conversation about fermentation of grapes with Luis, but I couldn't help feeling he was also listening to me and Pep. I got the impression Luis was listening in too. I wracked my brains to

304

think of something to say to Pep that wasn't about his visits to the Villa Naranja, but I couldn't think of a single thing.

'What about the oranges?' The question popped into my head, and it was Luis who looked at me in surprise. 'When are they harvested?' I asked. 'You've been talking about grapes but the trees in the Villa Naranja are laden with oranges. My friend told me that a neighbour picked them. When?'

'Usually between October and March,' replied Luis. 'The longer they are on the tree, the sweeter they become.'

Rosario, the grandmother, said something in Spanish, and Beatriz translated.

'She remembers the orange harvest when she was young,' she said. 'Men doing the picking, and she and her sisters bringing them water.'

The old woman said something else. Beatriz grinned.

'They wore big sombreros,' she said. 'Made of straw. They still do,' she added. 'Not the type you see in Mexico. Just big enough to shade you properly.'

'I love the idea of being able to pick an orange off a tree every morning for breakfast,' said Max. 'Unfortunately, I don't think it's ever going to happen in my garden. Well, it's more of a patio, really. And it's too cold and shady.'

'Last year there was snow,' said Miguel. 'The first snow in many, many years. I have photographs of the orange trees covered in it. And, of course, it was a worry for the grapes too.'

Suddenly the discussion turned to the weather. I thought it was funny that people in a country with a long, hot summer would complain about the weather just as much as the Irish, but they all had something to say. Meantime, Pep continued to play footsie with me under the table, which caused me to stifle occasional giggles. I caught Luis looking knowingly at me from time to time and remembered Max's words. That Luis fancied me. But he didn't. The only person Luis cared about was his brother.

It was Catalina who asked Max to tell them a little more about himself. He nodded, and began to speak slowly about his work, making sure that everyone understood him.

'It is good, then, what you do,' said Catalina. 'Is not just selling things to people.'

'Sometimes it is,' Max admitted. 'Our agency isn't an advertising agency but we are selling ideas.' He grinned. 'We've done projects for the Spanish Tourist Board. Mostly to raise awareness of Spanish food and wines.'

'Really?' Miguel looked interested.

'You can check them online.' Max told him the link. 'I hope they sent some business your way.'

'I hope so too.'

Suddenly, everyone was looking at Max with a greater warmth than before.

Even Pep.

It was Max who eventually told me that he should leave.

'If you don't mind, I'd love to have a shower and change my shirt,' he said. 'I didn't realise how hot it would be today.'

'Of course.' I looked at my watch, shocked to see that we'd spent nearly five hours at the Navarros'. The time had passed quickly, even though there had been some uncomfortable moments when either Luis or Pep made an ambiguous comment about my stay at the Villa Naranja, and I wondered what Max was thinking of me.

It was as I was kissing Catalina goodbye that she whispered into my ear that she was pregnant.

I looked at her in pleased surprise.

'I have not told anyone yet,' she murmured. 'But I wanted you to know, because you said you might be going back to Ireland soon and I thought it would be nice to tell you. Also,' she added, 'it proves that Magda is right. It is not the only thing she is right about.'

'What d'you mean?' We were slightly apart from the rest of the gathering as she glanced towards Max, who was shaking hands with Miguel.

'She promised you a man,' said Catalina. 'You did not believe her. But there is a man for you here, no?' Her eyes flickered towards Max again.

'Him?' I shook my head. 'Like he said earlier, he's an acquaintance.'

'Whatever you say.' She smiled at me. 'But I think you will be the first woman to break Pep Navarro's heart.'

I shook my head again.

I was the one who got her heart broken. I'd never broken one myself. And I never would.

'It really is a different life,' said Max when we got back to the Villa Naranja. 'And you seem to have embraced it pretty thoroughly.'

'I'm fairly sure we're seeing it through rose-tinted glasses,' I told him. 'Everyone's being really nice to me because I'm living in a haunted house on my own.'

'Do they believe it's haunted?' asked Max. 'Do you? Really?'

I shook my head. 'No. But the Navarros have rather taken

me under their wing, and Ana Perez, the owner of the house, has been very nice to me too.'

'I'm not surprised, after all the work you've done. It's a complete renovation.'

'Why does everyone keep saying that?' I demanded. 'I varnished the shutters, tidied the garden and did a bit of painting, that's all.'

He laughed. 'It'd take me months to do all that. You did it in a few weeks. You're a complete live wire.'

'I can't help it,' I admitted. 'I'm hopeless at doing nothing.'

'I can see why Brad fell for you.'

I stared at him.

'You're his kind of girl,' said Max. 'He always loved intelligent, active women.'

'But Alessandra was intelligent,' I said. 'So why did he cheat on her?'

'I don't know,' replied Max. 'I can only say that Brad was a man who liked new things all the time. He'd been with Alessandra for more than five years. Maybe . . .' He sighed. 'I hate to say this about my own brother, but maybe he was never cut out for monogamy. He loved her and he loved Dylan. But he also loved excitement.'

'And I provided that.'

'I'm sorry,' said Max.

'You don't need to apologise for him,' I said. 'You're not responsible for his behaviour.'

'I can't help thinking that maybe I enabled him a little.' Max rubbed the back of his neck. 'I told you I wasn't bothered when he asked Alessandra out, even though she'd come to the event with me, but I was, a bit. I never said anything because Brad . . . well, Brad always took what he wanted. He did it in the nicest of ways. He made you feel that he was doing you a favour. But in the end he was the kind of guy who got his own way. And I never really stopped him. Maybe if I had, things would've ended up differently.'

'And maybe if I'd asked more questions, I would've known he was cheating on me.' I shrugged. 'We can't blame ourselves, Max. He was the one who cheated. He was the one in the wrong.'

'You're a strong woman, Juno Ryan,' said Max.

'Have you forgotten you were showering me with paper napkins to mop up my tears at La Higuera?' I asked. 'I'm not strong at all. But I'm not going to live the rest of my life feeling guilty. I did when I heard about everything, at first. And then I came here and I had time to think, and Ana told me the history of the house and what had happened here. I realised that there will always be terrible things happening in the world. Some are big and dramatic and affect everyone. Some are small and only affect ourselves. But they can be equally devastating. I was devastated for a long time. I'm over it. Over him. Over everything.'

'I'm glad to hear it,' said Max. 'Maybe living here is good for you. Maybe you should stay.'

'It's a lovely idea but a few months in the summer isn't the same as living in a place forever.'

'I'm sure they'll all miss you when you go,' said Max. 'You seemed to be very in with the Navarros. Luis and Pep particularly. Which is an interesting situation, don't you think?'

I looked him straight in the eye.

'I'm just a passing paragraph in their lives,' I said. 'And

although Pep, in particular, has been very nice to me, he has a future mapped out and I'm not part of it.'

'Don't you want to be?'

'I had a similar conversation to this with my mother,' I said irritably. 'I don't need to be part of any man's future. I just need a future of my own.'

'Are you always this self-sufficient?' he asked. 'Always this practical?'

'Except for brief moments when I fall for married men and believe in ghosts – yes,' I said.

'Like I said, you're strong.' Max smiled. 'But it's nice that even strong women cry sometimes.'

I suddenly felt a lump in my throat. I was glad that Max Hollander thought I was strong and self-sufficient and practical. That's exactly how I liked to think of myself. But, quite unexpectedly, all of the grief and hurt in the aftermath of the earthquake came back to me. And I didn't feel strong at all.

'Have I upset you?' Max was looking at me with concern. 'God, Juno, I'm sorry. I didn't mean—'

'I'm fine,' I said as I turned away from him. 'Absolutely fine. Look, just go and have your shower, OK?'

He went upstairs and I went outside. I didn't know why I was feeling so rattled. I thought I'd put everything to do with Brad McIntyre in a box and sealed it shut. But some of the feelings still leaked out. The feeling of contentment I'd had when I thought he loved me. And the feeling of utter devastation when I realised I'd been fooled. And even though I was better, I'd never forget. And I'd never trust anyone with my heart ever again.

I walked around the garden. There was still no sign of

Banquo, although his food bowl was empty. I refilled it, but I was thinking I'd have to put him on a diet. He was eating me out of house and home and getting fatter by the day. Although I kept an eye out for him as I strolled around the garden, he didn't appear. I wondered if, despite him having allowed Max to pet him, he was put out by his arrival.

Twenty minutes later, Max came downstairs again. His fair hair was still damp from the shower, and he smelled of soap and a citrusy cologne. He was wearing casual trousers, a white shirt and navy jacket and suddenly looked more like a businessman than a tourist.

'It was good to have met you,' he said with a hint of formality. 'I truly am sorry about the circumstances.'

'Me, too.'

'Thanks for your hospitality the last couple of days.'

'You're welcome.'

'And thanks for being . . . well, just thanks.'

'Thank you for coming,' I said. 'I'm sure it wasn't easy for you, either.'

'No. But you made it . . . not as bad as I thought.' He took a deep breath and held out his hand. 'Goodbye, Juno.'

'I hope everything goes well for Dylan,' I said as we shook hands. 'That he gets better soon. That it all works out.'

'Thanks,' said Max. He picked up his bag and the car keys. I took the fob for the gate and followed him outside.

He put his stuff in the boot and got into the driver's seat. He started the car and then put directions to the airport into the satnav.

'Safe flight,' I said.

'Thank you.'

Chapter 28

Banquo still hadn't returned the next day. But as it, and the days following, were suffocatingly hot, I thought perhaps he'd found a cooler spot and was staying put, for which I couldn't blame him. According to my weather app, temperatures were in the high thirties (or 98° Fahrenheit, the app helpfully told me) and were likely to stay that way for another couple of days. I wasn't sure I could cope. It was as stifling in the shade as in the full sun, and even a morning dip in the pool was a very temporary respite from the cauldron. I was sweating again before I'd even towelled myself dry.

I brought an old electric fan to the patio and tried sitting outside, but it was still unbearable. So I returned to the house and switched on the air con in the living room. It was the first time in my life I'd ever been forced indoors because of the heat. As the air con slowly chuntered into life, I wondered how on earth people had managed when this sort of weather arrived in the days before air conditioning. The women especially would've struggled with their long, heavy dresses. It was no wonder they fainted all the time! I was wearing my flimsiest top and my shortest shorts – and I was still melting.

It took some time before the room became noticeably cooler, but then I felt myself perk up a little. I picked up my phone and fired off messages to Saoirse and Cleo, as well as to my mum. In all of them I apologised for moaning about the heat, hoped they were keeping well and reminded them that I'd be back home soon.

I could hardly believe that I was nearing the end of my stay. The time had flown by, helped by my sudden interest in home renovation and gardening. Helped too by my friendship with Rosa Johnson and my relationship with her former boyfriend, Pep. I exhaled slowly. I hadn't heard from Pep since Sunday lunch but he had to come to do the pool soon. I smiled to myself as I remembered him playing footsie with me under the table. I loved his openness and his sunny nature. I loved how he made love to me. I loved how he made me feel.

And yet I was going to go home and leave him behind. As I'd told Max Hollander, no matter how much fun I had with him, Pep was just a paragraph in the story of my life. I know not everyone would believe me. Women are supposed to fall in love with the men they sleep with. I usually do.

My phone buzzed and I picked it up.

The text was from Max himself.

Sorry I didn't get back to you sooner, he wrote. *This is just a quick message to say thanks again for meeting me and thanks again for your hospitality too. I realise it was difficult for you and I'm sorry if I seemed a bit high-handed about it all. I guess I was struggling with everything a bit. I loved my brother, I wanted him to be perfect and he wasn't. I'm sorry he hurt you. I hope everything goes really well for you in the future. Thanks again. M.*

PS, he added. *Love to Banquo.*

I read the message again.

Max had already thanked me and apologised to me before he'd left Spain. He hadn't needed to do it again. But he seemed to be a man who wanted to make everything all right. Our parting had been stilted and awkward after the easy familiarity we'd seemed to share earlier. It could be that he wanted to make sure I wasn't about to cause any hassle in the lives of the McIntyre/Hollander families, despite everything I'd said. Or perhaps, I thought, as I read the last few words again, perhaps he was just being nice.

Didn't realise you were a cat person, I typed, even as I remembered that he'd scratched Banquo behind the ears, and that the cat, clearly happy to share his affections, had let him. *I haven't seen him in the last couple of days. I'm beginning to think he's gone back to his original owner. Though someone (or something) has been eating his food.*

I hope he's OK. Max's reply came quickly. *I like to think someone is looking after you in the haunted house. Even if it's just a guard cat.*

Don't say 'just' a guard cat, I sent back. *He likes to think of himself as the one in charge.* I attached a photo of him I'd taken the previous week, stretched out beneath the table with his paws covering his eyes, totally relaxed.

Max sent back a string of laughing-face emojis.

I'm not great with emojis. I don't know what most of them mean. So I just sent a smiley-face one back.

I put the phone back on the table and went outside again. The air was still furnace hot. I returned to the air conditioning and picked up my phone. There were no further messages. Max clearly considered our conversation to be over. I picked up my iPad and opened my book. But I fell asleep before I'd got to the end of the chapter.

Not surprisingly, I got no sympathy from Saoirse or Cleo about the heatwave – they both messaged me to say it was cloudy and cold in Dublin and that I was lucky to be away. It suddenly struck me that most of us seem to be conditioned to focus on our irritations and misfortunes, rather than the good things that happen. Perhaps, at heart, we want to moan because we prefer to think that life is better for other people.

I'd thought that way for a long time. Not just when I'd found out about the tragedy that had befallen Brad and Alessandra, and not just when I realised how much he'd lied to me, but since childhood – when I believed that being the drunken mistake marked me out from my brother and sister as less wanted than either of them. And when I thought that not being creative made me less worthy of my mother's love. But I'd been wrong. Max Hollander had shown me that although I mightn't be an actress or a musician or a poet, I was creative all the same. And Mum, when she'd phoned, had been genuinely concerned about me. I'd heard it in her voice and realised that her trying to push me towards some kind of spirituality wasn't simply her attempt to gloss over a problem, but her very real way of trying to help. Just because it wasn't my way didn't mean it didn't matter. And just because I hadn't actually balanced my chakras or found my third eye, or whatever it was, it didn't mean that taking time out to review my life hadn't actually been a useful thing to do.

Bottom line, I was going to be a more thankful person in the future.

*   *   *

When Pep arrived to do the pool, he immediately started to grumble about the weather and I agreed that it was hot and uncomfortable but I didn't moan. But when he put his arms around me and began to kiss me, I wriggled away.

'Is too hot for you?' he asked.

It actually *was* too hot for sex, but that wasn't the reason. I'd known that this moment would come and I hadn't planned it for now, but I realised that the time was right.

'I'm sorry,' I said. 'You've been the best thing that has happened to me since I came here, but I can't do this any more.'

'What?' He stared at me.

'I've loved spending time with you. I've loved making love to you. But we're not a couple, Pep. We never will be.'

'You are breaking up with me?' His expression was one of astonishment.

'Yes,' I said.

'Is because of your Irish lover?'

'I don't have an Irish lover.'

'The man in the very pink shirt? He is not your lover?'

'Of course not,' I said. 'Don't be silly, Pep. He's a friend.'

'I thought you said not a friend,' said Pep. 'I thought you said acquaintance.'

I sighed.

'Friend, acquaintance, it's all the same.'

'I think you are trying to confuse me,' he complained. 'You said it was different before. And I do not think he looks at you like a friend.'

'How he looks at me isn't important.'

'No?' Pep snorted. 'He wants you in his bed. That much is very clear.'

317

'Pep—'

'But why would he not?' asked Pep. 'You are good in bed. One of the best I have ever had.'

I was unaccountably flattered by his remarks and I couldn't help smiling.

'You laugh at me,' he said, his tone injured.

'Not at all,' I assured him. 'I was just pleased you liked being in bed with me.'

'Of course I do,' he said. 'And I would like to be in bed with you again. There is no need to break up, Juno. You are staying here for some more weeks, no? We should be together all that time.'

'We were great together,' I said. 'I loved every minute of it. But things have changed.'

'What things?'

'I don't really know,' I admitted. 'It just feels different, that's all.'

'So if not your Irish man, who?' asked Pep.

'Nobody,' I said. 'I just want time to myself.'

'But that is a waste!' he cried. 'You are far too . . . far too sexy to be on your own!'

This time I laughed. He sounded truly upset on my behalf.

'We were never going to be forever—' I began.

'I know that,' he interrupted me. 'All I say is that while you are here we should do things that make us both happy.'

'You won't be broken-hearted when I go back to Ireland?'

'I will miss you,' said Pep. 'For some time my heart will be broken. Maybe even a long time because I have love for you, Juno Ryan. But then I return to college, and there, perhaps . . .'

'And there you'll find lots of other girls,' I finished for him.

'None like you.'

'But maybe someone long-term for you.'

'I told you before, I am too young for relationship,' he said. 'I do not understand why everyone thinks it must be forever. Why they cannot enjoy the moment. Always we want something more. But it is not necessary to think of the future to enjoy the present.'

His English had definitely improved if he could hold a philosophical conversation with me now.

I told him that, and he grinned. 'So, we will go now to bed?'

'It's changed for me,' I said. 'I don't know why. I'm sorry.'

'One more time?'

I still fancied him. How could I not? He was a Greek god, after all. And even if my attitude towards sleeping with him had shifted, I was allowed to change my mind, wasn't I? But I wouldn't.

'Over is over,' I said. 'I'm sorry, Pep.'

'You are strong woman, Juno,' he said.

I couldn't help smiling. Max had called me strong too. Maybe, despite everything, I really was.

Pep picked up the hose.

'I will go now,' he said.

'See you soon.'

'*Hasta luego.*'

He still gave me a kiss on the cheek before leaving.

Chapter 29

It was a relief when the heatwave finally passed and the temperature dropped to more comfortable levels. I hoped it would mean that Banquo would return to the house. I was missing him and, quite honestly, worried about him. I still left the kitchen window open, but although I checked the recycling box every morning he was never there. The house seemed very empty without his presence, and occasionally my earlier sensation of being watched returned. I knew it was because of being totally on my own – even though Banquo's appearances had been solely on his terms, he had been companionable.

I didn't like to think that something might have happened to him, but I couldn't dismiss the possibility that he'd run out beneath one of the cars that raced up and down the narrow road that led to Beniflor. Or that he'd been caught himself by one of the invisible nocturnal animals that might be eating his food. I didn't know if there were foxes in the neighbourhood, but I supposed there could be.

Concern about Banquo remained at the back of my mind as I took advantage of the relatively cooler temperatures and definitely cooler breeze to sweep up the dried bougainvillea and hibiscus blossoms on the terrace, and clear the purple carpet of petals from the sundial beneath the jacaranda tree. I was so engrossed that it took a moment before I realised the landline was ringing. Part of the reason why it didn't penetrate my consciousness, at first, was the fact that it had never rung before. It was an old-fashioned bell sound, like the phone in my parents' house.

I dropped the bag containing the dried flowers and sprinted back to the house, hoping that whoever it was wouldn't hang up before I got to answer it.

'Villa Naranja,' I gasped as I lifted the receiver.

'Juno? Are you all right?'

'Yes, yes, I'm fine. Who's speaking?' I recognised the voice but couldn't place it.

'It is me, Ana Perez.'

'Oh, Ana. Of course. How are you?'

'I am well, thank you,' she said. 'I hope you did not find it too uncomfortable during the heatwave?'

'It was pretty steamy,' I admitted. 'But it's grand now.'

'Grand?'

'Good,' I amended. 'Fine.'

'I am happy to hear it,' she said. 'I am ringing because I am coming to the house later this evening. I have someone who is thinking of buying it. Is it OK with you?'

'Of course,' I said. 'That's great news, Ana.' But my heart sank a little at the idea of the Villa Naranja ending up in a stranger's hands. I was a stranger myself, I knew. But I felt as though a part of me would always be here.

'It is good news,' she agreed. 'This is the first person in a long time who wishes to see it.'

'Do you want me to go out?' I asked.

She considered this for a moment, but then said it might be better if I stayed. It would make the house more of a home, she said, to have me there. I wasn't sure about that – in Dublin I doubt very much that prospective buyers want to meet the sellers, but maybe it was different here.

'I will be there at about seven o'clock,' said Ana.

'I'll make sure everything is tidy,' I promised. 'I'm doing the garden, anyhow.'

'You do not need to do anything,' protested Ana. 'I am sure it is already because of you that this man wishes to see the house. He liked the photos you sent me that I put on the website.'

'I'll tidy up anyway,' I said. 'And I'll see you later.'

'*Hasta luego*,' she said, and hung up.

There really wasn't much tidying to do, but I swept out the rooms, mopped the floors and plumped up the cushions. I made sure that all of my stuff was put away, and then I picked some of the oranges from the trees and put them in bowls in the dining room and living room. It all looked very *A Place in the Sun* when I'd finished. Except for the print on the wall, which was hanging at an angle again. I'd replaced the hook when I'd painted the wall, but when I tried to straighten the picture this time, the string snapped. Maybe the heat had dried it out, I thought, as I caught the picture before it fell on to the floor.

I remembered I'd seen a large ball of twine or cord in the shed where the Perez family stored their tools and outdoor furniture. Leaving the picture on the sofa, I went to investigate.

It took a minute or so for my eyes to adjust to the gloomy interior of the shed after the bright sunshine of the day. As

I stood there I was conscious, once again, of that feeling of being watched. But this time it seemed more real, more visceral. Because I *was* being watched. By a familiar pair of amber-flecked eyes.

'Banquo,' I said. 'What on earth are you doing in here – oh!'

The exclamation was because I'd made another realisation. And it was the realisation that I'd totally misnamed Banquo. If I'd wanted a Shakespearean character, then Ophelia would have been a better name for the cat. Because Banquo was nursing half a dozen kittens and was clearly a mum, not a dad.

'How the hell didn't I cop on?' I demanded as he – she – watched me studiously. 'I'm a health professional, for heaven's sake. I should have realised you were pregnant, not fat! I should've noticed your feminine attributes.' But, I consoled myself, even without her pregnancy Banquo was a very chunky cat. As a human, she would have been considered bootylicious. And she'd never rolled over on her back or let me rub her stomach. So I couldn't entirely blame myself. All the same, I felt very, very stupid.

No wonder she'd been eating all around her, I thought, as she looked at me intently. She'd been eating for seven. And she'd disappeared not because of the heatwave, but to have her babies in peace. Clearly, they were only a few days old. Their eyes were still firmly closed and their ears flat to their heads.

'I won't go near your family,' I told her. 'Don't worry.'

I could see the big ball of twine that I wanted, and I took two slow steps to get it. Banquo's stare followed me the whole time.

'I don't know much about kittens,' I said softly. 'But I'm

pretty sure I should just leave you to it until they're a bit bigger. I'll bring you food, though, so you don't have to leave them.'

I exited the shed, left the twine in the kitchen and returned to the new mother with the food bowl, which I'd filled. She didn't move as I put it within easy reach.

'I'll check on you later,' I said as I closed the door gently behind me.

Ana arrived at exactly seven o'clock with the potential house purchasers. By then I'd re-hung the picture and refilled Ophelia's bowl twice. I'd had to rename her, it would've been weird not to. It was only for my benefit, of course. Like all cats, she didn't bother to answer to any name.

'This is Señor and Señora Carreño,' Ana said as I walked out to greet them

'*Mucho gusto.*' Pep had taught me how to say that. The couple smiled at me and fired off a volley of words in return. I gave Ana a helpless look.

'They are delighted to meet you,' she paraphrased.

The Carreños were a couple in their late fifties, I guessed. He was tall and somewhat patrician, while she was shorter and more homely. But they were looking around the garden with delight and seemed eager to get on with the tour of the house. I stayed sitting on the patio while Ana escorted them, and was still there when she reappeared about twenty minutes later.

'They are looking around by themselves,' she said. 'But they seem very interested.'

'That's great news.' I smiled, and then asked if she knew much about them.

'They're from Valencia,' she replied. 'He's taking early

retirement from his job on a local council, and she's doing the same. They won some money on the lottery,' she added, 'and they've always wanted to live in the country.'

'But they're not from Beniflor,' I said.

'There's no chance of anyone from Beniflor buying the Villa Naranja,' Ana told me. 'It's sad, but that's life.'

The Carreños reappeared about ten minutes later and set off around the garden again.

'Do they know about looking after oranges?' I asked.

'I doubt it,' said Ana. 'But Paco Ramos is the farmer who harvests them now and I'm sure he can come to an arrangement with them.'

I nodded and then catapulted out of my chair as they made their way towards the shed.

'You can't go in there!' I caught Señor Carreño by the arm. 'There's a new mother with her babies.'

He looked at me in complete astonishment.

'Juno!' exclaimed Ana. 'What on earth are you talking about?'

'It's the cat.' I explained about Banquo/Ophelia and her kittens.

'She's only a cat,' said Ana. 'She won't mind if we have a peek into the shed.'

'She will,' I protested. 'The kittens are tiny. She's very protective of them. You can't let strangers go in. You just can't.'

Ana shrugged and then spoke to the Carreños. I got the impression that the Spanish people were looking at me and thinking I was a crazy English person who cared more about animals than people, but eventually Señor Carreño nodded and they walked away from the shed.

'I'm sorry,' I said. 'But they're just babies.'

'It's OK,' said Ana in amusement. 'I don't think seeing the inside, or not, of my storage area will affect the sale too much.'

She led the Carreños back to the house, where she offered them water. They stood on the patio chatting, while I wandered into the shade of the jacaranda tree. I wondered if Ana had told them anything about the history of the house. I supposed not. It might put them off. But without them knowing, the story of her grandfather might be lost forever. And that would be wrong somehow.

They finished their water and Ana waved at me.

'We're leaving now,' she said. 'They really like the house. They keep saying how bright and cheerful it is. If they buy it, it will be almost entirely thanks to your work. I'm very grateful.'

'Hopefully I didn't scupper the deal by jumping on top of Mr Carreño to stop him going into the shed,' I said.

'I do not understand scupper,' said Ana. 'But it was not a problem.'

'Let me know if they make an offer,' I said. 'They won't want to move in before I leave, will they?'

'No. It will take a few weeks to sort everything out,' Ana told me. 'Do not worry.'

She kissed me goodbye.

I was glad for her. But my heart was heavy as I watched them leave.

Pep came to clean the pool again the following day. He strode across the garden looking as much of a Greek god as ever. I came out of the house and said hello, asking him why he was cleaning it again so soon.

'Needs more treatment in hot weather,' he replied as he

uncoiled the hose. 'It was not perfect last time. I come with chlorine tablets for it.'

'OK.'

'You are well?' he asked.

'Yes.'

'You miss me?'

I laughed. 'I don't spend all day sitting around thinking about you, you know.'

'Pity,' he said.

'I've been busy,' I told him. 'I had to tidy the house. Ana had people to look at it yesterday.'

'To look at it?'

'People who might buy it.'

'What?'

I told him about the Carreños.

'They seemed to like it,' I said. 'They loved the pool and the garden and the house itself.'

'She would sell to people from Valencia?' He sounded aghast.

'Well, she did make the very valid point that nobody from Beniflor wanted to buy it,' I remarked. 'And I'm guessing that the Carreños aren't going to be too sticky about the price. They have the money to buy.'

'*Madre mía!*' He was clearly upset. 'I do not know how my mother will feel about that.'

'It's not up to her,' I said. 'To be honest, I feel a little sad about it myself. But it's always been Ana's plan to sell and buy her apartment on the coast.'

'Nevertheless . . .' Pep dropped a big chlorine tablet into the deep end of the pool. 'It is a pity to see the house go from the family.'

'I know.'

He looked up at me. 'This is your fault,' he said. 'Until you started the *reformas* nobody was interested.'

'Which is a pity,' I said. 'It means that nobody could see past the outward appearance and appreciate the house for what it was.'

'You are right.' Pep looked at me thoughtfully. 'You are very right, Juno. The people of Beniflor often do not see what is in front of them. It takes an *extranjera* to show.'

'I think you're exaggerating a bit,' I said. 'But I'm glad I've helped Ana. After all, she charged me hardly anything for the rental, and staying here has been a lovely experience.'

'For me, too.' He winked, and I burst out laughing. 'Are you one hundred per cent sure you do not want to sleep with me one more time?'

I'd moved on from Pep. I knew I had. So I repeated what I'd said before.

'OK.' He sighed. 'I am sad about it. But OK.'

'I'm sure the young women of Beniflor will be delighted to have you back on the market,' I told him.

'Excuse me?'

'Available to them again,' I amended.

He grinned. 'The young women of Alicante,' he corrected me. 'I will wait until I return to college to find my next girlfriend.'

'You're an arrogant sod,' I said with a laugh, which made him frown, and I had to explain it to him.

'But you tell me I am good in bed,' he said. 'And if I can be good for a woman and she is good for me too – then that is good for everyone, no?'

And I really didn't have a response to that.

328

I told him about Ophelia and her babies as he was getting ready to leave.

'Do you want me to get rid of them?' he asked.

'Pep! No! Of course not,' I said in horror. 'Actually, what I want is for them to find good homes.'

'Not so many people have cats in their homes here,' he said. 'In their gardens, perhaps.'

'That'd be fine,' I said. 'I don't like to think of them being feral, that's all. And I really feel that Ophelia should be sterilised. Goodness knows how many kittens she's had already, and what might have happened to them.'

He shrugged. 'Is not your problem,' he said.

And yet, like so many things in the Villa Naranja, I sort of felt that it was.

Chapter 30

The following morning, my phone pinged with another text from Max Hollander. It was a photo of Dylan holding a kitten. Although his hair had started to grow back, there was still a scar at his temple running to the top of his cheekbone. But he was smiling.

Meet the new member of the family, Max said. *Mac (short for Macbeth, obvs). Thought it would be a good idea for Dylan. Already inseparable. Hope Banquo has returned! M.*

I stared at the message for a while and then opened the photos on my phone. I selected one I'd taken of Ophelia nursing her kittens.

Banquo has transitioned, I typed. *Meet Ophelia and her family!*

My phone pinged almost instantly with a couple of horror-face emojis followed by a string of laughing-face ones. And then another text message.

I thought s/he was a bit porky, Max wrote. *But many congrats to the new family!*

Fat shamer! I responded.

Am off to check Macbeth, replied Max. *Tho will be making sure is neither male nor female in any event. One cat is enough.*

Who are you telling? I responded. *Am desperately trying to find homes for kittens. Not sure will succeed.*

Knowing you, am confident you will, typed Max. *Best of luck.*

I couldn't think of anything else to say. So I sent some thumbs-up emojis.

He didn't reply.

It was Rosa who finally solved the problem of Ophelia's kittens; although not until a couple of days later, and not until after Luis had called unexpectedly to the Villa Naranja first.

'Is it true?' he asked when he got out of his car. 'That there are buyers from Valencia for Doña Carmen's house?'

'It's true that people called around to look at it,' I replied. 'And they seemed interested.'

'*Joder,*' he muttered. 'This is not good.'

'It's good for Ana,' I told him. 'She's been trying to sell the house for ages. And, like I told Pep, nobody in Beniflor wants to buy it.'

'Nevertheless.' He frowned. 'Outsiders.'

'This is the twenty-first century, and you're not living in a backwater,' I retorted. 'I'm an outsider.'

'True.' He looked at me thoughtfully. 'And I wasn't very keen on you coming here, either.'

'Because of Pep?'

He shook his head 'No, no. I told you, I thought Pep would break your heart. And that you would be trouble for us. But I was wrong, and it has been nice to have you here.'

'I'm sure the Carreños are lovely people too,' I said. 'And

they'll settle into the community and be part of it in no time.'

'They may be lovely people,' he conceded. 'But it takes generations to settle into the community. That's just the way it is.'

'Well, I'm happy for Ana – and you should be too,' I said.

Ophelia chose this moment to take a break from her maternal duties and strolled across the garden. She stopped in the shade of a hibiscus bush and began to wash. I was still annoyed at myself for not realising she was female from the start, although there was no doubt that – even without the baby weight – she was definitely a curvaceous kind of cat.

'I must go,' said Luis.

'OK,' I said. 'But if you want to find out about the prospective buyers, you should really ring Ana Perez.'

'I might do that,' he said.

Perhaps he wanted to negotiate about the orange groves, I thought, as he left. Pep had said that the family had thought about buying some of the Perez land before, with the possibility of uprooting the orange trees and replacing them with vines. Obviously, if the property was to be sold, this would be the time to negotiate. And perhaps it would mean more money for Ana and her family too.

Ophelia came up and rubbed against my ankles. I scratched behind her ears.

'Everything's changing,' I murmured. 'Life moves on. For you. For me. For all of us.'

I went to Beniflor in the afternoon, and that's when I talked to Rosa about the kittens.

'What a hoot.' She laughed. 'You must have got a shock.'

'D'you know, I always felt there was something about that cat,' I admitted. 'Like he – I mean she – was keeping an eye on me. It must have been her maternal instinct kicking in. I'm worried about the kittens, though. Pep asked if I wanted to get rid of them, and he wasn't talking about finding them good homes!'

'Typical.' She snorted. 'The Spanish have their pets, of course, but they're not as sentimental as us about animals.'

'I'm not sentimental,' I said. 'But I don't want anything bad to happen to them.'

'Leave it with me,' said Rosa. 'I know one or two people who might like a kitten. It's going to be a few weeks before they're ready to leave their mum, anyway.'

'Eight weeks, according to Google,' I said. 'But the thing is, I'll have gone home by then.'

'Oh, really?' She picked up my empty coffee cup. 'When are you leaving?'

'At the end of the month. I can't believe it, to be honest. When I first came, the time stretched out in front of me, and now suddenly I'm thinking about getting back to work.'

'I'll miss you,' said Rosa. 'So will Pep.'

'I won't be keeping in touch with him,' I said. 'We were only ever going to be a short-term thing.'

'I'm sorry I was ratty with you over him,' said Rosa.

'How's it going with Tom?' I asked.

She smiled. 'Pretty well, so far. He's very attentive. It's nice.'

'I'm glad,' I told her. 'You deserve someone nice.'

'I'm in a better place with him than with Pep,' she said. 'Not as intense. But better. So you see,' she added, 'Magda

333

was right. And she was right about Catalina. She might be right about you and your man too.'

I laughed. 'I'm the exception,' I said. 'But that's fine. It really is.'

'Leave it with me, about the kittens,' she said. 'I'll call you.'

'Thanks.'

I finished my coffee and went home.

Although, of course, the Villa Naranja wasn't home.

Rosa was a quick worker. She sent me a WhatsApp the following day to say that she had homes for the kittens and asked if she could see them. She didn't have a car, so I picked her up from the café and brought her to the house.

'I've never been here before,' she said as she got out of the car. 'It's impressive, isn't it? I love the shutters!'

'Everyone's taken by the shutters,' I admitted. 'But it only took some sanding and a lick of varnish to make them look good.'

'Of course!' She turned to me. 'I'd forgotten you did all that. It looks great. So does the garden,' she added as she looked around. 'Did you do that too?'

I gave her a rundown of my DIY efforts over the past couple of months, and she told me that Ana had been lucky to find me. Everyone seemed to think of me as some kind of home-improvement fairy, I thought, as I brought her to the shed where Ophelia and her babies were. It was very satisfying to be lavished with praise, even if most of my work was superficial.

'Oh, gosh, how cute!' she whispered when I opened the door and she looked inside.

The kittens were latched on to Ophelia and feeding

hungrily. She opened an eye to look at us but she knew we weren't a threat.

'They're so sweet,' said Rosa as we left them to it. 'And I'm delighted to be able to find homes for them.'

'Where?' I asked.

'Two of them are coming to us at the hotel,' she said. 'We already have a couple of dogs the guests can take for walks through the countryside, but Mum has always liked the idea of some cats too. So she's happy to have them.'

'And the others?'

'Even better homes for them!' Her eyes gleamed with excitement. 'Hayley Carr is going to take them. She's Carola's sister – you remember Carola? She came to Magda with us.'

I nodded.

'Hayley is the manager of a retirement home in Altea. That's about twenty minutes or so from here. She wants to use pet therapy with the residents – apparently, it's good for them to interact with animals. At the moment one of the nurses brings her own cat to visit, and they love it. So Hayley wants to have animals actually living there with the residents too.'

'What a brilliant idea!'

'It is, isn't it? And ideal for Banquo's babies.'

'Ophelia,' I corrected her. 'Not that she cares one way or the other.' I looked at Rosa with concern. 'D'you think you could keep an eye on her too when I'm gone? I'd hate to think of her wandering around without anyone to care for her.'

'You're such a softie,' Rosa teased.

'I was going to bring her to the vet and have her sterilised,' I admitted. 'But the kittens have to be weaned first, and that takes about a month. I'll be gone before then. It's very frustrating.'

Rosa laughed. 'You could stay a little longer.'

'I wish,' I said. 'But I have to work.'

'I'm sure you could get a job as a house fixer-upper,' she said.

'Even if I could . . .' I shook my head. 'This isn't my life, Rosa. I love it here, but I also love my job. It would be a mistake to pretend I could change.'

'Even for Pep?'

'Especially for Pep.' I grimaced. 'How could I possibly live with a man who would've drowned the kittens!'

'He was just trying to be helpful. And he wouldn't have drowned them, he would've just brought them somewhere else and let them loose.'

'They still would've died!' I cried.

'Has that really changed your view of him?' asked Rosa. 'Might you have stayed otherwise?'

I shook my head. 'No. I told you, he was just a . . . a stopgap. And maybe I'm overreacting a bit about his attitude towards the kittens. All the same, Rosa, I need to go home. But I'm really glad I came.'

'Are you over your relationship with the married man?' she asked.

I nodded. 'He broke my heart. But it's mended again.'

'They do mend, don't they?' She looked pensive. 'I thought I'd never get over Pep, but I have. And even if Tom and I aren't forever, I've changed. I'm not as naive as I was.'

'It's such hard work,' I agreed. 'Having to change. Having to adapt. Having to move on. But everyone has to do it at some point.'

'I'm glad you came,' Rosa said. 'You were good for us, you know.'

'And you were good for me,' I said. 'Spain was good for me. I hope I'll be back.'

Chapter 31

And then, suddenly, it was almost time to go home. The week of my departure, I spent ages walking around the Villa Naranja, through the garden and along the orange groves, as though I could imprint every last centimetre of it on my heart. I'd grown to love the house, which was no longer even remotely eerie. I felt at peace there. And it would always be a part of me, even when it was finally sold and the outsiders from Valencia moved in.

I decided to ask a few people around for drinks two nights before I left. The Navarros, of course, Rosa and her mum, Carola and Hayley (who had yet to see the kittens), Catalina Ruiz and Ana Perez, who'd phoned earlier in the week to make sure that everything was OK before I left.

'I need to drop by in the next couple of days, if that's all right,' she'd said. 'I have stuff to do before I finalise the sale.'

'If you're here the day after tomorrow, I'm having some farewell drinks,' I told her. 'Please come.'

'That suits me very well,' said Ana. 'I finish early then.'

'Do you want to stay over?' I felt slightly awkward asking if she wanted to stay in her own house, and even more awkward hoping she'd say no because I wanted those last days to myself.

'No,' she replied. 'I'll stay in Eduardo's apartment.'

I'd forgotten about Pilar's brother, who I'd never met, but I told her he was welcome to come along too.

And so, at eight o'clock on Thursday evening, the people of Beniflor – who were now friends to me – assembled in the garden of the Villa Naranja, which was looking bright and colourful in the evening sun.

'It really is the most beautiful house,' said Luis. 'And excellent for a party.'

'It's not really a party.' I offered him a glass of his own wine. 'Just a gathering. And a thank you to everyone who's been so good to me.'

He smiled, and I remembered how I'd once thought he was hitting on me. And that Max had thought he fancied me. We'd both been wrong. There was no spark of electricity between Luis and me, and no frisson that would have alerted me. There's always something. You just know. The thought made me smile to myself. Mum would've liked to be part of my 'just knowing' about something. About tapping into that third eye, or sixth sense – or whatever it was that happened outside of normal everyday living.

Then Rosa arrived, along with Carola and her sister. About an hour later, as everyone was mingling quite happily, Ana turned up with her husband, Alonso, and Pilar's brother, Eduardo, who was home from Madrid.

The buzz of conversation grew louder. The atmosphere grew more relaxed. I chatted with Rosa and then Catalina, who told me that Xavi was back to his irrepressible self and had come home limping from his latest football match after a kick in the shins, bruised but happy that his team had won. Then I talked to Carola and Rosa again, and to Elena Navarro (who'd brought extra wine, and who was also charmed by the work to the Villa Naranja).

And then I talked to Pep, who asked me if I was sure I wanted to leave.

'Not entirely,' I admitted. 'But it's time. I know that.'

He gave me a quick hug, and it was a hug of dismissal. It was over for him too now. I was about to become a part of his past, as he was about to become a part of mine. I looked around at all the people who'd mattered to me. All, like Pep, about to become a part of my past. They'd probably gather together again like this in the future. But this time without me. I felt a pang of regret. But it wasn't enough to make me want to stay. Nevertheless, I'd never forget them.

My attention was caught by Ana and Luis, who'd been inside the house and who now walked out together, talking animatedly. They looked pleased with themselves, and Luis gave Ana a quick pat on the shoulder before she moved to one side and clapped her hands. The conversation immediately stopped as everyone turned towards her.

'*Hola, amigos*,' she said, and then, with a smile towards me, 'and friends.' Then she started talking to them all very quickly and, from my point of view, utterly incomprehensibly. I had no idea why there was a sudden gasp and a round of applause, and why Luis then started to speak, until Rosa appeared by my side and started to translate for me.

'He's bought the Villa Naranja,' she said.

'What!' I looked at her in amazement.

'Apparently, when he realised that it would be going out

340

of the hands of a family from Beniflor, he decided he needed
to step in and buy it.'

'But he could have bought it any time!' I exclaimed. 'Why
now?'

'Because . . .' She waited while he spoke a little more
and then turned back to me. 'Because he said it was only
when he learned it was going to be sold that he realised
how much it mattered. That his family and Ana's family are
family together. That they have lived and worked here for
generations . . . OK, he's losing it here a little bit. I
remember someone saying that you needed to have had
roots here for centuries before people truly accepted you
– anyway, his heart was moved and . . . yada, yada.' She
grinned at me.

'And a big thank you to Juno.' Luis switched to English,
and everyone looked at me. 'She has taken this house and
turned it into something really beautiful. And she has done
a good thing for Doña Carmen's daughter, because I think
that if she hadn't done this work – and there hadn't been
another offer – I would not have had to pay the money I
am paying now.'

Everyone laughed. He repeated it in Spanish, and they
laughed even louder.

'So I am thanking her, but I think Ana is thanking her
more,' concluded Luis.

She came over to me then and hugged me.

'The Carreños were good people,' she said. 'But they have
other options. Luis cares about this house and this land. It
would have made my mother happy to know it has gone to
the Navarros.'

'If I had anything to do with it, I'm delighted, of course,'

I said. 'But I bet it was just the whole idea of it going to someone from outside the town that made the Navarros realise what they'd be missing.'

'Yes, but the Carreños wouldn't have made an offer if you hadn't done it up,' Ana pointed out. 'So I do have to thank you. And if you ever want to come to stay in the apartment in Beniflor Costa, you're more than welcome.'

'Have you bought one already?'

'No, but I know which one I'm going to buy,' she said. 'Near the restaurant, with views over the sea. I could never have afforded it before, but thanks to you I can.'

'I'm very happy for you,' I said.

'And I'm happy too.' Luis joined us. 'It is true when I say I should have made an offer before now.'

'I'm glad it's worked out for everyone,' I said. 'I really am.'

'We will miss you,' said Luis. 'Everyone in the town likes you. You are sure we cannot persuade you to stay?'

Ana drifted away, her attention caught by Eduardo.

'You want me to stay?' I looked at him in surprise after she'd gone. 'I thought you were the one person in Beniflor who didn't like me.'

'I have to admit that I was suspicious of you,' said Luis. 'It seemed so strange, you coming to Doña Carmen's house and doing so much work, all for nothing. I thought you had an ulterior motive. That there was a reason for you being here I could not understand. And then, of course, you were with my brother . . .'

'Not any more,' I said.

'No.' He glanced towards Pep, who was chatting happily with Hayley.

'Being here was a summer break,' I told him. 'That's all.'

342

'To get away from that man?'

'What man?'

'The man in the pink shirt.'

'No.' I shook my head.

'You are still difficult to understand,' said Luis. 'But I thank you for making me see that I really did want to buy the Villa Naranja. It was only when it was nearly lost that I realised it.'

'And I want to thank you and everyone in Beniflor for your kindness.'

'I was not especially kind to you.'

'Ah, you're grand,' I said.

He looked at me in confusion.

'It's an Irish way of saying don't worry, everything is fine,' I told him.

'Fine is good.' He nodded. 'I hope you will come back sometime, Juno. Truly. You will be welcome.'

Then Rosa called over to me and asked if she could pair her phone with the speakers.

So I walked over to her and left Luis behind.

After my socialising with my Beniflor friends it seemed odd to simply pack up and leave on my own. I cried as I left a last bowl of food for Ophelia, who was still spending most of her time in the shed with her kittens. Beatriz Navarro had offered to check on her every day and to refill her bowl, which let Rosa off the hook.

'Are you sure?'

She'd made the offer during the party when a group of us had been laughing about my inability to distinguish a male from a female.

'But of course,' she replied. 'Actually, I think that cat used to sleep under the magnolia tree in our garden until you began to look after her.'

'Cats always go where they get the best attention,' observed Rosa.

'Anyway, I will take care of this one,' Beatriz said. 'So you do not need to worry.'

But I was still a little bit concerned about how Ophelia would get on without me. I was happy that Rosa had found homes for the kittens, though, and I'd told Hayley that I'd love to visit the retirement home sometime.

'Hopefully you'll be back to visit again,' she said.

Hopefully I would, I thought, as I heaved my bag into the boot of the car. I checked one more time that the door and the grille to the Villa Naranja were locked, and opened the car door. As I did, there was a beep from outside the gate and I looked up to see the Bodega Navarro van.

'I couldn't let you go without saying goodbye,' said Pep as I opened the gates. 'And thank you for a wonderful summer.'

'Thank you too,' I said in return. 'You made me . . . better.'

'I hope so.' He opened his arms and I moved closer for him to hug me. But it was a brotherly hug now, with none of the passion of the previous weeks.

'Have a great time at college,' I murmured. 'Don't break too many hearts.'

He grinned. 'I do my best.'

'You can take the keys,' I told him as I disentangled myself. 'Ana told me to drop them in the letter box. But I guess they're going to be Luis's keys soon, so . . .'

'OK,' he said.

I got into the car and drove outside. Then I hit the fob and closed the gates behind me. I wanted to cry again.

'Safe journey,' said Pep.

'Thank you.'

'You have many friends in Beniflor,' he reminded me. 'You will always be welcome here.'

'Thank you,' I said again.

Then I put the car in gear and drove away.

The airport was busy. It took ages to drop my bag and get through security, and, when I did, I joined the end of a long queue at Starbucks to order a coffee and a cookie.

I drank the coffee and nibbled the cookie, all the time wondering about the lives of the people around me – where they were going, why they were going there, who would meet them on their arrival and on their return. To judge from the bright-red arms and legs, many of them were returning from a holiday on which they'd happily ignored advice to slather on the sunscreen.

Having been almost pathological about it myself, my own skin was now a light biscuit colour and – despite having worn sun hats as much as possible – my dark brown hair had lightened by a couple of shades. Yet when I went to the Ladies before my flight was called, I could see that I looked healthier than I'd ever done. I applied some coral pink to my lips and sprayed myself with a rip-off perfume I'd bought in the Beniflor market (the scent was absolutely La Vie est Belle, it just didn't last for very long) and then went off to board the flight.

A few hours later, I was walking into the arrivals hall at Dublin. I always feel self-conscious as I step through the doors, knowing that the people waiting to meet passengers check out everyone who comes through. I could see the disappointment on the faces of the group who held up a banner saying 'Welcome Home, Sonia', while the bored drivers with their signs for 'Mr Murphy' or 'Kei Adachi' simply looked through me.

I turned towards the exit. My plan was to get the Aircoach to the Dundrum Town Centre, which would leave me a ten-minute walk to the apartment. I'd told Saoirse I'd see here there when she got home from work later in the evening. But as I dodged an embracing couple I heard my name being called, and I looked around in surprise.

'Sweetheart!' It was Mum's voice, clear and carrying. 'Over here.'

I don't know how I'd missed her – or Gonne, who was standing beside her. Mum was as vibrant as ever in a cerise dress and purple wrap, while Gonne wore slim-fitting jeans and a red jumper. My sister never bothers much with clothes, but truthfully she'd look beautiful in a bin liner.

'What on earth are you doing here?' I asked, after we'd hugged.

'I wasn't going to let you arrive without someone to meet you,' said Mum. 'Especially as you've been away for so long.'

'A little under three months,' I said. 'It's hardly a lifetime.'

'But we've missed you,' Mum said, turning to Gonne. 'Haven't we?'

'Of course,' said my sister. 'Did you have a good time?'

'Can we move out of here?' I was conscious that people

were looking at us. They'd probably been looking at Mum before now, recognising her as Imelda from *Clarendon Park*, but I didn't want to be dragged into the centre of attention.

'Follow me,' said Gonne, and she began to stride towards the exit.

We were stopped once by a middle-aged woman who asked Mum for her autograph. 'I wouldn't normally,' she explained. 'But I'm going to England to meet my sister, and she loves you in *Clarendon Park*.'

'No problem.' Mum signed the proffered piece of paper. 'I hardly ever get bothered by autograph hunters,' she said when we were settled in Gonne's car. 'Let's face it, the Irish hate asking you in case you think too much of yourself.'

I laughed. She was right. As a race we don't really revere our celebrities. Probably more than any other people in the world, we want them to know that they're nothing special. And maybe because I grew up around slightly famous people, I'm really terrible about even recognising them. Saoirse, Cleo and I were once in a bar where Bono was having drinks with some friends. I didn't even notice him. Afterwards, Cleo told me that nobody had approached him. We think we're too cool for that kind of thing.

Mum kept up a conversation about trivial family matters until we were out of the airport. But instead of taking the M50 to Dundrum, Gonne continued towards the city centre.

'Where are you going?' I cried.

'Home, of course,' said Mum. 'You're staying with us tonight.'

'But . . . but – that's not my plan,' I objected. 'I told Saoirse I'd see her in the apartment later.'

'You can see her tomorrow. You'll be back at work on Monday, and I won't have had time to talk to you at all,' said Mum.

'We can meet up and chat over the weekend. But I've got to get home myself.'

'*Mi casa es su casa*,' she said. 'I'm sure your Spanish is up to that by now.'

My house is your house. You didn't need to speak Spanish to know the phrase. And, of course, her house is the house I grew up in. The house I'd never one hundred per cent felt was home. Although that was my fault as much as hers.

I sighed. 'Fair enough,' I said. 'But one night only. I'm not a child, Mum. I haven't lived with you since I graduated.'

'I'm not asking you as a child,' said Mum. 'I'm inviting you as my daughter.'

And that put an end to my objections.

The house in Ranelagh had always been slightly chaotic. The hall was generally cluttered with coats, boots and umbrellas (Mum never remembered to bring one with her, so any time she was caught in the rain she bought a new one, each more vibrant than the last). The front room was Dad's domain and resembled any generic photo of a writer's studio. Overflowing bookshelves lined the walls, bound scripts took up much of the floor space, and his huge mahogany desk was covered in various piles of papers. The only nod to modernity was the open laptop and the printer in the corner.

Most of our family life took place in the kitchen. Originally a separate kitchen and dining room, the previous owners of the house had knocked down the dividing wall and so turned it into one big room, which took up the entire back of the house. We always ate at the kitchen table, and the dining area was now occupied by an enormous modular sofa in a faded green fabric. Mum and Dad had bought it when I was about ten and, although it was a bit lumpy in places now, it was still a comfortable place to hang out.

It was currently occupied by my brother, Butler, his husband Larry, Gonne's husband Gil, and Cian and Alannah, my niece and nephew. Through the large picture window I could see my dad in the tangled grass of the back garden. He was standing beneath the apple tree, smoking his pipe. Mum's ban on smoking indoors had preceded the government's similar ban by about fifteen years. Although I've never smoked myself, and hate the smell of stale cigarette smoke, I'd always found the slightly buttery caramel scent of Dad's pipes relaxing, and sided with him when he objected to Mum's rule. He was doomed to failure, of course. Nobody defeats Mum when she sets her mind to something.

'Desmond!' She rapped on the window. 'Juno's here! Come in.'

That was the signal for Alannah and Cian to get up from the sofa and hug me. Dad, after he'd put out his pipe, came inside and did the same. Only the men remained on the sofa, though all of them agreed it was good to see me again.

'You know, more than three months can go by without

349

me seeing any of you in Dublin,' I remarked in amusement. 'There's no need to make such a fuss.'

'Of course there is,' said Mum. 'You're the prodigal daughter. You were lost and you've returned.'

'I wasn't lost,' I protested. 'At least, not after the first night when I thought I might have been murdered on the road.'

'Oooh, what happened?' asked Cian.

I proceeded to tell them about my journey to the Villa Naranja, embellishing the eeriness of arriving at the house in complete darkness and Banquo's eventual appearance.

'You are so cool, Auntie Juno,' said my nephew. 'Nobody I know would stay in a haunted house on their own.'

'It wasn't really haunted.' I carried on about Banquo's metamorphosis into Ophelia and Ana's successful sale of the house to the Navarros. Naturally, I made no mention of the hot sex with Pep Navarro.

'Sounds interesting.' Dad looked at me thoughtfully. 'A TV series, perhaps. *A Year in Provence. A Summer in Spain.* Only grittier. You'd need more stuff going on, of course. Something sinister, related to the haunted house feeling, perhaps.'

'There was a murder.' I was revelling in my unaccustomed role as the storyteller of the family. 'During the Civil War.'

'Goodness!' exclaimed Mum when I'd finished. 'There's your story, Desmond. That poor man being strung up, and his wife and children watching. Think of the trauma. And the drama.'

'Maybe.' Dad put his unlit pipe into his mouth and started sucking on it. 'Historical is popular right now. Not for RTÉ, of course. They wouldn't do it.'

'Netflix,' suggested Gonne. 'Or Amazon Prime.'

'It was only a small incident in the overall horror of the war,' I said. 'I hardly think it's primetime Sunday viewing.'

'Oh, but it could be,' said Mum. 'I can see myself as the grandmother, looking back and remembering. You must write it all down,' she told me, 'before you forget. So that your dad can work on it.'

It was the first time my creative writing skills had ever been called on in the family. I felt a warm glow about it, even though I struggle to write memos, let alone accounts of civil wars and haunted houses.

'There has to be a modern story too,' said Gonne. 'Viewers need a bit of romance. Did you meet anyone while you were there, Juno?'

I felt the colour rise in my cheeks. Mum looked at me expectantly.

'I made lots of friends,' I said. 'Nobody special, though.'

'You can make that bit up,' Gonne told Dad. 'Give her a hot, hunky Spanish lover. And, of course, the husband and wife during the war can be a love story too.'

'Can you all cool it for a while?' I was conscious that my cheeks were flaming now. 'You're turning my stay into some kind of blockbuster romance. And it wasn't anything like that.'

Which was true. There was no romance with Pep. But, as we sat down to dinner that evening, I wondered what they would think if they knew everything. If I told them about Brad and Alessandra, about Pep and Luis, and about the arrival of Max Hollander. What kind of story would they think it was then?

And I could throw in Magda Burnaia for good measure

Chapter 32

Although I'd enjoyed my overnight stay with my parents more than I'd ever expected, it was good to get back to the apartment the following day, and even better to return to work on Monday morning. I called into the office, where Drina asked if I was feeling better.

'Much,' I replied.

'You look fantastic,' she told me. 'No more bags under your eyes, and I'm envying your healthy glow. I suppose a summer in the sun will do that for a girl.'

'Thank you for giving me the chance,' I said.

'We all need some time out occasionally,' she said. 'I like to think that we look after people's minds as well as their bodies here.'

'Thanks,' I said again.

'You're welcome. Now get back to radiology. It's a busy department and they've missed you.'

I wanted to think that maybe they had, but when I pushed open the double doors everything was humming along with its usual sense of efficiency. There was no time to chat, I got straight to it, X-raying a suspected fractured wrist, followed by a clearly broken clavicle (which reminded me of Xavi Ruiz and his dislocated shoulder) and then a patient with a badly swollen knee.

Later in the afternoon, Cleo and I went for a coffee in the hospital cafeteria where, like Drina, she commented on how well I was looking.

'Are you definitely over it?' she asked when we'd finished the coffee. I was going home but she still had a couple of hours to put in.

'Totally,' I said.

'Sure?'

'Absolutely.'

'I'm glad.'

'So am I.'

'What about the hot pool guy?'

'Over him too.'

'Shame.'

'Not really.'

I finished my coffee, gave her a quick hug and then left for the apartment. Saoirse had asked me the same questions the night before. So when I got in, the question of my time in Spain had already been dealt with and we settled down to watch TV. Except for my occasional efforts to watch the weather forecast, I'd spent hardly any time in front of the TV in Spain, but it seemed perfectly right to do it again now. I propped my feet on the corner of the coffee table and got stuck into the latest Netflix series that Saoirse had become addicted to.

It wasn't until after it had ended that I checked my phone. There was one message. It was from Max Hollander. It was a photo of an X-ray clearly showing a fracture of the metatarsal.

You? I texted back.

Yes. Took your advice. Had it seen to.

Told you.

The next text was a photo of a surgical boot with the message that it was a pain in the neck.

Better than in the foot, I sent back.

His reply was the laughing-face emojis again.

I've seen worse fractures, I texted.

You're strangely unsympathetic for someone who works in the health sector.

Not unsympathetic, I replied. *You should've got it looked at sooner.*

Was too busy.

That was true, I thought. He was busy with funerals and with the fallout from Brad and Alessandra's deaths and with looking after Dylan and chasing after the mysterious Ms Paycock – who'd turned out to be me.

How's Dylan? I texted. *And Mac?*

Doing great. You should meet Mac. You'd like him.

Maybe someday. Though not really, I said to myself, as I pressed 'send'. When would it ever be appropriate for me to be introduced to the cat belonging to my dead lover's son?

Meet for coffee when you're back in Dublin? suggested Max. *No cats obvs.*

I stared at the text. Why would he be suggesting coffee? Why would he even think it would be a good idea?

You can assess my broken foot. His second text arrived almost at the same time as the first.

I just photograph them, I sent in return. *I don't assess anything.*

You still knew there was something wrong.

Because you were LIMPING!!!!

Still. Shows professional interest.

I laughed. I couldn't help it. I sent back the emoji of a face covered with a surgical mask.

So . . . are you back soon?

Am actually back now.

In that case, would you like to do the coffee thing?

I hesitated before replying.

First day off is Saturday, I texted.

Sounds good. City centre? Or Dundrum?

City, I replied. *Dundrum manic on Saturdays!*

Carluccio's?

Works for me.

He sent the thumbs-up emoji.

I sent the same.

And then I wondered what on earth that had all been about.

Coffee with Max Hollander was at the back of my mind as I began work the following morning. Most of my day was scheduled at the ultrasound machine where, after a number of patients with abdominal pains, I saw a woman of about my own age who had fertility issues and had been referred by her GP. I smiled at her as she got on to the table and then applied some warmed gel to her stomach.

'I'm afraid I'll pee myself,' she said, a worried expression on her face.

'You wouldn't be the first.' I smiled at her. 'Having to drink a couple of litres of water followed by me pressing down on you isn't easy. But don't worry, you'll be fine.'

I kept talking to her as I moved the probe gently over her tummy, looking at the screen for signs of fibroids or endometriosis. I paused a few times as I studied the images.

'There isn't anything awful, is there?' she asked.

Patients ask this all the time. If you're doing an X-ray or a scan, it's easy to be non-committal because you're slightly distanced from them. But an ultrasound is the only procedure where you're right there with the patient, touching them. And you can't separate yourself quite as much.

'The thing is,' she added, before I had time to say anything, 'although I don't want terrible news, I'm sort of hoping it's me. Because if it is, I'm happy to have treatment. I'm prepared for IVF. But if it's Andrew, my husband . . . well, he wouldn't accept it, you know? The idea that there might be something wrong with him . . .' Her voice trailed off as I continued to slide the probe over her stomach.

'You can't tell me, I know,' she said when I remained silent. 'I have to wait for the results. But . . .'

I wanted to tell her but, even though I'd be the one to write the report, it would be the consultant radiologist who broke the news. Harry Mercer is a nice guy and he'd be sensitive when he told her that the reason she wasn't getting pregnant was that her antral follicle count was practically zero. Which meant she was producing hardly any eggs. There was almost no chance of her becoming pregnant naturally.

'We expected to have children before now,' she said. 'I don't mind him blaming me.'

'It's not a question of blame,' I said. 'Sometimes it just doesn't happen.'

'But there's always a reason.' She was dogged, she really was.

I agreed that there was nearly always a reason. But, I said, sometimes we don't know why things happen.

'Am I all right?' she asked.

'I didn't see anything sinister.' It was OK to reassure her a little. 'But Dr Mercer will talk you through it all and discuss the scan with you.'

'Thank you.' She smiled at me. 'You've been lovely.'

I wiped the gel from her stomach and she rushed off to go to the loo. Liz Munsen, the nurse who'd been with me, looked at me inquiringly.

'Hardly any antral follicles,' I said.

'Poor girl.'

I got ready for the next patient. But I was thinking about my own desire for children and wondering if there was anything that would prevent me having them in the future. Other than finding a father for them. Which would be difficult, seeing as I had no interest in men any more.

Saoirse was taken aback when I told her on Saturday morning that I was meeting Max Hollander. She was even more taken aback when I filled her in on his visit to Spain.

'You kept that very quiet,' she exclaimed. 'For crying out loud, Juno, why don't you share this stuff?'

'There didn't seem to be much point,' I told her. 'He came, we talked about Brad, he left . . . it wasn't important.'

'Clearly it was, if he wants to see you again,' said Saoirse.

'It's not seeing me in that kind of way,' I protested. 'It's just . . . we're linked because of Brad, that's all.'

That's what I'd decided as I'd thought about my coffee with him. That, despite everything, he was the one who wasn't over what had happened to his brother, and he was the one who needed to talk about him still.

'Nonsense!' Saoirse looked at me sceptically. 'He's been messaging you and he's asked you out for coffee. He wants to date you!'

'He doesn't,' I retorted. 'It's . . . it's that we've both lost someone, and we're both trying to cope the best way we can. He's struggling to know what's best for Dylan too. He probably wants my advice.'

'Are you for real?' she demanded. 'Read those texts again. They're not the texts of a broken-hearted brother. They're the texts of a man trying to sound cool with a woman he wants to sleep with.'

'Don't say that!' I cried. 'You're getting it all wrong, Saoirse. It's not like that. Really it's not.'

But, as I got the tram into the city centre, I wondered if she was right. There was no doubt, I admitted to myself, that I felt a certain connection to Max Hollander. But that was simply because he was Brad's brother. Brad was the thread that held us together. Nothing else. And it would be downright creepy to start seeing Max in a different light. It would be like dating Luis after sleeping with Pep. And I hadn't wanted to date Luis. Leaving aside the potential fallout it would have caused, it would've felt all wrong. Although . . . the thought suddenly flitted into my head . . . Max Hollander was Brad's stepbrother, not his biological brother. Which surely made a difference.

You don't want it to make a difference, Juno Ryan, I muttered under my breath as I walked down Dawson Street. You're not about to have a relationship with Max. This is coffee. This is two people using each other to get better. Even if you don't really need anyone to get better, because Spain and Pep and the Villa Naranja made you better. But

Max might need something, someone to help. And you have a responsibility to do what you can.

He was already there when I arrived, sitting at an outside table.

'Last available one in the fresh air,' he said as he stood up to greet me. 'Thought I'd better nab it. It's not quite as hot as Beniflor but nice to be outdoors.'

In fact, it was a beautiful day with the sun shining from an almost cloudless blue sky. Dublin is always great in the sunshine – not as hot and dusty as other major cities because, let's face it, it's not as big and crowded. The flowers of the street vendors added big splashes of colour, while the morning shoppers strolled rather than scurried around the town.

'What would you like?' asked Max when we were both sitting down and a waiter came over to take our order.

'A cappuccino and a croissant would be lovely,' I said.

'Americano and bread for me,' said Max, then turned to me. 'You're looking great,' he said.

'And you're not wearing your boot.'

He sighed. 'I couldn't. Not walking around town. Too much bloody trouble. And it honestly doesn't feel any better than before.'

'It takes nearly two months for a stress fracture to heal,' I told him. 'And if you've been pretending there's nothing wrong and running on it, it hasn't had a chance.'

'You sound just like the doctor,' he complained.

'Sorry.' I made a face at him. 'What I meant to say was, don't worry at all about your broken bone, it'll get better all by itself without you having to modify your life in any way whatsoever.'

He laughed.

'Sorry,' he said. 'I'm shit at being injured. Or being sick. Or anything outside my comfort zone of just getting on with my life.'

'So are most of us,' I said.

The silence between us was only broken when the waiter returned with our coffees.

'Why did you ask to meet?' I broke a piece off my flaky croissant and looked at him inquiringly.

He didn't answer straight away. I buttered the croissant, which I normally never do.

'I feel as though I should be keeping you in the loop,' he replied.

'I'm not sure you should.' I wiped my buttery fingers on a napkin. 'I'm nothing in your life, Max. In Dylan's either.'

'I wouldn't say nothing.' He frowned. 'I'd like to think we were friends. After all, we've been on holiday together. Sort of.'

'I split up with my fiancé after a holiday abroad,' I told him.

'You were engaged? Before Brad?' He looked at me in astonishment. I suppose he'd thought that I'd been naive and vulnerable when I'd gone out with his brother, not someone who'd already been around the block.

'Why did you break it off?' he asked.

'He suddenly realised he didn't want to settle down,' I replied. And then it struck me – Sean hadn't wanted to settle down with me. Brad had been two-timing me with his wife. And Pep had used me (as I had used him) for summer sex. Clearly, I wasn't the sort of girl men settled down with.

'So you sort of rebounded on to Brad?' asked Max.

361

'I wouldn't put it quite like that,' I said. 'I met him a year later. I got on well with him. I didn't throw myself at him, if that's what you're thinking.'

'Of course it's not,' he said. 'I know my brother. I know how he lived his life. I told you before. And, if you remember, his last message to me was about having got himself into a bit of a mess. I don't think he was blaming you for it.'

'I blamed myself,' I admitted. 'But not now. And I've put it behind me, Max. I've reached acceptance in the five stages of grief and, quite honestly, I don't think there's anything to be gained from talking about it any more. But if you need to talk, feel free. Just don't bring me and my decisions into it.'

'I thought I might be helping you.' His tone was unexpectedly cranky. 'I didn't realise you were perfectly capable of helping yourself.'

'For crying out loud!' I stared at him. 'What is it about men? Why do you all think women are hopeless without you? When the truth is that most of the time we're clearing up after the mess you've made of things. Especially the messes you leave behind when you've lied and cheated and hurt the people who matter most in life.'

'Generalise, why don't you?'

'Every time I've had a relationship with a man he's the one who's been a dick,' I returned. 'My ex-fiancé, then your goddam brother – both of them suiting themselves and not giving a shit about me.'

Max didn't say anything.

'But you're blaming me, aren't you?' I continued. 'You're thinking I'm the deranged woman who couldn't keep a man. Because that's how you all think!' I pushed my chair away from the table and stood up. 'I'm sorry if I'm not the person you wanted me to be. I'm sorry if I've managed to get over it all by myself, without giving you the therapy of fixing me. I'm sorry you can't fix yourself by meddling in my life.'

He still didn't speak.

I picked up my bag and stalked down the street, leaving him to pay the bill.

Chapter 33

I was halfway up Dawson Street before I halted my angry stride and asked myself what on earth had just happened. Why had I flown off the handle so inappropriately with Max? Why had I dumped all of my resentment over Sean and Brad on him? And why had I been so determined to show him that I didn't need anyone? Perhaps he'd been a bit patronising – and I hate being patronised – but there'd been absolutely no need for me to lose it in such a bizarre way.

I released the breath I'd been holding and walked briskly back to Carluccio's. I was an idiot. I needed to apologise right away.

But, of course, he wasn't there. I went inside the café to see if he was paying at the till (I was already embarrassed at having walked off without even leaving money on the table), but there was no sign of him. I walked up Duke Street to Grafton Street but I couldn't see him among the throng of people in the city. I rambled around for a while, keeping an eye out for him, before finally stopping outside Brown Thomas and taking out my phone.

Sorry I lost it just then, I typed. *Perhaps we could meet again and this time I'll buy the coffees.*

I waited in case he was nearby and replied.

But he didn't.

Quite suddenly, I didn't want to go home. Saoirse was out for the day and I didn't want to sit in the apartment alone, where I'd have time to think again about my habit of sabotaging my own life. I'd got it together so well in Spain, I couldn't quite believe I seemed to have morphed into someone completely different in Dublin. I'd thought I was better. But, clearly, I was utterly hopeless. And I didn't want to drown in my hopelessness alone. I needed to be some-where, anywhere with other people.

So, almost without realising it, I walked to the Luas stop and got on the tram for Ranelagh.

Although I had a key to my parents' house, I didn't use it but rang the bell instead. I heard the sounds of a door opening and the barking of a dog – a dog? Where had that come from? – and then the clipped sound of high heels on a tiled floor.

Mum opened the door and her eyes widened in surprise.

'Juno!' she exclaimed. 'What are you doing here? Not that it isn't lovely to see you,' she added as she scooped up the miniature dachshund puppy before it shot out of the door, 'but I wasn't expecting you to call by so soon. Isn't he a dear?' She thrust the dog into my face. 'I know it's a bit bonkers to get another dog after years without one, but Betsey Freeman's daughter's dachs had a litter, and I couldn't resist. His name is Seyton.'

Seyton is a character in *Macbeth*, the servant who stays with the king when everyone else is abandoning him. I was pretty sure I'd never mentioned Banquo to her by name, so it was odd that she'd chosen to name the puppy after another character in the play.

'Not at all odd,' she remarked when I said this to her, 'because you and I are connected spiritually, and it's quite possible that you passed the idea to me subconsciously. He's a dote, isn't he?' She closed the hall door and let the puppy run along the hallway again.

He shot out of the kitchen door into the garden, and we followed him.

'You brought the good weather home with you,' she said. 'I've been sitting out. Well, sitting isn't really the word because I've been spending a lot of time cleaning up after this guy. He knows he's only meant to poop at the back of the garden but, of course, he's trying to go everywhere. Seyton, no!' And she was off after him as he squatted on the grass.

Why on earth had I come here? I wondered as I watched them. Why had I opened myself up to my mother's scatter-brained lunacy? But deep down I knew. There was no way I could mope when I was in Mum's company. The woman simply didn't know the meaning of the word.

'So are you OK for that osteoporosis thingy?' she asked as she sat beside me on a wooden bench beneath the apple tree.

'Sure,' I said. 'No problem.'

She said nothing as Seyton bounded over to her and she patted him on the head.

'He's definitely not a bitch?' I asked.

'No. Why on earth would you think that?'

I told her about Banquo, and she laughed.

'How could you possibly have made such a basic mistake?' she demanded.

'She's a very chunky cat.' I took out my phone and showed her some pictures of Ophelia during her pregnancy.

'Not very Ophelia-like,' agreed Mum. 'More of your Kardashian cat with that behind.'

I laughed.

'That's good to hear,' she said. 'You've had a long face on you since you arrived. What's the matter?'

I think the last time I sobbed on Mum's shoulder was when I was about six and Tiffany Lorrimer, who sat next to me in school, told me that she wasn't going to be my friend because I had a funny face and wore silly clothes. She was partly right, both about the face and the clothes. I wasn't pretty as a child and, although we wore a navy uniform at school, Mum's selection of non-school wear for me was bohemian at best, without any concession to current fashions. I remember Tiffany and one of her friends looking at me in such a disdainful way that, when Mum met me at the school gate that afternoon, I hadn't been able to contain my tears. And I wasn't able to contain them now, either.

'Juno. Juno.' She put her arms around me and gathered me close. 'It's OK, my sweetheart. Whatever it is, don't worry. We'll sort it out. It's OK.'

'It doesn't need to be sorted out.' I sniffed. 'It's fine, really.'

'It's not,' said Mum. 'You don't cry when everything is fine. You don't cry at all.'

That was completely true. Or at least it was true for the period between the Tiffany Lorrimer episode and the day I saw the news about Brad. Since then, though, I seemed to be able to cry at the drop of a hat.

Mum stroked my hair while my tears continued to flow.

Seyton came and sat at my feet. I could see him out of my watery eyes, looking solemnly at me. He yapped and then licked my ankles. I gave him a feeble smile, then pulled away from my mother.

'Are you all right?' she asked.

'Hard to blub like a baby when there's a dachshund licking your legs.' I sniffed as I reached down and picked him up. He started to lick my face. 'That's disgusting,' I cried. 'Please stop.'

He licked me again.

'I need to go and splash some water on me,' I told Mum.

I put Seyton on the grass but he followed me into the house and into the downstairs loo.

'You're like Banquo,' I said. 'I mean, Ophelia.'

He yapped.

'She made me feel better. You're doing the same.'

He sat and looked at me, his eyes wide, his tongue hanging out.

'Let's go,' I said. 'I'm fine now.'

Mum hadn't budged from the bench beneath the apple tree.

'OK?' she asked as I sat down again.

I nodded.

'Want to share?'

It's not my thing, sharing. In a world where we seem to let everyone know everything about our lives, I prefer to do it all by myself. To work it out for myself. To get through the feelings by myself. That's why Spain had been so good for me. I'd dealt with it all on my own. I'd reached acceptance. I'd sorted out my issues. I'd tried to become the strong person that Luis Navarro and everyone else in Beniflor seemed to think I already was.

As I looked at my mum I suddenly realised that I didn't

want her to know that I made mistakes. Or that I was vulnerable. I didn't want her to know that my strength was nothing but an illusion. But who was I kidding? She knew already.

So I took a deep breath and told her everything. Meeting Brad, the accident, the discovery that he was married, going to the funeral, talking to Max Hollander. All of it. The only part I glossed over was my relationship with Pep Navarro. She might have told me to find someone to love and have some sex with, but I wasn't prepared to share that with her.

'Oh, Juno!' she cried when I was finished. 'You poor, poor pet.' And she enveloped me in her arms again.

We had tea afterwards. She made it in her big rose-patterned teapot and served it in the matching china teacups, with a couple of slices of apple pie. It was very English country garden and very restful. She didn't talk about what I'd told her until we'd finished, and then she asked about Max.

'I guess I felt a connection to him, at first, because he was Brad's brother,' I explained. 'I thought we were helping each other. But Saoirse said he wanted to meet me because he fancies me.'

'Does he?'

'I don't think so.'

'How do you feel about him?'

'I like him,' I said. 'We have stuff in common. But . . .'

'But what?'

'It's gross,' I told her. 'They were brothers.'

'So what?' she demanded. 'If you care about him . . .'

'I don't!' I cried. 'Not like that.'

'And yet he's reduced you to tears.'

'Not him. I've done that myself. Maybe it all got too much

369

for me,' I added. 'Maybe going back to work, having to deal with people again, just triggered something inside me.'

'Are you busy in work?' Her question was bland.

'Very,' I replied. 'It's been all go, all week. And . . .'

'What?'

I sighed. I hadn't been able to get the woman with hardly any antral follicles out of my mind. By now she'd know that her chances of conceiving a baby of her own were more or less zero. So she'd have to make choices about her future family. A donor egg was one answer. But not every woman wanted to do that. And I wasn't sure how her husband would feel about it, either. I don't know why her situation had bothered me so much. After all, in radiology we see life-threatening situations. We know when the road ahead is going to be rocky. We know that not everyone will have a good outcome. But even though this woman's situation wasn't life-threatening, it would change her life as she knew it. Like me, all her dreams and hopes for the future would be altered forever. And I'd never know how it turned out for her. That's the other thing about radiology. Once you've identified a problem, you see patients at the start of their journey. You don't see how things have panned out.

'Are you getting worried about having children yourself?' asked Mum when I'd finished talking about the patient. 'You shouldn't be. You're still young and, don't forget, I was in my forties when you came along.'

'True. But we don't know how many eggs I started out with. And I'm at an age where they start decreasing more and more rapidly.' I sighed. 'It's not about babies, Mum, not really. It's just . . .' I thought for a moment, '. . . it's lost opportunities. Opportunities I thought I had with Sean and then with Brad that weren't real opportunities at all. And it's not that I want to jump the first man I see and have children with him, it's just that my life isn't working out the way I thought.'

'Maybe I shouldn't have talked to you about opening up your chakras.' She gave me a sympathetic look. 'Maybe you weren't ready to have everything come at you.'

I gave her a shaky smile. 'I don't think it's my chakras or the fortune telling or—'

'Fortune telling?' She looked at me in disbelief. '*You* went to a fortune teller?'

'Obviously, it was nonsense,' I said after I'd told her about Magda.

'What did she say to you?'

'Oh, the usual. Difficult life, difficult times, nobody understood me. And a tall, dark and handsome prince would ride to my rescue.'

Mum laughed. 'Did you believe any of it?'

'It was generic,' I said. 'She got some things right. But they always do, don't they?'

'What does Max look like?' she asked.

'Oh, don't you start.' I snorted. 'He's fair-haired, for a start – and although he's not bad-looking, he's not here to rescue me.'

'Yet you thought you were rescuing him.'

'Don't try to turn it into something.'

My phone beeped and I scrambled for it straight away. But the text was from Saoirse, telling me that she wouldn't be home till Monday as she was staying an extra night at home and going straight into work from there.

'Not him?' asked Mum.

371

'No. I guess I really pissed him off.'

'If he cares about you, he'll call,' she said.

'I don't care if he cares. I was annoyed at him for thinking that it was all about being looked after, anyhow. I just wanted to apologise for walking out and leaving him to pay. I don't need him. I don't need anyone.'

The hurt expression was only on her face for an instant.

'I'm sorry.' I rubbed my already sore eyes. 'That's not true. I do need people. I needed you today, Mum. I'm glad you were here.'

'I know you've always felt a bit out of the loop because you were a late baby,' she said. 'But I love all my children equally.'

'It's just that I thought Gonne and Butler were more . . . more like true Ryans,' I admitted. 'Her music and his poetry. It fitted in with everything. Whereas I was an outlier. But Max,' I smiled at her, and this time there was no wobble in it, 'Max told me that being a radiographer was just as creative. Because I had to think intuitively. And he was right.'

'He sounds like a nice person,' she said.

'He is.'

'He'll call.'

But he didn't. He sent a text later that night.

I planned to give you this earlier, he wrote. *I found it on Brad's computer and thought it would be better to hand it over in person. It's probably best we don't meet again, though. You're right, there's nothing to be gained from it. M.*

There was an image attached. It was a sheet of paper headed 'Pros & Cons' set out in two columns. Under 'Pros' it said: *Amazing. Lovely. Intelligent. Soulmate?* Under 'Cons' it said: *I can't.*

It didn't have to be about me, of course. And, even if it was, I wasn't necessarily under the 'Pros' column. But I knew it was. And it made me feel a little better to think that he'd agonised about us. Even if it was clear that, ultimately, he was going to stay with his family. Which was the right choice for him to make.

I read it again. And again. And again.

Finally, I wiped away the tears that had rolled down my cheeks. They were the last I would shed for Brad McIntyre. I had no more crying to do for him now.

I deleted the text.

As for Max Hollander, I thought, the phone still in my hand, Saoirse had been wrong about him. His only reason in wanting to meet me had been to give me this note.

I hesitated for a moment, then sent him a new message, saying *Thank you*.

There was no reply.

I hadn't expected one.

So that was that.

I put my late lover's brother out of my mind and concentrated on my life. Work was as busy as always, and in the evenings I went out a lot with Saoirse, who'd broken it off with her boyfriend, Conal.

'I feel guilty that this is all my fault, after what you said in Spain about me losing Brad,' I told her one night when we'd gone to our local for a drink. 'You were perfectly happy before my meltdown.'

'I can't have been,' she said. 'Otherwise nothing that happened to you would've made the slightest difference.'

'All the same . . .'

'Better now than after swanning up the aisle in a long dress.' She grinned. 'I think I'll be one of those older brides who get married in neat little suits and look chic and sophisticated.'

'You and me both,' I said. 'If I ever get married at all.'

'Still off the men?'

I nodded. I'd given her an edited version of my meeting with Max and finished by saying that it had been good to meet him but we wouldn't in any way ever be involved.

'Oh well.' She raised her glass and clinked it against mine. 'Girl power.'

Girl power.

I had a hangover the next day.

The next time I saw Mum was at the osteoporosis lunch. She looked fabulous in a purple-and-orange dress while I, in my suitable-for-all-occasions navy shift, was drab by comparison. Everyone at the event came up to her and talked to her, and she kept our table of ten entertained all afternoon with her theatre stories while my admiration for her ability to be all things to all people grew by the second.

After the meal, she introduced me to the chairperson of the charity, a woman who reminded me of Drina, the head of our radiology department. Sinead Curtin was around the same age as my boss, bright and vivacious and full of enthusiasm for the work they were doing. Mum drifted off while I chatted to Sinead about the value of quantitative heel ultrasound scans in predicting bone density.

'I know this is a little out of left field,' Sinead said when we'd finished the discussion, 'but would you be interested in becoming involved with us?'

'I've already signed up for the direct debit to help,' I assured her.

'I didn't mean as a donor,' she said. 'I meant as someone who could add value to our board. Two of our members will be retiring this year. I think you'd be an excellent addition.'

'Really?' I was both surprised and flattered. 'Obviously, I enjoy what I do, but I don't know if I have the qualifications or experience to make a contribution.'

'Of course you have,' she said. 'You spoke so eloquently just now. You'd be great.'

'Well . . .'

'I won't pressurise you to make an immediate decision,' Sinead said. 'But how about I give you a call next week?'

I nodded and gave her my number.

'They'd be lucky to have you,' Mum said, when I told her about Sinead's offer.

'You say the nicest things,' I teased.

'I mean it.' Mum turned to look at me. 'You were the one who made me go for the scan. You explained it so well. And I'm grateful to you.'

I smiled.

'Why don't you and I go away for a weekend together?' she suggested. 'A bit of mother and daughter time. You could take me to Beniflor.'

'There's nowhere to stay except the posh hotel,' I said. 'Pilar's mum has sold the Villa Naranja.'

'The posh hotel sounds wonderful,' Mum said. 'Look at your schedule. See what works. I've got a couple of weeks of filming for *Clarendon Park*, then I'm free for a while.'

Going back might not be a good idea, I thought. Even in a short space of time people would have moved on. But, I reminded myself, so had I. And Mum had been good to me. I'd put her off during the summer. It would be ungrateful to put her off again now.

Chapter 34

While I was considering the possibility of spending a weekend away with Mum, Pilar actually went to Spain herself for a few days, to celebrate her brother's thirtieth birthday. She posted lots of pictures of the party on Facebook, and then emailed me another picture of the Villa Naranja, looking as beautiful as ever in the evening sun.

The sale completed while I was here, she said. *I went to say goodbye to it with Mamá. I know you said you'd done some painting but I didn't realise how lovely it was. It made me very, very nostalgic. Mamá too, I think. But Luis will be a good owner. He invited us for drinks on the evening of the signing, which was the day before Eduardo's birthday.*

I felt a small stab of envy as I thought of them enjoying drinks in the tranquil garden, but I knew that the Villa Naranja was part of my past. A healing part, obviously, but the past nonetheless. And so I was prepared to tell Mum that somewhere other than Beniflor might be a better option for our trip, when she rang and asked to know what dates I was free because she wanted to book the flights.

'Are you sure—' I began before she interrupted me.

'Absolutely.' Her tone was bossy. 'I wanted to visit while

you were there but you put me off because, you said, it was too hot. Clearly, you thought I was some frail old woman who couldn't cope with a bit of heat. But it's October now, Juno, and the days are getting shorter. I need some heat before the winter. Besides, the vitamin D will be good for my bones.'

'It's not that I don't want to go away with you,' I told her. 'It's just that the hotel is expensive, and maybe we should think about somewhere else entirely.'

'Oh, for heaven's sake, I was always going to pay for the hotel!' cried Mum.

'But—'

'No buts.' She was quite determined. 'Let me know your next available weekend. I insist.'

And so, against my better judgement, I found myself at the departure gates for a flight to Alicante once again a fortnight later – although this time with Mum in tow.

'I do so love the Internet,' she said as we waited to board. 'I love being able to pick anything I want from anywhere in the world right from the comfort of my armchair.'

'Funnily enough, I wouldn't have thought of you as a tech sort of person,' I remarked.

'Just because I'm old doesn't mean I can't learn new tricks.'

'It's not about your age,' I told her. 'It's about being you. About liking plays more than the cinema, and proper books not Kindles, and preferring to phone people rather than sending texts and all that sort of stuff.'

'Plays are more personal than movies,' she said. 'You're in the same room as the characters and you're totally involved with them. Printed books are works of art. They look beautiful, they feel beautiful and they smell beautiful. So why

378

wouldn't anyone want them? As for picking up the phone to talk to someone – doesn't that make perfect sense, if you want to have a conversation? I can't bear watching people tapping away at their keyboards like woodpeckers, when it would be just as easy to have a bloody conversation. But this,' she continued as we moved forward and she opened her app to retrieve her boarding pass, 'this makes perfect sense to me.'

'Thea Ryan.' The staff member at the gate looked at her ID and then at her. 'You're very welcome on board. I love you in *Clarendon Park*. That Imelda one is a right bitch, isn't she?'

'I do my best to be as bitchy as possible,' Mum assured her, and the agent laughed.

'I wouldn't have expected to be recognised at the gate,' Mum said to me as we settled into our seats. 'The staff are from so many different countries now that you don't assume they watch Irish TV.'

'Clearly, your fame goes before you.'

'Well, *Clarendon Park* has been sold to other European stations,' she said with satisfaction. 'Maybe I'm big in Poland and Romania.'

Despite Mum's surprise at being recognised, and her general experience of not being asked for autographs, two elderly women did stop by our seats and asked her to sign the back of their snack boxes for them.

'You make older women acceptable on TV,' said one of them. 'We're not all passively sitting there letting life go on around us, much as the youth of today might like to think that's all we do.'

'Absolutely right,' Mum agreed. 'Seventy is the new sixty.

The new fifty, in fact.' She signed her name with a flourish. 'I hope you have a great holiday.'

'We're here until New Year,' said one of the women, whose name was Trudy. 'Me and my husband bought a lovely apartment in Torrevieja when he retired. He died last year, it was the cigarettes that did for him, the poor love – dreadful habit but, of course, he'd been on them all his life – anyway, I thought about selling it, but then I said to myself, "What would Imelda do?" And I knew that you'd never sell somewhere like that but you'd come back, over and over again, and live your life and be a pain in the arse to everyone around you, and I decided that's what I'd do. Not be a pain in the arse, mind,' she added. 'But everything else.'

'I'm sorry for your loss,' said Mum. 'But I'm glad you're doing well.'

'Ah, you have to get on with it, don't you?' said Trudy. 'We'll be long enough dead.'

After which they returned to their seats, while the pang I'd felt when they spoke about death was masked by the genuine amusement I'd got from listening to them talk to Mum.

'I never thought of you as an icon for the older woman before,' I murmured. 'I always saw you as a kind of grande dame. But those women just think of you as someone out for a good time.'

'And they're right,' said Mum. 'About all of it. No point in moping, no point in not getting on with it, life is for living. You should know that by now.'

'I do.' I clipped up the tray table in front of me as a cabin crew member told us that we were commencing our descent. 'If anyone knows that, it's me. Hell, I'm on a jaunt to Spain with my mother. If that's not living it up, I don't know what is.'

'Cheeky thing.' But she laughed.

And so did I.

Although Mum had insisted on organising the flights and hotel, she allowed me to be the one in charge of the car hire. The queue was considerably shorter than it had been at the start of the summer, and there was no delay in picking up the keys. I didn't bother with the satnav, as I was confident about where I was going, but when I turned off the motorway and took the twisting road to Beniflor, Mum gasped.

'If I'd known what this was like before, I'd have worried about you a bit more,' she said.

I laughed and took another bend with practised ease.

'You're actually liking this, aren't you? You're enjoying the fact that I'm terrified.'

'Kind of,' I admitted.

'I underestimated you,' she said. 'Maybe I always have.'

And maybe I'd underestimated her, I thought, as the road straightened out and we approached the hotel. Maybe we all underestimate each other in a whole variety of ways.

I turned into the driveway that led to the hotel building and brought the car to a stop under a covered bay.

'Oh, my goodness!' Mum exclaimed as she got out. 'It's beautiful.'

And it was. Even more beautiful in the slightly softer light of the late October afternoon, I thought, than it had been in the full glare of the summer sun. The air was still clear and balmy and a soft breeze rustled through the oleander bushes.

'This way.' I led her to the building. As we mounted the

steps I could see the face of a small tabby cat in an urn of pink and purple flowers.

'Oh!' I gasped. 'It's one of the kittens.'

'Ophelia's kittens?' Mum looked at the cat with the same level of curiosity as it was giving her. 'You know my views on them. But he – or she – is endearing.'

I moved towards the kitten who leaped gracefully from the urn and then disappeared into the box hedge.

'After all I did for you, you could show a little gratitude,' I called after it.

'Like I said,' Mum observed. 'Selfish creatures. But elegant. At least she hasn't inherited her mother's arse.'

I was choking with laughter as we walked into the hotel together. Bridget Johnson, Rosa's mum, was sitting behind the large table they used as a desk. I wasn't sure she'd remember me, but her face lit up in recognition and she came from behind the table to greet me.

'It's lovely to see you again,' she said. 'I saw your name on the reservation, but I didn't know if it really was you or not. I thought, if you came back, you'd stay with the Navarros. Or maybe with Ana Perez.'

'Navarros? Perez?' asked my mother.

'The Navarros are the neighbours who bought the house I was staying in,' I reminded her. 'Ana is Pilar's mother, she originally owned it.'

'Yes, yes, I know about Pilar,' said Mum.

'She was here with her family recently,' said Bridget. 'It was Eduardo's birthday and they had a lovely celebration. They booked the entire terrace.'

'She sent photos,' I told her. 'It looked like a great night.'

'It was,' Bridget said. 'Pilar spent a lot of time talking to Luis Navarro. The whole Navarro family were there. Pilar and Luis seemed very taken with each other.' She gave me a knowing smile.

Luis. And Pilar. Could they become a thing? She hadn't said a word about it, despite giving me and Cleo what I thought had been a full rundown of the birthday night. I'd enjoyed hearing about it and hearing about the people I'd come to know. I'd felt as though I was there again myself. I thought about Luis and Pilar. It would keep the Villa Naranja in the Perez family, if they became a thing. But that was medieval thinking. People didn't actually get married to do things like that. And Pilar didn't care about the house. All the same, I was going to ask her when I got back to Ireland. If only because she'd kept very quiet about meeting Luis.

'Pep was here too,' Bridget said. 'He's keeping well.'

'How's Rosa?' I wasn't going to talk about Pep, least of all in front of Mum.

'She's great.' Bridget smiled at me. 'She's doing really well this term at college.'

'She's not here now?'

Bridget shook her head. 'She's sharing an apartment in Alicante with her girlfriends. Far more exciting than here.'

'Tell her I said hello.'

'You should've let her know you were coming,' said Bridget. 'I'm sure she'd have dropped by. She still might, if you call.'

'Oh, I wouldn't drag her away from her studies,' I said. 'Besides, Mum and I are just here for a little R&R.'

'Juno told such lovely tales about her time here that I had to see it for myself,' said Mum.

'Well, I certainly hope you'll enjoy your stay with us,' Bridget said. 'Let's fill in some info, then I'll give you the key and you can chill out.'

Ten minutes later, I was opening the door to our room.

'A suite! Mum . . .' I turned to her. 'You didn't have to book a suite, for heaven's sake.'

'I didn't,' she told me. 'I just asked for a room with a sea view.'

I looked around the room, which was divided into a living area and a sleeping area, both beautifully decorated in delicate shades of off-white and apple green. The all-marble bathroom was even bigger than the fantastic one in the Villa Naranja and contained bales of fluffy towels, Acqua di Parma toiletries and a couple of luxurious robes.

'This is very satisfactory,' said Mum as she opened the doors to the balcony. 'Very satisfactory indeed.'

But while she was standing outside, revelling in the evening sun, I was ringing Bridget to check that there hadn't been a mistake.

'Of course not,' said Bridget. 'Like I said, I saw your name on the reservation. I thought that, if it was you, you'd like to sample La Higuera at its best. And if it wasn't, well, it would have been a nice surprise for the other guests.'

'It's a nice surprise for us,' I said. 'Thank you very much.'

'Actually, I wanted to thank you,' said Bridget. 'You were a breath of fresh air for Rosa this summer. Since meeting you and talking to you, she's become far more focused on her studies. She told me that you'd inspired her and she hoped to be like you some day.'

'What?' I was astonished. 'I'm not . . . there's nothing about me that's particularly inspiring.'

384

'She said you were very clued-in,' said Bridget. 'And that you knew what you wanted and that, even though you'd had a setback, you were getting yourself together. Like all of us, she was very impressed with how you looked after Xavi Ruiz. Truth is, Rosa really looks up to you, and I'm delighted about that.'

I put the phone down with a profound sense of shock. I hadn't realised that Rosa had seen me as someone to look up to. I didn't see myself like that at all. But I was someone who'd made mistakes and forgiven myself for them. So perhaps that was something worth celebrating.

'Champagne?' Mum came in from the balcony. 'I do think that evenings in the sun should be celebrated with champagne, don't you?'

'Yes,' I said, still dazed after Bridget's words. 'I do.'

There were heaters on the terrace, even though the air was still warm. About half of the tables were occupied, and a charming waiter led us to one at the far end. I didn't say anything but I could feel my entire body tighten as I realised it was the same table I'd sat at with Max Hollander when he'd told me everything about Brad, Alessandra and Dylan. I shivered involuntarily.

'OK?' asked Mum. 'Do you want to sit closer to the heater?'

'No, I'm fine.' I pushed thoughts of my previous time here to the back of my mind as the waiter returned with our two glasses of champagne and a food menu.

'Hungry?' she asked.

'Not very,' I admitted, even though the only food I'd had since breakfast had been some cheese and crackers on the plane.

'I need something to pick at.' Mum took her glasses from her bag and began to study the menu.

'*Para picar*,' I said.

'Huh?'

'To pick at. *Para picar.*'

'Did you take lessons while you were here?' she asked.

'No. But some things sink in anyhow.'

'Who's Pep?' She closed the menu and looked inquiringly at me.

'Pep?'

'Yes. The lovely woman at reception said that he was at that birthday celebration. She said it as though it should mean something to you.'

'He was the pool cleaner at the Villa Naranja,' I replied.

Mum's deep-blue eyes regarded me thoughtfully.

'And?'

'And another of the Navarros,' I said. 'The pool cleaning was his summer job. He's a student in Alicante.'

'And?'

'For heaven's sake, Mum!'

She grinned. 'Just checking. That there was someone.'

I shook my head. 'You're impossible. Yes, all right, I had a bit of a fling with him, but that's all it was, honestly.'

'You needed a fling,' she said. 'I told you before.'

'I know. And I wish you wouldn't.'

A few months ago, her probing would have annoyed me. But now, even though I made a face at her, I didn't really mind. She wasn't asking about Pep to judge me or to measure me against anyone else in the family. She was asking because she was interested and because she cared.

'I love you, you know,' she said.

386

'And I love you,' I told her.

Then the waiter came and she ordered *jamón ibérico* and a variety of bread, which we shared as the sun slid behind the mountains and the stars appeared in the cloudless sky.

After we'd finished the food, Mum declared herself exhausted and said she was going to bed. Although I was tired, I wasn't sleepy. So I said goodnight to her and moved into the small lounge area of the hotel, which overlooked the pool. I took out my phone and messaged Cleo and Saoirse, who both hoped I was having a good time with my mum (they knew that my relationship with her had always been edgy and had been surprised when I told them I was going away with her). *So far so good*, was my response, which was perfectly true. Somehow, for the first time, I was seeing Mum as a person and not as a mother who'd been shocked at my arrival, nor as the actress who was bewildered by my love of practical things. I sent a message to Pilar too and added *Luis Navarro??* at the end. Then I sent a text to Dad telling him that everything was great and that Mum had retired early.

I'm sitting in the kitchen smoking my pipe, he sent back. *The back door is open. Don't tell her, though.*

You want me to hide your sins?

You're usually on my side. Especially about the pipe.

I sent back some laughing emojis. It was true that I nearly always sided with Dad in every argument with Mum. But those arguments were few and far between, because they were united on so many fronts. And Dad, to me, was a somewhat distant, literary figure, never to be disturbed when he was working – the head of the household without actually laying down the law, because Mum did it for him.

I might not always have appreciated them, I realised, but I did now.

I put the phone on the glass table in front of me as two small cats strolled through the open doors of the lounge and stopped in front of me. I recognised the one I'd seen earlier. The other was obviously his or her sibling. Both Ophelia's offspring. Their eyes were fixed on me, and as I leaned forward I half expected them to run away. But instead they came closer and began to rub against my ankles.

'Do you remember me?' I scratched them both on their heads. 'I knew your mother.'

The cats purred like tractors and then settled beneath my chair. The same sense of peace I'd always felt at the Villa Naranja settled over me. I closed my eyes.

My phone beeped and I picked it up again.

Hi, I read. *I'm truly sorry about my last text to you. No excuse, just bad manners and grumpiness. Are you still available to buy me that coffee? Max*

Chapter 35

I stared at the text in disbelief.

What on earth had prompted Max to send me a text? And why would I even bother answering his message now? Who the hell did he think he was?

There was movement beneath my chair and the two cats appeared at my feet again. Both of them looked at me, unblinking.

'What?' I asked them.

They kept staring.

Bridget Johnson walked into the room.

'Are they bothering you?' she asked. 'I'll scoot them out if—'

'No,' I replied quickly. 'They're not. I like them.'

'Of course, they're from the Villa Naranja!' she exclaimed. 'I don't know how I forgot that. Rosa brought them because you were worried about them.'

I nodded.

'Ben and Jerry,' she said. 'That's what we named them, although Jerry's a girl and Ben's a boy. Ben is the one with the white socks. Jerry is the tabby.'

I was glad she'd worked out the sexes already. And that she hadn't picked theatrical names for them.

'The guests love them,' she added, 'but I know not everyone likes cats, even when they're still at the kitten stage, so I'm always ready to shoo them away.'

'Their mother was great company at the villa,' I said. 'It's nice to see them here.'

'They seem to have taken a shine to you,' she said as Ben suddenly jumped on to my lap. 'Are you sure you don't mind?'

I shook my head and rubbed the cat beneath his chin. He started to purr again. His sister lay across my feet. Bridget laughed.

'If you're totally sure,' she said. 'Can I get you anything else? Wine? Spirits?'

'A coffee would be nice. Decaf if you have it.'

'No problem,' she said.

She went to get the coffee and I kept rubbing Ben. But I was thinking of Brad. And Max.

Of course, I'd never truly believed that Brad's spirit was somehow in Banquo. I believed it even less when he'd transitioned into Ophelia. But it was strange how she, and her offspring, seemed to be attracted to me. It didn't happen in Dublin. Keisha Washington, who lived in the apartment next door to Saoirse and me, had a black-and-white cat that occasionally jumped on to our balcony. But it didn't stay if I opened the doors. It had never rubbed against my ankles or stared at me with that knowing look that seemed to be a feature of Ophelia's family.

'You're losing it again,' I muttered. 'Something happens to you here. Your mind goes AWOL.'

I picked up the phone and looked at it again.

It would be stupid to reply to Max Hollander.

What would be the point?

I was about to put the phone down when it pinged again. My heart skipped a beat.

Haha, Pilar had sent. *Actually, Luis Navarro was very nice when I met him. Talked about his plans for the house. Interesting.*

Interesting in what sort of way? Texting Pilar was happily distracting.

He's an interesting man.

That's all?

'Yes!!!! Well . . . maybe.

OMG, I texted back. *Really??*

I don't know. He's there. I'm here. And we only talked for an evening.

I sent back the laughing emojis. I was getting good at them.

Pilar and Luis. It would be amazing.

Bridget returned with my coffee and I picked Ben from my lap. He and his sister padded after her when she walked back through the hotel, leaving me on my own again. Then a group of guests came into the lounge and arranged themselves around one of the low tables. They were English and I gathered they'd been celebrating a twenty-fifth wedding anniversary.

Twenty-five years. How lovely it was to think of being with the love of your life for twenty-five years. To know that you'd got it so absolutely right.

Mum and Dad had been together for longer, I realised. We'd never had celebrations for them because, despite their love of parties, they always liked to mark their anniversaries by being on their own. But there was no doubt Mum was the love of Dad's life, and he of hers. They were a long-haul couple.

I finished my coffee and put the cup back on the table. I picked up my phone.

No more messages.

I looked at Max's again.

I'm truly sorry about my last text to you. No excuse, just bad manners and grumpiness. Are you still available to buy me that coffee?

I breathed in deeply and exhaled slowly.

No problem, I typed. *But I'm back in Spain so can't make good on my coffee offer. Sorry.*

The reply came back immediately.

For good?

No. With Mum. Mini-break.

Oh. Till when?

Sunday night. Same flight home as you took when you were here. I added a smiley face.

Staying at Villa Naranja again?

No. La Higuera.

Lovely hotel.

Yes. Never thought I'd be staying in it.

Meeting up with all your friends?

Haven't made plans. Just here to chill with Mum, really.

Sounds perfect.

How's Dylan?

Doing well. Mac has been really good for him.

Glad to hear it. How's foot?

Much better. Kept boot on as instructed. Think maybe the pain was partly responsible for grumpiness.

392

A picture followed. It was another X-ray. I could see the healing fracture.

Looks good. Wear better trainers and stay off the roads.

Yes, nurse.

Am not a nurse.

No. I forgot.

Though they are very qualified and would give you the same orders.

Women are always right.

There are male nurses too.

You always know the way to put me down.

I stared at the text. Was that what I was doing? I didn't mean to. Bloody texts, I thought. They're too stark. Too emotionless. They don't get the sense of what you're trying to say. They can be misconstrued.

Sorry, I typed. *Was meant as joke.*

No need. Obvs am still a bit grumpy.

You need a mini-break too.

Maybe.

Perhaps we can do that coffee soon?

Would be lovely.

I was the rude one, I typed. *When we met last time. I flared up at you for no reason.*

You'd been under a lot of pressure.

No. I was back from lovely stay in Spain. I was fine. Just rude.

You'd reached acceptance. But that doesn't mean you still weren't hurting.

Once again, I stared at the text. He was right. I was better, but the hurt was still there beneath the surface. It would go eventually, but maybe never completely. Because everything that happens is part of who we are. It can never be erased. It simply adds to the layers that we are made of. Although I'd gone to pieces, at first, Brad's betrayal and his death had also hardened me. I was tougher than I'd been before. Less trusting. Maybe Max was too.

You were hurting just as much, I sent after a moment.

Let's agree neither of us was at our best. Better next time. Hopefully soon.

Hopefully.

He sent a smiley face.

I sent one back.

Then I went to bed.

It was a long time before I fell asleep.

Mum was awake before me the following morning. I'd slept fitfully, my dreams a series of jumbled encounters with Brad and Pep and Max and Luis. Sean made an appearance too, as did Magda Burnaia. She shuffled a pack of tarot cards, then threw them in the air so that they rained down on top of me.

'The Lovers,' she said. 'It was always about the Lovers.'

That was when my eyes snapped open and I realised that the sun was slanting through the gap in the curtains where Mum had parted them so that she could go outside. I got up and put one of the soft robes on over my skimpy pyjamas before joining her on the balcony, where she was having tea.

'Are you up long?' I asked.

'About an hour,' she replied. 'I've been sitting here reading Joyce.' She nodded towards a dog-eared copy of *Ulysses*.

I've never been able to read *Ulysses*. I've tried on numerous occasions but always fall at the hurdle of long sentences without commas that don't make a lot of sense – at least, not to me. My last attempt had been over ten years earlier, before I'd left home, when Mum was doing a reading of the book for a literary festival. She'd spent ages practising, and hearing her say the words somehow made it seem more accessible, but when I opened the pages I gave up in despair again. I comforted myself regarding my lack of intellectual ability by deciding that the book on diagnostic imaging I was studying would have been gibberish to her. But truthfully, I felt like a failure. Especially as Gonne and Butler both considered it to be a masterpiece.

'Would you like breakfast?' I asked.

'Yes.' She grinned at me. 'I'm ravenous. If you hadn't woken up yourself, I was prepared to dig you out of the bed.'

I laughed and got ready.

We went downstairs, where we both feasted off the lavish buffet provided by the Higuera. Afterwards, Mum said that she'd like to visit the town, so we drove into Beniflor.

I parked in my usual space, outside the supermarket, and then we walked to the town square, which was busier than I'd expected. The usual parade of people were going in and out of the *ayuntamiento* building, the old men were sitting outside the bar, and the umbrellas were up in front of the Café Flor where three of the half-dozen tables were occupied. It looked peaceful and unchanging, and I felt a wave of tranquillity wash over me. Then I realised that one of the people at the café was Catalina Ruiz, her pregnancy now obvious. When she looked up and saw me she smiled.

'You are back,' she said as she stood up and embraced me. 'How nice.'

'Only for a short visit,' I said. 'I'm here with my mum.'

I introduced them, and Catalina told Mum that it was lucky I'd been around when I was. Otherwise her son might not have recovered as quickly from his dislocated shoulder.

'You never said anything about that.' Mum looked at me in puzzlement after we'd said our goodbyes to Catalina. 'Honestly, Juno, it's like you live your life in a bubble sometimes.'

'She's making it out to be a much bigger deal than it was,' I said. 'People do, when they get a fright. It was a pretty basic dislocation, and all I did was provide first aid.'

Mum shook her head but said nothing. I walked with her around the town, which took all of fifteen minutes – including cultural highlights like the DIY shop – then I suggested we went to Beniflor Costa for a proper walk along the beach.

'We could visit the Arab baths tomorrow, but it's lovely and sunny right now, ideal for the beach.'

'Whatever you like,' said Mum, who still seemed miffed because I hadn't mentioned Xavi Ruiz's shoulder sooner.

It was much easier to find a parking space near the beach in Beniflor Costa, and the sight of the blue sea and the fine, biscuit-coloured sand restored Mum's good humour. She insisted on going down to the water's edge to paddle and, as the sea lapped around our ankles, I explained how lots of people from around the area had apartments near the coast and how they sometimes moved to them for the summer months.

'For the breeze,' I explained. 'It can be stifling inland, even though it might only be a few kilometres.'

'How far is it from here to the house where you stayed?' she asked.

'Not very. Eight, ten kilometres,' I replied. 'But you could feel the difference. I guess that's why Pilar's mum wanted to sell it. A weekend home near the sea is probably a better idea.'

She nodded. 'But you must take me to the house, all the same.'

'It's been sold,' I reminded her. 'We can't go in.'

'Just a drive-by,' she said. 'Then we can go back to the hotel, have a light lunch, and I can spend the rest of the afternoon relaxing with my book.'

'OK.'

After we'd sat on the promenade for long enough to allow our feet to dry, we got into the car and I drove to the Villa Naranja.

I felt my heart constrict a little as I rounded the bend in the road and saw the whitewashed walls behind the green metal gate. I pulled to a stop, and we both got out of the car. That was when I realised that there was someone in the gardens.

'Luis Navarro,' I said to my mother. 'The man who bought it.'

Luis had seen the car pull up and was walking towards us. When he recognised me, he looked surprised.

'I did not expect to see you here so soon,' he said as he reached into his pocket and took out the remote that opened the gates. 'Welcome back.'

As with Catalina, I introduced my mother and explained about being on a mini-break with her.

'At La Higuera. That's very nice,' he said.

'Indeed it is,' said Mum.

'No need for renovations there.' He grinned at me. 'I have been doing more work here. Would you like to see?'

'Of course,' said Mum before I could speak.

The house was definitely more cared for than before, and not just because of my painting and varnishing and gardening. There was a subtle change in the atmosphere about it, a feeling that it mattered to someone now.

'Have you moved in?' I asked Luis.

He nodded.

'It is nice to have a place entirely for myself. Well, not entirely,' he corrected himself as a familiar cat stalked through the garden. 'I have to share.'

'Banquo! I mean, Ophelia!' I hunkered down and stroked her.

'The famous cat,' said Mum. 'I'm glad she was here to keep you company. But truly, Juno, I'll never understand your affection for felines.'

'I like their unpredictability,' I said. 'And the way they're always in charge of their lives.'

She laughed. 'Unpredictability! From my daughter who likes things to be rational, explainable and predictable. Although,' she conceded, 'I never would have predicted you'd have taken a summer break like this.'

'We are all glad Juno came to stay,' said Luis. 'I'm afraid Pep isn't here,' he added as he turned to me. 'He is in Alicante.'

'I didn't expect to see him,' I said.

Mum gave me a knowing look but I said nothing.

'Do you want to see the place where Pilar's great-grandfather was hanged?' I asked.

'Oh, yes!' Her enthusiasm wasn't ghoulish but born of a real interest in the past.

I brought her to the spot beneath the jacaranda, and she

stood there in silence looking at it. I stayed quiet too. I could see that she was living it in her head.

'We need to remember these things,' she said eventually. 'They shape our lives, our futures, our children's futures.'

'You are right, of course,' said Luis. 'But I do not want the garden to be a place of sadness.'

My mother nodded her agreement. 'Memories are enough.'

And then Luis invited us into the house, where he offered us juice along with some nuts and olives. He wanted to give us some Navarro wine to take home but I pointed out that we couldn't bring it in our carry-on luggage. He snorted in disgust.

'It is so annoying,' he said. 'I would like to share our wines with more people outside Spain. I must contact your friend,' he added. 'The one who worked with the Spanish Tourist Board.'

'Which friend?' asked Mum.

'Max Hollander,' I replied.

'Oh.' Her expression was unfathomable as she looked at me. 'I take it you still haven't heard from him?'

She'd asked me once or twice already, when we'd talked about the trip, and I'd told her to stop because it was perfectly obvious I wasn't going to hear from him and I was absolutely fine with it. The day I'd called to her and broken down in tears had been a bad day but I'd got over myself now and I was fine. I would tell her about his text, but not in front of Luis. I shook my head.

'If you have time later today, or tomorrow, you should drop by the finca and say hello to my mother,' he said. 'I know she would be happy to see you.'

'That'd be great,' said Mum before I could reply. 'My husband is thinking of writing a script about this place.'

'He is a writer?'

'A playwright,' I clarified, before turning to Mum. 'He's not seriously thinking about it, is he?'

'Of course,' said Mum. 'The Civil War story is very interesting. And I'm sure he'll weave in a modern-day love story too.'

'So you're here as a research trip?' I asked.

She laughed. 'I'm just the actress, sweetheart. Your dad does everything else.'

I shot her a sceptical look while Luis frowned as he tried to follow the subtext of our conversation.

'We'd better go,' I told him. 'Thank you for showing us around, Luis. It looks fabulous. I hope you're very happy here.' And then, because I couldn't resist it, I added that I hoped Pilar would visit again soon.

His eyes narrowed, and I grinned.

'You know lots about me,' I said. 'Now I know a little about you too.'

'She is nice woman,' he said. 'And we are just friends.'

I'd always meant it when I referred to myself as 'just friends' with someone. But now I realised how lame it sounded.

'I hope it works out,' I said.

'There is nothing . . . well . . .'

'It would be so lovely,' I said. 'You and Doña Carmen's granddaughter.'

'Perhaps.' His voice was suddenly serious. 'But only if she was the right one for me. It is important, Juno, to know who the right one is. You must think about this yourself.'

He kissed me briefly on the cheek, then turned to Mum and told her it had been a pleasure to meet a famous actress and that he hoped she would visit again soon.

As we walked out of the house I gave Ophelia a goodbye scratch on the head.

And then I drove Mum back to the hotel.

'What was all that about Pilar and Luis and the importance of knowing the right one?' Mum demanded as I parked outside La Higuera.

I told her about Bridget's belief that there was something between Luis and Pilar and she looked thoughtful.

'I'll have to tell your dad that. It would make his story stronger.'

'You can't take people's lives and muck around with them in a screenplay,' I protested. But Mum just snorted and said everyone was fair game to Dad – and besides, it would make a perfect ending.

'Clichéd,' I said.

'But what if it's true?' she asked. 'What if your friend and that man fall in love, and she moves into her grandmother's house? Then it's life. And the ripples of the past echo to the present and beyond, Juno.'

I didn't say anything but chivvied her along to the terrace for lunch, where we had salads along with a glass of wine each. Then Mum retrieved *Ulysses* from the room and found a shady place beneath one of the wide awnings to read, while I braved the heated pool for a swim. I emerged glowing and refreshed and then went upstairs and had a shower. I didn't bother drying my hair – it was longer than in the summer but still not long enough to worry about – and got dressed in a comfortable striped cotton dress that I'd bought in the sales when I'd returned home.

I felt good again. And happy again. And pleased that I'd come here with Mum, even if I'd been dubious at the start. I was glad I'd gone to the Villa Naranja too, glad that it had looked so lovely, and glad that Ophelia was still around.

The feelings of unfinished business I'd had when I'd left for Dublin were gone. Beniflor had moved on. So had the people. So had I.

I'd intended to show Mum Max's text when I came downstairs, but she was asleep in the shade of the awning and I didn't want to disturb her. She'd obviously dozed off while reading, because *Ulysses* had fallen from her hand and was upturned on the ground. I picked it up and replaced it on the table in front of her. Her bookmark had fallen out and, as I picked that up too, I hoped she'd have some idea of where she'd been in the novel. I glanced at the bookmark as I placed it within the pages, and caught my breath.

It was a customised bookmark with individual headshots of me, Gonne and Butler on one side. On the other was a quote from Frederick Douglass. It said: 'It is easier to raise strong children than to repair broken men.'

Was that what Mum had wanted for her children? For us to be strong? And had she succeeded? I thought of all of us. All doing what we wanted to do. Butler, an acclaimed poet, who'd finally had the opportunity to marry the man he'd shared his life with for so long. Gonne, who combined her love of music with her talent as a mother. And me, the practical one, back doing the job I'd always wanted to do after picking up the pieces of my personal tragedy. The one who everyone else did indeed think was strong. I'd doubted my own strength for a long time but now I knew it was still there. Just as she'd raised me. Just like her. Just like Dad. Just like my brother and my sister.

I left her to her snooze and went for a walk around the gardens. They were more extensive than I originally thought, with the more cultivated areas eventually leading to a small forest of pine trees.

It was very quiet. Very still.

Until my phone beeped and, in taking it out of my pocket, I tripped over a sprawling root and landed on my behind while the phone itself skittered across the fallen pine leaves on the track I'd been following. I lay there for a moment, winded and shocked. When I eventually tried to get up, I yelped in pain. My ankle was already swelling up and was really hurting.

'Bugger,' I muttered as I ran my fingers over the joints, which felt tender. 'Bugger.'

I pulled myself into a sitting position at the base of the tree and made myself breathe slowly and evenly. My heartbeat returned to normal and, even though my ankle was throbbing furiously, I'd already recovered from the shock. I felt it again. The swelling was bigger. If a patient had presented at the hospital with an ankle as swollen as mine, he or she would have been immediately referred to radiology for an X-ray to see if it was fractured. I doubted mine was. Yes, I'd jolted it when I caught it in the tree root, but the fall hadn't been that bad. Nevertheless, without an X-ray I couldn't be certain. Many ankle fractures can be quite minor, especially when the bone actually stays in place. Usually, in that case, a doctor will recommend a high ankle shoe, or sometimes a short cast, while it heals.

I suddenly laughed at myself. They say that doctors and nurses make the worst patients, but radiographers are just as bad. We always go for the doomsday scenario.

My phone beeped again, reminding me that I hadn't picked up the text from a couple of minutes earlier. I edged my way over to it. I assumed Mum had woken up and had texted me to find out where I'd got to. I was running through the excuses I could give her for having been so stupid as to trip, when I actually looked at the message.

How about today for that coffee? Max

Max. I'd nearly, possibly, probably broken my ankle because of Max Hollander! Asking me for coffee when he already knew I was in Spain and so couldn't meet him, anyway. Honestly, I thought, how inconsiderate could one man be?

I told you. Am away, I texted in return. *So can't make coffee.*

I'm away too. The response came quickly. *You recommended a mini-break, remember?*

Away where? I typed.

In Spain.

What???

I couldn't wait for coffee. Thought maybe we could have it here.

Where are you? My fingers flew over the keypad.

La Higuera.

I stared at the screen. Max Hollander was here. He'd come here. To La Higuera. But he knew I was here with Mum. So why . . . ?

Why are you here?

I told you. For coffee. You said you were buying.

Maybe the fall had slowed my brain. I hadn't quite got my head around what he was saying.

You're in La Higuera now? I texted.

Yes. On the terrace. Looking out over garden. Are you here?

Yes.

Where? I can see three people on sunloungers and an older woman asleep in a chair. But not you.

The older woman is my mum.

I didn't recognise her, he texted. *She has a sun visor over her face.*

She always protects her face.

So . . . am I standing here like a complete idiot or will you meet me for coffee?

I can't.

Why?

I was composing my reply when another message from him arrived.

Have I made a tit of it? he asked. *Coming here? Was it a massive mistake? It seemed like such a great idea yesterday. Meet again in a place where we seemed to get on so well. Apologise again for my grumpiness. And for being a bit overbearing too. Sometimes ideas aren't as good in practice as they are when you think about them. I'm an idiot. Certainly every time I think of you.*

I read this message three times.

I can't meet you, I typed. *I can't walk at the moment.*

What?

Went for a stroll in the garden. Tripped and crocked my ankle.

Where?

In the little forest.

The pine trees at the end of the garden? Not some other pine trees miles away?

405

Yes.
On the way.

I stayed where I was, sitting against the tree, nursing my ankle. Five minutes later, I heard footsteps on the trail I'd been following. And then Max Hollander appeared.

He was wearing jeans and a polo shirt; a pair of aviator sunglasses pushed on to his head. He stopped when he saw me.

'Juno! Are you badly hurt?'

'My pride certainly is,' I said. 'My ankle aches but I'm pretty sure it's just badly sprained.'

'Ice,' he said.

'I know. But there isn't much here.'

'Plenty at the hotel.'

'Yeah.'

He grinned. 'I've always wanted to do this.'

'What?'

'Rescue a damsel in distress, of course. What man doesn't see himself as a knight in shining armour?'

'If you help me up, I'm sure I can limp my way back to the hotel. And Bridget will give us some ice.'

He did as I asked, taking my hand and helping me to my feet. And then, just as I was steadying myself, he lifted me into his arms.

'Ow!' I yelped. 'What are you doing?'

'Rescuing you, of course,' he said. 'I'm carrying you back to the hotel. You don't think I'd let you hobble on that ankle and make things worse, do you?'

'I'd be perfectly capable—' I began, but he interrupted me.

'You lectured me about my foot,' he said. 'Clearly, you're a do-as-I-say-and-not-as-I-do sort of person.'

'Possibly,' I admitted.

'Now keep still and let me do my Galahad thing,' he said.

I put my arms around his neck.

It was nice to be rescued.

It was even nicer to be rescued by Max.

He carried me all the way to the hotel, and as he drew near, I heard a horrified exclamation from my mother.

'Juno! What on earth has happened? Are you all right?'

I lifted my head from Max's shoulder and slid out of his arms, wincing as my foot touched the ground.

'I'm fine,' I said. 'I turned my ankle, that's all.'

'For a second I thought . . . I thought . . . well, I don't know what I thought.' Mum's expression was concerned.

'I'll be fine. I just need to ice and elevate it,' I told her.

'Sit here.' She gestured towards the cushioned chair she'd vacated.

I hopped over and did what she asked.

'I'll get the ice,' said Max.

'Can you see if they have an elastic bandage too?' I asked.

He nodded and went inside the hotel.

'You're very pale,' said Mum. 'Are you sure you're OK?'

'It's pretty sore at the moment,' I admitted. 'But I'll be fine.'

'Maybe you need a cast or something,' she said.

'No!' I shook my head. 'Not when we're flying home so soon. It'd probably be OK, but I'm not going to risk it.'

'This is all my fault,' said Mum. 'I was the one who wanted to come. If I hadn't . . .'

'Don't be silly,' I said. 'I wanted to come too. With you. It's been lovely.'

'Really?'

'Yes,' I said. 'I'm glad we did it. And I'm sorry if I some-times . . . if I've been . . . well, stroppy with you, I guess.'

'I'm glad you're stroppy,' she told me. 'It means I did a good job.'

'I saw your bookmark.'

'I always wanted you to be independent. All of you. I suppose Gonne was the closest to me in attitude. But, obvi-ously, Butler went through some hard times, especially when he was younger. All the same, he didn't compromise who he was and I'm proud of that. And I'm proud you didn't, either. You did what you wanted to do too.'

'I thought I was breaking the mould,' I said.

She laughed. 'I hope you were. Anyway, getting back to the here and now, what happened? You were lucky that man was around to help you. Is he a guest?'

Before I had a chance to reply, Max returned with a bag of ice and a long elastic bandage, which I used to strap up my ankle.

'Wow,' he said when I'd finished. 'That was impressive.'

'Easy-peasy.' I eyed my handiwork with satisfaction.

'Thank you for helping her,' said Mum. 'We haven't been introduced. I'm Thea Ryan.'

'I know,' said Max. 'I'm a big fan.'

'Thank you.' Mum looked pleased. 'I wasn't expecting to be recognised out here.'

'I had a little bit of prior knowledge,' admitted Max.

'Who are you?' she asked.

'A friend of Juno's,' said Max.

408

'Sorry?' Mum looked at him in astonishment. 'A friend? You're from around here? You knew her when she stayed before?'

'Not exactly,' said Max.

'He's Max,' I told her. 'Brad's brother.'

She stared at Max, and then at me.

'Your lover's brother?'

'Mum!'

'What are you doing here?' she asked him.

'Inviting me for coffee,' I answered, before he had a chance to reply.

'What?' Mum was completely bewildered.

'Juno told me I needed a mini-break. And I thought I could combine that with having coffee with her.'

'Well, this is an interesting turn of events.' Mum looked at him and then glanced sidelong at me. 'I've never had a man fly a few thousand miles to ask *me* for coffee.'

'I'd be happy to have coffee with you too,' said Max.

'Huh.' Mum snorted. 'I hope you're not going to ruin it all by suggesting a double date!'

Max smiled at her. 'I'd insist on an entirely separate coffee date with you,' he said. 'As a fan, I wouldn't want to share.'

'Goodness.' Mum looked at me. 'He's quite charming, isn't he?'

I hadn't thought of Max as charming before. Just . . . well . . . nice.

'I don't think Juno regards me as charming.' Max echoed my thoughts. 'Actually, I think she thinks I'm a bit of a pain in the arse. And I have been, I suppose, even though it's always unintentional. The bottom line is I wanted coffee with her, and I couldn't wait, and so I came here. But, Juno,' he turned to me, 'if you think I am definitely being a pain in the arse, or if you want me to get out of your life and never return, I'll go.'

There was a sudden movement in the garden. The two young cats stalked across the grass. They were followed by a third.

'Banquo!' I exclaimed. 'Ophelia.'

The cats stopped in the distance. Then Ophelia left her two children and padded through the grass until she was in front of me. She began to purr.

'Oh, Ophelia,' I said.

She rubbed against my uninjured ankle.

'You've walked miles!' I cried.

'The cat,' said Mum. 'The one at the Villa Naranja.'

I nodded.

Ophelia looked at Mum, then at me. And then she strode deliberately over to Max and began to rub against him too.

'She approves of me,' said Max. 'That has to count for something.'

'I feel like I'm in a play where nobody has told me the ending,' said Mum. 'And I'm not sure if it's got to the point where I should be exiting stage left.'

'The ending is up to Juno,' said Max. 'It always was.'

'So, are you saying yes to the coffee?' asked Mum.

'We met for coffee before,' I reminded her. 'It didn't end up well.'

'But you can always rewrite the script,' she told me. 'It happens all the time.'

'You think?' I glanced at Max and then at Mum.

'You do know,' she said, 'that the chemistry between the pair of you is practically electric? And that the audience will be looking for a lot more than coffee at the end of this play.'

'Mum!'

'I might be an old woman, but I'm not a stupid woman.' She stood up. 'My sensible little girl is the leading lady in a drama of her own making. I'm making my grand exit now.' She picked up *Ulysses* and walked quickly into the hotel.

Then Max and I were alone.

'So . . . coffee.' He grinned.

'Oh, stop with the coffee.' But I grinned too.

'Sorry,' he said. 'For everything.'

'Nothing to be sorry about. I should be the one apologising, really. I lost it when we met before, and I don't know why.'

'And you texted me, but I was too angry with you to reply. Which was ridiculous, because I was only angry for about ten minutes. And then I was stubborn. And then I was confused because I thought about Brad and you and the note on his computer, and I was suddenly more jealous of him than I'd ever been in my life before. And I hated myself for it.'

'The past is the past,' I said.

'But Brad,' said Max. 'He'll always be there. There's Dylan, you see. I know he's with my parents, but he's also a part of my life – and he always will be. Which would be messy, don't you think?'

'Everything's messy till you look at it clearly,' I told him. 'That's what happens with an X-ray or an ultrasound. We have ideas, we have theories, possibilities . . . and then we look at it and we figure it out. And we find a way to make it better.'

'Only sometimes you can't.'

'But lots of times we can.'

'Can we?' he asked.

'If we can't, then I'm not the person I thought I was. Or that my mother thinks I am. Or wants me to be.' I smiled at him. 'She's up there in the room and I know she's peppering to be here and stick her nose in and be involved. Yet she's holding back, which is a big, big thing for her. But she wants it to be a massive romance. I know she does.'

'And you?'

'I'm not a romantic person,' I said. 'I wanted to be. I got engaged to Sean because I was desperate to find romance. I fell for Brad because it really did feel romantic. But with you . . .' I looked at him, and sensations I'd never felt before coursed through my body. 'With you it's more than that. It's . . . it's something different. Something I never thought I'd feel. And I didn't want to feel it, because – you're right – it's complicated. But only complicated if we want it to be. Do we?'

'No,' said Max. 'I want it to be perfect.'

'Nothing's perfect,' I said.

'Maybe that's a good thing.'

Ophelia, who'd been lying in front of us, suddenly jumped up, mewed and stalked away through the garden.

'She thinks so too,' I said. 'She's kept an eye out for me, you know. All the time I was at the Villa Naranja. And today. For a very, very short time I thought she was Brad's spirit.'

Max raised an eyebrow.

'But that was me being silly,' I said. 'She's a cat, that's all. There are no spirits. There is nothing else, only the here and now.'

412

'You can't be sure of that.'

'No,' I conceded. 'But what I can be sure of is that we have to make the here and now as good as it can be. We have to grab it and enjoy it and make the most of it.'

'And can we?' said Max.

'I hope so.'

'Do you want to talk about it a bit more over that coffee?'

'Don't be bloody ridiculous,' I said. 'I'm Thea Ryan's daughter. All of my important conversations happen over champagne.'

He laughed.

I remembered Magda Burnaia's words: *A man is coming to you. He will travel some distance. He is important. He has a message for you. Something you will want to hear.*

I hadn't believed her. I still didn't, despite the fact that Max really had come some distance with a message. A text message that had left me flat on my face in the forest. But he'd picked me up and looked after me. And he'd said some things that I was very happy to hear.

In the distance I saw Ophelia disappear into the trees. She didn't look back. And neither would I.

Max put his arm around my shoulder.

'OK?' he asked.

'Very OK,' I said.

I was ready for the future.

No matter what it held.

Acknowledgements

Writing is a solitary process, but I know that while I'm hiding away in front of my laptop lost in the world of my characters, there is an army of people behind me helping to turn my manuscript into the final product.

As always I have to thank my wonderful publisher and editor, Marion Donaldson, who has been with me for so many books. Her famed editorial notes may now be digital but they are as wise as ever.

Thank you to Isobel Dixon, my agent. It has been a pleasure to work with you on Juno's story. Thanks also to the entire Blake Friedmann team who continue to bring my books to new readers in different countries around the world.

The teams at Headline UK and the worldwide Hachette family are a joy to work with and I know my books are in safe hands with all of you. Thank you so much to every single one of you for the effort you put in on my behalf and for those wonderful, friendly meetings where everyone makes a unique contribution. Extra thanks to Hannah, Helena and Becky who are always just an email away, and to Yeti for her beautiful cover designs.

A special thanks to Hachette in Ireland – Breda, Ruth,

Jim, Joanna, Bernard, Siobhan, John, and the two Ciaras, who are always so warm and welcoming while being very professional in what they do. Thanks also to Sharon and Mark of Plunkett PR who do a great job of organising me, and to Jane Selley for always spotting the not-so-deliberate errors.

Much of *The Hideaway* is set in the beautiful province of Alicante in Valencia, Spain. I've been very fortunate to be able to spend a lot of time here and would like to extend a huge thank you to all of the people who have made me feel so welcome and who have shared their knowledge with me – especially Mari Carmen Perez Parres, José Monllor Perez and everyone at the Academia Berlingua. *Muchísimas gracias a todos.*

Huge thanks to Audrey Nagle who was so helpful and informative about the work of radiographers and radiologists. Naturally any mistakes are mine alone.

Thank you, as always, to my extended family, who are always there for me and who never lose an opportunity to champion my books.

Thank you to Colm for everything, especially for spotting the deliberate mistakes, and for dragging me away from my desk . . .

And, of course, thank you to all my readers wherever you may be. Thank you for buying my books, for getting in touch and for being so lovely and supportive and friendly. It's always a joy to meet you both virtually and in person. I hope you enjoyed *The Hideaway*.